THE CASE OF THE
MICHAELMAS
GOOSE

ETCHWORTH TOWER

THE CASE OF THE
MICHAELMAS GOOSE

by
CLIFFORD WITTING

GALILEO PUBLISHERS, CAMBRIDGE

Galileo Publishers
16 Woodlands Road, Great Shelford,
Cambridge
CB22 5LW UK

www.galileopublishing.co.uk

Distributed in the USA by SCB Distributors
15608 S. New Century Drive
Gardena, CA 90248-2129, USA

Australia: Peribo Pty Limited
58 Beaumont Road
Mount Kuring-Gai NSW 2080
Australia

ISBN 978-1-915530-12-7

First published in 1938
This edition © 2023 The Estate of Clifford Witting

Illustrations by J. E Kelly

Series Consultant: Richard Reynolds

Printed in the EU

TO
ERIC CROFTS

CONTENTS

BOOK I—THE GOOSE

BOOK II—THE KILLING

BOOK III—THE GOLDEN EGGS

BOOK ONE

The GOOSE

I.

ON HIGH DOWN

"WELL. I'll be danged!"

Old Tom Lee slowly straightened his back as far as it would go and looked vaguely round for assistance; but, except when tourists came, there was seldom anyone within call on the top of High Down, and the glance from Tom's watery old eyes drifted back to what he had found at the foot of Etchworth Tower. He stood for a while making up his slow mind, then turned and broke into a hurried shamble down the lane towards Etchworth village, mumbling, as he went, the fine tale that he was going to tell.

Police-Constable Collins was standing in the High Street in the slight mist of late September, with his mind as nearly blank as a human mind can be; but old Tom's circumstantial and toothlessly imparted tidings sent him running to the telephone-box on the corner outside the grocer's.

Station-Sergeant Harrison had a newspaper spread out on his desk and was engrossed in the weekend's news when the bell rang. With his eyes still running down a column, he reached out his arm, felt for and lifted the receiver.

"Officer on duty, Lulverton police station," he said absently across the space that separated him from the transmitter.

But as Collins's official monotone droned out its message, the Sergeant stiffened and pulled the instrument over the newspaper.

"Right," he said at last. "I'll see to that this end. You stand by until the Super gets someone along and—Hullo!... Hold that witness.... Right."

He replaced the receiver, waited a few seconds, then rang Dr. Lorimer's house and exchanged a word or two with the maid. It was barely eight o'clock and Superintendent Kingsley had not yet arrived. Harrison put through a call for the

3

ambulance, then rang the Superintendent at his house and made his report.

"Get Charlton," ordered Kingsley briefly.

Three miles away, in Southmouth-by-the-Sea, Inspector Harry Charlton of the C.I.D. was having his lonely breakfast. Outside in the hall the 'phone-bell trilled and, laying aside his napkin, he rose to answer it.

"Confound you, Harrison," he said without heat.

Etchworth Tower, a fluted column of the Doric order white stone, stands on the summit of High Down to the north of the village, and is something of a show-place in Downshire. Visitors to the neighbourhood who feel in the mood for the exercise and are ready to pay threepence to the representative of the Lulverton U.D.C. who controls the turnstiles from the tiny cubicle inside, can climb the one hundred and sixty-six winding stairs and enjoy, on regaining breath, one of the finest views in the county. Superimposed on the balcony is a stone cylinder on top of which is a metal vase of flames that years of exposure have deprived of the fine brilliance of its first golden lustre. The rim of this vase is a hundred and eight feet above the ground below.

High Down's five hundred feet does not, of course, compare with gigantic Butser, away to the west in Hampshire, from whose top certain liars report having seen the spire of Salisbury Cathedral; but it is not the least among the vast hills of chalk that run from Petersfield to Beachy Head.

In a way Etchworth Tower is rather like the place in Grove Park that was built for a lark. It is said that in the year 1782, when the village of Etchworth and his own country house were completely destroyed by fire, Richard Cathcorn, fourth and craziest Duke of Redbourn, remembered the Monument that Wren had built near London Bridge to commemorate the Great Fire and caused to be erected an exactly similar memorial of the local conflagration. This Tower, which cost him ten thousand pounds and ruined him so thoroughly that he could not afterwards afford to have his own gutted mansion rebuilt, was not on so grand a scale as the Monument; but then, as His Grace is reputed to have handsomely conceded, neither was the fire.

With the police photographer sitting by Inspector Charlton's side, the big black Vauxhall saloon swung into the narrow lane off Etchworth High Street and purred up the hill. Another private car was standing in front of the Tower entrance and three men were grouped near it: Tom Lee, P.C. Collins and a tall young man in horn-rimmed spectacles, who walked across as Charlton pulled up his car and jumped out.

"Good morning, Dr. Lorimer," Charlton greeted him. "Is he dead?"

The doctor nodded. To the east of the Tower, a few feet away from the square plinth, the twisted body of a man lay on the yellow, sun-baked grass. He wore a raincoat, his face was brown-bearded and near him was a rough green felt hat, pressed into the shape known as pork-pie.

"Spine's broken, by the look of it," said Lorimer. "There was nothing I could do for him, so I've left him for you. It seems to have been a fancy-dress affair," he ended dryly.

"Them whiskers is false, sir," added P.C. Collins smartly.

The Inspector stepped across the grass and went down on one knee by the body.

"False, but good," he said, looking across at the doctor. "Not the crepe-hair-on-wire variety."

He got to his feet and nodded to the photographer, who was standing ready with his camera.

The dead man's left, contorted arm lay under him. When the photographs had been taken, they turned him gently over on to his back and found on the grass where he had lain an unbreakable watch-glass. Charlton examined the watch on the left wrist. It had stopped at 8.32.

"The winding-shaft's been pulled out," he said to Collins,

"and half the minute-hand is missing. We must find that."

While Lorimer produced a thermometer and carried out a more detailed examination of the body, the two policemen searched the grass, and it was five minutes before they found the quarter-inch fragment of hand.

"As I thought," said Lorimer, "the spine's broken and the left arm, leg and collar bone. That was the side that took the whole brunt of the fall. I'll let you know later if there are any internal injuries. You notice the stains on the palms of the hands?"

Charlton nodded agreement. "Looks like rust," he said.

The dead man was wearing a grey pin-stripe flannel suit and heavy brown shoes. Charlton examined the soles, which were of patterned rubber. Inside the green felt hat he found the initials: "C. H."

"How long do you think he's been dead, Doctor?" he asked.

As he put the question, he glanced at Collins and jerked his head meaningly. The constable escorted the gaping Tom out of earshot.

"Roughly?" enquired Lorimer.

"As near as you can estimate. It's obvious that *rigor mortis* has already set in. That's a matter of two to four hours, isn't it?"

"Usually; but with sudden death after great nervous excitement—and I should say that's the way this poor devil felt—it would be nearer two than four. Temperature will help us more than that. Assuming he was healthy, his normal temperature would be somewhere about 98°. His present temperature is 88½°. That means a drop of—let me see...."

"9½°," supplied Charlton.

"My arithmetic's foul," grinned Lorimer. "Now, other things being equal—that is, assuming this hilltop hasn't been too draughty overnight—he ought to have lost 3½° during the first three hours after death, about 3° during the second three hours—and so on. So that if his temperature dropped 9½° altogether, that would be.... Will you again oblige me with the calculation?"

"3½ for three hours, 6½ for six hours.... What's the figure for the next three hours—?"

"More or less," said Lorimer guardedly. "It *can* only be approximate."

"Then it would be 9° for nine hours, making it nearly ten hours before you took his temperature, which was at 8.30."

"But the whole thing, Charlton, depends on so many other things. I know we've argued about this before and you can smile like a Cheshire cat if you like, but it's impossible to narrow it down to within a few minutes. On the evidence of his temperature only, I'll be prepared to tell the coroner's jury that he's been dead between eight and twelve hours. How's that?"

"Good," answered Charlton, and caught the sound of an engine changing noisily into low gear, as the ambulance climbed up from the village.

He beckoned to Collins, who brought Tom back to them.

"You'd better go with the ambulance, Collins," he said, as he unclipped the silver expanding bracelet from the dead man's wrist, "and ask them at the mortuary to be particularly careful with those stains on the hands. I want to make sure that they're rust-marks."

He knelt down again by the body, deftly ripped the beard, and then the moustache, from the dead face—and drew in a sharp breath.

"It's young Mr. Harbord of Sheep village!" exclaimed Collins over his shoulder, and he grunted agreement.

He felt in the pockets. From the raincoat, he gingerly produced a small, unlabelled bottle of yellow liquid; and from the grey suit, a half-filled box of matches, a twenty packet of Craven "A" in which nineteen cigarettes still remained, a picture-postcard of the Tower, and a wallet containing two ten-shilling notes and a few papers of minor importance. He turned to Lorimer.

"I won't keep you any longer, Doctor."

Lorimer nodded and walked over to his car, near which the ambulance was now waiting. Charlton took carefully by the neck the bottle he had removed from Harbord's pocket, removed the cork and sniffed the contents. Then he held it out to Collins, who inhaled noisily.

"Varnish, by the smell of it, sir," said the constable.

"And varnish it is, Collins. Tell the mortuary officer that I'm keeping it for the moment, as well as these other things. Ask Detective-Sergeant Martin to go to Old Forge House in Sheep village and break the news to Mrs. Grey and afterwards bring her over to Lulverton to identify Harbord. I'll see her later."

After the body had been transferred to the ambulance and taken off with Collins and the photographer, Charlton turned his attention for the first time to Tom Lee.

"Did *you* find him?" he asked, taking out his note-book.

"That I did," answered Tom, who had been kept silent far too long for one of his chatty habits, "and it prop'ly took me breath away when I come up the 'ill and found 'im lying there like a sack of mangels. 'Well, I'll be danged!' I said to meself——"

"What's your name?"

"Tom Lee, and I was that taken aback——"

"Tom or Thomas?"

"Dang me if I know! Tom it's always bin since first I can call to mind, but it might be Thomas be rights. You set me prop'ly thinking!"

"Splendid! While you're still in that fortunate condition, perhaps you can answer a few questions. What time did you find the body?"

"I don't rightly think," asserted Tom stoutly, "that I ought to be telling that to nobbut the p'lice."

Charlton smiled gently down at the old man.

"I *am* the police."

In slow amazement, as if, for the first time in his sixty-eight years, he was watching a lift go up, Tom allowed his glance to travel from the soles of the dark-tan shoes, *via* the snugly fitting double-breasted light grey suit, to the crown of the dark brown hat.

"Dang it!" he said. "And there was me taking you for a gennleman with no more to pass the time but poking 'is nose into other folks' business!"

"A very accurate valuation," approved the detective; "but please tell me at what time you found Mr. Harbord's body."

"I saw 'im just as soon as I got 'ere."

"The coroner's jury will appreciate your testimony," said Charlton, who seldom allowed himself to be sarcastic. "And when was that?"

"'Cep when me twinginess keeps me abed, which is when young Bert Parsons, old Bill Parsons's lad—not the eldest one that's in the Air Force and doing very well for 'isself, by all accounts—but young Bert, the second boy, does it for me, 'im working as well for the Council, though not for all the years that I 'ave. Why, dang me if it mustn't be gone fifty years that I——"

"What time did you get here?"

"That's what I'm working round to. When the twinginess don't stop me, I allus catch the blue bus from Lulverton. Course, with the turn and turn about and the keen composition, as you might say, 'tween the drivers running the buses for two different companies, times it's the red bus; but most ways it's the blue bus that I catches from Lulverton, which is a matter of three miles as the crow flies, which is only another way of saying as the road runs, it being as straight as straight's ever likely to be in a crooked world and——"

"What time did you get here?"

Charlton's deep, caressing voice had a sudden rasp in it.

"All right. Aren't I trying to figure it out?" demanded Tom fretfully.

"The first bus from Lulverton arrives at Etchworth at 7.30. You caught it this morning and got out at Etchworth. Is *that* right?"

"If you like to put it like that, yes."

"How long did it take you to climb the hill?"

"That's where you've stumped me. Times when I've got the twinginess, it'll take me double as long as——"

"Confound this infirmity of yours! Had you any— twinginess this morning?"

"No, for all that dratted mist. I came up as frisky as a——"

"You left the bus at 7.30. You reported to the constable at 7.55. That leaves you five-and-twenty minutes to climb the hill, discover the body and hurry down again. I take it you *did* hurry?"

"*Hurry?*" exclaimed the aghast Tom. "Dang me if I weren't down in the village again like an 'awk on a leveret!"

"Did it take you as long as ten minutes to reach the village?"

"Less'n that. I put up a tidy turn of speed for an old 'un."

"We'll assume, then, that you discovered Mr. Harbord at about a quarter to eight. Do you agree?" Tom nodded several times, then snapped his fingers in exasperation.

"I mighter known," he lamented, "that the p'lice would be asking, and ought to've looked at me clock, but I was that dumbgasted that me wits ran off and left me alone with the corpse."

"By clock, I suppose you mean watch?" asked the Inspector, glancing at the chain across the waistcoat that had been made for a far bigger man than Tom.

Tom shook his head.

"This 'ere elbert," he explained, "is fixed in me weskit pockets with a couple of safety-pins. It's me only vanity. The clock's in the office, else I wouldn't know when to lock up."

"When to lock up what?"

"Why, the Tower."

"Good Lord, man! You're the attendant? Why the devil

didn't you tell me that before?"

"Mighty fine chance I'd of telling you, with all yer questions!" retorted Tom with spirit.

The Inspector threw back his head.

"That's one to you!" he laughed. "Were you on duty yesterday?"

"Yes. It were me Sunday on. One in three I 'as off. And a lovely day I 'ad for it, too. It's the fine weather as brings the visitors. Why, I've known it when we didn't even get an American from one week's end to another. It's lonely, I tell you, all by yerself up 'ere on 'Igh Down, with never even the click of the turnstiles to break the monot'nous 'ush."

"When is the Tower open to the public?"

Tom closed his eyes and rattled off:

"Nineter six, April ter September; nineter four, 'Tober ter March."

"I wish," smiled Charlton, "you'd answer all my questions like that."

"I've got that one off pat, as you might say. It's part of me job. Many's the time——"

"So today is the last day that the Tower stays open until six o'clock. What's the procedure when you close for the night? How d'you warn visitors that time's up?"

"There's a notice up on the balcony, saying a bell will be rung at" —he broke again into his rapid sing-song—"teminitzer six, April ter September——"

Charlton waved a protesting hand, but Tom's eyes were too tightly shut.

"—and teminitzer four, 'Tober ter March; and when the clock in the office points ter that, I presses me thumb on the push and down they all come."

"What if someone gets left behind?"

"We *thought* of that," answered Tom proudly. "I waits till the stroke of the hour, then I locks up the doors and climbs the stairs to the balcony. Every day I does it. Hunnerd and sixty-six of 'em and me sixty-nine next May. Time was when there was a couple of us to run it—one up, one down—but the Council took it inter their 'eads to cut down expenses like, times not being what they——"

"Then after making sure that all visitors have left the balcony, you come down again, let yourself out and go home?"

Tom agreed.

"Did you go through that routine yesterday evening?"

"Yes," said the old fellow. "I locked the doors just like what I always do, climbed up to the balcony——"

"You satisfied yourself, in fact, that everyone had left the place?"

"That's what took me so aback when I found 'im an hour since. I'll stake my Bible oath that there wasn't a living soul in there when I turned the key in the lock last night!"

II.

AN EYE FOR DETAIL

THE front of the Tower, in which was its sole entrance, faced due west. It was the only side of the plinth having the additional protection of iron railings, badly in need of paint, that curved from its corners, like the neck of a bottle, to the two central gates. Charlton strolled across the grass and Tom, in his worn suit with laden pockets—one of them with the added burden of a half-pint bottle of milk—sagging below the flaps, shambled after him. They stopped before the gates, which, together with the doors behind, were closed.

"You haven't been inside this morning?" Charlton asked, and Tom shook his head. "Does everything seem as usual?"

"Yes, by the looks of it. You'll probably be wanting to go in? I got the keys on me chain."

He pulled them from his pocket and, at Charlton's request, unclipped the ring from the chain. The gate key was large and very old, but the door key was a modern 6-lever Chubb "Detector." Charlton unlocked the gates and pushed them open. The paintwork of the doors was shabby and blistered, and initials and loving devices were carved on their solid panels; but there was no indication that they had been tampered with and the key turned properly in the lock when he tested it. A peculiarity of Chubb "Detector" locks is that if a wrong key has been tried in them, the right key will not operate unless it is turned in the reverse direction of that usually employed. Charlton stepped back on to the path and returned the keys to Tom.

"When you lock the doors from inside," he asked, "and go upstairs for your last look round, do you take the keys with you? Yes, I suppose you do, as you keep them on a chain. This third one—but I'll go more closely into the question of keys later on."

He lighted a cigarette and waggled it at Tom.

"Now think carefully before you answer this next question. When you came down from the balcony last night, what exactly did you do after you got to the foot of the staircase?"

Lee pushed back the bowler hat, grown soft, pulpy and very slightly green with the years, and thought carefully.

"Went through the turnstile," he said, slowly and with weight, "stepped outside, locked the door again, then the gates, and went off down the 'ill, little knowing that when I next come up again——"

"You relocked the doors at once? You didn't leave them open while you took a stroll round the Tower, or anything of the kind?"

Tom was very definite on that point. He had lost no time, he said, in locking the doors behind him.

"That's that," said the Inspector. "Now let's turn our attention to the next thing. Before they took away Mr. Harbord's body, you were able to have a good look at him. Did you pass him through the turnstile yesterday?"

"Yes. It muster bin——"

"Was he wearing a beard?"

"Yes, just like 'e was when I came on 'im this morning. It muster bin round about four when 'e came——"

"Please be as brief as possible."

The old man looked pained at this demand, but went on:

"I'd bin tidy busy most of the afternoon—the fine Sunday brought 'em out like flies; but this chap came along by 'isself and put down 'is money. A shilling it was and taking me wages every Friday from the Council and always 'aving their best interests at 'eart, I asked 'im if 'e'd like a pitcher—a real fortygraph, twopence, or coloured beautiful for no more cost—or 'The 'Istory of Etchworth, With Some Account——"

"Lee," threw in Charlton in humorous despair, "you're as

14

difficult to question as a bishop's motives. For heaven's sake cut out the flapdoodle!"

"I got to do things in me own way," Tom defended himself. "Once get me flustivated and I'm done. This chap in the beard bought a card and told me to keep the change out of the bob; and that's why"— triumphantly—"I can call 'im so clear to mind!"

He paused for effect, then added:

"It isn't everybody 'oo slips me anything at all, let alone the price of a pint of old-and-mild."

"How did this man behave?"

"Very well. I've no complaints at all. Course there '*ave* bin folks, 'tick'ly young lads—"

Charlton stopped him hastily.

"I'm not interested in breaches of the bye-laws," he explained. "Did he seem normal? Or was he excited or anxious? Did his voice sound natural?"

"Quite ordinary."

"Could you describe his voice? Was it rather high and did he speak quickly?"

"Can't remember anything about that. 'E spoke like a gennleman, if that's anything. Passed the time o' day. Said the rain was keeping off, but e'd brought 'is raincoat, just in case. Asked me a thing or two—"

"It was *he* who said he'd brought the coat? You didn't mention it first?"

"No, it was 'im started the talk about it."

"Was he wearing it or carrying it on his arm?"

"Wearing it."

"Was he also wearing a green felt hat, such as you saw earlier this morning?"

"Yes, 'e was. Then 'e asked me one or two things about the Tower: height, how many stairs, and all the other questions I'm always being put."

"You had no suspicions that he was Mr. Harbord of Sheep?"

"I didn't know the young gennleman, never going to Sheep but once or twice a year."

"Then you passed him through the turnstile, I suppose, and he went up the stairs? And at that particular time, were there many other people in the Tower?"

"A tidy few."

"How many do you mean by that?"

"Well, it be 'ard to say, with folks in and out all the afternoon. Mebbe ten or a dozen."

"You didn't leave your office between the time this man arrived and the time you locked up for the night?"

"No, I was there, sitting in me chair all the time."

"Did the bearded man leave the Tower later in the afternoon?"

"Muster done."

"That is not an answer," said Charlton sharply. "Did you see him leave?"

"Not so far as I remember," admitted Tom grudgingly.

"Didn't it occur to you, while you were getting ready to lock up, that you hadn't noticed him go?"

"I never give 'im a second thought till I saw 'im lying there earlier on."

"Do you recall any man who left the Tower who might have been he? Assume that he took off the beard and his raincoat, changed into a different hat and perhaps put on a pair of glasses."

"There were quite a few different sorts of young fellows in and out of 'ere on Sunday. 'E might well 'ave bin one of them."

"Did you pay any attention to those who passed you on their way out?"

"No more than usual, which isn't much if the truth must be told, what with me paper and one thing and another. When they come in, I 'as to attend to them, but when they've 'ad their three-penn'orth, they can see theirselves out, in a manner of speaking. Sometimes, of course, they've got a word or two to say to me as they go past the office."

"Did anyone do that yesterday afternoon?"

"Yes, the Bank manager from Lulverton brought some friends over in 'is car and stopped to ask 'ow me twinginess was getting along, me 'aving an 'Ome Safe and 'im being took up with the 'ealth of 'is customers, as a Bank manager rightly should——"

"There are five Banks in Lulverton. Which one do you mean?"

"Why, the Old Bank," answered Tom, as if the Southern Counties were the only one of which he had ever heard—an odd characteristic in countryfolk. "Mr. Scott-Brown."

"Did he and his party arrive after the bearded man?"

"No, a bit before."

"And what time did they leave?"

Tom pondered. "I was making meself a cupper tea when Mr. Scott-Brown spoke to me, and that would be about arpars four."

"Were there any other visitors whom you recognised?"

Tom shook his head.

"Right," said Charlton, and pulled out his cigarette-case.

The examinee heaved a thankful sigh that the ordeal of using his brains was not to be prolonged.

"You'll almost always find me 'ere if you want to know anything else any time," he said, turning towards the entrance doors.

"Thank you," smiled the Inspector, "but our present little *tête-à-tête* is not nearly finished yet. We've only touched, up to now, on the more general points."

As Tom's face dropped almost audibly, Charlton stepped up to the turnstiles.

"Tell me about these," he requested, and Tom came and stood by his side.

"This one's 'IN'," he explained, pointing to the right "and the other's 'OUT'. You come along and put down your threepence, which I take and presses me foot on that bar, which lets you swing the turnstile and go through."

"And the apparatus records it?"

"That's it."

With a grimy thumb-nail, he pulled out a narrow strip of wood——an obviously amateur replacement——from the brass top of the turnstile, and revealed a row of five figures resembling an overgrown cyclometer. Charlton bent over.

"3952," he read. "I suppose the total is checked periodically with your takings?"

"Every Saturday evening. Mr. Lambert or one of the other gennlemen from the Council offices comes over from Lulverton to do it. There's a strong-box in me office there"—he pointed behind the right-hand turnstile—"which I locks the takings up in every night, and Mr. Lambert writes down the total in a little book and takes the money away with 'im."

"Did Mr. Lambert come last Saturday evening?"

"Yes, and precious little there was for 'im. 'Ardly paid for the petrol to come over." He shook his head mournfully, as if for an ailing child. "The Tower's bin badly 'it by the talkies."

"So the present total, less the amount noted down by Mr. Lambert in his book on Saturday, will give us the number of visitors to the Tower yesterday?"

A slow smile spread over Tom's face.

"Dang me," he marvelled, "but so it will!"

"Which is more popular with visitors—the morning or the afternoon?"

"Afternoon," was the prompt reply.

"This other turnstile has no recording attachment?"

"No, 'e swings quite free, but only the one way, clockwise, so's you can't get in without paying."

"How do *you* manage? Do they pass you a credit every Saturday?"

Tom looked vastly crafty.

"There be a trick about it," he confided.

"Surely you don't climb over the top?" asked the detective in disbelief.

"You'll keepitcher self?"

"If it doesn't affect my case."

The old attendant turned his bowed shoulders and scanned the deserted miles of downland. Then he nodded his head towards the left-hand turnstile.

"Pull it till it clicks four," he muttered conspiratorially.

Charlton did as suggested. At the fourth click of the ratchet, the arms of the stile were at their furthest distance from the dividing rail; and the two men were able to slip through. In front of them a wooden door with upper panels of glass led to the staircase; fixed to the wall on the left was a glazed showcase displaying picture-postcards of the Tower, Etchworth Village, the famous Tall Man with its adjacent chalk-pit, and other local views, together with copies of "The History of Etchworth Tower": and on the other side was the "office," which was no more than a recess cut in the solid stone of the Tower's square plinth.

Behind the waist-high door of Tom's niche were a chair, a very small table and, down on the floor against the wall, an oil-stove with a kettle on the top of it. The table was covered by an evening paper, which, where the many months' accumulation of stains permitted, still trumpeted bravely about the Abdication; and there stood upon it a Woolworth's teapot, a saucerless cup with a spoon in it, and, propped against the wall, Tom's National Health Insurance card with (Charlton had an eye for detail) thirteen stamps attached. On the wall behind the chair was the Electric Company's switch-box, beneath which three keys on a ring hung from a nail.

"What are *they* for?" asked the Inspector, pointing to the keys.

"The big un's for the grille up top and——"

"Which grille up top?"

"When you get to the balcony," explained Tom, "there's a door leading out onto it. That's for the public. But the stairs go on right up into the upper cylinder, where only me and the other officials is allowed. To stop the public from going where they oughtn't, which is what they like doing more than anything else I know, there's an iron grille across on a level with the balcony door."

"Is there a key to the balcony door?"

"Yes, it's one of them two." He pulled the milk bottle from his pocket and placed it on the table. "I mind the time when we 'ad some fun with that door, which was before we put glass in it." From his other pocket he took a brown-paper parcel, presumably containing his lunch. "A bunch of them suffragettes—it muster bin round about 1912 or '13—got up there fine and early and fixed the door with a bit of wood wedged against the railing so's we couldn't get it open. And there they stayed all day, waving flags and shouting, 'Votes for Women'—not that there was anyone to 'ear 'em 'cept a few sheep, 'oo don't care much one way or the other about tom-fool politics sich as that."

He chuckled at the recollection.

"Do you lock the balcony door at night?" Charlton asked.

"Reg'lar."

"You locked it last night?"

"When I 'ad me look round."

"Did you go into the upper cylinder?"

"No. Sometimes that grille's not opened for a year at a stretch. The last time was—when would it be? May or early June this year, when nothing would satisfy a friend of one of the Councillors—some big bug or other from London—but poking 'is 'ead out of the top. Plumb in the middle of the flames is a couple of trap-doors, which we keep padlocked from inside. That there's the key of 'em."

"I'll go up to the balcony now. You'd better stay down here—and don't let anyone in. Say that the Tower is closed for the time being."

He reached across and unhooked the keys.

"I didn't ought to let you 'ave those," said Tom doubtfully. "I got strict orders about letting the public past the grille."

"I'll take the blame," Charlton reassured him, as he slipped the keys into his pocket.

"You do it at yer own risk," came Tom's salvo from behind his official defences; then, as if all further responsibility were no longer his, he went on: "You'll find a candle on the stairs just past the grille. There's an electric light at the bottom of the cylinder, but if you're going any further, you'll be wanting a candle."

He reached up and switched on the current for the staircase lights.

"You'll get danged dirty," he added contentedly, as he dropped into his chair and felt in his pocket for his pipe.

The Inspector pulled open the door and began to climb the spiral staircase, which, as he got higher, became narrower. Periodically, there were openings in the shaft, but they were mere slits through which very little could be seen. On the wall were painted "Keep to the Right" notices and, at one point, one of those chatty little announcements that add such a welcoming and homelike note to all public buildings and places of carefree recreation. This particular manifesto read: "It is strictly forbidden to write upon or deface the walls of this building. The attendants have instructions to give into custody any persons found misconducting themselves. By Order of the Council, June, 1894." Beneath this, at one time or another, some staunch upholder of the liberty of the subject had diligently pencilled, in a hand of exquisite neatness, a single devastating word.

Charlton had looked at his watch before starting from below. He glanced at it again when he reached the balcony door. The climb had taken him three minutes. The wooden balcony door was locked—he made sure of that; and so with the grille leading to the upper cylinder, which was to his right as he faced the door. He unfastened the door, noting that the key would operate from both sides, and went out on the balcony.

The mists had cleared, the sun shone and the view that tourists so much prized was there for his delight: the undulating Downs with occasional rows of stunted yews and man-made clumps and rings of beeches, the finest of which is Chanctonbury; to the south, the gradual drop to the sea-plain, and, across the Solent, the wooded coast of the Isle of Wight; to the north, at the foot of the steeper inland slopes, meadows and tiny villages and beyond them the forests of the Weald; to the south-west, the bustling, commonplace town of Lulverton, with the bright red chimney of its rubber-heel factory belching black smoke; to the east beautiful little Sheep: and directly below, from which the fastidious visitor averted his flinching eyes, Etchworth, surely the ugliest village in all southern England, with its long, long High Street of vile rough-cast villas, its corrugated-iron garage, its dreadfully drab public-house and Memorial Hall, all festooned about with the thick wires, the squat poles and the big white insulators of the Downshire Electric Light & Power Company.

But Charlton saw none of these things.

III.

THE VASE OF FLAMES

HE slowly made the circuit of the balcony. Unlike its model in Monument Place, it was not entirely caged in, the grille around it having been fitted rather to guard against accident than the more purposeful business of *felo de se*. The breast-high railing that his Grace's architect had considered sufficient in the 1780's had certainly been added to, so that the present grillework was fully eight feet high; but the top had been left unbarred. Undoubtedly, it was a deplorable state of affairs, but the Lulverton U.D.C. were not as cautious as the City Lands Committee of the Corporation of London, perhaps because *they* had never had the stimulus of six suicides and one accidental death (all of them, be it added, before 1843) to rouse them to action.

As with the railings outside the entrance below, all the ironwork sorely needed painting. Charlton worked his way round, carefully examining the bars, particularly those on the eastern side, for any evidence of someone having climbed over. The floor of the balcony was covered with a fine dust, but none of it seemed to have been transferred to the only available footholds on the grillework, which were the original handrail and the bottom rail of the upper grille, a few inches above it. These had no discernible coating of dust, probably because visitors were constantly gripping them. He took a hold high up on the bars and pulled himself to a standing position on the handrail. Looking down, he felt that it needed more than ordinary courage to fling oneself over. When he lowered himself on to the balcony, his hands were marked, by rust and dirt, but the leather soles of his shoes had left no traces behind them. A good many cigarette-ends were scattered about, among them a Craven "A"; and in the southeast corner, close up to the railing, he found the clear imprint of such a rubber sole as that on Harbord's right shoe.

His attention was next directed to the upper cylinder.

He took the keys from his pocket, unlocked the grille and switched on the light. Here the evidence was of a completely definite nature. According to Tom, the cylinder had not been entered for the better part of four months, and the stairs were thickly laid with dust that nowhere showed the slightest indication of footprints or other recent disturbance. Harbord had not hidden *there* while Tom Lee shuffled round the balcony outside.

The stairs wound up to where the cylinder sloped inwards to meet the crowning vase, and they were littered with odds and ends: dusty, crumpled flags and lengths of bunting and rope, the candle mentioned by Tom and, as evidence that the cylinder had afforded a private though uncomfortable, retreat for the attendant who had once assisted Tom, a shabby cushion on a stair, empty, crushed cigarette-packets and match-boxes, a broom and a tightly rolled ball of silver-paper, intended, possibly, for some hospital, but now forgotten.

From the landing at the top of the staircase, for the examination of which Charlton had to light the candle, four rusty bars ran up through the gilded vase. To these were fixed, at intervals of about a foot, a series of iron rungs, the first six being half-loops and the remainder complete circles. He held up the candle, but it was not sufficient to illuminate more than a few feet of the dark funnel, which could not have been more than twenty-four inches wide. After a moment's hesitation, the very human impulse of curiosity triumphed and, placing the candle on the floor, he began to climb.

When his foot reached the twelfth rung, his questing hand came in contact with the trap-doors above him. He pulled out the keys and felt about for the padlock. The hinges were rusty, but he managed to push up the trapdoors—and the sudden rush of blazing daylight blinded him for a moment or two.

He climbed further, until he stood on the last rung but one, immediately getting the impression that he had come up through the bottom of a shallow saucepan with yellow, and very rigid, flames surrounding it. It was bigger than he had expected—three feet six across, he estimated—and with the trap-doors down, would have given seating accommodation to two generously proportioned men. There was so little protection, though, that it would have been dangerous for anyone fearing heights to stand erect on the closed trapdoors.

He stayed there for some minutes. The feeling of detachedness was rather fascinating.

Tom Lee was just taking the steaming kettle from the oil-stove as Charlton pushed open the door at the foot of the staircase.

"Fancied you could do with a cupper tea," he said without turning round.

"Thought-reader," applauded Charlton, checking by his watch that he had taken two minutes to descend from the level of the balcony. "Not too strong, please, and no sugar."

The old man had magically produced a second cup from somewhere.

"Hope you're not in a great 'urry," he said in all seriousness, "'cause there's no saucer."

"I can blow on it," replied the detective with equal gravity.

While they waited for the tea to draw, he replaced the keys on the nail below the switch-box and asked:

"Can you remember whether the bearded man was smoking when he arrived here yesterday?"

"Not then. As we was chatting, 'e brought out a packeter fags—"

"Craven 'A'?"

"Far as I remember. 'E offered me one."

"Was it a fresh packet?"

"Wait while I think.... Yes, I remember 'im tearing off the

wrappings. 'E threw it outside."

Charlton slipped through the turnstile and found a crumpled ball of cellophane and the detachable inner foil flap that is a characteristic of that particular brand of cigarette. He put the fragments carefully away and went back to Tom, who was pouring out the tea.

"Did you accept the cigarette?"

"No, I told 'im I'd no time for the things; that I preferred me pipe. Then 'e said 'e could never get on with a pipe. Made 'is teeth ache and wouldn't keep alight. Give 'im fags every time, 'e said."

The detective picked up his cup and sipped for a while in silence.

"Where d'you keep the strong-box?" he asked so suddenly that Tom spilt his tea down his waistcoat.

With elaborate stealth, Tom showed him. Under the shabby mat in the office was a trap-door, which opened to reveal a foot-deep box of rough boards. In it were a collection of oddments and a Ratner bent-steel Haffner pattern cash-box.

"Please get the box out. I want to check your receipts."

Tom pulled it up and put it on the table. He unlocked it with one of the keys on his chain and together they counted the money inside. It amounted to three pounds, six shillings and sixpence. Charlton took out his note-book.

"You probably keep a floating balance," he said. "How much does that come to?"

"Mr. Lambert 'e always leaves me a couple of pounds in small change."

"That reduces yesterday's takings to one-six-six." He scribbled down the sum. "That's 318 pence. Divide by three: 106. Thank you—I've finished with that."

Tom kept the box out, but lowered the trap-door and replaced the carpet.

"What's underneath there?" Charlton asked.

"Mother Earth," answered Tom facetiously. "They do say

there used to be an 'idden passage, but that's all me eye."

"Coming back to those keys, Lee. There are six altogether: three on one ring and three on the other. Ring No. 1 holds the keys of the outer gates, the entrance doors and the strong-box. Ring No. 2 holds the keys of the balcony door, the cylinder grille and the trap-door padlock. Is Ring No. 2 kept permanently on that nail?"

"Yes. There ain't no sense in carrying about more keys than you can 'elp, what with the wear on the pockets and———"

"Do *you* keep the other keys overnight?"

Tom shook his head.

"They don't trust me that far. I've only worked with them 'alf a century and they 'aven't 'ad the time to make up their minds about me honesty. I give the keys in at the office on me way 'ome every night and pick 'em up agen next morning."

"You passed them over yesterday evening?"

"To Mr. Matthews 'isself. 'E's the Clurk, you know."

"And was it he who gave them back to you this morning?"

"No, it was Mr. Lambert give 'em to me."

"One more question: What's the height of this Tower?"

"'Unnerd and eight feet overall; eighty-three to the abacus; cylinder and vawse, twenty-five."

"What's the abacus?"

Tom scratched his head. "Dang me if I rightly know," he admitted. "You're the first as ever asked me that. 'Eight-three to the abacus,' I tell 'em; and it never goes further than that."

"It must be the level of the balcony." He slipped his note-book into his pocket. "That's all for the time being. When news of this business gets round, High Down's going to be crowded with rubber-necks, but don't let anyone inside here. I'll go along to the Council offices now and get that confirmed. In return for the cup of tea, Lee, I'll give you a word of advice: when you're called at the inquest, there's one thing you must remember to say."

"What's that?" asked the intrigued Tom.

"As little as possible," answered the Inspector, and with a smile and a nod, he went to look round outside before he drove off towards Lulverton.

Before he went to the Council offices, Charlton called in at Mr. Selby's shop in Low Pavement and spent ten minutes with the old watchmaker in the congested little back room. When he came out, he lighted a cigarette and immediately threw it away.

Mr. Matthews, Clerk to the Council, was a little man with a big nose. He wore horn-rimmed spectacles and had the quick, jerky manner of an anxious sparrow. He received Charlton in his office and answered his questions with a briskness that was a refreshing change from Tom Lee's exasperating wordiness.

"I've instructed Lee to keep the Tower closed until further notice," said Charlton after explaining the reason for his visit, which came as a disagreeable surprise to the Clerk.

"Quite right. I'll have a notice prepared. We're entirely in your hands, Inspector. Is there anything else?"

"There are one or two points on which you can help me, Mr. Matthews. Firstly, Lee tells me that the keys of the Tower are deposited here at night."

"That is so."

"He gave them to you yesterday evening, on his return from Etchworth. What happened to them after that?"

Mr. Matthews pointed to a safe in the corner of the room.

"They were locked up in there," he said, then smiled brilliantly for an instant. "They are not very important keys, Inspector, but we like to be methodical. The offices were closed yesterday, of course, but I have arranged with the Tower attendants, Lee and a young man named Parsons, that on Sundays they come to my private quarters upstairs. A few minutes after Lee had gone, I brought them down and locked them in the safe."

"And this morning....?"

"I didn't hand them to Lee myself. That was done by one of my young assistants, a Mr. Lambert. Perhaps you know him?"

Charlton shook his head.

"He also has a key of the safe?"

"Yes. Would you like a word with him?"

"I should, if I may. I've something else to ask him."

Mr. Matthews reached for his house telephone, but Charlton stopped him.

"Before you ask Mr. Lambert to come in," he said, "I have one more question for you. Is Lee to be trusted? I don't mean is he honest, but is he dependable?"

The Clerk smiled suddenly again.

"He's getting an old man and he's the biggest chatterbox in the district—with the exception of some of our revered Councillors!—but we've no complaints to make about the way he does his work, if that's what you mean. We've been trying for years to pension him off, but he hangs on like a limpet. Young Parsons is getting to know the job and we hope soon to take some definite step about Lee." He shook his head. "I'm afraid, though, that it will kill the old fellow."

"Let's hope not," smiled Charlton. "Now, perhaps you'll ask Mr. Lambert to come in."

Lambert caught Charlton unprepared. He did not expect to find as clerk to a Clerk the exquisite young man who drifted languidly, like a lazy cloud, into the room. He was not very tall—five feet ten or so—but his slimness seemed to increase his height. He wore a grey flannel suit, suede leather shoes, a polo-collared shirt of some elusive shade of pastel blue and an Old Boys' tie pulled to the tiniest of knots. His hair, which was not so dark as brilliantine made it, was faultlessly smooth and on his lip had been etched a moustache that just missed sharing the geometrical definition of a line, which has—or so one is told—length, but no thickness. Altogether, he was *too* beautiful, reminding Charlton of Harry Hotspur's "certain lord." Admittedly, he held no pouncet-box 'twixt his finger and his thumb, but that, Charlton thought, was more the pity. A pouncet-box would have suited him.

"Lambert," said Mr. Matthews, "the body of a man was found at the foot of Etchworth Tower this morning. Inspector Charlton is inquiring into the matter and wishes to ask you a few questions."

Weary eyes were turned towards the detective.

"Delighted," said Lambert, as if that was the last thing he could ever be.

Charlton was glad to note that, although he drawled annoyingly, he did not "talk so like a waiting-gentle-woman."

"Did you check the turnstile figures last Saturday evening?" he asked.

Lambert hung himself over a filing-cabinet, like some rare tapestry.

"Ran over in the car."

"Can you give me the total?"

"3846."

"That is definite?"

"Oh, quite."

"The point is important, Mr. Lambert. Would it not be as well to get the book?"

"There's no need to. I've given you the figure."

"I should like to see the book, please."

Lambert raised his eyebrows disdainfully, but went to fetch the book. The last total recorded agreed with the figures he had quoted.

"How much cash did you leave behind in the box?"

"Exactly two pounds."

"Thank you, Mr. Lambert. Now, there's one more thing. Did you hand the keys of the Tower to Lee this morning?"

"Yes."

"Was the safe locked when you came to open it?"

He turned swiftly to Mr. Matthews. "I mean no disrespect

to you, sir," he smiled.

"I admire your attention to detail, Inspector," the Clerk smiled back.

"Everything was as usual," said Lambert wearily. "I gave the key to Lee and that was really all there was to it."

"I'm obliged to you, Mr. Lambert. I think that is all for the moment."

When they were left alone, Mr. Matthews dropped his head and looked solemnly over his spectacles at Charlton.

"You probably share my keen desire, Inspector," he said, "to give that preposterous popinjay a kick in the pants."

He pulled forward his chair and placed his elbows on the desk.

"Now," he asked, "is there anything else I can do for you? For fifteen years I have been telling the Council about the dangerous conditions on that Tower balcony, and now the thing I feared has happened. I knew some crazy fool would chuck himself off there one day. *Now*, perhaps, they'll sanction the expenditure."

"Another halfpenny on the rates," smiled Charlton. "Are you and Mr. Lambert the only key-holders for that safe?"

"Not exactly. It is true that there are only two keys in general use—besides, of course, the duplicate, which is deposited at the Metropolitan & Provincial Bank. I am the permanent holder of one key, but Lambert is only in temporary possession of the other. Business begins early in Lulverton, especially on market-days, and I have made it a rule with the younger members of my staff that one of them must be here by seven o'clock each morning. It's not a very popular regulation, but circumstances forced it on me. They take it in turns and the man concerned holds the office keys and the key of the safe during his period of early duty. Today begins Lambert's week. His colleague passed over the keys at the close of business on Saturday."

"What time was that?"

"One o'clock."

"I understand that Mr. Lambert regularly devotes a part of his Saturday evenings to collecting the cash takings from the Tower."

Mr. Matthews gave him a shrewd glance.

"Which, I take it, Inspector," he smiled, "is your way of asking whether that is another of my harsh mandates?"

"Not at all," lied Charlton shamelessly. "It just struck me as a little odd."

"It's funny you should mention it. Until a few months ago, such visits to Etchworth were—desultory. The care of the Tower forms only a small part of our responsibilities and the advisability of closing it to the public has frequently been considered. Financially, it is a dead loss. It doesn't even pay for Lee's wages. It is a white elephant, Inspector—one of many in this district. In spite of that, a member of the Council one day recommended that we should check the turnstile figures every week, which would supply us with useful comparative statistics. What benefit we should derive from the analysis was—and still is—a little beyond me, but that is by the way. *My* business was to give effect to the Council's wishes, so I had Lambert in and instructed him to check the turnstile once a week without fail."

"Was it you who suggested the hour of his visits?"

"Strangely enough, no. My original idea was that he should go on Saturday mornings, but he came back to me the next day and said he thought Saturday evenings would be better, because the complete week would then be represented by the figures. He has a car and he said it would be no trouble for him to drive over a few minutes before six o'clock."

He paused before adding:

"I was very agreeably surprised."

"Your staff seem to be enthusiastic workers, Mr. Matthews!" smiled the Inspector. "Even old Lee arrives at the Tower an hour and a quarter before he is due to open the doors to the public."

"It's his life. I really believe he loves the thing. They tell me that even on his free days, he goes along to see that no misfortune has befallen it; but that is probably an exaggeration. A facetious junior clerk of mine once christened the Tower 'Uncle Tom's Cabin'."

They laughed together, then Charlton said:

"I'm sorry to keep harping on those keys, sir, but they're rather important. There are three keys on the ring handed out every day to Lee and three others that are kept permanently in the Tower. Are there any duplicates of those six, particularly those that pass the locks on the outer gates and the entrance doors?"

"Yes, for all of them. They are with our other duplicates at the Metropolitan & Provincial Bank."

Charlton rose to his feet and picked up his hat. After he had gone, the Clerk to the Council sat thinking for a minute or two; then lifted his telephone receiver and asked to be put through to the District Surveyor.

IV.

WHILE AT OLD FORGE HOUSE...

BEAUTIFUL little Sheep. It would be foolish to say that it had been entirely unaffected by modern progressiveness or that life under its thatched roofs had gone on unchanged since George III was King. It *had* been affected, but it had not been spoiled. There are those who shout to high heaven when a beauty-spot is threatened by some beneficial ugliness: when their aesthetic eye is offended by gaunt pylons clutching a foothold on the hills, or chromium-plated taps in place of a picturesque, moss-encrusted well, from whose dark depths the bucket each time brought up a pop-eyed, anæmic frog. But let it be noted that *they* do not live in the country. They drive—or are driven—out in their cars in search of pastoral loveliness; and when they find Sweet Auburn, they sit in some tiny cottage or in a garden under old, twisted trees, sipping their tea with little fingers refinedly hooked, and pecking daintily at home-made bread; or stand in public-bars, revelling in skittles, shove-ha'penny and the now modish darts. Then, emotionally soothed by their brief contact with the simple life of the countryside, they drive—or are driven—back to London and all the comforts of their everyday existence. But let those chawbacons, with whom they fraternize with such palpable condescension, venture to ask for the same conveniences as they themselves enjoy at home, and they are up in arms against the vile Goths who disfigure England's green and pleasant land with pylons, transformers, telephone-boxes and petrol-pumps, and who destroy the primitive beauties of cottages and farmhouses by hanging out wireless aerials and having such vulgar things as electric light, radio-gramophones and gas-cookers in place of the delightful oil-lamps, harpsichord (or, as a concession, harmoniums) and vast open fires. They even seek to deny Tony Lumpkin the greatest blessing that man ever bestowed upon man: Main Drainage.

Sheep village had been enriched by civilization, but, unlike Etchworth, it had not fallen victim to the jerry builder. There is probably no other hamlet like it in England. As one came into it from the direction of Etchworth, the village green, with its lovely old chestnut trees, spread out on either side of the road in two almost perfect half-circles. Separated from the grass by curving pathways, just wide enough for a grocer's van, were the two rows of thatched, half-timbered cottages. The last on the right, before the road went on to Eastbourne, was the "Sun in the Sands," outside which the two buses, red and blue, turned round to go back to Lulverton. Each half of the green, with the cottages skirting it, was independently named. As one faced east, with one's back to Etchworth, to the left was Plestrium Sinister and to the right, Plestrium Dexter. Because of these names, scholars have tried to prove that Sheep is a survival of the Roman occupation of Britain; but although their Latin dictionaries are clear about *Sinister* and *Dexter*, none of them has ever traced *Plestrium*. Maybe it was born in the mind of an idle monk upon some sleepy mediaeval afternoon.

Old Forge House, a comfortably large thatched cottage, was the fifth building in Plestrium Sinister. It had a short, white-fenced garden. On the low green door, which led straight into the larger of the two front rooms, a brass knocker and letter-box shone brilliantly and over it hung a small sign announcing:

"OLD FORGE GUEST HOUSE
LUNCHEONS & TEAS"

The garden was well-kept and there was about the whole place an air of pleasant orderliness.

At half-past eight, while Dr. Lorimer was carrying out his examination of Harbord's body, Mrs. Grey sat at breakfast with her daughter, Judith, and her son, Peter, who was more concerned with his newspaper than with the others' idle talk.

When her husband had died, Ruth Grey had managed, somehow, to keep her children on at their schools. Later, with their education finished, she had bought Old Forge House; and it was fortunate that she had not sunk all her capital in the enterprise, for the income from it was not very large.

Judith helped her with the Guest House, while Peter worked for Cooper & Silcock, the Lulverton architects. Peter was twenty-seven, five feet ten and a typical product of his school, where he had been a pretty useful stand-off half. His eyes and teeth were his best features and he had considerable artistic ability. Old Mr. Silcock considered him the firm's best draughtsman. His sister was three years his senior, nearly as tall as he and very like him. Her hair was brown and curly, her face full of character; and she had a smile for which, in more chivalrous times, most men would have fought and some ardent few would have died.

Mrs. Grey, whose hair was scarcely flecked with white, stopped talking about the village's new baby and asked:

"What happened to Courtenay last night? Do you know, Judy?"

"Haven't the vaguest idea," admitted Judy. "Probably stayed with the Quentins."

"Did he say anything to you, Peter?"

The answering grunt might have meant anything.

"Peter, dear," persisted Mrs. Grey. "Did Courtenay tell you he might sleep at the Quentins' last night?"

"Didn't know he was going. Who *are* the Quentins, anyway?"

"You know as well as I do."

"Well, His Excellency the Weasel didn't open his heart to me."

"That's not a very nice thing to call him, Peter. And I don't think *you* ought to laugh either, Judy!"

She sipped her coffee.

"I hope nothing's happened to him," she went on.

"No such luck," growled Peter, as he turned over the pages of his paper.

"Peter!" said his mother sharply, if such a delightful and amiable lady could ever speak sharply, "you mustn't say that!"

"The man's a wart," retorted Peter firmly.

"He's your cousin and I think you ought to——"

Peter threw out his arm dramatically.

"'Am I not consanguineous?'" he declaimed; "'am I not of the same blood?'"

"I think 'wart' suits him," meditated Judy. "A wart on the nose of democracy."

This was too much for Mrs. Grey, who laughed in spite of herself.

"You're both very cruel to Courtenay," she said at last.

Her son and daughter took no notice of this accusation. They knew that she was on their side.

"A wart on the nose of democracy," she said slowly, then burst again into a fit of laughing that suddenly stopped, as she turned to look through the mullioned windows. "There goes the red bus. Hurry up, Peter."

"Plenty of time," he assured her and buttered another piece of toast.

"You were late home last night, dear, weren't you?" she asked him.

"Twelve-ish. Missed the last bus."

"*My* watch said well after one when you woke me up with all the noise you made."

"Oh, that was a long time after I came in. I couldn't remember if I'd bolted the front door and when I came down to find out, I fell over that confounded stool. Sorry I woke you."

Mrs. Grey rose from her chair and walked over to peer

through the window.

"The bus has turned round," she said over her shoulder. "Are you proposing to go to the office today?"

"I have yet to receive the summons," answered Peter calmly.

He replaced his cup in its saucer, lighted a cigarette and leant back in his chair, seemingly at peace with the world and especially with Peter Grey.

"It'll go without you," his mother warned.

"Not before old Triton blows his wreathèd horn."

"It might be a new driver."

"And so might pigs."

"So might they what?"

The obvious answer was never given, for at that moment there echoed round the empty village a peremptory "ER-er! ER-er!"

Peter leapt from his chair, folded up his paper, kissed his mother, snatched his hat and pulled open the green front door in one swift continuity of movement.

"How much longer are you going to wear that hat?" asked Judy before he disappeared. "It makes you look like a cross between a Swiss mountaineer and a Buff Orpington."

"As long as it continues to annoy Courtenay—and not a moment longer," he grinned, gave the offending hat a still more rakish tilt and, with a poor attempt at a yodel, ran down the garden path and across Plestrium Sinister towards the waiting bus.

The others began to clear away the breakfast things.

"I wish," said Mrs. Grey, piling china on a tray, "that you and Peter were kinder to Courtenay."

"We *are* kind to him," responded Judy. "You'd be surprised if you knew how hard we work at it. When I wake up in the morning, I say 'Every day in every way I must be kinder and kinder to Courtenay.'"

"Now you're being silly, dear."

"Certainly I am. But really, Mother, you can't expect Peter

and me to *love* Courtenay. He's completely insufferable—and you *know* it! The other day he found a toad in the garden and before I could stop him, he'd picked it up and flung it at the wall with a simply beastly laugh. That's the sort of nice little boy he is!"

While Mrs. Grey looked miserable, Judy pursued her advantage.

"The only thing to do," she said stoutly, "is to throw him out on his ear, preferably the left ear, because that was the one he had an ache in last winter."

"Judy!" protested her mother.

"I mean it! He's caused nothing but trouble since the first day he came here, which seems more like fifty years ago than five."

"I couldn't do that. If it weren't for us, he would be alone in the world."

"Serve him jolly well right. He's a crafty, deceitful, stuck-up, callous, self-opinionated, supercilious, sneaking little... little... *wart!"*

In her excitement, Judy dropped a cup on the red-tiled floor.

"Peter and I put up with him," she went on, as she stooped to collect the fragments, "but I don't see why we should go on doing it indefinitely. You know Peter's a bit impetuous. One of these days, he'll knock Courtenay's block off good and proper—and if *he* doesn't, I will!"

She jumped to her feet and waved her finger accusingly at Mrs. Grey.

"How much money did you give him last week?"

"Two pounds," was the meek reply.

"Well, that's just four pounds too much. What does he do for us in return? Nothing. He doesn't even hang up his clothes. What does he think this is—a free hotel? He's got talent and if we don't fling him out in the cold, cold snow, he'll never use it, except to think up new ways of being warty."

"I do wish you'd stop using that word!"

"And I wish you'd stop being sentimental and silly. Courtenay's sniggering up his sleeve at all of us."

"He's your Aunt Minnie's child."

"She couldn't help that, poor dear."

So their talk went over the same ground as had been covered many times before; for Mrs. Grey's kind heart and sense of duty to her dead sister had always deterred her from taking the step that would have fulfilled their dearest wish: riddance of Courtenay Harbord.

Detective-Sergeant Albert Martin had no liking for his task. In his forty-six years, the first twenty-five of which had been divided between the drab and overpopulated district having Camberwell Green as its centre and that other afflicted region that lay around Verdun, he had been given many unpleasant things to do; but there had been few he had relished less than this one.

He got off the blue bus outside the "Sun in the Sands," walked slowly round to Old Forge House, closed the gate behind him and went up the path. On the worn doorstep, he paused, adjusted his bowler, squared his shoulders under his neat blue serge suit: then lifted the shining knocker on the low green door.

It was 11.30 that same morning. Mrs. Grey and Judy had formally identified the body of Courtenay Harbord and the first wild grief of his aunt and the lesser, but sincere, distress of his cousin had now abated. They were both still pale from the shock of it, but calm enough to face Charlton's interrogation. They sat in his room at Lulverton police station with Sergeant Martin in attendance.

When Charlton's deep, cultured voice was at its gentlest and most persuasive, it usually meant trouble for his *vis à vis;* but now his questions were quietly put for quite another reason.

"I think Mr. Harbord was your nephew, Mrs. Grey?" he began.

"He was my sister's son. She and my brother-in-law are both dead and he came to live with us."

"Has he any other close relations—brothers or sisters?"

"No, we were his only relatives. My sister and I were the only two in our family and my brother-in-law was an only child."

"How old was Mr. Harbord?"

"He would have been twenty-six in November."

"He was quite a—normal young man?"

"Oh, yes."

"How long has he lived with you?"

"Just over five years. His parents died in a typhoid epidemic and ours was the only home that he had to go to."

"Had he any occupation?"

Mrs. Grey hesitated. "He was very artistic and sold some of his etchings and paintings. He once had a poem published in *Verses of Tomorrow*."

"But he had no regular employment?"

Again she hesitated. "No."

"I expect his parents left him provided for," he nodded, seeming to dismiss the subject. "Now, Mrs. Grey, please turn your mind——"

"Just a moment," Judy interrupted him. "Mother, the Inspector is being misled. Let *me* tell him."

"No, dear. It can't possibly have anything to do with poor Courtenay's terrible accident."

"Inspector," said Judy, leaning eagerly forward in her chair, "my cousin's mother and father did *not* provide for him. My uncle left only a few pounds. Since they died *we* have kept him—or rather, Mother has."

"It's a difficult business finding a post these days," said Charlton sympathetically.

"Yes," Mrs. Grey took up the theme far too avidly. "With all this unemployment, it's a wonder any young man can get a job."

Which answered the question that he had been careful not to ask: Courtenay Harbord had been a shirk-work.

"Did this worry Mr. Harbord?"

Mrs. Grey felt herself falling into the trap. She vainly played for time.

"I don't quite understand what you mean, Inspector."

"Was he depressed by his position? By his failure to find work?"

The trap clicked shut. Mrs. Grey began to stammer something, but Judy touched her arm.

"Please excuse my mother," she said with a faint smile. "Courtenay was one of our family and she is anxious to say nothing to hurt him. Your question puts her in a very difficult position."

Charlton rose from his seat at the desk and walked to the window.

"It's not a very important point," ventured the girl. He swung round and looked down at her, his handsome face very grave.

"Miss Grey," he said softly, "in a few days from now, a coroner's jury will decide how Mr. Harbord died. I think you would both like their verdict to be Accidental Death."

For a second or two, there was silence in the room, except for the furtive squeaking of Martin's new boots.

"My questions may seem trivial," Charlton went on, "but I do assure you that they are not."

Judy made up her mind.

"Courtenay was living on our charity, and he was doing it deliberately. He never had——"

"Judy, darling——"

"He never had the slightest intention of earning a living, so long as we made his bed and cooked his meals and gave him all the money he needed. I know that it's horrible to say it about him now that he's dead, but I've told you what you want to know!"

Charlton, having gained his point, sat down. Martin's discreet cough denoted approbation.

"You say that he had all the money he needed. Do you think he had any financial anxieties?"

It was Mrs. Grey who answered:

"I feel sure he hadn't, or he would have told me."

"Did he usually tell you his troubles?"

"When they were money troubles, yes," supplied Judy.

"Did you ever receive the impression, Mrs. Grey, that he was spending more than you gave him?"

"No, I don't think so."

"And you, Miss Grey?"

"It's difficult to say, Inspector. You see, *we* weren't there when he spent it. There isn't very much you *can* spend money on in Sheep. He had friends we've never met."

"Perhaps you know some of them by name?"

"There are people here in Lulverton he spent a lot of time with. Their name's Quentin. When he missed the last bus back to Sheep, he used to stay the night at their house."

"Do you know the address?"

"It's that house on the corner of Vanbrugh Road at the top of Beastmarket Hill. I've never been inside or even met the Quentins, but that's where they live."

"He spent last Friday night there," added Mrs. Grey.

"Can you think of any other friends of his?"

Mrs. Grey pursed her lips and Judy delayed replying.

"Yes," she said eventually. "He used to visit a house in Etchworth village. He hasn't been going there so much lately. It's a Mr. Greenhill and he lives in Etchworth High Street. The house is on the left-hand side going from here, the first one past the Memorial Hall."

"Thank you, Miss Grey. Now, there's just one other small question before we come to the events of yesterday. Did Mr. Harbord smoke?"

"Yes. Cigarettes."

"Many?"

"Quite a lot. I can't tell you exactly, but at least twenty a day."

"Which brand?"

"Craven 'A'."

"Did he always smoke those?"

"Yes, he liked the cork tips."

"Did he smoke a pipe at all?"

"I've never seen him with one. Have *you*, Mother?"

"No, dear. He always used to say it was too much trouble. Poor Courtenay!"

"Did either of you see him yesterday?"

They both agreed.

"Will you please describe to me just what happened, Mrs. Grey. Did he sleep at Old Forge House on Saturday night?"

"Yes. He came down on Sunday morning at about nine o'clock and we all had breakfast together. Usually, we have ours first, because Peter—my son—has to be at his office soon after nine."

"I should like to speak to Mr. Grey. He's with Cooper & Silcock, isn't he?"

"That's right. After breakfast, Courtenay went out and I didn't see him again until he came home to lunch at one. I had some visitors—customers, you know—to see to and I didn't notice what happened to him after lunch. My daughter says——"

"Perhaps Miss Grey will tell me herself?"

"He went out at about three o'clock—almost exactly three, I should say," answered Judy, "and that was the last time I saw him alive."

"Did he tell you where he was going or when he would be back?"

"He said something about 'the wind on the heath, brother' and a tramp across the Downs blowing the cobwebs from a busy man's brain."

"Obviously in high spirits. Did he say anything else to you?"

"Only good-bye, or words to that effect."

"Can you remember the exact phrase?"

"Yes. It was, 'So long, cheerful!'"

"Was that a favourite expression of his?"

"Not particularly."

"Had he any reason for using it then?"

"It was just another way of saying good-bye."

"But why 'cheerful'? Because you *were* cheerful?"

"No. Because I *wasn't*."

Charlton's smile was disarming.

"It's a quaint custom in this country," he seemed to drift off into idle speculation, "that when we mean one thing, we usually say the opposite. After a day's incessant rain, we call it lovely weather and when anything especially pleases us, we describe it as frightfully nice or terribly attractive."

Judy relaxed in her chair, but Martin, who knew his chief, waited for the blow to fall. "Lull them, Martin," was the advice he had so often heard, "wrap them in comforting assurances, croon them a lullaby of honied words and then, when they are soothed and unaware, rap out your question suddenly."

"I don't know whether it is," Charlton mused on, "that we are a cross-grained, contrary lot, or whether it is that we, as a nation, instinctively hide our real thoughts, or whether it's only a kind of humorous sarcasm. Probably," he smiled, "it's a mixture of all three. Was Mr. Harbord the cause of your depression, Miss Grey?"

"I'm quite sure he wasn't," Mrs. Grey replied with animation. "We all get scratchy at times and it's a worrying business catering for customers who are difficult and purposely awkward. *If* my daughter wasn't in her usual good spirits, it was most likely some little thing like that that had irritated her."

He patiently heard her out.

"But Mrs. Grey," he said, "didn't I understand you to say that you did not notice what happened to Mr. Harbord after lunch?"

She looked puzzled.

"The Inspector means, Mother," explained Judy, "that you tried to answer a question that was meant for me."

She turned back to him.

"Mr. Harbord and I had a fearful row," she told him with a frankness that made her mother gasp. "*If*," she continued after a pause, "it doesn't take two to make a quarrel."

"Your discussion was one-sided?"

"Yes. *I* did all the talking. The only thing my cousin did was smirk, and that, as you'll guess, increased my—cheerfulness."

"I always thought you and Courtenay were such *good* friends," wailed Mrs. Grey.

But on that morning *esprit de corps* did not weigh very heavily with Judy Grey.

"I was trying to knock some sense of decency into him. It was about time somebody told him what a nasty, sarcastic, cadging little fellow he was."

"But darling——"

"Be *quiet*, Mother! I know what I'm saying—and that is that if anyone was less likely than anyone else in all the big, wide world to commit suicide, it was my cousin, Courtenay Harbord!"

V.

MARTIN'S AUNT

THERE was an odd look in Charlton's grey eyes.

"Don't you think," he said, "that your remonstrances made any impression on Mr. Harbord?"

"Of course they didn't," scoffed Judy. "I knew, right from the beginning, that it was a waste of time, but I was silly enough to try. I caught him at the front door and asked him to come and talk to me in the summer-house in the back-garden. He was so *infuriating* that I lost my temper and said things that would have made him lose his if he'd been more of a man and less of a parasite. Then, when I'd reached the point of hitting him, he picked up his hat and left with the words I've already told you. I didn't think, as I watched him walk across the lawn and disappear round the side of the house, that that was the last thing he'd ever say to me."

"What sort of hat was it?"

"It was green—a rough fur felt, pushed into a pork-pie shape. There were some feathers stuck in it."

"Can you recall what else he was wearing?"

"A pin-stripe grey flannel suit, a grey sports shirt with a tie of the same material and brown shoes."

"Can you describe the shoes more fully?"

"They were heavy golf shoes with barred rubber soles."

"Wasn't he also wearing a raincoat?"

"He took one with him, but when I last saw him, he was carrying it over his arm."

"How many hats had he altogether?"

"Mother?"

"Four," answered Mrs. Grey. "The green one, an ordinary brown felt, an opera hat and a check cap."

"Would you mind confirming when you get home that the

brown hat and the cap are still where they ought to be?"

"Of course not. Judy, please remind me." Charlton broached his next subject.

"Was Mr. Harbord interested in amateur dramatics?"

Mother and daughter both looked startled. They had been told nothing of the dead man's disguise.

"Not as far as I know," said Judy at last. "He loved the sound of his own voice, but that was as far as it went."

"He didn't possess any stage properties: grease-paint, wigs and so forth?"

"Oh, no!" Mrs. Grey said.

"Had he anywhere to lock such things away?"

"No. He never did lock anything away. There's a chest of drawers and a dressing-table in his bedroom, but I'm always going to those when I see to his clothes."

"Would you say that he was fussy about his clothes?"

"Not so much fussy as funny. The poor, dear boy liked to be *different*. He used to wear the strangest ties sometimes, just to express his individuality, I really believe. I remember how cross he was when my son bought himself a green hat just like the one he was wearing when he died." She looked piteously at her daughter. "He's *dead*, Judy. I'm still trying hard not to believe it, but he's *dead*."

The girl rose swiftly from her chair and put her arm around her mother, who burst into a wild fit of tears.

It was some little time before Charlton could ask his next question.

"Did Mr. Harbord ever wear spectacles?"

"Never," said Judy.

"Do *you*, Mrs. Grey?"

"Yes, I have a pair of horn-rims for reading and sewing."

"You did not miss them yesterday?"

"Good heavens, no! Why should I?"

"Does your son use glasses?"

"No."

"Have you any sun-glasses or anything of that kind in the house?"

"What about that pair, Judy, that Peter bought for a joke years ago? Those ones with plain glass in them. We've still got those somewhere, haven't we?"

"We'll have to ask Peter. *I* don't know."

"Perhaps you'll be good enough to let me know if you manage to find them. I suppose that you yourselves have no stage properties in your possession?"

"None of any sort," said Judy decisively. "Peter and I have never been interested in theatricals. I *really* don't understand all these strange questions!"

"It is right that you should know," said Charlton gravely, "that when Mr. Harbord's body was found this morning at the foot of Etchworth Tower, he had on a false beard, and, according to the evidence, he was wearing it when he went to the Tower at four o'clock yesterday afternoon."

He got to his feet and Martin relaxed his rigid pose.

"I won't keep you ladies any longer. I need hardly say how much I regret having to bother you with my questions so soon after the tragedy."

The Sergeant opened the door and Judy followed Mrs. Grey out of the room, When the two detectives were left alone, Martin, the film-fan, enquired with a rising inflection:

"What do you know about that?"

"Not nearly as much as I fear," Charlton answered seriously, then went on in a more matter-of-fact tone, "Did you find the son, Peter Grey?"

"No, sir. They told me at Cooper & Silcock's that he'd gone off in the firm's car and wasn't expected back until this afternoon—about two o'clock, they thought."

"I'll see him then. In the meantime, Martin, there's something else you can do. You heard Miss Grey say that Harbord left Old Forge House at three o'clock yesterday afternoon. I want you to find out where he went after that. It's quite likely that he caught one of the buses, so I should begin by having a word with the conductors who were on yesterday."

"I'll see to that, sir."

"One other thing. Make general enquiries in Etchworth for anyone who saw a man on the Tower balcony after six o'clock last night. There's no parapet round the balcony, you know—only an iron railing—and anyone up there would have been clearly visible from the village, and, of course, from a good many other points. We're not concerned with anyone seen up there *before* six o'clock. You heard Miss Grey mention a man named Greenhill? Leave him out: I'll see him myself. I shall also be interested to know whether Harbord was seen in the village after four o'clock; and to hear about a man with the following description. Get out your tablets and write it down."

The Sergeant produced a note-book.

"Aged twenty-five or six; height, five feet ten; carrying a raincoat folded inside out; possibly hatless, but if not, wearing a cloth cap or a brown or grey felt; grey pin-stripe flannel suit; smoking a pipe; cleanshaven or fairly full moustached (that's beautifully vague, but it can't be helped): and very likely wearing spectacles, horn-rimmed or otherwise. Have you got all that?"

Martin was looking interested.

"Yes, sir. How are things shaping, sir? Looks as if you're making progress."

Once Martin had been sergeant in charge of Paulsfield Sub-Division, but a few months previously, when the detective-sergeant at Lulverton Divisional Headquarters had been transferred to another part of the County, Martin had taken his place. He had once confided to Charlton (who was, although neither of them ever dropped a hint of it, his best friend, whom he followed with a dog-like devotion) that he always got the fidgets out of uniform, never knowing where to put his thumbs; and even now he spoke dolefully of the days at Paulsfield when he had been "a little tin god in me own right and not one of them black-coated workers." But, in the secret places of his heart, he had been a proud and delighted man ever since Superintendent Kingsley, in a confidential interview, had told him of the appointment that had been later officially confirmed in the General Orders.

"The only thing that's clear at the moment, Martin," said Charlton, "is that a series of singular events have taken place in this neighbourhood during the last twenty-four hours."

"But it's a plain case of suicide, isn't it, sir?"

"Have you an Auntie Flo, Martin?"

"No," chuckled the Sergeant. "I've got an Auntie Fannie 'oo lives a few doors away from the 'Marquis of Granby' at New Cross—and a proper old so-and-so she is, too!"

"Well," smiled Charlton, "suicide *her*."

"Don't you think 'e done 'imself in?"

"Not for a moment. I'll give you a rough idea of what I've discovered so far."

He pulled a Gold Flake packet from his pocket and lighted a cigarette.

"At approximately four o'clock yesterday afternoon, a brown-bearded man presented himself at the Tower turnstile. On the evidence of old Lee, the attendant, he was wearing a raincoat and a rough green felt hat. He bought a picture-postcard from Lee and told him to keep the change out of the shilling. He said that he had brought his raincoat in case the weather changed, and offered Lee a Craven 'A' cigarette from a new packet. Lee refused, explaining that he preferred his pipe, and the visitor said that he himself never smoked a pipe. Lee passed him through the turnstile—and that was the last Lee remembers having seen of him yesterday. He has no recollection of his leaving the Tower, but admits that his attention was not on the turnstiles all the time. What do you deduce from that?"

"That this Whiskers was still 'iding in the Tower when Lee locked up for the night."

"To me it suggests just the opposite. What did he do when he met Lee? He tried to impress his appearance on Lee's mind. He gave him a fairly handsome tip—and, after what you've heard of him, can you imagine Harbord throwing his money about like that?—chatted with him for some time, drew his attention to his raincoat and told him that he never smoked a pipe."

The Sergeant roughed up his thin sandy hair.

"Where does that get us?"

"Doesn't it suggest that he wanted to distract Lee's notice from the unobtrusive exit, later in the afternoon, of a man *without* a beard, wearing any other hat than a rough green felt, smoking a pipe and carrying a raincoat neatly folded inside.

"Oh-HO," said the comprehending Sergeant.

"It's only a theory, of course, but this bearded man— Whiskers, I think you christened him—does seem to have been more than careful to leave a clear picture of himself in Lee's mind. If *you*, Martin, were proposing to skulk behind after everyone had gone and then fling yourself from the Tower balcony, would *you* do all the things this fellow did? Would *you* draw attention to the way you were dressed and stand chatting with the attendant quite long enough for him to take in all the details about you? Surely not! You would be deliberately hazarding your chances of being left in the Tower after Lee had locked up and gone home. There would be a big danger of Lee being on the watch for you and making a very thorough search when he found you missing."

"But," suggested Martin, who had been following closely, "this bloke that you think left the Tower after pulling off the whiskers and getting 'is pipe nicely under way was running the same risk by chin-waggin' with Lee."

"Certainly he was; but it was a sporting chance that it was a part of his plan to take."

"Did Lee's description of Whiskers tally with young 'Arbord's body when it was found this morning?"

"In every way. The clothes were the same and I found a picture postcard in his pocket, as well as a packet of Craven 'A' with one cigarette missing. *That's* another interesting point."

"What is?"

"While he was talking to Lee at the turnstiles, Whiskers opened a new packet of cigarettes. That was at four o'clock in the afternoon. Dr. Lorimer suggests that Harbord did not die until after half-past eight in the evening. What do you suppose he was doing during that long period?"

"Trying to pluck up courage to do the job. It'd take me the best part of a week to make up me mind to jump off that balcony—and even then I wouldn't do it!"

"According to Miss Grey, Harbord got through at least twenty cigarettes a day. Do you mean to tell me that, under such conditions, a confirmed smoker wouldn't light more than *one* cigarette? Why, in his state of horrible indecision, he'd chain-smoke like mad!"

"Perhaps 'e'd a stand-by supply."

"Where? There was no case in his pockets when I went through them and I made a special search, in and round the Tower, for discarded empty packets."

"No matches?"

"I found a half-filled box on him."

"'E might 'ave carried the smokes loose."

"That's hardly likely."

"Neither is togging yourself up in false whiskers of a fine Sunday afternoon," retorted Martin, and respectfully added, "if I may say so."

"'A hit, a very palpable hit!'" laughed Charlton. "Let's say that I can't see any earthly reason why Harbord should have done so."

"No more can I," Martin was forced to admit.

"Apart from that, I found only one Craven 'A' cigarette-end on the balcony. Reverting to my masterly summary, Lee told me that, between four o'clock, when he saw Whiskers go up the staircase, and six o'clock, when he locked up the Tower, he himself did not leave the office. You know it, I suppose?"

The Sergeant nodded. "Little cubby-hole just inside the doors. Took my nipper up there one Sunday."

"So Whiskers couldn't have slipped back into the Tower and up the stairs after Lee had made his last inspection of the balcony, which is a regular routine."

"What about keys?"

"There's a Chubb 'Detector' lock on the entrance doors which had not been tampered with. You know the idea of a 'Detector' lock? If you try to use a wrong key, the detector-lever locks the bolt, which can then only be released by turning the correct key the other way."

"Don't tell my missus," grinned Martin, "or she'll be fixing one on the sideboard."

"The key of the Chubb lock is on a ring with the keys of the outside gates and the strong-box in the office. Lee deposits them every night at the Council offices. Yesterday evening, he handed them over to Mr. Matthews, and this morning, he got them back from a man named Lambert."

"'E's a queenie, if ever there was one!"

"You know him? I met him this morning for the first time and disliked him nearly as much as I do boiled cod."

"It's tomatoes with me," sympathised the Sergeant.

"You might find out whatever you can about that lovely young man—tactfully, of course. He seems to have had quite a lot to do with the Tower. And if you want any help on these inquiries, take Bradfield or Emerson."

Martin got out his book and scribbled a note.

"So nobody without a key," Charlton went on, "could have got into the building after Lee closed up last night. I think we can go further and say nobody without the key on Lee's ring, because the only duplicate in existence is lying cosily in the strong room of the Metropolitan & Provincial Bank."

"Lee might 'ave left 'is lying about."

"I don't think that would matter. It needs more than average ability to cut a six-lever key from a hurriedly made wax-impression. Besides, Lee keeps the keys on a chain attached to a trouser-button."

"But in spite of anything that 'appened later on yesterday, your theory boils down, doesn't it, to this: that the bearded man who went up the Tower yesterday wasn't 'Arbord."

"Precisely."

"Then you and your 'umble servant are on the threshold, as you might say, of another murder mystery?"

"It's beginning to look like it."

"That's the idea!" enthused Martin, but his superior did not smile.

"I only wish I could agree with you," he said quietly, "but I'm not easy in my mind."

Martin had not been made detective-sergeant for nothing.

"They certainly didn't *seem* to think any great shakes of 'im," he wisely observed.

"No."

"Mrs. G did 'er 'poor Courtenay' turn and she's very likely cut up about it; but it looked to me as if anything short of murder to get the fellow out of the 'ouse would 'ave been just her cup of tea."

"Yes."

"And the girl. By the way she went on, he was just as much to 'er taste as a dose of cyanide. I wouldn't put it past *her*—"

"*Stop that!*"

There was white fury on Charlton's face. He swung round from the astonished Sergeant and stared out unseeingly into the sunlit street. It was a full minute before he turned back into the room.

"I'm sorry, Martin," he smiled weakly. "I forgot myself for a moment. Carry on from where you left off."

The Sergeant's round, red face had an anxious look. For the first time in ten years, he had seen Charlton lose his temper. He managed to stammer:

"That door at the top of the staircase. Was it locked when—"

"I asked you to go on with what you were saying when I interrupted you."

"It wasn't anything very much, sir."

"Let's have it. I promise not to fly at your throat again."

Martin hesitated before he blurted out:

"Mrs. Grey let fall that 'e bought 'imself a green hat just like 'Arbord's."

"I was wondering if you'd noticed that."

"Course it all depends on what this—on what Mr. Grey looks like. I've never set eyes on 'im."

"He's very similar to Harbord—not in looks, but in build. Five feet ten or thereabouts, middling brown hair parted on the left, with a bit, but not much, of a wave in it. He's about a year older than Harbord, but a far pleasanter fellow. Harbord was a supercilious, disdainful little worm. Grey played fly-half for Kent Public Schools and he's got an open-air look about him: tanned and healthy."

"I didn't know you knew them."

"I met the whole family some months ago. Don't you remember?"

Martin snapped his fingers.

"Of course I do now! I hadn't connected 'em up. I'm wondering what you kept on at Mrs. Grey about them glasses for."

"In order to slip out of the Tower unnoticed, Whiskers had not only to make himself look different from Whiskers, if you follow me, but also to make himself look different from himself, if you still follow me. Horn-rimmed glasses are wonderful things for disguising one's appearance and would be the first idea of anyone with that intention."

For a time, they were both busy with their thoughts. Martin broke the silence with the question:

"Will you get any help from the whiskers?"

"A lot, I hope. *Someone* must have bought them."

"They'll take some tracing."

"Not necessarily. I went into the subject a few years ago and I learnt that there are four general grades of false beard. Firstly, the crepe-hair beard described in the catalogue as, 'Whiskers on wire, 2/-.' This wouldn't deceive anyone and is the kind worn by Father Christmases—or is it Fathers Christmas?"

"Santa Clauseses," suggested Martin, who was always ready to give advice.

"I mean the ones outside big stores in December. The beard usually hooks over the ears and is very convenient for lightning changes in concert party burlesques. Secondly, human hair on a gauze foundation, which is the type most employed for serious stage performances. Thirdly, human hair knotted on a *net* foundation. That one's largely used for film work. The telescopic camera would instantly show up the faults of a gauze foundation, but this third quality not only defies the camera, but is also sufficiently convincing to trick the man in the street. Finally, there is the beard that is applied by an expert directly to the face, hair by hair, and is so completely like the real thing that it will stand up to the closest examination.

"The beard I pulled off Harbord's face this morning was Grade 3—human hair knotted on a net foundation, which probably isn't stocked by smaller firms of theatrical costumiers. It costs about a guinea and is much too good for ordinary amateur dramatics."

"That's a bit of fat," said Martin. "We'll soon find where that was bought. Isn't it a bit of a job getting a thing like that off your face, once it's stuck on?"

"Not really. The best way is to rip it off quickly."

He felt in his pocket and brought out the bottle he had taken from Harbord's body. It had been carefully wrapped in tissue paper.

"A solution," he imitated the manner of a platform lecturer, "of mastic in alcohol, known in the building trade as white hard varnish and sold for one-and-six a pint; but known in the theatrical profession as spirit gum and retailed at sixpence the tiny bottle."

"Made," appended Martin, "by Contented Workers in our Sunshine Factory."

"The label's been taken off," said Charlton. "We'll have the bottle tested for fingerprints. I found it in Harbord's pocket."

He refolded the paper round it.

"Well, Martin," he continued, "that's about all there is for the moment. You carry on as I suggested and we'll compare notes this evening."

"Right, sir."

In the room known as the "Inspector's Office," where members of the public came to report across the counter that they had either lost a bicycle or found one, Station-sergeant Harrison was speaking on the telephone.

"I've been perusing that charge of yours," he said to the distant subscriber, "and I notice that you've got the date of the offence as the Ist October, which is tomorrow. Is that all right? ... No, I thought you were a bit previous.... O.K. So long."

As he replaced the receiver, Martin came up behind him, took his arm and looked earnestly round into his face.

"Sarge," he said, "in your long and not very virtuous life, 'ave you ever found yourself face to face with a wounded tiger in a room fourteen foot by twelve?"

"Can't say I have."

"Neither 'ave I, but I know now what it feels like." He slammed his bowler on his head, tapped it crooked with the flat of his hand, and pushed through the wicket out into the autumn sunshine.

VI.

ONE NAMED PETER

MRS. GREY and Judy caught the blue bus outside the Library and had very little to say to each other on the journey back to Sheep; but in the privacy of their own home, they went over the whole matter again and again. Neither could think that Harbord had deliberately killed himself and the thought of murder did not, for a moment, enter their heads. Accidental death was the theory to which they both desperately—and against all reason—clung.

"If *only* it was an accident," sighed Mrs. Grey for the tenth time, as they prepared the lunch that neither felt she could face.

"I keep on telling myself that it *must* have been," replied Judy, "but every time a little voice says, 'How?'"

"Perhaps he wanted to look at something and leant over a bit too far."

"He couldn't. There's a high railing all round the balcony."

"He might have climbed up it to get a better view, and fallen over the top."

"That's our only hope. But why the false beard?"

"Just a practical joke, I expect. I can think of all sorts of reasons."

"For instance?"

"Well. ..." For a moment she was at a loss. "Well, suppose somebody had bet him that he wouldn't climb up and sit on top of the railings; and he didn't want anybody else to know who it was, in case he got into trouble, so put on a false beard. That's *quite* likely, isn't it?"

"No."

"Well," she tried again, but a car pulled up outside, a door slammed and they heard someone coming up the path. "That'll be Gerrish's," she said.

It was not Gerrish's. The front door was flung open and a smiling young man burst into the room and rocketed his hat expertly across to a chair.

"Good afternoon, girls!" he greeted them.

"Why, Peter!" exclaimed his mother. "What are *you* doing here?"

"I thought I'd give you a treat. I've been over to Eastbourne and popped in here for lunch on my way back. Is there any? A steak and chips, a few mushrooms and a Guinness, followed by apple-tart and cream and a nice ripe piece of camem—"

His smile faded.

"Is anything the matter?" he asked anxiously. "You both look like death. What is it, mother?"

"We've bad news for you, Peter, dear."

"What's happened?"

"Courtenay has had an accident."

"Tough luck! Shock and bruises and all that?"

"It is far, far worse than that. Courtenay is—dead, Peter."

"Good God!"

"They found him early this morning lying with a broken neck at the bottom of Etchworth Tower."

Peter dropped into a chair.

"That's rotten. Poor chap! How did it happen?"

"Nobody knows yet. Inspector Charlton—you remember him?—is looking into it. We think he must have slipped and fallen off the balcony."

"What a horrible business. That tower must be a hundred feet high."

"Judy and I haven't been back very long. We had to go to Lulverton to identify the poor boy and then we went round to the police station and were asked a lot of questions. Inspector Charlton wants to see you as well."

"I'll call in there before I go back to the office."

The cold lunch was ready and the three of them sat down

to it without much appetite.

"I don't see," said Peter, as he took his plate from Mrs. Grey, "how Courtenay could have accidentally fallen off the balcony. I can't remember very clearly, but surely there's a high grille to prevent any trouble like that?"

"We think," firmly asserted his mother, "that he climbed up the grille and missed his footing."

"Why on *earth* should he climb the grille? When did this—accident happen?"

"He went to the Tower yesterday afternoon."

"And he wasn't found till this morning? But isn't the Tower closed at six o'clock? If he did it at all, mustn't he have done it before then? Why wasn't his body discovered last night? The attendant was there, wasn't he?"

He ceased to fire off questions and helped himself liberally to mustard.

"He must have got left inside when the place was locked up," suggested Judy.

"That's it!" fluttered her mother. "Courtenay found himself trapped on the balcony for the night and tried to escape by climbing over the railings."

"And what do you think he proposed to do after that?" Judy dashed her rising spirits. "The Tower shaft is quite smooth and there wouldn't have been anything for him to hang on to."

"He may not have thought of that until it was too late."

"It's not very convincing, Mother," contended Peter. "Is it possible that he *meant* to get left in the Tower and hid himself until everyone else had gone?"

"Why?" asked his matter-of-fact sister.

"He might have been up to his tricks again."

An understanding glance passed between him and Judy.

"The very thing I was saying to Judy before you came in, dear. You remember how he always loved his little joke."

"Very clearly," agreed Peter with bitterness, "and the worse taste it was in, the better he loved it."

He caught the look on Mrs. Grey's face.

"I'm sorry, mother," he said repentantly. "I ought not to have said that."

"It's all right, dear," she answered sadly. "I knew Courtenay as well as you did, probably better; but we should try to forget his little weaknesses now that he's...."

Her voice trailed away.

"The thing I can't understand," Judy tried to create a diversion, "is the beard. It seems so fantastic."

Peter's eyes were enquiring.

"When they discovered his body this morning," she explained, "he was wearing a false beard."

"Why! That must have been the—"

His knife fell from his hand and clattered on the tiled floor.

"Must have been what, dear?" asked Mrs. Grey when he had retrieved it.

He helped himself to some more mustard before he replied:

"That must have been the reason ... What you said just now must have been the reason for wearing a false beard ... He was—playing a practical joke and used the beard for that."

Mrs. Grey beamed happily.

"I'm sure it was," she said. "Aren't you, Judy?"

"I can't believe that he committed suicide," was all her daughter had to say.

They ate in silence for a time. Then:

"Peter, dear, the Inspector asked Judy and me a lot of strange questions. Can you remember what happened to that pair of horn-rimmed glasses you bought once?"

"I ... don't know what you're talking about."

"Those horn-rimmed glasses. It was a long time ago. Just ordinary glass, they were. Don't you remember how we all said you looked like Harold Lloyd?"

"Oh, those. They're upstairs somewhere. Aren't they in the trunk on the landing?"

"I must look. The Inspector wants to know whether we've

still got them."

"Why?"

"I don't know, dear, but he probably has his reasons. The police are rather mysterious in their methods."

Peter rolled his napkin and slipped it in the ring.

"Any clean handkerchiefs in my drawer?" he asked. "Couldn't find one this morning."

"Of course there are, dear. I put some there on Saturday."

She started to get up, but he was already at the foot of the stairs.

"Did you find them?" she asked when he came down.

"Yes," he said. "I must have been blind!"

At two o'clock he left them. Mrs. Grey took up some knitting, while Judy found a book. But in ten minutes both work and reading were abandoned.

"What a nice man Inspector Charlton is," mused Mrs. Grey. "So sympathetic and kind and with such pleasant manners. He's nothing like the detectives you see on the films, who never take their hats off and keep on saying, 'Wait a minute.'"

"They're American detectives," laughed Judy.

"Ours are quite different."

"He has such an intelligent face and his hair just turning grey gives him a very distinguished appearance, like an important diplomat. I think he wears very well, for he must be well on the wrong side of fifty."

"*Fifty?* He can't be more than forty-five or six."

The light of the gossip came into Mrs. Grey's eyes.

"I don't *know,* but they say he's got money of his own and that he comes from a good family. Do you remember reading in the papers three or four months ago the account of a wedding of a girl called Arnold—Molly Arnold, I think it was—with a man named Parkinson?"

"Rutherford, Mother. John Rutherford of Paulsfield."

Paulsfield was four miles to the north of Lulverton, just on the other side of the Downs.

"Well, dear, this Molly Arnold is Inspector Charlton's niece. She used to keep house for him. Now he is living alone, poor man, and I haven't the *least* doubt that he sleeps in *wringing* wet sheets every night of his life. Men have no idea of airing things."

"But doesn't he keep a servant?"

"*Servant?* You know what servants are, dear; and he can't always be there to see she does things properly. Servants have to be watched every *minute*. When he comes home after a hard day's detecting, he doesn't want to go round finding out if she's dusted everywhere. It's so exhausting. And Mrs. Fowler—Mrs. 'Inglenook' Fowler, not Mrs. 'The Hollies'—says it's a big house, a great *barn* of a place at the back of Southmouth."

She paused to breathe.

"Yes," she continued, "Molly Arnold must have been married to the Parkinson man just about the same time as the Inspector came over to see us."

Judy was perfectly well aware of that, but it was taking her mother's mind off the tragedy. Besides, the topic pleased her.

"Really?" she answered. "I'd forgotten about that business."

"Was it ever cleared up, do you know?"

"I'm sure it must have been. I should think that once *he* starts on anything, there's no stopping him. Look at the marvellous way he questioned us this morning. He kept on until he got what he wanted and yet he had such a comforting way with him. You felt you simply *had* to tell him everything, even where you kept your vaccination-marks. If I had a horrible, guilty secret right down inside me, I don't think I could keep it from him for long. I'd love to tell him the story of my life. When he turned round from the window and looked down at me with those eyes that you're never quite sure aren't laughing at you, and said that about the verdict of the jury, I went all squirmy inside."

Mrs. Grey felt that this was the moment for her rebuke.

"I don't think, dear, that you should have spoken as you did about Courtenay. We don't want everybody to know and it had nothing to do with the Inspector."

"It had a very great deal to do with him; and, as I just told you, I felt I couldn't keep anything back. Courtenay was a little beast and the Inspector had the right to know. You got yourself into a knot when you tried to make him think that Courtenay had been worrying himself sick looking for a job."

"I thought it was for the best, dear. I felt that otherwise I'd be betraying Courtenay."

Judy got up from her chair.

"You're a loyal old darling, and I'm sorry your daughter's not more like you. What do you say to a nice hot cup of tea?"

With his pleasant young face set in hard, thoughtful lines, Peter Grey turned the car northward, away from Sheep and Lulverton and the tall, white monument on the summit of High Down.

VII.

THE ROUTINE OF IT

WHEN Charlton arrived at the Southern Counties Bank, which is not to be confused with the Metropolitan & Provincial Bank, Mr. Maurice Scott-Brown, M.C., was just about to go to lunch, but he willingly laid aside his hat and took the detective into his room. He was a big, hearty man with a voice that had the deep richness of a moving-coil loudspeaker, and he took a prominent part in Lulverton affairs. The two knew each other well and, in a few words, Charlton explained what brought him to the bank.

"I understand, sir," he said, "that you arrived at the Tower a little before four o'clock?"

"Yes, somewhere between a quarter and ten to."

"And you left at four-thirty?"

"More or less. Can't be too exact, you know. Couple of minutes either way, perhaps."

"That's quite near enough. Did you see a bearded man wearing a rough green felt hat and a raincoat?"

Mr. Scott-Brown shook his head decisively.

"Won't be too definite about the hat and raincoat, but certainly saw no beards."

"You took some friends to the Tower with you, I think? Will you please tell me who they were?"

"My wife, my eldest daughter and Mr. and Mrs. Eric Rothbury. Mr. Rothbury is my nephew and they were down from London spending the weekend with us. Went back by the 7.50 this morning."

"Can you give me their address?"

"23a, Gleneagles Road, Blackheath, S.E. 3."

"During the time you were in the Tower, did you meet anyone you knew, either personally or by sight?"

The manager gave a deep-mouthed chuckle.

"Can't go anywhere in this district without doing that!" he said. "That's the trouble with most of us poor bank-men. Knew two of them. One my customer and very good friend, Major Stallard. He and another man were already on the balcony when we got there. Don't know who the friend was. Other was Mrs. d'Eyncourt, whose daughter goes to the same school as my youngest girl. She'd a friend with her, too. Heard 'em talking about the trains back to Waterloo, so it looks as if she was another Londoner."

"That's fine," smiled Charlton. "Any others?"

"There were a couple of young Americans. Heard the girl say, 'Whether Shakespeare is performed in Stratford-on-Avon or in Harlem, he's *good.*' Fine praise, that! Stuck in my mind. Suggests they'd recently been to the birthplace."

Mr. Scott-Brown's conversation had few trimmings. He was particularly sparing in his use of the first personal pronoun.

"You didn't catch any mention of where they were staying, I suppose?"

"No. Take it various other people came up and went down, but can't remember a thing about them. Chiefly concerned with the view."

"You didn't notice a brown-haired young man in a grey flannel suit? It's not much to go on, but he was either wearing or carrying a raincoat and possibly had a moustache. The hat was probably soft felt, or he might have worn a cloth cap."

"'Fraid not. You know how it is on that balcony. If you both walked at the same speed, two of you could go round and round it for a year and never catch sight of each other."

"As you climbed the stairs, did you meet anyone coming down?"

"Not a soul. Sure of that."

"And when you went down?"

"Caught a couple up near the bottom. Small man and a fat woman. Don't know how she got through the turnstile.

Amazing performance."

"Did you know Mr. Courtenay Harbord?"

"No."

The Inspector got up from his chair.

"I should like to see Mrs. Scott-Brown and your—"

"Just a moment!" interrupted the manager. "Thought of something else. Two boys of twelve or so, wearing Paulsfield caps."

"Splendid! *They* won't be hard to trace. Were they by themselves?"

Mr. Scott-Brown admitted that he was not sure. The distinctive pink caps were the only things he had noticed. Charlton took out his note-book and wrote down all the available names and addresses.

"Pretty quick worker," complimented Mr. Scott-Brown as the book was put away. "Didn't waste much time in picking up *my* trail!"

"I had it from a customer of yours," smiled the detective. "Old Tom Lee is very proud of his Home Safe account with you."

"Home Safes," said the manager, and there was a wealth of sincere feeling in his tone.

Mrs. d'Eyncourt was undoubtedly "County." She lived in a big house set back in its own extensive grounds from the Southmouth road. Charlton drove there after lunch and was graciously received.

"No," said Mrs. d'Eyncourt in answer to his first enquiry, "I didn't know the young man. It must have been a great shock to his family."

"I think you visited Etchworth Tower yesterday afternoon?"

"Yes, a friend of mine from London insisted on our going. It was the first time I have ever climbed it and it will certainly be the last."

"Mr. Scott-Brown of the Southern Counties Bank has told me that he met you on the balcony. Did you see anyone else you knew?"

"I don't think so."

"Or a bearded man wearing a rough green felt hat?"

"Definitely no."

"Or a young man with brown hair, in a grey flannel suit and a soft felt hat or a cloth cap? He was wearing or carrying a raincoat and may have had a moustache."

He thought wryly of the times he would probably be compelled to ask those same questions.

"Not with a moustache. There *was* a man—quite young—in a grey flannel suit and a brown felt hat. I *think* he was wearing horn-rimmed glasses. My friend spoke to him: asked him about a building we could see in the distance. He was very pleasant and nicely spoken; raised his hat and said he was very sorry, but he didn't know what it was, although it looked to him like a ruined castle."

"Do you think you would recognise him again?"

"Quite possibly. My friend, Miss Mortimer, is more likely to remember, for it was she who spoke to him."

"Will you kindly give me her address?"

"34, Boreham Court House, St. John's Wood, London."

The rest of his questions elicited only one piece of useful information. Mrs. d'Eyncourt and Miss Mortimer had been driven to the Tower in the Daimler (she thought it was the Daimler) and Robson, the chauffeur, had waited below while they made the ascent. Charlton asked if he might speak to him and was taken by a maid to where Robson, a young man smart in appearance and manner, was hosing down a Humber in the yard.

"You took Mrs. d'Eyncourt and a friend to Etchworth Tower yesterday afternoon, didn't you?" the Inspector began.

"Yezzir."

"What time did you get there?"

"Ten-past four, sir."

"And you waited in the car until the ladies were ready for

you to take them home."

"Yezzir."

"What time did you drive them away?"

"Just about four-twenty-five, sir."

"While you were sitting in the car, did you notice a bearded man leave the tower?"

"No, sir. I'm certain of that, sir."

Charlton repeated his description of the young man in the flannel suit, now adding the possibility that he wore glasses with horn-rims; but Robson was certain that no such person came out of the building while he was waiting.

"Sitting outside places half your time like I 'ave to do," said Robson, "you get the trick of taking an interest in everything that goes on round you. I weigh people up, trying to guess what they are and what they do for a living, if anything. I'll stake my oath that, while I was waiting for Madam, no such chap as you've described came out—*or* went in, for that matter."

"Good. Now let me test your powers of observation. Tell me about everyone you saw at that time, arriving and coming away."

Robson pursed his lower lip with his finger and thumb.

"After I'd been there a matter of ten minutes, p'raps not quite so long, a pair of Paulsfield College boys went in. One of them was tall for 'is age, which I'd put at twelve, and the other was a little chap. Just afterwards, they were followed by a fat woman and a little shrimp of a man 'oo looked silly enough to be 'er husband. By their talk as they went by me, I'd say they came from the same part of the world as I do—Bromley-by-Bow. No one else went in and there were only two as came out. A couple of oldish men. I thought I knew one of them by sight, but I can't be certain. Perky little gent, 'e looked. A bit 'igh and mighty, so to speak. Swung 'is walking-stick as if 'e'd got the massed bands be'ind 'im."

"What time would you say that was?"

"Twenty-past four or thereabouts."

"Does the name 'Major Stallard' convey anything to you?"

"Might very well 'ave been the small one. 'E looked military. But I can't say for sure. I've *heard* of a Major Stallard and that's all."

"And these persons you've mentioned were the only ones to come or go during your wait for the ladies?"

"Yes."

"You're sure of that?"

"Dead sure."

"Thank you, Robson. You've been very helpful."

"Granted," said the chauffeur magnanimously, and returned to his hosing.

Major Stallard was the next on the list. He was spraying his gooseberries with liver of sulphur when Charlton was announced and laid aside his syringe with reluctance. He wore a dreadfully shabby hat, but had all the appearance of Indian Army (ret. pay). His present manner was testy.

"Well, Inspector, what is it?" he demanded. "About that damned dog I complained of?"

"No, sir. I'm inquiring into a rather serious matter. The body of a man was found at the foot of Etchworth Tower this morning and I have been given to believe that you yourself visited there yesterday afternoon."

"What interfering busybody told you that?"

Charlton had questioned far too many difficult witnesses to be put off by any such brusqueness.

"I found it out in the course of my investigations, sir," he smiled. "It is purely a matter of routine."

"The whole of this town," snorted the Major, "is a seething mass of tittle-tattle. It makes me sick sir!"

"I need only take a moment or two of your time," the Inspector tried to mollify him. "Perhaps you will confirm that you arrived at the Tower with a friend some little time before 3.45 and that you left, still in the company of your friend, at

71

about twenty-past four?"

"Impudence! *Damned* impudence! By whose authority am I being spied upon? This is not Russia sir!"

It was rather like having a chat with a jumping cracker. Just as another explosion impended, Charlton did some quick thinking and said:

"My informant was Mr. Scott-Brown."

The Major's choler was immediately dissipated. "Mr. Scott-Brown. That puts an entirely different complexion on the matter. It was his duty to tell you, Inspector, just as it is my duty to answer your questions."

"That is very kind of you, sir. Perhaps you can help me to find out how this young man died. His name was Courtenay Harbord and he lived at Sheep with his aunt, Mrs. Grey. You may know the family?"

"Mrs. Grey I have met, and her daughter. *There's* a girl for you, Inspector! A thoroughbred, with class written all over her. If I had had a daughter instead of a son who's damn fool enough to waste his time in the Navy, when he could have chosen a *gentleman's* career in the Army, I should have been a proud man to rear a girl like Judith Grey."

Duty, with Inspector Harry Charlton, always came first. Therefore he changed the subject.

"Yesterday afternoon at four o'clock," he said, "a brown-bearded man passed through the Tower turnstile. Did you see him on the balcony, Major?"

"No. I saw Scott-Brown and his party, and a woman I've seen about Lulverton a good deal. She had a friend with her. Woman about the same age. Fifty-ish."

"Do you recall a young man in a brown hat and a grey flannel suit? I think he had horn-rimmed glasses on and was about five feet ten."

"Yes. Fellow with a moustache."

"I have been told that he was clean-shaven."

"Very likely. I didn't pay much heed to him. Thought he

had a moustache, though."

"You can't say definitely? It's an important point."

"Not in the witness-box. Perhaps Mr. Townsend will be able to say. He was up there with me. Came over with his wife from Whitchester and I took him out, so that the ladies could tell each other all about it. Beginning to wish we'd stayed at home!"

"Mrs. d'Eyncourt, who I think was the lady you mentioned just now, has told me that her friend spoke to this man. Did you see the incident?"

"No. The fellow I saw was wandering round by himself. But you ask Townsend, 72, Blossom Street, Whitchester."

"Can you tell me about anybody else on the balcony?" asked the detective as he wrote down Mr. Townsend's address.

"There were a young couple, but I think they were with the Scott-Browns. I've no doubt he's told you about them." He paused to think. "Oh, yes. I'd almost forgotten the Americans. Two of them; and the girl kept on saying how much she admired Shakespeare. He was apparently the only English institution to meet with her unqualified approval!"

"Was anyone coming up when you and Mr. Townsend were on your way out?"

"Yes. First we met a couple of young hooligans, who were racing each other up the stairs. I remember speaking to them rather sharply. Further down, we had difficulty in passing a female of immense bulk, who should never have embarked on the—ah—ascent. There was some sort of a man with her."

After five more minutes of unprofitable conversation, they parted on the best of terms.

At the offices of Messrs. Cooper & Silcock in the Thoroughfare, they had no news of Peter Grey. He had been expected, they said, at two o'clock, but he had not yet arrived. Charlton said he would call back later and went round to see Mrs. Scott-Brown and her daughter, Vera, who had just left school for good.

They were able to add a little to the sum of his knowledge. They were both certain about not having seen a bearded man, but less forthright on the question of the young man in the flannel suit. Vera said she had a hazy recollection of someone answering the description, but her mother's mind was a complete blank.

"I was concentrating more on my own troubles," she admitted with a smile. "I don't like heights and only went to please the others. Vera almost had to drag me there, didn't you, dear? If there had been *fifty* men in flannel suits and every one of them had had a flaming red beard and a bright blue *beret,* I doubt if I should have noticed!"

Vera had something interesting to say about the Americans. She had noticed them starting off down the staircase and had caught the man's remark about catching the bus to Sheep and having tea there.

Which was much to Charlton's liking. There was only one place for tea in Sheep.

At three-thirty, Peter Grey was still missing. After five minutes' talk with Superintendent Kingsley, in which mention was made of the British Broadcasting Corporation, Charlton continued on the round of district visiting. He could do little more at the moment about the visitors to the Tower, so transferred his attention to Courtenay Harbord's friends. He turned the car up the steep slope of Beastmarket Hill and pulled up outside the house on the corner of Vanbrugh Road.

It was a fine house and its name was "Capri." A uniformed servant answered his ring. He handed her his card and asked to speak to Mr. Quentin. It was ten minutes before she returned and invited him to follow her. The room into which she showed him was as richly furnished as the hall in which he had tarried. While he was thinking that space might have been found for a few marble pillars and an impressive musical-comedy staircase a smiling man came forward with outstretched hand.

"So sorry to keep you waiting, Sergeant," he gushed. "Please do sit down."

Charlton lowered himself into a square-armed easy chair that he thought would never stop sinking away from him. Mr. Quentin produced a box of cigars and offered it with a flourish, but Charlton politely refused.

"Perhaps you prefer a cigarette?" fussed Quentin and brought a big silver box from an inlaid table by the window. "Turkish, Egyptian, Russian," he recited, pointing with the chubby white finger of a hand that should have been grilled, like a jeweller's window, "and the common gasper."

"I'll have a common gasper," smiled Charlton.

He took one and felt for a match, but Mr. Quentin forestalled him with a petrol-lighter that took the shape of a Transatlantic liner. When Charlton thought that his host's anxiety for his comfort would urge him to the point of helping to smoke the cigarette, Quentin sat down on the edge of the chair opposite and said:

"Now, Sergeant, what can I do for you?"

He was about forty-five, short and fleshy without being fat, and perfectly dressed in a black jacket and striped trousers, with spotlessly white linen. His hair was black and smooth, and was brushed straight back from his forehead. His complexion was unhealthily white, as if from eating too many vegetables out of season.

"Do you know," asked the detective, "a Mr. Courtenay Harbord?"

"Harbord?"

"Yes. I understand from his aunt, Mrs. Grey, that he has visited here quite a lot."

"Oh, yes. My wife and I keep open house, you know, and all sorts of people pop in and out, just as they please."

"He was not a particular friend of yours?"

"I have so many friends, Sergeant."

"Then my news, if you don't know it already, won't come

as so great a shock to you."

Mr. Quentin's face grew solicitously long.

"Don't tell me that something has happened to the poor fellow?"

"He was found dead this morning at the foot of Etchworth Tower."

"My God! Had he thrown himself off? What a terrible thing for a man to do, especially one so young."

"When did you last see him, Mr. Quentin?"

Charlton's note-book was on his knee.

"Let me see ... When was it? ... One evening the week before last. Tuesday? No, we were out. Wednesday. That was it. Last Wednesday week."

"I am informed that he came to this house three days ago. Friday. Perhaps you were out *then?*"

"Of course! How silly of me! On Thursday my wife reminded me that we hadn't seen him for some time and I phoned him to ask him if he would care to make up a couple of tables of bridge on the following evening."

"Did he pass the Friday night here?"

"Yes, the bus services in this part of the world are not so good as they might be, and frequently we have to put our friends up—especially when the last rubber *refuses* to be finished!"

"You saw Mr. Harbord on Saturday morning?"

"No; he left the house before I was up."

"He didn't spend Saturday night here?"

"I can be quite definite about that. The last time I saw him was on Friday night, just before we retired to our rooms. Poor young fellow! Snuffed out like a candle. I'll admit, Sergeant, that I am more shocked than I can say."

"Was it your habit, when Mr. Harbord visited you, to play bridge for money?"

"Nominal stakes, you know, just to make the game interesting. As you've probably experienced yourself, Sergeant, bridge played for love always leads to persistent over-calling and general carelessness. Threepence a hundred was our maximum."

"Have you any knowledge of Mr. Harbord's financial affairs?"

"That's a thing," parried Mr. Quentin, "that one does not inquire into. I can only say that he seemed able to live up to his position in life."

It occurred to Charlton that Harbord should have had no trouble about that.

"I'll put my question more bluntly, Mr. Quentin," he said, leaning forward. "Did Mr. Harbord owe you any money?"

Quentin looked horrified. Then his features relaxed and he waved the question aside as unimportant.

"It was all part of the give and take among friends, easy come, easy go, you know!"

"Did Mr. Harbord owe you any money?" repeated Charlton with ominous gentleness.

"You're getting me in a corner, Sergeant," chided Mr. Quentin. "One hardly likes to mention private matters like that. It isn't quite the thing."

"I shall appreciate a plain yes or no, Mr. Quentin."

"Yes, then."

"How much?"

"A mere trifle. A few pounds. Something till the end of the month, sort of thing. Nothing for either of us to lose any sleep over."

"How much?"

"This is very unpleasant for me, Sergeant."

"That is unavoidable, I'm afraid. How much did Mr. Harbord owe you?"

Mr. Quentin opened his mouth, closed it again, and then said with extravagant unwillingness:

"As you insist upon knowing, ninety-seven pounds."

It was all Charlton could do not to jump.

"Don't think," Quentin went on hastily, "that I was at all

anxious about it. I knew Court would pay me back when the tide turned. We all have our ups and downs; and if, for a little while, we are lucky enough to be up, it's the least we can do to lend a hand to a friend who is temporarily down. He'd do the same for us. After all, Sergeant, it's only Christian, isn't it?"

He leapt up to supply Charlton with an ash-tray.

"You have heard," he said piously, "the story of the Good Samaritan?"

"I know *one* version," was Charlton's soft response.

VIII.

NIL NISI MALUM

"THAT debt of Harbord's," said the detective. "Was it for losses at cards?"

"My *dear* Sergeant! At threepence a hundred? Come! It was a loan."

"Did he borrow it for any particular purpose?"

"I should have said that it was a series of loans over a considerable period. A fiver here, a tenner there—and so forth. I liked the boy. That's really what it amounted to. He'd drop a hint that things were a bit tight and I'd call him an improvident young rascal, pull out my wallet and think no more about it."

"Yet you remember the total."

Mr. Quentin held up a white hand.

"There you wrong me, Sergeant. It was not I who remembered, but Court. He used to note down each—er—advance, in order to keep track of his indebtedness to me."

"Did he ever make any attempt to pay you back?"

"Very seldom, I'm forced to admit. And that was my reason for having a fatherly little chat with him last Friday evening, after my other guests had gone."

"Was he trying to borrow some more?"

"No. One must be fair to the boy. I found myself alone with him, which was the opportunity for which I had been waiting for some time. I felt that it was in his best interests to act as I did. I broached the subject by asking if things were getting easier for him financially. He replied that they were much about the same. Then I said that I had hoped that he would try to pay off some of his debt to me. Mark you, Sergeant, ninety-seven pounds or so doesn't give *me* much concern, but I thought that Court should be pulled up before he went too far."

"Did he make you any offer?"

"He said that it was impossible: that he hadn't a penny. 'Make an effort, Court,' I said. 'Get yourself a job and put aside a fixed amount each week. It's wonderful how soon it mounts up.' He promptly retorted that I was sermonizing like a silly old woman and that to ask him for money then was trying to get blood out of a stone. He said I might just as well demand the whole ninety-seven pounds, for all the chance I had of getting a brass farthing out of him. That irritated me, as you'll probably guess, Sergeant. I was rather short in my reply. I said that I expected something and suggested five pounds on account. 'Haven't I just told you,' he laughed, 'that I'm broke.' Then I had the idea of frightening him. I said that if I did not receive twenty pounds in cash by Monday morning—that was *this* morning—I should be compelled much against my wishes, to take an unpleasant step."

He laughed merrily.

"I had no notion of what that step would be, but it had the desired effect on Court, for the cheeky smile disappeared from his face and he turned and went up to bed without another word, not even 'Good-night'."

"And this morning his body was found on High Down."

Mr. Quentin looked suddenly appalled.

"My God!" he said in a hushed voice. "You don't mean … You can't possibly mean that he committed suicide because of that?"

"It will interest the coroner's jury."

"How terrible! I had no idea that the poor boy would take it so much to heart. If I had thought, for a single instant, that he would do such an awful thing, I would willingly have foregone every penny he owed me. What a frightful tragedy! And I'm to blame. Don't try to excuse me, Sergeant. The responsibility for Courtenay's death is mine—entirely mine!"

The Inspector, who had listened to this self-denunciation as if Mr. Quentin were remarking how the rain was keeping off, now took a grip on each arm of his chair and forced his body from its soft, embracing depths. Mr. Quentin was out of his in a flash.

"Can I offer you something before you go?" he asked.

Charlton declined and picked up his hat. Quentin swept across the room and opened the door.

"I am more than obliged to you, Sergeant," he said, as he followed the detective into the hall and, by a swift flanking movement, beat him by a short head to the front-door knob. "It was kind of you to come and tell me about poor Court. My wife will be desolate. I hope that I shan't be called at the inquest. It would show me up in a very bad light."

"I can't promise anything about that, Mr. Quentin."

He paused in the porch.

"One last question," he said. "Do you hold any documents or papers relating to Mr. Harbord's obligations?"

The enquiry seemed to shock Mr. Quentin.

"I.O.U.'s, do you mean? Certainly not. It was a gentlemen's agreement throughout. If Court had offered me an I.O.U., I should have torn it up in his presence. I took *his* word, Inspec—Sergeant, and I feel sure that his family will take mine."

From his superior height, Charlton looked down on the little man. His lips were smiling, but his grey eyes were hard.

"I hope," he said, "that the occasion will not arise."

By four-fifteen, when Charlton called again at Cooper & Silcock's, Peter Grey had not returned. Old Mr. Silcock, who happened to be in the outer office, admitted that he could not understand it. Grey, he said, had taken the firm's car to Eastbourne, but he could not think that the necessary business should have taken him so long. Perhaps, he suggested, the car had broken down.

"We close," he added, "at five."

Harbord's other friend, according to Judy, was a Mr. Greenhill. Charlton drove to Etchworth and pulled up in front of the house bearing on the fanlight over its door the name, "Pro Bono Publico." A shabby, unshaven man in a stained grey hat and a pair of cricket boots, was clipping the privet hedge in the front garden. As Charlton pushed open the gate and walked up the path, the man turned round.

"'Oojer want?" he demanded.

"Mr. Greenhill. Is he in?"

"No. Out."

"Do you know when he'll be home?"

"Yes. Now."

"But you said he was out."

"So 'e is—out in the back garden."

"You can defer your music-hall turn," said Charlton acidly, and continued towards the front door.

"If you knock till you're sick," said the man amiably, "'e won't take no notice. 'E's pottin' out the chrysanths. I don't mind telling 'im you're 'ere. Any partic'lar name?"

"Inspector Charlton of the County Police."

"Fid. Def. Ind. Imp.," grinned the gardener, "*etcetera, etcetera.*"

He laid down his shears, went through the gate and, with toes turned out and arms swinging, marched on his heels round into the passage between the garden fence and the Memorial Hall, noisily advising the Inspector and everyone else within a quarter of a mile to make a bonfire of their troubles and see them blaze away.

"Guv'nor!" Charlton heard him call. "Comp'ny to see you."

Charlton did not catch the reply, but he was forced to smile at the brazen impudence of the gardener's answering bellow:

"It's a busy fellow. They've nosed out yer dirty past."

He marched back to the same tune, picked up his shears and returned to clipping the hedge.

"Turned out nice again," he called over his shoulder.

Mr. Greenhill came through the house and opened the door. He was a small man with a large head covered by a wig that made no more attempt to deceive than a barrister's thirty-something little curls. His jacket was high-necked, in the fashion of a quarter century ago, and he wore a tall single collar with a tie of light blue, patterned silk secured in a huge, loose knot. Charlton guessed him to be in the early sixties.

"Good afternoon," said Mr. Greenhill. "Pray come inside."

He led the way into the front room and urged his visitor to take a chair that fell far short of Mr. Quentin's idea of comfort. The furniture was of heavy carved mahogany, and the room was crowded with it: a table with a fringed red cloth; a glass-fronted cabinet crammed with china knick-knacks and presents from here, there and Brighton; an upright piano with shaded candles in the sticks. The windows were covered with thick lace curtains and on a bamboo table in the bay was an aspidistra in a green-glazed pot. The overmantel laboured under a mass of fretted enrichments, the fire-irons were laid across the brass fender and on the mantelpiece, under a glass cover that hid none of its secrets, there stood an ormolu clock that had stopped at three minutes after some long-gone noon or midnight, perhaps as a protest against the indelicate display of its intestinal functionings.

"I am sorry," said Mr. Greenhill, "to have kept you waiting. I understood Philp to say that you were a busy man."

"He didn't quite mean that," smiled Charlton. " 'Busy fellow' is a slang phrase for a detective. I am Inspector Charlton."

"Very pleased to make your acquaintance, Inspector."

When Mr. Greenhill spoke, odd things happened to his face. His chin wobbled. It was as if it were not very securely fastened, pulling his lower lip into strange shapes and giving his speech a queer, munching sound.

"Do you know a young man named Courtenay Harbord, Mr. Greenhill?"

"Yes, and Philp has brought me some very sad news about him. Have you come to see me in that connection?"

Charlton nodded. "I have been told by his aunt, Mrs. Grey,

that he was in the habit of visiting you, and I wonder whether you can tell me anything about him."

Mr. Greenhill fidgeted uncomfortably in his chair and looked miserable.

"It is very, very sad," he said with a shake of his head.

"Very."

"A calamity," Mr. Greenhill continued to mourn. "A terribubble calamity."

He shook his head again and blinked his pale blue eyes.

"Terrible," said Charlton.

"It came as a great shock to me—a very great shock."

The Inspector began to feel like a Greek Chorus and was tempted to wail, "Aie, Aie, Aie!" He was the most human and sympathetic of men, but he did hate sentimentality.

"I'm sure it did," he agreed; and then went on swiftly, "When did you last see Mr. Harbord?"

"Last Thursday evening. It was all very distressing and my daughter and I have been caused immense unhappiness."

Charlton prepared to cut short any further obituaries, but Mr. Greenhill was on a different theme.

"I have an only daughter, Inspector. My dear wife died many years ago and Phyllis is all I have left. About a year ago, perhaps longer—one loses count of time—she met Courtenay Harbord at a dance in the hall next door. A day or two later, she brought him in to tea. I had always trusted her discretion implicitly and so I welcomed the young man to my home. For some months he was a frequent visitor, and I was beginning to think that their friendship would ripen, as once her mother's and mine had done, into the beautiful bloom of love, when certain disturbing rumours came to my ears."

He went on after a pause:

"You may think, perhaps, that I am lacking in respect for the dead when you hear what I am going to say; but I do it deliberately, for the sake of my daughter. In my long life, I have learnt only too well the damage that slanderous tongues can do. During the early days of the friendship between Harbord and my little girl, he told us both that he had a private income that enabled him to live in comparative comfort. We had no reason to doubt his word. He was a well-spoken boy, always wore good quality clothes, even though his tastes were a little extravagant, and did not spare expense when he took Phyllis into Lulverton or Southmouth for the evening."

He glanced anxiously at the Inspector.

"I hope I am not taking too much of your time?" he asked.

"Not a bit," Charlton reassured him. "You interest me immensely."

"One day," Mr. Greenhill resumed, "I was talking with a friend of mine who lives in Sheep. He did not know that Courtenay and my daughter were—ah—walking out. I happened to mention the young man's name in the course of the conversation, and his reply, which took me completely by surprise was, 'That young waster?' He went on to tell me that Courtenay was living entirely on the charity of his aunt and that he seemed to have not the slightest intention of ever doing anything else.

"I am not one to pay much attention to malicious gossip, but my friend's remarks worried me for a long time. At last, when I managed to get Courtenay to myself, my daughter being in the kitchen preparing tea, I told him frankly what I had been informed. He blustered at first and then agreed that it was true, adding that it was his pride that had made him lie to us. I felt I could forgive him the deception. It was a degrading thing to have to admit. I pressed him on the question of finding employment and said that surely he was not going to depend all his life on the generosity of his relations. His reply put fresh heart into me. He stoutly asserted it was unfair to say that he did not want to earn his own living, and that the problem of finding a job was seldom out of his thoughts. Then he told me that he had been following up an advertisement in a daily paper and there was every chance that he would secure the position. An influential friend in Lulverton was putting in a word for him."

"Did he mention the friend's name?" asked Charlton, thinking of the unctuous Mr. Quentin.

"No, but he was very well thought of in Lulverton." He sighed heavily. "It was too good to be true. When next I approached Courtenay, he told me that the post had been filled by another applicant. So matters rested until one day he came to me and asked for my daughter's hand in marriage. To put it mildly, Inspector, I was flabubblegasted. I demanded to know what he proposed that they should live on and he muttered some foolishness about love in a cottage. I am an even-tempered man as a general rule, but this last piece of impudence made me lose my temper. I told him flatly that I thought he had taken leave of his senses; that until he obtained regular employment and could produce proof of its continuance, I should not dream of allowing him to marry my daughter. He took my decision very calmly, as if it was what he had expected."

At this point, Mr. Greenhill hesitated for several moments.

"Up to that time," he said at length, "my only thought had been that Harbord was a careless, improvident young man, with no sense of his responsibilities. Charming when he liked to be, but absolutely undependabubble and totally unfitted to be entrusted with my little girl's future. I imagined that he had the intention of marrying Phyllis and then looking to me for their upkeep.

"Then it was that I began to hear the rumours I have already mentioned. I was told of—ah—incidents on the Downs. It was nothing to do with my daughter. Please don't think that for a single instant. But there were certain *episodes* in which I have reason to believe Courtenay was concerned. It is not necessary for me to go into details, but the reports were too well substantiated to be no more than tittle-tattle. There was the case"—he dropped his voice to a murmur "of a little girl of twelve, who was running home in the gathering dusk, when a man leapt out at her from behind a bush and brutally sheared off her plaited hair. I was horrified that a grown man should be guilty of such disgraceful behaviour."

"It's a recognized form of perversion," nodded Charlton.

"The parents took no action, but the child's description of her assailant left *me* in no doubt of his identity.

"In the face of these unsavoury stories, Courtenay's association with my daughter still continued, until I felt that she should be told. She was as horror-struck as I had been. Although I had anticipated that she would roundly deny any suggestion that his conduct was not all it should be, she admitted having noticed signs of an unpleasant streak in his character. Undoubtedly, he was on his best behaviour when in her company, but he could not have been able to hide his weakness entirely.

"Phyllis promised me, there and then, that she would break with him; and she was as good as her word. When he next called, she told him quite clearly that she did not wish their friendship to continue. He wrote to her, but she tore the letters up without answering them. Last Thursday, he came to see me."

The detective sat up in his chair.

"Will you tell me what took place?"

"It was a most distressing interview. Happily, my daughter was not at home. He said he loved her to the point of desperation and almost went down on his knees, imploring me to agree to their marriage. I was adamant. I said that if they married at all, it would be without my consent and that neither of them would ever be allowed in this house again. He said that nothing would persuade him to take that step. He wanted my benediction on their union. I replied that even if I changed my views, which I should never do, Phyllis had no wish to be further associated with him. Thereupon, he accused me in the strongest terms of having poisoned her mind against him; and then he broke down entirely. He said that, since his parents had died, everything had gone against him. His father had been an improvident, careless man and, after failing to provide for his son's future by putting him into some business or profession, had died and left him without a penny in the world. Courtenay told me, with tears in his eyes, that if he could only get a proper chance, he would make a brilliant success of his life and be abubble to come to me, without fear of dismissal, to ask for my daughter's hand. That very morning, he solemnly swore, he had been offered a partnership in a flourishing bookselling business in Paulsfield Square."

Charlton's mouth fell open.

"This offer, however, was contingent upon his bringing a hundred pounds of capital into the firm. I said that I sympathized with his position, but if he was suggesting that I should put up the money for this enterprise, he was to understand that I unconditionally refused. Neither I nor my daughter had anything further to say to him. He protested and made wild charges, but eventually left the house, leaving me in a condition of acute nervous exhaustion."

Mr. Greenhill looked at Charlton sadly.

"Now you will appreciate," he said, "my horror when Philp brought me word of this morning's tragedy, and my anxiety that you should know the true facts of the case. I do not want it to be said that it was because of her callous breaking off of their friendship that he was driven to the horribubble step of taking his own life. Nothing, Inspector, was further from the truth. I am convinced that my firm attitude last Thursday was fully justified."

"I appreciate your feelings, Mr. Greenhill," murmured Charlton.

A face appeared at the window and two cupped hands were pressed against the glass.

"'Ave you told 'im where you put the body, Guv'nor?" yelled Philp.

His employer, with a hasty word of apology, went out

into the hall and opened the front door. Charlton heard him chiding his manservant.

"All right, Guv'nor," said Philp cheerfully. "No offence meant or taken, I'm sure."

Mr. Greenhill closed the door and came back.

"I really must apologize for Philp," he said. "Although he is far too ready with his tongue, he doesn't mean to be impudent, A bad shell-shock case, I'm afraid, and I haven't the heart to discharge him, because of his real devotion to myself and my daughter."

He smiled.

"The other day he had the effrontery to twit me about my toupee, which I wear to guard against chills, rather than for reasons of vanity. One ceases to be conceited, Inspector, when one reaches the age that shifts into the lean and slipper'd pantaloon, as the Bard of Avon so finely put it."

Charlton was sufficiently a lover of Shakespeare to shiver when he heard him called the Bard of Avon, and directed the conversation back to the point where Philp had interrupted it.

"Is it convenient for me to speak to Miss Greenhill?" he asked.

"She is not in now, but I expect her home before very long. If you consider it essential to question her, perhaps you would care to call back in an hour's time. I do hope you will not make it too troublesome for her, Inspector."

"Does she know?"

"Yes, Philp rather foolishly shouted the news up the stairs instead of telling me first, so that I could break it to her gently."

Charlton got up. "I'll call later, if I may," he said, and went out to his car.

As he pressed his thumb on the starter, a head popped up over the hedge.

"Bung-oh!" said Philp.

IX.

BEFORE THE NEWS

IT was only at weekends and during the holiday months
that Mrs. Grey saw a useful profit on her teas and light
refreshments, and at five o'clock on that Monday afternoon,
there were no customers at all in Old Forge House.

Judy's face broke into a smile when she opened the door
to Charlton.

"I'm sorry to bother you again, Miss Grey," he smiled back.

The tables in both front rooms were laid for tea; but while
the chairs in the large room were inflexible wheelbacks, those
in the small room, which was a foot lower than the other, were
of comfortably cushioned wicker. It·was down into the small
room that Judy led him.

"Now," she said, as they sat down.

"Since you left me this morning, Miss Grey, I have
interviewed a good many people."

"Did you see the Quentins?" she demanded eagerly.

"I saw *a* Quentin."

"Male or female?"

"Male."

"What was it like?"

His lips twitched. "Privately?"

"Yes, *Mister* Charlton."

"Plump and oily, like a well-fed sardine. If he comes here,
let me know and keep him here until I've had time to change
into my heavier shoes."

"Is he likely to?"

"I don't know. According to him, your cousin owed him
ninety-seven pounds. He may try to collect the money from
Mrs. Grey. Please tell her not to pay him a penny."

"*I'll* deal with him," said Judy confidently. "But ninety-seven pounds! It's a lot of money. I could buy myself a hat with that. Courtenay *must* have been going the pace."

"I wonder he dared to get into debt like that."

"He always depended on mother to get him out of any trouble."

"Even to the tune of ninety-seven pounds?"

"If she hadn't had all that in the Bank, she would have sold some shares and, if necessary, mortgaged Old Forge House. She felt that Courtenay was her responsibility and would have made any kind of sacrifice for him, although I really think she loathed him as much as I did. And Courtenay knew it. It didn't worry him a scrap that we should have all been delighted if he'd gone to Africa or somewhere and made a tasty snack for a tiger. He enjoyed the way we disliked him and used to say that we'd want him back when he'd gone."

"Gone where—to Africa?"

"When he was dead, I suppose he meant."

"He said that, did he?" His tone was thoughtful.

"Quite often, but he was like the little boy who sneezed: he only did it to annoy."

Charlton smiled and changed the subject by asking:

"Have you seen your brother since he left home this morning?"

"Yes. He came in to lunch. We were rather surprised to see him, but he was on his way back to Lulverton from Eastbourne, Mother told him you wanted to see him and he said he'd go straight to the police station before he went back to the office. Didn't he?"

"I must have missed him. I've been out most of the day. Had he heard about Mr. Harbord?"

"Not until we told him."

"There's another question you may be able to answer, Miss Grey. You described to me this morning a hat belonging to Mr. Harbord. Had it a feather stuck in the band?"

"Oh, lots! I'm not quite sure what the score was."

"The score?"

"It was all very silly, really. You remember mother telling you that after Courtenay bought the hat, Peter got himself one exactly like it? That was *my* idea and it annoyed Courtenay more than we'd dared to hope. To make his different from Peter's, he stuck another feather in the band. Peter immediately did the same. It was marvellous! Courtenay put up with it for a week and then added a third feather. I think the score was about five-all yesterday. It sounds beastly petty, but it was nice for the joke to be against *him* for a change."

"Did he often play jokes, then?"

"Yes; and they weren't very pleasant, either."

He did not pursue the matter.

"Had you many customers here yesterday afternoon?" he asked.

"A good many. Why?"

"Do you remember a young American couple?"

"Mother told me some had been in, but I didn't see them. Would you like to ask her? She's upstairs."

She was going to get up, but he stopped her.

"Don't trouble her just now," he urged. "I have one or two other things to ask you."

"Certainly," she agreed and sank back into her chair.

He seemed strangely reluctant to put his next question. He shifted his position and pushed back his cuff to study his watch. Judy sat waiting. At last he said:

"Is your mother resting?"

"No!" laughed Judy. "She never rests. I often suspect her of secret midnight knitting."

He picked up his hat, looked at the maker's name inside the crown and replaced it carefully on the chair by his side. Across Plestrium Sinister, a frisky mongrel puppy dragged a small boy by a string. He craned his head to watch them until they had gone out of range.

"I don't want to disturb her if she's resting."

"She isn't."

"Splendid."

"When you've asked me those other things, I'll call her down."

"Thank you very much ... I shall be glad if you will ... I'm interested in those Americans ... Mrs. Grey may be able to help me."

A sudden anguished "Chi-ike!" came from the other end of Plestrium Sinister. The boy had caught the dog up. Then peace descended again on the sundrenched Plestriums and a silence followed in the raftered little room in Old Forge House. Judy broke it with the enquiry:

"What do you want to ask me?"

"I've nothing to *ask* you, Miss Grey ... I only wanted to say ... I wanted to say that ... if your mother can spare me a few moments now, I shall appreciate it."

He jumped to his feet as she rose from her chair. She stepped up into the other room, where she turned back to him and gave him a smile in which he thought he read perfect understanding.

Mrs. Grey came down to him, but Judy stayed behind. He apologized for worrying her again, and then asked:

"Did you have some American visitors to tea yesterday, Mrs. Grey?"

"Yes. They were a young married couple and very amusing to listen to. The man wanted to talk about Etchworth Tower, which they'd just been up, but the girl kept on saying how much she admired Shakespeare. It was quite a complex with her! I heard her say that everything in England reminded her of Shakespeare and that altogether he was just too—how did she pronounce it?—dairndy."

"I'm glad you remember them," smiled Charlton, "because I am very anxious to get in touch with them. Did they say where they were staying?"

Mrs. Grey shook her head.

"They asked me for a railway timetable and I heard them agreeing that the 5.58 from Lulverton would suit them nicely."

"Do you mind letting me see the timetable?"

She got it from the window-sill in the other room. He turned to the "up" trains for Sundays, but there was no 5.58 to Waterloo. In the "down" section, however, he found it.

"That means they went to Southmouth," he said. "Were you able to find out about Mr. Harbord's hats, Mrs. Grey?"

"Yes. They were all where they should be."

"Including the brown felt?"

"Yes, that was there."

"And the horn-rimmed spectacles?"

"I found those, too. They were pushed down the side of the big trunk I keep on the landing outside our bedrooms. It's full of all sorts of odds and ends. Anything we don't know what to do with goes in there!"

"May I take them away with me?"

"Certainly."

She went off to fetch them and on her return, was followed by Judy with a loaded tray. He got up to take the spectacles from Mrs. Grey and wrapped them in a piece of tissue paper. Judy was laying a table.

"I mustn't take any more of your time," he murmured.

"Your tea is ready," announced Judy. "I hope you like crumpets?"

He smiled with delight.

"They are my greatest vice."

"Will twelve be enough?"

"I'll try to make them do."

"Mother," instructed Judy, "you go upstairs and get on with whatever it was you were doing. The Inspector will excuse you. I'll stop and pour out tea."

As Mrs. Grey obediently left them, Charlton noticed that there were only two cups on the tray.

"Thank you for staying to tea," Judy said softly.

"Thank you for thinking of it," he replied.

"I was afraid you would go all business-like and inspectorial."

"I ought to have done," he admitted. "If you had offered me anything less sublime than crumpets, I should have resisted."

"Would you?"

"No," he said, and they laughed together.

Judy poured out the tea. "I was hoping," she said, "that you would eat those crumpets. Do you always look at them for half an hour first? I had my tea at four o'clock."

By tacit consent, they put aside the serious business that had brought him to Old Forge House, and talked of many things—not why the sea was boiling hot and whether pigs had wings, but of books they had read, plays they had seen, broadcasts they had heard. Then, when the crumpets had disappeared, the tea had all been drunk, and it was two minutes to six, Charlton said:

"I noticed a radio in, the other room. May we switch it on for a moment or two? There's something I particularly want to hear."

They were in time to get the time-signal. Then the announcer said:

"This is the National Programme. Before I read the news, here is a police message. At 7.45 a.m. today, the body of a man was found lying at the foot of Etchworth Tower, three miles from Lulverton, Downshire. Will all those who visited the Tower yesterday, or who can throw any light on the tragedy, please communicate with the Chief Constable, Whitchester (Telephone Number, Whitchester 2000) or with any police station ... The weather forecast for tonight and tomorrow. An extended ridge of high-pressure—"

Charlton rudely switched him off.

"I wonder if all my hundred-and-six heard that," he pondered; then turned to the girl. "You weren't very anxious to tell me this morning about your cousin's visits to a house in Etchworth with the incomprehensible name of 'Pro Bono Publico'. Do you know anything about Phyllis Greenhill?"

"Not a great deal. She's pretty in a babyish sort of way, but with no personality at all. She's just the submissive, brainless type to appeal to Courtenay. At one time, he was always out and about with her; but three or four months ago he stopped going there. I suppose old Mr. Greenhill discovered what sort of a thing it was that he was nursing in his bosom, and gave him his marching orders."

"I'm going along to see her now."

"I expect she'll say, 'I'm afraid I don't know,' to most of your questions. Or giggle. She's a great giggler."

Charlton went back into the other room to get his hat.

"Miss Grey," he said when he returned, "will you do something for me?"

She made an elaborate curtsey. "Your Grace's obedient servant."

"I want a photograph of Mr. Harbord." He paused. "And one of your brother."

"*Peter?* Why Peter?"

He looked down at her gravely.

"It is my duty to ask you for those photographs. You are quite at liberty to refuse."

Without a word, she turned and left him. She came back with two postcard-size photographs, which he placed in his wallet.

"A little while ago," he said, "I tried to tell you something, but my courage failed me. Even now I find it difficult to say."

Judy's lips curved in a tiny, encouraging smile.

"I think I know what it is," she said.

"Do you?" he asked eagerly. "Do you understand that I am two men: one a soulless keeper of the King's Peace, a hireling of justice, with no right to any private fads and feelings; and the other an ordinary sort of fellow, who has no liking at all for the things that his other self has to do? Do you understand that?"

"Yes," she said simply.

"I believe there are anxious times ahead for all of us. There's something about the death of Mr. Harbord that I do not understand. It frightens me. A clever and vindictive brain has been at work, and it's my business to find out the truth. But I want you to know, right from the beginning and whatever happens, what my private feelings are."

He stopped, then went on in a brisker tone:

"As soon as your brother comes home, please ask him to ring me, either at Lulverton police station or at my home: Southmouth 8321. Tell him the moment you see him and urge him to get in touch with me without delay. It's most important that I speak to him at the earliest possible moment."

He pulled open the front door.

"Don't forget," smiled Judy bravely, "that we are always open for teas, light refreshments and, if you can stand them, minerals."

"I certainly won't," he said and went down the path between the flowers.

As he closed the gate behind him, he muttered:

"You *poor* fool!"

A passing cat turned its head in contemptuous surprise, but Charlton was not speaking to him.

His interview with Phyllis Greenhill did not take long. As Judy had said, she had the insipid, characterless prettiness of a doll. Her hair was bobbed and fluffy, and, like most girls of her lack-brained type, she gave the impression, in any but the simplest of conversations, that she thought her interlocutor was not quite right in his mind.

He questioned her in the room where he had spoken earlier with Mr. Greenhill, and he had the feeling that the old gentleman was anxiously crouching outside in the hall, ready to interrupt if his daughter's feelings became too harrowed.

"Miss Greenhill," he began, "I am sorry to intrude at such a time, but I am forced to ask you one or two questions. When did you last see Mr. Harbord?"

"Oh, ever such a long time ago."

"How long?"

"I couldn't really say. Several months."

"Your father has told me about your friendship with Mr. Harbord and how it came to be discontinued. I expect it made you very unhappy."

"Oh, it did."

"It isn't a thing one easily forgets, is it?"

"Oh, no."

"You'll probably remember your last Sunday afternoon together as long as you live."

"It wasn't a Sunday. It was the evening when he came to take me to the flannel-dance in Buckingham Park. I had a new dress for it and I couldn't wear it."

"You haven't seen Mr. Harbord since then?"

"Not to speak to. I've seen him go past in the bus and he's come here several times to try to see me, but Daddy wouldn't let him and he had to go away again."

"But he wrote you letters?"

She sniggered for no apparent reason.

"Oh, yes; but Daddy said I mustn't answer them and I tore them up, because I was going out with another boy then."

"Are you still going out with him," Charlton smiled, "or have you exercised the privilege of your sex?"

"Oh, no! We're still friends. Philip is ever such a nice boy— and *he* behaves properly."

"What's his other name? Perhaps I know him."

"Lambert. He's quite a big official at the District Council offices. They're ever so pleased with him."

If Charlton had been alone, he would have whistled, not tunefully, but with astonishment. Things were taking an unexpected turn.

"Have you received any letters from Mr. Harbord recently?" he asked.

"Not for ever so long. He stopped writing when I didn't write back."

"Did the letters suggest that Mr. Harbord was—how shall we say it?—desperate?"

"The last one said his heart was broken and that, if I didn't change my mind, he'd kill himself. It was a lovely letter. I hated tearing it up."

"Do you think he meant it?"

There was a stir in the hall and Mr. Greenhill opened the door to poke in his large head.

"I hope you won't prolong the poor child's ordeal, Inspector," he champed. "I am sure that she is abubble to tell you very little."

"I have just asked my last question. Miss Greenhill was about to answer when you came in."

He turned to the girl enquiringly.

"I really couldn't say," was her reply. "He was such a funny boy."

Mr. Greenhill fussed around Charlton until he had shepherded him out of the house.

"Of *course* he threatened to take his own life," he said with his chin working like a flail. "All disappointed suitors do that."

Charlton smiled as he went towards the gate. Mr. Greenhill *had* been listening in the hall.

On the High Street corner of Paulsfield market-square was a little seventeenth-century building. It had been many things in its time, but it was now a bookshop. Between the mullioned bay-windows, one facing the High Street and the other looking on to the Square, was the low door, over which hung an orange and black sign announcing that the shop was called "VOSLIVRES." It was John Rutherford, tired of a lazy life, who had started the business in 1935; but he had met Molly Arnold and, when he had married her in the June before the Etchworth Tower incident, had deserted trade, leaving his assistant, George Stubbings, in sole charge of the shop and lending-library.

It has been said that appearances are deceptive. George Stubbings conclusively proved it. At that time, he was nearly twenty and, despite his neat blue suit, looked a typical country yokel. His face was rubicund, round and witless; his eyes placid and with no sparkle. His tow-coloured hair was parted in the middle and, for all his oiling and furious brushing, curled upwards on each side of his scalp. But George was a "village Hampden." He was a farm-labourer's son, but books were so much his passion that now he talked like one. Further, he read every thriller as soon as it came to "Voslivres" from the publishers, and accounted himself an expert on the novel of detection. He and Charlton were firm friends and the detective always called in when he happened to be in Paulsfield. But that evening, after leaving "Pro Bono Publico," Charlton went to the bookshop on a more precise mission.

"Well," was his greeting, "and how is the great Hanaud today?"

"Fine, thank you, sir," grinned George. "I hope that Chief-Inspector French is the same?"

"Far too busy to bother. You weren't near Etchworth in a false beard yesterday, I suppose? No, it was rather too much to hope."

"False beard, sir? I thought they went out years ago. They did in fiction."

"Fiction is always a little more headlong than fact; but, for all we know, false beards may be coming back, as they write in the fashion notes."

"Far too reactionary," decided George. "Facial disguise in Crime is bad art. It's like Death-Ray's and Underground Rooms connected to the Water Main. So much Piffle."

The outcrop of capitals was distinct in his tone.

"Don't be so sweeping, young man. You listen to this and *then* air your opinions."

George did not utter a word while Charlton gave him a rough outline of the Harbord case.

"There!" said the Inspector eventually. "What do you think of that?"

"Marvellous," replied George in a reverent voice. "It couldn't have been accidental, it obviously wasn't suicide, so it must have been murder. Whoopee!"

"I don't agree that it *obviously* wasn't suicide, but do you take back what you said about false beards?"

"Without reservation, sir. Would you mind if I gave you *my* theory, based, naturally, on the available evidence, which is far from complete. Not," he added hurriedly, "that I mean to be rude, sir. We must give you time."

"I shall make full use of the concession. Fire away, George."

"Confidentially, sir? Strictly between ourselves?"

"Absolutely."

"Of course, you haven't investigated his alibi, but, on the face of it—on the *prima facie* evidence, six—I should say that the man called Grey did it. He had a first-rate motive and was most likely to have been the man in the beard."

"I hope to be able to prove that you're wrong.... Now, George, I came over here on serious business. Tell me this: is 'Voslivres' the only bookshop in Paulsfield Square?"

With a perfectly serious expression on his bumpkin face, George opened the door and went out to look.

"Yes, sir," he announced on his return. "There has been no mushroom development since lunch-time."

"Will you now kindly confirm that my nephew-in-law, Mr. John Rutherford, has been in the South of France for just over three weeks?"

"That's right, sir. They're at a little place called Peira-Cava. I had a picture-postcard from Mrs. Rutherford last Friday."

"How many partners are there in this firm?"

"There aren't any *partners,* sir. Mr. Rutherford owns it."

"And you manage it for him?"

"Yes, sir," answered George and added with sudden solicitude, "Are you feeling all right, sir?"

"Perfectly, thank you, George."

"But you know all that, sir."

"I am a police officer and I am interrogating you as a witness."

"Witness, sir? You're joking."

His expression was so dazed that Charlton burst out laughing.

"I'm serious, George, Answer my questions like a good boy and *don't* argue.... You, as the manager of this shop, are aware of everything that goes on, are you not?"

"Yes, sir."

"You are directly responsible for its supervision."

"Yes, sir. Mr. Rutherford gives me a free hand, but I always refer important points to him."

"Although Mr. Rutherford has a perfect right to take any steps he likes without any reference to you, do you think that he would do so?"

"Not before telling me, sir."

"He would not, for instance, take a partner without having previously consulted you?"

George began to look really anxious.

"He's *not* going to do that, is he, sir?" he asked with apprehension.

"That's what I'm asking *you.*"

"No, I'm sure not. Mr. Rutherford would never do a *thing* like that."

"I have been told that a certain person was offered a partnership, provided he put up a hundred pounds."

"A hundred pounds in a firm like this? Why, that's chicken-feed! Just a moment and I'll show you the turnover."

The scandalised young man was halfway up the stairs to the office above before Charlton could call him back.

"Don't worry, George. I only wanted you to confirm what

I knew already. I'll now ask you my final official question: In your knowledge, has a partnership in 'Voslivres' ever been offered to a Mr. Courtenay Harbord on the understanding that he brought one hundred pounds into the business?"

"No, sir,"

"Then that is that."

"Shall I have to give evidence in court, sir?"

Charlton cocked an eyebrow at him.

"Would you like to?"

"Unquestionably, sir."

"I'll see what I can do for you."

"Whoopee!" said George for the second time that day.

As Charlton drove through Paulsfield on his way back to Lulverton Headquarters, the same throaty voices sounded from almost every house he passed. He smiled gently to himself.

Inspector Homleigh was investigating.

X.

THE PLAY-BOY OF WHITCHESTER

THE sergeant was waiting at Lulverton police station.

"Well, Martin," Charlton asked him, "what have you found out? Anything interesting?"

"Acting on instructions received," declaimed the Sergeant, "I proceeded to——"

"Keep that for the Petty Sessions," suggested Charlton rudely. "I want facts, not flummery."

The unabashed Sergeant merely grinned.

"I've seen both drivers and both conductors of yesterday's buses," he began again, "and I've got one or two tasty tit-bits."

His superior sat down, waved him to another chair and lighted a cigarette.

"From the beginning," he enjoined.

"The conductor of the red bus, whose name is Steeple, knew young 'Arbord well, and 'e remembers 'im getting on the bus yesterday afternoon at 3.5, which was just as it was starting for Lulverton."

"How was he dressed?"

"Green hat with feathers in it and a raincoat on his arm. Grey flannel suit and brown shoes. 'E got Steeple to stop the bus for 'im just 'alfway between Etchworth and Lulverton, and, as the bus went on, Steeple saw 'im strike off the road—there's no hedge or anything on that stretch, you know—and make for a biggish clump of beeches on the side of the Downs."

"Waltham Hanger," nodded Charlton.

"That's the spot. Steeple doesn't call to mind seeing 'im reach the Hanger, 'cause its a fair way up from the road and the bus soon took Steeple out of sight; but 'e was certainly making in that direction. The driver of the bus was off duty, but I ferreted 'im out and got 'im to confirm that 'e'd stopped the bus where Steeple said they'd put 'Arbord down."

"Commendably thorough of you, Martin."

"Thank you, sir. None of the other busmen remember seeing 'Arbord. That was the last time 'e was set eyes on, as far as our inquiries go."

"What about the young man in the flannel suit?"

"I managed to pick up a trail." There was pride in his voice. "I went along to Etchworth and slipped into the public of the 'Tower Arms,' where I ordered up and stood against the bar. A couple of yobs were shoving good money into a pin-table, which they 'ad to kick every time they wanted another ball up. Two old grandads were sitting on a bench with pots of rough on the table in front of 'em. I passed the time of day and, when kicking and shaking didn't do the trick and the young chaps 'ad lifted up the table between 'em and dropped it on the floor and been told by the old crow be'ind the bar to go easy or there'd be—"

"Martin," he was interrupted, "you'd run old Tom Lee a close second in the Windbag Stakes."

"I asked the four of 'em what they'd take and we all fell to chatting. I brought the talk round to yesterday's beano and said I wondered if the police were trying to trace all the visitors to the Tower, because I knew a bloke 'oo'd been up in the afternoon and was wondering if 'e oughtn't to tell someone about it.

"'I don't know whether you know 'im,' I said. 'Name of Fleming. Middling height. Wears 'orn-rimmed glasses.'

"That didn't seem to mean a thing to any of 'em. They just sat round sponging up the beer I'd stood Sam for and not caring much about my old pal, Fleming. Then another man came in and I roped 'im into our matey little circle.

"'Just talking about Fleming, my friend from Lulverton, 'oo was up the Tower yesterday,' I said, 'E's on the jump about whether the coroner'll want 'im for the inquest. Nice chap. Youngish. Five feet ten or so. 'Orn-rimmed glasses. Did you see 'im yesterday?'

"'What?' 'e says, 'D'you mean the auctioneers' clerk? Thought 'e'd been shifted to Waterlooville.'"

Charlton chuckled. "You picked the wrong name!"

"'Ow was I to know?" answered Martin plaintively. "I said 'e must be thinking of a different Fleming, as my pal kept a wireless shop."

"'Didn't 'appen to 'ave seen 'im yesterday, I suppose?' I said. 'Wears a grey flannel suit, as a general rule, and a brown felt 'at. Good-looking, to my way of thinking.'"

Martin leant back and clasped his hands contentedly across his waistcoat.

"That got 'im, sir."

The Inspector leant forward.

"'E took a good swig at 'is beer and, after 'e'd come up for air, said, 'Wouldn't 'ave been green, by any chance?' I kept my head and said it was more than likely; that I seemed to remember 'aving seen 'im in it and that 'e was a great one for sticking feathers in the band.

"'Then I saw 'im all right,' says this chap, 'over on the other side of High Down.'

'That'd be Fleming,' I said, and switched the talk to other things. After ten minutes or so, 'e said 'e must be getting along and I said p'raps 'e was going my way. When I got 'im alone outside, I took 'is name and address and got a full statement."

Charlton carefully stubbed out his cigarette in the ash-tray on his desk.

"Was it Harbord?" he asked.

"It was *not!*" exulted Martin.

"Give me the details," said Charlton quietly.

The man's name was Allwork. He was a farm-labourer and he lived at Etchworth. The previous afternoon, he had taken a walk with his girl friend, and they had chosen, very naturally, an unfrequented route. On the north side of the Downs ran a lonely lane called Leaves Lane. It had hedges on each side of it and it could be reached from Etchworth either by toiling over High Down, or by walking a mile towards Sheep to the point where the lane branched off the major road and swung through a gap in the hills. Allwork and his lady-love chose the less arduous way and, as they strolled along the lane arm-in-arm, saw a young man walking briskly towards them and away from the Tower. He was wearing a green hat richly trimmed with feathers and was carrying a raincoat on his arm. He smiled at them as he passed and cheerily wished them good afternoon. Allwork told the Sergeant proudly that, as they had walked on, he had sent his Nellie into fits of laughter by suggesting:

"'Un ought to fly like a bird with all they feathers."

When asked what time they had met this man, Allwork was doubtful, but said it was probably between half-past four and a quarter to five.

"Any reason to think it wasn't Harbord?" Charlton asked the Sergeant.

"Description didn't tally, sir. Allwork was a bit hazy, but 'e did remember that this chap 'ad a healthy open-air sort of colour and that, when 'e smiled, 'is teeth were like an advertisement for somebody's paste. Was *that* the dear departed?"

"Harbord was a sallow little devil and his teeth were about the same shade."

"There you are, then."

"Did you go any further with it?"

"Left it at that, sir. I didn't fancy going all round Etchworth, asking if they knew my pal, Fleming. It might 'ave got back to 'im and 'e's a bit touchy like that. Just in passing, sir, and outside the present inquiry, 'ave you been into the 'Tower Arms' lately?"

"No; why?"

"Besides the old eyesore 'oo's drawn the beer off short every time I've been in there, they've got a little Irish girl and she's the neatest little barishna you could wish to see. Dark, with big brown eyes and a smile like another ten bob a week. I could listen to 'er Ballymena brogue for hours on end——"

"That's more than I'm prepared to do with you. Some of you young fellows have your heads turned by every pretty face you see. You're a policeman, Martin, not a Lothario. Ballymena, was it, you said she came from?"

Martin chuckled and murmured something about pots and kettles that should, by rights, have resulted in his instant reversion to the uniformed branch.

"That other matter," said Charlton, returning to the business on hand. "Did anyone see a man on the balcony after six o'clock?"

"Young Bradfield covered that. It wasn't such a confidential inquiry as mine, so 'e went in all the splendour of 'is office, knocking at the doors and putting 'is questions to everyone 'e saw."

He shook his head regretfully.

"Human beings are funny things, sir. You step up to a man in the Rother'ithe Road and ask to be directed to Surrey Docks, and like as not, 'e'll say 'e's never heard of them. And it's the same with the Etchworth people. They *do* know the Tower's there. Somebody must 'ave told 'em. But they never take a blind bit of notice of it. Bradfield couldn't find anyone who'd seen a chap on the balcony, but that's because they never looked. Life marches on in Etchworth without a thought for Redbourn's Crowning Folly. 'E didn't carry 'is inquiries any further than Etchworth and Barns Bottom, that little village this side of the Tall Man on the other side of the Downs from Etchworth. You can see the Tower for miles around. A chap with a telescope on Ryde Pier could 'ave picked out a figure on the balcony, so you've got to draw the line somewhere."

Charlton shrugged his shoulders.

"It's only routine," he said. "I had no hopes whatever, but I would have given a month's salary to the War Memorial Hospital funds if a man *had* been noticed on the balcony."

He paused to light another cigarette. "And I still would," he added.

"At the same time," Martin went on with his report, "Bradfield asked about Harbord, but, though some of them knew 'im by sight, he wasn't seen in Etchworth yesterday afternoon. There are a dozen farms scattered about on both sides of High Down and Bradfield went to them all; but there was nothing doing. 'E carried on to Sheep and found a couple of women 'oo said they'd seen 'Arbord leave Old Forge House and walk across to the bus stop outside the 'Sun in the Sands.'"

Martin stopped short and his face took on an expression of doubt.

"There's one other thing Bradfield found out, sh—all in the course of duty," he said at last. "One man 'e questioned told 'im that he'd not seen Harbord, but as 'e was on the way back from Lulverton on 'is bicycle, 'e saw Mr. Peter Grey, who'd been walking towards 'im, turn off the main road into the Leaves Lane that I was speaking of. The man said Mr. Grey was wearing a green hat at the time, which would've been about two-thirty."

He did not pause again, but went swiftly on:

"Coming to Master Lambert, Mr. Matthews's assistant, 'e seems to be a bit of a lad. 'E's the son of a Captain of Industry, who's a Bart, and a J.P. into the bargain."

"What? Sir Percy Lambert of Whitchester?"

"As ever was. Young Philip kicked over the traces until the old man got a bit tired of it. He found a two-pound-ten a week job for the boy with the Lulverton U.D.C. and said, 'Phil, me lad, keep that place for five years and all will be forgiven: lose it, and the Lambert millions go to the Hendon Police College or some other deserving charity.' Philip couldn't stick the thought of that, so 'e closed with the offer. That was two years ago, leaving three more to run."

He broke off to add ominously:

"I doubt if he'll stay the course. Spots can't change the

leopard and it's just as much a leopard in one spot as another. The Council offices 'ave certainly cramped Lambert's style a bit, but 'e's still carrying on the old business at the new address."

"What's his speciality?"

"'E's not partic'lar, being able to turn 'is hand to almost anything. That's not to say that he's overdue for a visit from you, me or the Super, but 'e's working up for it. Drink and horses, chiefly; and that means that, sooner or later, he'll be dipping into the Petty Cash or rigging the Poor Rate. Have you met that man, Quentin?"

Charlton stiffened. "I called on him today."

"Did you, though? We seem to be working along the same lines. Lambert goes there a lot and I don't think it's for the company. If you ask me, I'd say it was about time we got that Quentin taped. That young chap we found with 'is throat cut last March was always round at 'Capri', not that his was anything but a plain case of suicide."

He added darkly:

"I wouldn't put a gambling-hell past Mr. Smarmy Quentin."

"Neither would I. Get Bradfield on it. The Yard may know something about him. Quentin's a bad actor and a poor liar, and there's no doubt that he'd got Harbord mixed up in some kind of funny business. When I saw him this morning, he first tried to suggest that he'd never heard of Harbord, then admitted having noticed him about the house from time to time, but not since last Wednesday week. I persuaded him to agree that their last meeting was only three days ago, when there had been a scene between them about ninety-seven pounds that Quentin told me Harbord owed him."

The Sergeant whistled. "Ninety-seven jimmy o'goblins! *That* proves they didn't play for beans."

"Quentin said it wasn't card-losses, but a series of small loans to help Harbord out of his continual money troubles."

"And last Friday 'e foreclosed?"

"According to him, he did it in Harbord's interests. He thought the boy needed pulling up with a jerk, and demanded twenty pounds on account, with the promise of big trouble if he wasn't paid by this morning."

"There's been a good many suicides for less than that."

"But not this time. Everything points to murder—not a casual affair done in hot blood, but a carefully thought out piece of homicide. Whether or not the coroner's jury will agree with me remains to be seen."

He drew a fanciful design on the blotting-pad.

"Is there any information about *Mrs.* Quentin?" he asked.

"That's what she calls 'erself," was Martin's slanderous reply. "She looks like one of those females we used to call 'vamps' in the old silent days. Tall, dark and swognay, with a long cigarette-holder. Sort of woman 'oo'd seduce the 'ole Russian army before breakfast and make a regular thing of going round with the plans of the fortifications stuffed down the front of 'er dress—if it had one."

"Martin, Martin!" despaired Charlton. "What *is* the matter with you today?"

"Sorry, sir, but I'm a bit above meself."

They were quite alone, but he leant forward and muttered into Charlton's ear. Charlton smiled broadly.

"Really?" he said. "That's fine. Congratulations, Martin! It'll be company for young Ted."

"Now, sir," said the Sergeant briskly, "to come back to Mrs. Quentin. There's nothing against her locally. Big accounts with the grocer and the wine merchants, but all bills paid prompt. Two maids and a chauffeur 'oo looks after the garden, or a gardener 'oo drives the car, whichever it is. They've been in Lulverton three years. Nobody knows where they came from, but their credit's good."

"Talking about credit, is Lambert in debt?"

"Yes, but I can't say how deep. He moved 'is lodgings a fortnight ago and the previous landlady gave me to understand that 'e still owed her for four weeks' bed and board, which is why 'e left. I went the round of the bookies and found 'e runs an account with our old college chum, Tom Starling. Tom says Lambert dropped five pounds on the St. Leger and a couple more on the Doncaster Cup, and hasn't seen fit to settle yet, though Tom hasn't had much trouble with 'im in the past."

"Thanks very much, Martin. You've done well. There are two other little jobs for you before you knock off for the day. One, ask the Headmaster of Paulsfield College to find out which two of his boys were up the Tower yesterday afternoon. If he rings you back, go over and see the boys and ask them these questions." He jotted them down on a sheet of paper. "Two, when was the flannel dance in Buckingham Park?

"Tomorrow, there's another inquiry for you. Mr. Greenhill has told me that he strongly suspects Harbord of fun and games with the maidens of Etchworth. He quoted the case of a small girl of twelve, who had her plaits sheared off. We mustn't neglect the possibility of a revengeful parent, so look into it, will you?"

He got up and took down his hat from the stand.

"I," he said, "am off in search of a lover of Shakespeare. Tomorrow morning, I'm going up to London, so I shan't see you until the afternoon. Make a point of being here between two and three. I may ring you."

"Right, sir. Any news of Mr. Grey, sir?"

Charlton had crossed the room, but paused at the door.

"Not yet; and that reminds me that there's another thing for you to arrange."

He explained to Martin what it was, and Harry Charlton would have enjoyed kicking Inspector Charlton all the way out to the car.

Martin stood stroking his chin reflectively.

"Looks to me," he said to the hat-stand, "as if Master Grey 'as hopped the dolly."

It was at the "Metropole" on Southmouth Promenade that Charlton eventually found Mr. and Mrs. Theyer Claft of Ridgeway Drive, Rochester, N.Y. They were a delightful pair, in whose laughter and gay talk there was an unaffected zest for life. They were "doing" Europe, but they did not mind if it took them more than one day. Charlton was received as if they had waited on tip-toe all their lives for him and, within thirty seconds, he had been supplied with an Angel's Rapture and the whole resources of the most lavish hotel in Southmouth placed at his disposal.

He explained his mission and they marvelled.

"We heard on the radio in the lounge," said Claft, "that you were keen to make our acquaintance, but we didn't figure you'd get on our trail till we called on the District Attorney tomorrow. Our Homicide Bureau back home are quick movers, but they've got to hand it to you folks sometimes!"

Charlton smiled his acknowledgment of the compliment.

"You weren't very difficult to trace," he admitted, "and now that I've found you, perhaps you'll answer a few questions?"

They both warmly agreed to help in every possible way.

"I think you got to the Tower some time before four o'clock?"

"At about a half after three," Claft replied.

"And when did you leave?"

"Apprahzimately four o'clock."

"Can you remember anyone who was on the balcony at the same time as you?"

Claft turned to his wife. "What do you say, honey?"

"There was a big man whose voice seemed to come up at you from the bottom of an elevator-shaft," she said. "He had a party with him. There were two girls, one of them, I reckon, still at school, and a woman who called old Foghorn 'Horace' or 'Morris'. Then there were two, maybe three, other men — "

"Three, honey," confirmed her husband, "one old and tall, one young and tall, and the other a military little guy with a mustash, who talked like a sub-machine gun."

"I remember him! 'Jenkins! Confound the fellow! Where's he put my dinnah-jacket?'"

It was a wonderful imitation of Major Stallard's staccato manner, and Charlton smiled his approbation.

"Was there anyone else?" he asked.

"Sure," agreed Claft. "I never guessed your old Tower would be so appreciated. It was as crowded as our Elevated Railroad back in New York."

Unfortunately, they had not so clear a picture in their minds of any visitors. They remembered a father and mother of the Buggins type, with two small children who could not be kept from climbing the railings and who had been dragged down the stairs to safety by their anxious parents soon after the Clafts arrived on the balcony. Mrs. Claft thought she recalled a Panama hat in conjunction with a long, drooping moustache.

"But," she added, "maybe it was only a beautiful mirage."

Charlton then asked his most important question:

"Did you see a bearded man on the balcony?"

"No," answered daft, "but we saw him on the descent."

"Sixty-five stairs down," chimed in his wife.

"Being of a suspicious temperament," grinned Claft, "my wife was checking up on the figures in the brochure we bought from the ticket-agent."

"And old man Fungus nearly stalled me."

"Was he wearing a green felt hat?"

They looked at each other and Mrs. Claft shook her head doubtfully.

"That's where we fall down, Inspector," said Claft. "The illumination in the Tower is not so hot."

"Did you notice anything else about him besides the beard?"

"We didn't have much worry in passing him on the stairway, so he wasn't any sort of a Carnera."

"He had a weatherproof over his arm," added his wife.

"I've reason to believe," said Charlton, "that between the

time he passed you and the time he reached the balcony, the man stopped for a few moments. Did you notice any break in his footsteps?"

They feared not, and he left it at that. His visit to the "Metropole" had not been an entire waste of time, for these two were the first visitors he had questioned who could testify to the existence of Whiskers. Before he met the Clafts, he was beginning to wonder whether Tom Lee suffered from hallucinations.

After being prevailed upon to take another Angel's Rapture and promising to spend some weeks with them when next in Rochester, N.Y., he left them. It was not until he was on his way out through the magnificent vestibule that he realized that Mrs. Claft had been strangely dumb about William Shakespeare. Which was a pity. He would have enjoyed her eager praise.

At 8.45, after he had finished his meal, changed into his slippers and settled in his easy chair with an evening paper, Judy phoned him. She had received a telegram, she said. It had been despatched from Croydon and read:

"Don't expect me tonight detained Peter."

After she had rung off, he put through a call to Whitchester Headquarters and afterwards to Croydon police station. His enquiry was promptly answered. A car with the registration number supplied to him by Whitchester had been standing outside the Post Office in Croydon High Street for three hours and nobody had yet returned to face the constable who stood guard over it with a note-book ready.

Charlton slowly replaced the receiver.

XI.

THREE MEN TOO MANY

D R. ROBERTS, the Head-master of Paulsfield College, made a brief announcement after prayers the next morning, and two apprehensive boys, Punchard 2 of the Lower Fourth and Wood I of the Third, crept later into his study. They were pleasantly surprised at their reception and strode back to their classrooms with the stern expressions associated by themselves with Men of Moment, but suggesting to the observer that they should go up to the Linen Room to see if Matron could give them something for it. Their preoccupation persisted throughout the morning to such an extent that, when Punchard 2, who had been staring out across Big Field with his thoughts strayed far from the subtleties of the pluperfect subjunctive, was sharply recalled from his daydreams by Monsieur's, "*Faites attention!*" he answered abstractedly, "Pardon, m'lud?"

At 9.15 Sergeant Martin was being told that the last flannel dance in Buckingham Park had been on Saturday, the 29th June.

At 9.30 Detective-Constable Bradfield, who had called at "Capri" on the pretext of taking an order for a copy of *The Comprehensive Guide to Household Management,* was talking to the Quentins housemaid and had just reached the point in the conversation when, with a facility born of long practice, he asked whether she went out much.

At 9.35 Judy Grey walked into Lulverton station and bought a cheap day ticket to London.

At 9.40 Inspector Charlton strolled into the Post Office by the Main Line platform in Waterloo Station and asked for a copy of the Classified Telephone Directory. On page 1091, under the heading, "Theatrical and Fancy Costumiers," he found thirty-four names and addresses. Ten were printed in heavy type and he noted them down.

By 10.20 he had visited four of them with no success, and at 10.30 he went into Wight & Son's premises in Gray's Inn Road. The spacious shop and the gallery above were tastefully panelled in light oak, and round the walls stood suits of armour with empty gauntlets limply holding halberds and lances. Across the table in the centre had been carelessly flung a magnificent plum-coloured coat with fine lace ruffles; and at a desk by the door sat a girl.

Charlton was now word-perfect in his opening speech.

"Good morning," he smiled. "I should like to speak to somebody about false beards."

"Will you please take a seat?" invited the girl with an answering smile.

She lifted the receiver of the house-telephone on her desk and said a few words into it. Charlton heard a door open up on the gallery. The man who came down was middle-aged. His morning suit was without visible blemish and his smile was one of real welcome as he asked Charlton in what way he could be of assistance. The detective felt that, had he been a *bona fide* customer in such quiet and dignified surroundings, he would have had a beard of human hair applied immediately to his face, strand by strand and at great cost, rather than dare to ask for "Whiskers on wire, 2/-." He offered his card and, with a comprehending nod, his host (he could think of him as nothing but that) invited him to step that way, and led him upstairs into a comfortably furnished office.

"Now, sir?" said the costumier, when the door had been closed and Charlton had taken the proffered chair.

"In the case I'm working on," explained Charlton, "a false beard is concerned. It is a good quality beard—human hair knotted on a net foundation—and I wonder whether you can identify it."

He opened his case, took out the beard and handed it across

the desk. The man examined it carefully and then looked up at him.

"It looks like some of our work," he said.

"Good. Can you remember having sold such a beard recently?"

"Not for some months. It may have been my colleague. I'll ask him to come in."

The man who joined them, in response to a request on the house-telephone, was younger than the other, but just as perfectly dressed.

"Yes, Mr. Butterworth?" he enquired.

"Mr. Harraway, do you remember selling this to anyone?"

"It may not have been that particular one, but I certainly supplied a brown beard of that quality last week."

"Can you describe the person who bought it?" asked the detective, trying to keep the excitement out of his voice.

"Not very well, I'm afraid. We have so many customers in and out. He was young, of medium height and, by the way he spoke, fairly well educated."

Charlton took out his pocket-book, extracted the two photographs that Judy had lent him and passed them to Harraway.

"Was it either of those?"

The young man studied them both.

"Yes," he said, indicating Peter Grey's. "That one."

"There's no doubt about it? I want you to be sure."

"I *may* be wrong, of course," admitted Harraway.

"Photos can be very deceptive. But I'm practically certain that was the man. One thing I'm ready to swear on oath: it wasn't the other one."

The photos were replaced.

"Will you please tell me everything you can remember about his visit here."

"He came last Friday afternoon and explained to Miss Drakeley, whom you probably saw downstairs, that he wanted to buy a false beard. Miss Drakeley only deals with orders for grease-paint and things like that, so she rang for me. I asked him what kind of a beard he required and he said, one that would look realistic off the stage. He wanted to go to a fancy-dress dance and be so well disguised that none of his friends would recognize him.

"'What's the best beard for that?' he asked me.

"I told him that the most convincing shades were mouse and middling-brown, and that the best quality for his purpose was the same as that one there. I said it would cost him a guinea and he chose the brown shade.

"'How do I fix it on?' he said.

"I got him a bottle of spirit gum and explained how to use it. Then he asked me how he would be able to get it off in a hurry and I explained *that* to him. He gave me twenty-one and six, I wrapped the stuff—and that's really all that happened."

"Is a brush included with the spirit gum?"

"Yes, a small quill-handled affair."

"It isn't fixed to the cork?"

"Not in the cheap quality, which is what he bought."

"You are sure you didn't omit the brush?"

"Perfectly sure."

"Would you be able to say that that beard on the desk was the one this young man purchased?"

"I'm afraid not, but it's of exactly the same quality and unquestionably one of our manufacture. I could tell our man's knotting anywhere."

"I'm obliged to you, Mr. Harraway. There's one more thing on which you gentlemen can, perhaps, advise me. Would you say that that beard has been worn more than once? It's a difficult question, but you may be able to answer it."

The experts took the beard to the window and conferred. Then Mr. Butterworth delivered their decision:

"We would say that it *has*. It really amounts to this, Inspector: However carefully one applies spirit gum to one's face, the beard does not adhere perfectly at every point, and parts of it, therefore, are not touched by the gum. This particular beard has not been cleaned with benzine and the layer of hardened gum is spread over the net foundation so evenly and with so few untouched patches, that it seems against the law of averages, that it has been used only once. Apart from that, the layer of gum is rather thicker in some places than we should expect after only one contact with the face."

"Thank you, gentlemen," said Charlton, "You have been extremely helpful."

He went by Underground to Baker Street, where he changed on to a bus that took him to Boreham Court House, a vast white block of flats. He took the lift to the third floor and rang the bell on the door marked "34."

Miss Mortimer was at home. She was tall and gaunt, with a face like a horse of great docility, but unimpeachable pedigree. When he had introduced himself, she invited him inside. The rent could not have been less than £125 per annum, yet there was hardly room to swing a kitten, let alone a cat. Miss Mortimer bestrode it like a Colossus and, when Charlton had wedged himself inside with her, he felt that their propinquity demanded a chaperone.

"I have been referred to you," he said, "by Mrs. d'Eyncourt of Lulverton. You have probably read in the papers of the tragedy at Etchworth Tower? I am looking into the matter and I am told that you went there with her on Sunday afternoon."

Miss Mortimer nodded and he pulled out his note-book.

"I understand," he went on, after referring to his memoranda, "that you arrived at the Tower at ten minutes past four and left just after 4.25. Can you confirm that, Miss Mortimer?"

"I should think it was very likely. I can't be *certain*, you know. That's the trouble in all these police cases. If one only knew *beforehand* that one was going to be asked *afterwards*, one could be so much more alert *at the time* and a great deal more helpful to *you* gentlemen, don't you think? I'm sure if Mrs. d'Eyncourt gave you those times you need have *no* hesitation in accepting them. She is so very dependable."

"They were supplied by Robson, the chauffeur."

"That clinches it," she said with a wave of her hand. "Robson is a treasure."

Charlton smiled. "Mrs. d'Eyncourt told me yesterday that while you were both on the Tower balcony, you spoke to a young man. You asked him, I think, if he could identify a building. Could you describe him to me?"

A delighted expression came to Miss Mortimer's craggy features like a shaft of sunlight striking a forbidding mountainside.

"I can help you there!" she said brightly. "Time means very little to me, but human beings interest me *enormously*. He was young, as you've just said, clean-shaven and *most* attractive. Not *handsome,* but good-looking. He was not very tall or very thin or very fat. Just *well*-proportioned. I don't think you'll misunderstand me, Inspector, when I admit that, as a lover of all the Southern Counties, I knew perfectly well that they were the ruins of Belforth Abbey, which was partially destroyed by Henry VIII. But I wanted an excuse to talk to the young man. When one is nearing the end of the Roaring Forties, Inspector, one cannot be accused of forwardness, and I was very anxious to know whether his voice was as pleasant as his appearance."

"And was it?"

"Entirely so. To give you a few more details, he was wearing a well-cut suit of pin-stripe grey flannel, a brown felt hat with the brim pulled down at the front, a pale blue shirt with a soft, pointed collar and a dark red tie. He was carrying a raincoat or mackintosh over his arm and was wearing horn-rimmed spectacles, which were the only things about him that I didn't like. When he raised his hat to me, I noticed that his hair was medium brown and that it had a slight, but not at all objectionable, wave in it."

He produced Peter Grey's photograph.

"Would you say that was he?"

Miss Mortimer studied it eagerly.

"Without any possible shadow of doubt," was her verdict, "The spectacles don't make very much difference, although I prefer him without them."

"Was he smoking a pipe?"

"Definitely not."

"I know you are doubtful about the period of your visit, Miss Mortimer, but could you give me any idea of when you spoke to him?"

"Let me see. Belforth Abbey is to the north-west of the Tower and the door on the balcony faces west; and as we obeyed the notice and went round in a clockwise direction, we hadn't got very far when I put the question to him. So it must have been soon after we arrived on the balcony."

"And did you see him again, after your little talk was finished?"

"No, he drifted away from us."

"Can you describe to me any other persons you noticed on the balcony?"

"There were a party of people who were friends of Mrs. d'Eyncourt's. I think she said their name was something-or-other hyphen Brown. Then there were two boys of eleven or twelve, wearing school caps. They came up a minute or two before we left, when we were standing quite close to the door. The caps were pink."

She sat thinking deeply for a time.

"There were two elderly gentlemen, one tall and the other short. They exchanged a word or two with Mr. Hyphen Brown.... And there was a group of young people, most of them in the twenties, I should say, with nothing noticeable about any of them....

I remember catching a remark by one of the girls. I think

it was, 'He's in the Country Clearing,' or words to that effect. Which suggests that they were Post Office employees."

Charlton knew better, but did not say so.

"That's all, I think.... Oh, yes! As Mrs. d'Eyncourt and I were going down the stairs, we met a very large woman with a very small man trailing behind her. She was in great difficulty with her breathing, but managed to gasp out at us as we went by her, 'I'll do it, if it's the last thing I do!'"

"A real Spartan!" His smile was automatic, for his mind was filled with troubled thoughts.

He made a move to go, but Miss Mortimer restrained him.

"Have you ever read any books by Patrick Dumayne?" she asked. "*Blood on His Hands, Syncopated Death, Revenge Impatient Rose* or any others?"

"Didn't he write *Potassium Cyanide?*"

"Yes, that was the last one, published in March." After a pause, she added diffidently, "I am Patrick Dumayne."

"That's very interesting. Are you writing anything now?"

"It's about half finished and it is to be called *Twelve Good Men and Wrong*—and that's why I brought up the subject. The idea is that a coroner's jury return a verdict of *suicide,* while the police believe it was *murder*, which it does, of course, actually turn out to be. You are a detective and can very likely advise me on something that is worrying me: after the 'twelve good men' have decided that the man killed himself, can the police go on with their inquiries, or does the jury's decision close the matter for *good?*"

"To begin with, Miss Mortimer, there aren't twelve men on a coroner's jury, but nine."

"Good heavens!" she cried. "I've made them twelve in every book I've written!"

"It doesn't seem to have affected the sales, Miss Mortimer," he gallantly risked.

She beamed upon him. "That was nice of you."

"Your question is easy to answer. The decision of a coroner's jury does not hamper the police. If we think it's murder, we carry on with our investigations. The only thing is that, if we do have our suspicions, we usually ask the coroner to adjourn his inquiry, so that if a man is arrested, the inquest can be further adjourned until after his trial. The proceedings at an inquest are—or should be—entirely formal, and are concerned with three questions alone: When? Where? and By what means? It is not the custom nowadays—except in fiction—for the police to use the inquest as an easy way of getting evidence."

"Inspector," lamented the authoress, "you have not only altered my title; you have also completely ruined my plot!"

"I found no fault with *Potassium Cyanide*, Miss Mortimer."

Which, as he had not read it, was perfectly true.

On the way from St. John's Wood to Charing Cross, it occurred to him that Miss Mortimer's new thriller had certain things in common with the case of Courtenay Harbord; and that just as he had wrecked her plot, so also was he now slowly wrecking the murderer's plot—and wrecking, too, his own chance of happiness.

He caught a Bexleyheath line train from Charing Cross to Blackheath, resisted the temptation to charter one of the three old horse-cabs that wait outside that station, and went by a 75 bus across the Heath. He got off at the War Memorial on the corner of Greenwich Park and walked round into Gleneagles Road.

Eric Rothbury, the nephew of Mr. Scott-Brown, lived in the upper part of No. 23, which was a big, unlovely basement house, with a heavy, wide gate marked "Please Keep Shut," but now wedged open with a brick. A small car stood in the front garden and, as Charlton walked towards the house, a girl came out and ran down the many beautifully hearthstoned steps. He paused in doubt, not knowing if she were Mrs. Rothbury, but:

"Are you calling on me?" she asked. "I'm Mrs. Rothbury."

"Yes," he said. "My name is Charlton—Detective-Inspector Charlton."

Her face went suddenly white and she gave a little cry.

"Has anything hap—?" she began, but his smile was reassuring.

"There is no need for you to worry," he said. "If you can spare me a few minutes, I'll explain...."

"It's not... my husband?"

He shook his head and she smiled with relief.

"I'm sorry to be so silly," she said, "but we haven't been married very long and when he's not here, I always imagine terrible things happening to him."

Briefly he explained what he wanted to know and, standing in the front garden by the little Austin car, she answered his questions. She remembered Major Stallard and his friend, Mr. Townsend of Whitchester; Punchard 2, Wood 1 and the Clafts: but she had no recollection of Mrs. d'Eyncourt or the authoress of *Potassium Cyanide*. She had been a long time on the balcony with her husband and the Scott-Browns, and many other visitors must have come and gone.

"There was a fat woman," she added, "who came panting out on to the balcony, took one look through the railings at the ground a long way below us, instantly had an attack of vertigo and fell into the arms of the little man a fat woman always seems to marry. He had to take her down again at once, which was such a pity. She must have had a lot of trouble getting up there."

She had seen no bearded man, but there lingered in her mind the picture of a man in a brown felt hat. She thought he had a moustache and was carrying some sort of overcoat, but she was not at all sure. He showed her the photographs, but they meant nothing to her. She was able to confirm, though, that Mrs. Claft had not seen a beautiful mirage, but a very much alive old gentleman in a Panama hat and a drooping, tobacco-stained moustache.

Charlton wrote it all down. His note-book was beginning to look, he thought, like a timetable compiled by a certifiable railway official with a weakness for hrn.-rms., flnnl. st. and brd.

He asked the girl where he could find her husband, was given the address of an insurance company in the City, and caught a train to Cannon Street.

But Eric Rothbury told him nothing new.

XII.

HIS OWN FREE WILL

HE lunched at a place in Newgate Street, where he had often fed in the days when much of his time, as a young plain-clothes man and later as a detective-sergeant, had been devoted to giving evidence at the Old Bailey. The proprietor was delighted to see him again and they talked of old times; of the choruses round the piano upstairs, after the wearisome days in the courts were finished, when often the C.I.D. Male-Voice Choir's impromptu rendering of "Lily of Laguna" and "Little Dolly Daydreams" nearly brought their uniformed colleagues in, with truncheons drawn, to quell the rough-house that sounded as if it were assuming dangerous proportions. They chuckled over the tricks they had played, when they had both been young enough to enjoy them and when their favourite joke against newcomers to their gatherings had been to persuade them, by example, to stand on their hands against a wall and then to pour a pint of beer down each trouser-leg.

They nodded their heads portentously and agreed that those had been the days.

After lunch, Charlton phoned Martin; and it was only by hard sprinting from the bus that he caught the 2.30 from Waterloo. As he went along the corridor in search of a smoker, he caught sight of a girl in a brown tailor-made suit. It was Judy. She looked up and saw him; and her smile of welcome was rather wan as she invited him to join her.

"I hardly expected to see you so far away from Lulverton, Mr. Charlton," she said when he had sat down opposite to her.

"I had to come up on business. What a glorious day it is. Even Vauxhall Station looks cheerful."

"It does, doesn't it." There was no interest in her tone. "It

127

must be irritating for you when business in London drags you away from a case."

The question was carefully wrapped up, but he answered it as if it had been bluntly put.

"I've been interviewing Tower witnesses. I was in two minds whether to bring the car, but thought a comfortable electric train would make a change. Any news of your brother?"

"He's not come home yet," she answered and opened the *Punch* that had been lying on her lap.

They clattered through Clapham Junction and it was not until they were nearing Earlsfield that she spoke again.

"Why are you so keen to see Peter?"

"I want to question him, just as I have questioned you and your mother and everyone else who had any connection with the affair."

"Do you think he can tell you anything?"

"He can tell me a very great deal; and the longer our meeting is delayed, the more difficult will the situation become. If your brother comes to me of his own free will, I shall be sincerely pleased."

"Suppose his business keeps him away from home longer than he first thought?"

"Then I must wait until he returns."

"You don't intend to … try to get in touch with him?"

He looked at her with steady eyes.

"Not unless it is forced upon me, and then I shall go with a warrant for his arrest."

"*My God!*" she almost whispered.

He leant impulsively towards her.

"Miss Grey," he said earnestly, "I told you yesterday that there were anxious times ahead of us. Today I am more convinced of it than ever. As I go further with my inquiries, every fresh clue that I find leads me nearer to one terrrible conclusion … And I must go on. I can't stop now … Unless your brother comes to me in time, nothing—*nothing* will prevent his being charged with the murder of Courtenay Harbord."

Judy clenched her teeth on her quivering lip and gazed out of the window.

"Will you please tell him that?" he added gently.

She swung back to him and her words came quickly.

"I went to see him this morning. He phoned me and I caught the next train. The poor boy was in a terrible state and he made me promise not to tell you where he is."

He shook his head impatiently.

"It's madness! I *know* where he is—51, Warne Road, Sydenham,"—Judy drew in a sharp breath—"and it's desperately important that he should come back home today and go to Cooper & Silcock's tomorrow with a convincing excuse for having stayed away. Tell him to call at Croydon police station for the car. I'll arrange for them to hand it over."

He threw out his hands in a gesture of resignation.

"I can't say any more. I have said too much already."

"I'll ring him up as soon as I get home," she murmured. "I had an awful time with him. He was sitting in a wretched little bedroom at the top of the house. The only time he had left it since he'd arrived was when he had slipped downstairs to ring me from the 'phone in the hall ... I couldn't get a really sensible word out of him. All he did was curse Courtenay for playing him the filthiest trick he'd ever seen. He kept repeating that he knew Courtenay had hated him, but never thought he had hated him as much as that ... I told him I thought he'd gone crazy and he glared at me and said in a horrible whisper, 'Can't you see that they're going to hang me for murdering him?' I tried to laugh it off and told him not to be silly, but he still insisted that there was no way out of it: that he'd behaved like a trusting fool and, although he'd thought about it for twenty-four hours, couldn't see a single gleam of hope. ... With him in that state, it wasn't any use my staying, so I gave him some more money and came away."

Charlton grunted and sat in deep thought. Then he slowly raised his head and looked at her.

"If only I can prove it," he said.

They got out at Lulverton. Judy caught the red bus back to Sheep and Charlton walked round to the police station. As he flung open the door of his room and strode in, Sergeant Martin got his feet down off the mantelpiece only just in time.

"Afternoon, sir," he said, jumping up.

Charlton looked at the pile of papers laid neatly on the blotting-pad. Martin followed his glance.

"Fan-mail, sir," he explained, "after our broadcast last night. Thirty-six reports covering seventy-four visitors."

"And I've questioned—how many?"

He took a sheet of paper from a drawer and wrote down these names:—

Scott-Brown	Major Stallard
Mrs. Scott-Brown	Mrs. d'Eyncourt
Vera Scott-Brown	Miss Mortimer
Eric Rothbury	Theyer Claft
Mrs. Rothbury	Mrs. Claft.

"Then," he said, "there was Townsend, the Major's friend."

"I think there's a report about him," answered the Sergeant and Charlton ran through the papers to confirm it.

"What about the two Paulsfield boys?"

"Dr. Roberts, the 'eadmaster, rang this morning and I went over and took statements. The boy's names are Wood and Punchard and they've each got a number because there are other Woods and Punchards in the school. These two are Wood I and Punchard 2. They went up the Tower at 4.20 and came down at 4.45. They didn't see any man, with a beard and don't remember any 'orn specs. The boy called Wood saw some friends of 'is Mum on the balcony. Chillingham is the name, and they live in Chesapeake Road on the edge of Paulsfield Common. The lads couldn't tell me any more than that, so being on the spot, as you might say, I went round to Chesapeake. Mrs. Chillingham was in, and she told me they 'eard the broadcast last evening and 'er 'usband went round to tell the sergeant at Paulsfield first thing this morning. The report's with the others. Three of them, there were in the party: Mr. and Mrs. and young Dudley, 'oo works on the Gold Coast Railway and is home on leave for three months. Old man C's an estate agent in the High Street and I interviewed both him and the son."

The Sergeant dropped his voice.

"As they were on their way up, which was, as near as dammit, 4.30, they met 'orn-rims coming down. Grey flannel suit, soft brown hat, raincoat over 'is arm—and a pipe going."

Charlton accepted this news without comment and took up his pencil.

"I'll put the boys on my list. That makes twelve altogether. Twelve plus—what was it? Twelve plus seventy-four is eighty-six ... Whoever he really was, we must include Whiskers ... Eighty-seven ... The turnstile total was a hundred and six, leaving a balance of nineteen visitors still to be traced. We'll wait until the last minute and then, if necessary, ask the B.B.C. to repeat the message. It'll help a great deal if I can find those nineteen."

"Why? It's nice to know these things, but why, sir?"

"The turnstile total was a hundred and six. If we can get evidence of a hundred and five other visitors, and we can satisfy ourselves that they were not concerned in Harbord's death, there will remain no possible doubt of the bearded man's identity."

"Go on!" said the Sergeant incredulously. "And who would it be, might I ask?"

"Peter Grey."

Martin whistled discordantly and ran his hand through his sandy hair.

"By the way," Charlton went on, "have yon discovered anything to confirm old Greenhill's suspicions about Harbord's delinquencies with the Etchworth girls?"

"Nothing definite yet, sir. You've got to be discreet about inquiries like that, but I'll 'ave another try."

"Did you find the child who was assaulted?"

"I saw the mother and she implored me not to question the kid about it. They're afraid it'll affect her brain. The mother passed on to me the kid's description of the man: young, middle height, cleanshaven. That covers a fair proportion of the population."

"Right, Sergeant. That's all, for the time being. I'll run through these reports now."

After Martin had gone, he sat at his desk drawing pictures on the blotting-paper, with his mind busy on his problem. Courtenay Harbord had been deeply in debt to a man who, however much he protested the purity of his motives in doing so, was dunning him for the money. Harbord had been given his *congé* by Phyllis Greenhill and, according to her, had threatened, if she did not change her mind, to kill himself. There was also Mr. Greenhill's story of his last interview with Harbord, but that seemed more like an attempt to get money out of the old gentleman than the action of a desperate lover. There was no other evidence in support of suicide and even those two possible motives were not strong. Mrs. Grey was not a rich woman, but she would doubtless have been able to find ninety-seven pounds to save the young man whom Mrs. Harbord had left in her care. It hardly seemed that Harbord would have hesitated to ask for the money. It hardly seemed, either, that, with such a character as his, he would have fretted himself overmuch about a broken romance. He was a nasty little rat and might very well have taken a mean revenge on the girl and her father, but not by depriving himself of anything, least of all his life.

From his talk with Judy on the train, he gathered that Peter imagined himself the victim of a trick; and the only trick that Harbord would appear to have played was to commit suicide and throw the blame for his death on Peter. If that was so, Harbord had been the bearded man. He had gone to the Tower disguised, managed to get left behind after everyone else had left, and, when darkness came, flung himself off the balcony. He had also managed to persuade Peter to climb the Tower as well, after altering his appearance by wearing horn-rimmed spectacles; and Peter's visit had had to be so adjusted that nobody should notice him entering the building.

From the accumulated evidence of witnesses, no bearded man had been seen on the balcony. The Clafts had passed him on the staircase and he must have pulled off the beard and changed his hat before he reached the balcony door. If Tom Lee's evidence was to be relied upon, Whiskers had not been in the Tower at closing time.

Everything suggested, therefore, that Harbord had not committed suicide. How, then, had Peter Grey been concerned, unless he had been Whiskers? And Peter's motive? Wasn't he weary to the point of desperation of living under the same roof as Harbord, listening to his cheap sneers, suffering his callous jokes and watching Mrs. Grey grow daily more unhappy at the ungrateful cuckoo who monopolized the nest and gave nothing in return?

Charlton sighed heavily and pulled the pile of reports towards him.

First he divided them into two piles: those who had climbed the Tower in the morning, and those who had gone during the afternoon. The proportion was twenty-three to fifty-one. He put an elastic band round the smaller pile and laid it on one side. The other pile he sub-divided under two headings:

(*a*) All those who left the Tower before four o'clock.

(*b*) All those who left the Tower after four o'clock.

To (*b*) he added the twelve names already listed.

The totals of the sections were then.

(*a*) 24.

(*b*) 39.

He concentrated on the second section, as those who left the Tower before the bearded man arrived at four o'clock were not likely to be of any assistance to him. He took the reports and copied out the names. When he had finished, his full list read as follows:—

The Scott–Brown party	5
Major Stallard and Mr. Townsend	2
Mrs. d'Eyncourt and Miss Mortimer	2
The Clafts	2
Punchard 2 and Wood I	2
Frank and Roy Davison, both of Southmouth, and Mr. and Mrs. Brian Stevens of Woodford Green, Essex	4
Miss Kathleen Harding of West Dulwich, London, S.E., and Miss Jean Turner of Stanmore, Middlesex	2
Mr. and Mrs. John Chillingham and Mr. Dudley Chillingham	3
Mr. and Mrs. Herbert Haggett of Leyton, London, E	2
Mr. Francis Conway, Miss Stella Conway and Master Derek Conway of Bromley, Kent	3
Miss Patricia Chalmers of Ealing, London, W., and Miss Majorie Loder of Mitcham, Surrey	2
Mr. H.L. Burtenshaw and Miss Doris Horniman, both of Horsham, Sussex	2
Miss Pamela Hart-Manning and the Hon. John Morvenden, both of Mount St., Grosvenor Square, London, W	2
Mr. and Mrs. Arthur Presland and Master Michael Presland of Shoreham-by-Sea	3
Miss Muriel Smith of St. Albans, Herts.	1
Mr. Arthur Perks and Miss Mary Tibbs, both of Forest Gate, London, E	2

TOTAL 39

He studied the names and tried to identify them with the scraps of information he had picked up. Mr. and Mrs. Herbert Haggett certainly suggested themselves as the small man with the fat wife, who fell back swooning into his arms. There were two pairs of girls who might have been those whom Miss Mortimer, the novelist, had heard speaking of a man in the Country Clearing, which *she* thought to be a section of the G.P.O., but which he knew to be a Head Office department of one of the big Banks. The old gentleman in the Panama hat could not have been anyone who arrived after the Clafts had left and that, according to the times quoted on the reports, was everybody on his list *after* the Davisons and Stevenses.

At five o'clock, when he was having a cup of tea, two more reports came in. One of them covered a party of visitors during the morning and the other related to a Mr. and Mrs. Theodore Halfpenny and Mr. Jack Halfpenny, who fell under his second heading for the afternoon. He sipped his tea and studied the names. Halfpenny, he decided, went very well with a Panama hat and a long stained moustache; and Theodore seemed to clinch it.

He went along to the Superintendent's office and arranged with him for the message to be broadcast again.

Soon after six, a constable knocked on his door to announce a caller and, at his request, showed in Peter Grey.

XIII.

FIVE POUND NOTES

"I THINK you want to see me?" said Peter.

"Sit down," the Inspector invited him with a smile.

He proffered his cigarette-box and Peter helped himself automatically.

"It is good of you to come along, Mr. Grey. I have been anxious to have a chat with you about the tragic business of your cousin. Things seem to be getting more and more complicated as I proceed, and you may be able to give me some useful guidance."

"Do you think he committed suicide?" demanded Peter.

He had not lost his healthy colour, but his eyes looked tired and his manner was distrait. He drew so hard at his cigarette that brown stains ran down it.

"I'm not in a position to answer that question, Mr. Grey. Now, before you give me your story, which I hope is your motive for coming here, let me tell you certain things that I have discovered."

This was directly contrary to his usual procedure, but Charlton had his reasons.

"Please hear me out," he added, "without interruption."

Peter inclined his head. His eyes were fixed unwaveringly upon Charlton.

"Last Friday afternoon, you bought a false beard and a bottle of spirit gum from Wight & Son in Gray's Inn Road, London. An identical beard was attached to Mr. Harbord's face when his body was found yesterday morning. Some little time before 2.30 on Sunday afternoon, you left home wearing your green hat trimmed with several feathers, and walked towards Lulverton. When you reached the lane that branches to the right—Leaves Lane, it is called—you turned into it.

At four o'clock, a bearded man wearing such a hat as yours went through the Tower turnstile. On the way up the staircase, he was passed by two persons coming down—and that was the last time he was seen in the beard. At about 4.15 a tall woman in the late forties, who had a companion of the same age, asked you a question. At that time, you were wearing a brown felt hat and a pair of horn-rimmed glasses. At 4.30 or thereabouts, you went down the stairs and passed a party of three on their way up. You were then still wearing the brown hat and the glasses, but, a short while later, when you passed a courting couple in Leaves Lane, you had taken off the glasses and changed back into your green hat."

Peter opened his mouth, but Charlton held up his hand.

"Yesterday afternoon, after lunching with your mother and sister, you left home in a car belonging to your firm and drove to Croydon, from where you sent your sister a telegram saying that you were detained. You abandoned the car outside the Post Office and took a tram to Sydenham, where you engaged a bedroom in 51, Warne Road, Sydenham, under the name of John Hurst.

"That is all I have to say. Thank you for listening so patiently. Now, perhaps, you will give me your explanation. You do so, of course, entirely at your own wish and you are not compelled to make a statement. I shall write down everything you say and I must warn you that it may be used in evidence."

"I'll tell you everything," Peter replied, "right from the beginning. I have been over it again and again, and I hope"— he smiled without humour—"that it won't sound so damned improbable to you as it does to me. Last Friday I went up to London on the firm's business. They'll confirm it, if you ask them. Just before I left home in the morning, my cousin took me on one side and asked me to do him a personal favour. I wasn't too keen to do anything for him, but I asked him what it was. He said——"

"Just a moment, Mr. Grey. Did Mr. Harbord know beforehand that you proposed to go up to London?"

"Yes, I remember saying something about it to the family earlier in the week."

"Thank you. Please go on."

"He said he was going to play a joke on some friends and needed a false beard. It seemed fairly reasonable, though I wondered how his friends were going to enjoy it. Courtenay's little bits of clean fun were usually highly unpleasant for somebody! He told me that the beard had to be a good one, and gave me thirty shillings, impressing on me not to breathe a word about it to my mother and sister, in case they got peeved at the way he was wasting his money. He asked me to get full particulars of how to stick the blasted thing on his face and was very anxious that I should find out the quickest way to get it off again.

"I had to go to some Quantity Surveyors in Holborn Bars and I had heard of Wight's in Gray's Inn Road, which is just round the corner, I bought the beard, got the man in Wight's to explain the technique, and passed over the beard and the advice, when I met Courtenay in the evening. I gave him his change and he thanked me very much, which wasn't like him."

"You gave an explanation to the shop-assistant. Can you remember what you said?"

"I told him I was going to a fancy-dress dance. I know it was a lie, but there was no need to tell him that I was buying the beard for my cousin, who wanted to play a dirty trick on some friends of his."

Charlton controlled his features. It was not the time for smiling. But it had been a temptation.

"Did anyone see you hand Mr. Harbord the beard?"

"No. I took it up to his room and he hid it away. Well, I suppose he hid it. He said he was going to."

"So nobody besides yourselves knew anything at all about it?"

"Not as far as I was concerned."

"A pity—but go on."

"Courtenay may have told somebody, of course. …. On Saturday evening he asked for a few minutes in private in our summer-house. I was getting a bit fed up with his hush-hush conferences, but, like a fool, I went—and fell for it. That's the amazing part. With all my five years' experience of his splendid, open character, I let him take me in with the filthiest piece of trickery he'd ever. …. May I have another cigarette?"

The box was pushed across the desk.

"I'll try to remember the whole of our conversation," he continued, throwing the spent match in the ash-tray, "though I won't promise that it's word for word. He began by saying how sorry he was that he and I didn't get on better than we did, and that he was afraid that it was largely his fault, but he had such a funny temper that, when he was worried, it made him behave very badly. That ought to have warned me. A weasel doesn't apologize for being a weasel. But it didn't put me on my guard. …. I don't think I answered. I may have mumbled something, but I'm not sure. He said that, in spite of having tried hard to stop it, he was getting worse in his ways—and all because of one thing: money. I thought I could see which way the conversation was going and assured him quickly that that was my trouble, too. He took no notice, but went on something like this:

"'I owe a packet to a moneylender, who's beginning to be damned difficult. It's seventeen pounds and I haven't got anything like that. This fellow has threatened that, if I don't pay him back p.d.q., he'll go to Aunt Ruth. The last thing I want is for that to happen. I daren't sponge on her myself, in case she gets shirty and throws me out to shift for myself, as she's every right to do.'

"I began to say that I was sorry, but if he *would* waste his money on false beards … when he stopped me. He said he knew he'd behaved damned foolishly and I mustn't think that he was asking for a loan. It wasn't that; but I *could* help him in another way. He pulled a letter out of his pocket and passed it to me. I struck a match and read it. It said that the signatory's representative——"

"Who was the signatory?"

"I couldn't make out the name. It was one of those that are written straight up and down, like 'aluminium' or 'unanimous' scribbled in a hurry. There was no address at the top. It said that this representative would be waiting on the Tower balcony, with a red flower in his buttonhole, at 4.15 on Sunday; and that if Courtenay didn't meet him there with the money, he had instructions to go straight along to my mother. I gave the letter back to him and I believe I said, 'So what?' Courtenay said he had told the moneylender that he was sorry he wouldn't be able to go to the Tower, but he was ill in bed. Then he showed me the reply. It simply said that he must arrange for someone else to go. 'That,' smirked my charming cousin, 'is where you come in. Will you do me that little favour?'

"I said it was all very well, but, even if I went where was the money coming from? He had a quick answer. He hadn't the whole amount, but he'd managed to borrow a fiver and hoped to fob the Shylock off with that. To give the pretty little affair a realistic touch, he took five pounds from his wallet, produced a plain envelope from somewhere, gave me the notes to count, then put them in the envelope and stuck it down. He held it out to me.

"'Is it on?' he asked.

"I admitted frankly that I wasn't one bit enthusiastic. How was I to know, I said, that someone I knew wouldn't see me furtively passing over a mysterious letter to a usurer's nark? And if it came to that, why choose a beastly public place like the Tower balcony for the meeting-place? Courtenay said that he couldn't answer that any more than I could. *He* hadn't suggested the Tower. Then he pretended to have a brilliant idea."

Peter wriggled in his chair.

"When I *think* what a damned fool I was to swallow it, I

want to kick myself from here to Sheep! The whole thing fairly stank of trickery. ... Courtenay must have guessed I would raise that objection and fitted it into his plot. Why, couldn't I, he suggested, disguise myself a bit? I asked, more as a joke than anything, if he meant that I should wear the beard I'd bought for him. At once, he was all denials. The beard wouldn't do at all. It was all right to wear as a joke, but it was no good for my purpose. All I needed to do, he felt certain, was to wear an old hat pulled well down over my face, and put on a pair of horn-rimmed glasses. If I liked, I could take a raincoat and keep the collar of it turned up.

"'Don't,' he said, 'leave home like that. Wear your new green hat, just as if you were going for an ordinary stroll. Stuff the old brown one in your raincoat pocket and make the change behind a bush when you get near the Tower. Go *via* Leaves Lane, not through Etchworth, where you'd be noticed, and come home the same way. The man you're to meet, as you saw in the letter, will be alone and will be wearing a red flower in his buttonhole. He'll give you a fairly thick packet in return for that envelope.'

"I wondered what the packet would have in it, but decided that it wasn't any real business of mine. As a matter of fact, I was getting rather interested. It promised to be rather good fun—the disguise, I mean, and the man with the buttonhole. . . . *Blast* it! Why was I so half-witted?"

He quietened down and continued:

"Anyway, I told Courtenay I was game. I left home on Sunday afternoon, in good time for the appointment. About twenty-past two, I should think. I took the three-mile walk gently and, when I got near the Tower, hid myself in some bushes to make my change. Then I marched boldly up the hill, laid down my threepence and went up the staircase. When I got to the——"

"One moment, Mr. Grey. What time did you get there?"

"Eleven minutes past four. I looked at my watch."

Charlton thought instantly of Mrs. d'Eyncourt and Miss Mortimer.

"Were any other visitors there at that moment?"

"No, but I saw a big car coming up the hill and skipped through the turnstile before it arrived. It was a near thing. I didn't want to be spotted too early in the proceedings."

"Previous to that, did you meet anyone at all during your walk along Leaves Lane and your climb up High Down?"

"Not a soul."

"Did you speak to the attendant?"

"No."

"And did you meet anyone on the staircase?"

"Not actually met, but I nearly caught a party up. I was leaping up the stairs, so as to get to the balcony by 4.15 when I heard children's voices above me. I slowed down and kept behind them, but managed to reach the balcony by 4.14."

"Did you see anything of the children?"

"Yes, on the balcony. They were a little boy and girl with their father. Kids of about seven or eight."

The Conways, was Charlton's notion.

"I looked round," said Peter, "for the man with the buttonhole, but didn't see him. The first person I *did* set eyes on was Mr. Scott-Brown, the Bank manager, which rather made me wish that I'd insisted on the beard! I kept well away from him and his party, and I don't think he noticed me—or was he one of the people who told you about me?"

"Who else did you see?"

"Two boys with Paulsfield caps on. . . . The gaunt female you've already mentioned and her friend.

I went into a flat spin when she spoke to me. . . . A couple of girls in the early twenties. . . . That's all I can think of."

"There was no bearded man?"

Peter shook his head vigorously.

"Do you think anyone saw you come up the last few stairs and walk out on to the balcony?"

"There was nobody on that side just then. I hung about for some time, on the watch for Buttonhole, but there was no sign of him. Then at 4.30, after I'd seen the Scott-Brown circus go down, I felt I'd had enough of it and slipped away myself. I remember saying good afternoon to the love-birds in Leaves Lane.

"Yesterday, coming back from Eastbourne in the firm's car, I called in at Old Forge House for lunch. It wasn't till mother told me then that I knew Courtenay was dead. After we had sat down to grub, Judy—my sister—mentioned the beard he'd been found in and immediately a ghastly thought flashed into my mind: he'd committed suicide and tried to put the blame on me. That's what I still think. Why did he get *me* to buy the beard? Why did he kid *me* into going disguised to the Tower to meet a man who never arrived? Why did he ask *me* to keep the whole thing dark? Because it delighted his nasty little soul to think that I should suffer by his death!

"I'm afraid that, after that, I went absolutely dippy. How I sat through the rest of lunch, I don't know. Then mother suddenly sprang a question on me about horn-rimmed spectacles and told me that it was you who were asking about them. They were an old pair of fake ones we've had kicking about for years. When I got back on Sunday, I pushed them into a drawer of my dressing-table. Before I left after lunch yesterday, I slipped upstairs and put them back where I'd found them—in a big trunk we keep on the landing. But when I heard you'd been asking questions about them, I went into a flat spin. I got into the car and, almost unconsciously, steered away from Lulverton. I wanted time to think; time to work it all out and try to find a loophole. . . . Before I realized it, I was in Croydon—and it looks as if you know the rest. I phoned my sister this morning and asked her to come and see me. It was a silly thing to do, but I wanted her advice. When she gave it, I wouldn't take it. This afternoon she rang me back and absolutely begged me to come and tell you the whole impossible story.

"And here I am, Inspector. If you have any questions, I'll answer them as fully as I can. Is there any need for me to deny flatly that I was the man in the beard? If there is, I do."

"What shoes were you wearing last Sunday?"

"These." Peter held up his right foot and Charlton studied the rubber sole.

It corresponded exactly with the imprint on the balcony.

"That five pounds he gave you. Did he tell you where he had got it from?"

"No. He just said he'd borrowed it."

"What happened to the envelope?"

"It's still in my pocket."

"I should like to see it, please."

He took it from Peter, taking care to hold it by the edges, slit it open with a paper-knife and confirmed that it held five one-pound notes.

"I'll keep this for the time being, Mr. Grey," he said. "You shall have a receipt for the money. Now, tell me, please, exactly what you did after you had passed the lovers in Leaves Lane."

"I went home, getting there about 5.30. I asked my sister where Courtenay was, so that I could explain to him what had happened, but she said that he had gone out at three o'clock and she hadn't seen him since. I told her it didn't matter and had some tea."

"And after tea?"

"I put in a couple of hours' swatting, then went to Lulverton to see a girl friend of mine."

"What time did you leave her?"

"About half-past ten. We stood talking at her gate longer than either of us imagined. I missed the last bus, which goes at 10.15. I had to walk the six miles back to Sheep and didn't get home until after twelve."

"Did you meet any other pedestrians?"

"No, there was no one else about. The whole of the district was in bed and asleep by that time. A car caught me up a little way out of Lulverton and I hoped I was going to be offered a lift, but they drove on without stopping."

"Mrs. Grey and your sister were in bed when you arrived?"

"Yes. I slunk upstairs quietly, because, if Mother's roused in the night, it sometimes takes her hours to get to sleep again."

"Did you disturb her?"

"Not then, so she told me the next morning; but after I'd been in bed about an hour, I suddenly woke with the idea in my head that I hadn't bolted the front door. We keep it on the latch all day and bolt it before we go to bed. You know how things like that worry you? I kept remembering I'd done it and immediately felt sure that I hadn't. Eventually, I got sick of arguing with myself about it and losing sleep over it, and went downstairs—to find, of course, that it *was* bolted. On the way back across the room in the dark, I fell over a stool and made a devil of a row. Mother called out to me when I got back on the landing. I told her that everything was all right, but I'm afraid she lay awake for a long time afterwards."

"Did you know that Mr. Harbord was still out?"

"Yes, I looked in his room when I first went upstairs."

"You hadn't been told that he was spending the night elsewhere?"

Peter shook his head.

"Then why did you bolt the door?"

"It was getting late and I assumed that he wasn't coming in. I didn't like to leave the door on the latch, so risked having to get out of bed to let him in. His friends, the Quentins, often put him up, because the buses don't run very late to Sheep. If he *had* been coming in, he would have been home long before midnight. *I* walked, but I'm darned sure Courtenay wouldn't."

Charlton did his best to hide the disquiet of his mind.

"Before you go, Mr. Grey," he said, "I shall be glad if you will allow us to take your fingerprints."

"Of course," was the ready agreement. "You're thinking

about that envelope, I suppose. You may not find any of Courtenay's on it. I remember now that he was just going out when we had our talk in the summer-house and kept his gloves on all the time. He might have touched it with his bare hands earlier in the day, of course."

Peter's fingerprints were taken.

"Thank you, Mr. Grey," said the Inspector. "If I want you, I don't expect I shall have any trouble in finding you."

"I shan't panic again," asserted Peter firmly.

Left by himself, Charlton sat slouched in his chair, drumming on the desk with his pencil, until Martin knocked and entered, hat in hand.

"Will there be anything more today, sir?" he asked.

Charlton's lips twitched.

"If there is," he said, "I shall swoon."

XIV.

WALTHAM HANGER

STUART LORIMER, M.R.C.S. Eng., L.R.C.P. Lond., had just shown his last panel patient to the door when Charlton called later that evening. He took him into his consulting-room, gave him a cigarette, lighted one for himself and lay back in his chair with a weary sigh.

"I've washed my hands forty-six times today," he announced without emotion. "I counted them."

He had not been many years in Lulverton, this young, hard-working doctor, but he and the Inspector were already good friends, although they never resisted an occasional gentle dig at each other. He was a fine surgeon and, though he affected a certain flippancy, was never at fault in a diagnosis.

"I suppose you've come on business?" he went on. "The only things you and I ever have a heart to heart talk about are corpses and *post mortems* and *rigor mortis*. Can't we sometimes discuss the international situation or my iron shot at the eighth last Saturday?"

"We can try," smiled Charlton, "but I don't think_it would be very long before we drifted back to the unfortunate deceased."

"I'm not so sure. When I'm on the subject of my iron shot at the eighth, there's no gainsaying me. I'm a juggernaut."

"The trouble with you and me, Lorimer, is that we have no clear division between our work and play. *You* must be ready to lay down your golf club at a moment's notice and I to put away my *Snakes-and-Ladders* board. I often wonder if I should like a steady nine-to-five job with a fixed hour for lunch."

"Of course you wouldn't!" scoffed the doctor. "After a month of it, you'd run screaming—and so would I."

"Then let's talk about *post mortems,* in particular of Courtenay Harbord's. I've seen the statement of your P.M. findings for the coroner, but it doesn't answer my most important question: Was he killed by falling off the Tower?"

"My dear chap!" protested Lorimer. "Be reasonable! That's *your* pigeon. I spent the whole of a glorious afternoon, while outside in the trees were thousands of gaily twittering birds——"

"More of my pigeons," murmured Charlton.

"Pigeons don't twitter. There are I, on that perfect afternoon, when Autumn, close bosom-friend of the maturing sun, was doing something or other that Shelley described quite prettily."

"Keats."

"Same thing. Picture me spending my time in a draughty, uncomfortable, miserable hole that's more like some London theatres than a mortuary, while you were probably sprawling in a deck-chair in the Pier Pavilion listening to the band playing 'The Chocolate Soldier.' And now you expect me——"

"This is rank ingratitude!" threw in Charlton with a solemn face. "Who is it always helps you with your sums?"

"That's because you can work 'em out in your head. It's only a question of practice. Give me a piece of paper and a pencil, and I can do anything—even long division."

"Let me put it another way: were Harbord's injuries *in keeping* with a fall from the Tower?"

"That's a very different thing. The answer is, Yes. But they might just as well have been caused by a fall over Beachy Head."

"They couldn't have been faked?"

Lorimer looked doubtful. "It would have taken some doing, unless he could have been given a straight drop from some other high point. It's easy enough to knock a body about with a crowbar, but you've got to do more than that. If a man falls eighty feet or so, his inside gets stirred up something cruel. His liver and spleen are never the same again. It's like throwing a clock from a third-floor window and expecting to find only the glass broken and the case a bit dented."

"Odd you should say that."

"Why? It's perfectly true."

"That's why it's odd."

"If you must talk in riddles, don't ask me about the door that isn't a door. I've heard it."

"So Harbord undoubtedly fell?"

"And a fairly long way. He landed, if you follow me, with *violence*. It might have been faked by chucking him out of an express train or a fast-moving car; but he wasn't killed and afterwards ill-treated, because there were no signs of any other attack on him. His skull was intact, so he wasn't killed by a blow on the head; nor was he poisoned or shot or stabbed or suffocated or drowned. He died because he broke his spinal cord."

Before Charlton went home to Southmouth, he called in at the police station and asked for an Ordnance Survey map of the district. It took him fifteen seconds to find what he wanted—and it was then that he remembered the picture-postcard he had seen in the show-case just inside the Tower entrance.

The Tall Man chalk-pit. . . .

Early next morning, he said to Sergt. Martin:

"Would you like to come motoring with me?"

Martin brightened considerably. He had a profound respect for his superior's driving ability, and a beautiful October day spent sitting by his side, watching England go swiftly and smoothly by, was just to his taste.

"At your service, sir," he replied. "Would you like me to get some sandwiches put up?"

"There's no need. We're only going to the Tall Man. We may as well take Bradfield."

Martin bravely hid his chagrin and, with a jaunty step, went off to find the young detective.

They did not take the Eastbourne road, but bore to the

north of the Downs along a lane connecting, at the tiny village of Barns Bottom, with Leaves Lane. Three-quarters of a mile past Barns Bottom, carved centuries before in the chalk, but now, by the good offices of the Downshire Archaeological Trust, picked out with white tiles, was the Tall Man, a figure two hundred feet high, with each outstretched hand holding a staff. He was the twin of the Long Man of Wilmington, near Eastbourne. Immediately to the east of him was the chalk-pit and, four hundred yards further, the Tower.

Bradfield was left in the car, while the others climbed a footpath that led them to the bed of the pit, which was half-way up the hillside. Martin was hot and breathless when they stopped.

"And all for six-two-six a week," he gasped.

The pit had not been worked for many years and the bed of it, which was flat, roughly elliptical in shape and about fifty yards across, had precisely the same surface as the Tower's surroundings. They explored every inch of it, but the ground was hard after the dry summer and they could find no marks to show where a body might have fallen. Charlton threw back his head and scanned the face of the pit. It seemed from eighty to eighty-five feet high and, as is the way with so many disused chalk-pits, was not quite perpendicular, but sloped at an angle of 100°.

"If you fell off there," observed Martin, "you'd *roll* down."

"Just what I was thinking," Charlton agreed. "Dr. Lorimer said Harbord hit the ground with considerable force and, although this would give him a shaking and perhaps a broken collar-bone, I doubt if the fall would kill him. I suppose you wouldn't care to try?" he added diffidently.

"Looking at it from 'ere," replied the Sergeant, "I almost would, but if you put me at the top, I'd probably think twice about it."

"Let's go and see."

They skirted the pit and clambered up the steep side of

High Down, until they drew level with the pit's brink, along which ran a very old wooden fence, so inadequate that, for a space of six feet in the centre, where its presence was most needed, it was entirely non-existent. They peered over the edge and, as Martin had foretold, found that the view from there was not so pleasant as from down below.

"In answer to your kind invitation of even date," said Martin, "I regret that another engagement forces me to decline."

But the Inspector was not listening. He was staring intently down at the grassy face of the pit.

"Follow my finger," he instructed, "and tell me what that looks like."

Martin puckered up his face and squinted along Charlton's arm.

"I can see it," he said, "but I can't make out what it is. Might be a black pebble."

"I think I know, but how are we going to get at it?"

"Rope," was the terse suggestion.

"The only thing. There's some in the car. Stay here, while I get it."

He brought back the rope and Bradfield, who was twenty-five and as agile as a monkey. They tied the rope round the young detective's waist. After Martin had insisted on shaking him sadly by the hand, he slithered down until he could reach their object.

"Take it by the stem!" Charlton called down to him, as he and Martin hung fast to the rope.

They lowered him the rest of the way. He released himself from the rope, climbed back to where they waited to hand the prize to Charlton. It was an imitation briar pipe of very cheap quality—he placed its value at sixpence—and it had been very little smoked. There were but the smallest traces of teeth-marks on the mouthpiece and the bowl was only slightly scorched. With a satisfied grunt, he wrapped it up and slipped it in his pocket.

"Up to now, Martin," he said, "fingerprints haven't helped us much, but it looks as if our luck has changed."

"Bit of luck you noticed it. Fancy it lodging there."

"The stem," explained Bradfield, "was caught in a fissure."

The Sergeant raised his eyebrows in extravagant surprise.

"Teach 'em some words these days, don't they?" he remarked to High Down.

Further searching of the immediate surroundings produced no fresh clues, and they went back to the car.

"Which is the quickest way to Waltham Hanger, Bradfield?" asked Charlton, with his hand on the starter.

"We can't turn here, sir, or we'll be in the ditch. We'll have to drive straight on and back along the other side of the Downs."

Martin sighed contentedly and settled back in his seat. It was only a few miles' run, but it was better than nothing.

"But it's quicker to go back?"

"Much, sir. It's less than half the distance."

"Then we turn."

And turn they did, to Martin's vast displeasure. As he said later in the day to Bradfield:

"Who'd 'ave thought 'e could get round in that space? 'E *wears* that car like a pair of trousers."

Waltham Hanger was a compact, oval clump of beeches in a combe on the southern slope of High Down. It was a hundred yards or so from the main road and it had been towards it that Steeple, the bus conductor, had seen Harbord walking on the Sunday afternoon. There were no footpaths through it, as it was too far from Lulverton and Etchworth to be much frequented. Both the town and the village had more accessible retreats for couples who wanted to be by themselves. There was practically no undergrowth, but the ground was thickly laid with beech mast. Even on that fine, bright morning, it was a melancholy place.

Charlton and his two assistants spread out and sought evidence of Harbord's entry. It was Bradfield who first picked up a trail on the northern margin, where a sliding foot down the slope had ploughed through the mast and left a furrow. Charlton came in answer to Bradfield's call, but Martin was round on the other side and did not hear. Had they been Cherokee warriors, their steps through the Hanger would not have faltered; but as neither of them had more than a smattering of woodcraft, it was largely luck that directed their uncertain feet towards the trunk of a fallen tree, some eighty yards from the boundary of the wood. As they neared it, Charlton leapt forward and picked up by its stiffly matted hairs a small quill-handled camel's-hair brush.

"Bradfield," he said, "I think we can safely claim that we progress."

"But why the paint-brush, sir?" enquired the puzzled young man.

"Not paint, Bradfield, but spirit gum." He smiled suddenly. "You know, in these surroundings, I feel rather like Mr. Robinson on that overstocked island, explaining some quirk of nature to Fritz, Jack and Ernest!"

"And little Francis," appended Bradfield.

They scouted round the tree-trunk and found an empty Craven "A" packet lying near it. Trodden into the mast by the side of the trunk was an accumulation of cork-tipped cigarette-ends. Charlton sat on his heels and collected ten, but although he extended his area, found only one match, six feet away from the trunk.

"A chain-smoker of some distinction," he smiled up at Bradfield.

"Or a party of people."

"Hardly. This match has scarcely more than the head of it burnt. It looks clear to me that a man sat down on the trunk, lighted a cigarette, threw the match away, smoked the cigarette, lighted another from it and trod it out with his foot. All the butts were in a bunch, so he probably didn't move far away from this trunk. He was waiting patiently for someone or something. How long does a Craven 'A' take to smoke? All of these are burnt to within a quarter of an inch of the cork. Twelve minutes? Twelve times ten. That's two hours. What do you make of it, Bradfield?"

"Only what you said just now: that he either had an appointment here, or was deliberately keeping out of other people's way for a couple of hours."

"We're now four and a half miles from Sheep. The buses take twenty minutes to do the whole journey, so if Harbord caught the 3.5 from Sheep, he got here at about 3.20. That means he sat here until nearly half-past five—if, naturally, he *was* the smoker."

"Does Mr. Grey smoke Craven 'A'?" asked Bradfield, greatly daring.

Charlton laughed. "I envy your poetic gift, Bradfield! No, he doesn't. He smokes a pipe."

From some distance below them, there came a shout.

"The Sergeant," said Bradfield and they called back to him until he caught sight of them through the trees.

"Talk about Snow White and the Seven Dwarfs," he gasped, pushing back his bowler and wiping his forehead. "I thought Bert Martin was lost for ever to the world."

He restored his hat to a normal angle and settled it with a final pat on the crown.

"Inspector, sir," he said, "I don't know how *you're* going, but as I was fighting my way up to you just now, I came across something. It's either a clue or someone's been trying to keep a bull prisoner against its wishes. Would you care to follow me, sir?"

It was only a few yards down the hill: a place where the mast had been churned up, as if some creature had struggled desperately on the ground.

"There!" said Martin. "Was that a wrestle or a Dorcas meeting?"

With his hands in his pockets, Charlton prowled around. By

the foot of one of the beeches, he bent down to pick up two lengths of knotted rope.

"Someone's been tied up and then cut free," suggested Bradfield.

"Looks like bits of clothes-line," was the Sergeant's addendum.

Waltham Hanger might have had other things to tell them, but it remained dumb. Charlton took the rope and they went down the hill to the Vauxhall. He drove on to Etchworth.

"They seem to 'ave got the decorators in," Martin remarked as they swung into the lane and climbed towards the Tower.

A builders' board fixed to the railings round the balcony announced that the work was in the hands of Edmunds, Son & Carfew (Contractors) Ltd. of Lulverton and Guildford. Ladders were roped to the vase and, at that dizzy height, two men were working as carelessly as if they stood upon the ground. Over the flames at the top of the vase the head and shoulders of another man were visible, and Charlton recalled his own expedition on the previous Monday morning. Other men were on the balcony, busy with hammer, hacksaw and chisel. Already a steel hoop had been fixed round the cylinder on a level with the top of the railings.

"The U.D.C.," chuckled Charlton, "haven't wasted time getting the balcony caged in. Harbord must have frightened them badly."

A builders' lorry was standing outside the entrance. He pulled up the car behind it and, telling the others to stay where they were, went in. The Tower was still closed to the public, but that had not kept Tom Lee away. The old fellow welcomed him with a grin and laid down his pipe.

"See what's going on up there?" he asked. "Monday morning, the Borough Surveyor 'e comes round. 'Lee,' 'e says, 'we don't want this to 'appen again,' 'e said. 'Quite right, sir,' I said. 'It gets the place a bad name,' I said. 'We'll cage it right in,' says 'e, 'and while we're at it, we'll 'ave some gold-leaf on that vawse. It's 'igh time it was done,' 'e says."

"It should look very nice," smiled the detective. "But I came here to talk to you about something else. There were two visitors here on Sunday and I want you to try to remember them. I'll take them separately."

Tom twisted his face to show eagerness to help.

"At 4.11 a young man passed through the turnstile. He was dressed..."

He described Peter.

"There were a tidy few folks coming and going last Sunday and it ain't easy to——"

"Do you remember him? Think hard, because it's very important."

"No," said Tom, "I can't pick 'im out. Might if I saw 'im again. When you've done this job all the years I've done it, you get not to notice people. Mechanical, as you might say. Threepence and eight clicks of the stile. That's 'ow I've come to think of most of 'em."

"The other man was of about the same height and he *left* the Tower some time after four o'clock. I can't give you all the details, but he was probably moustached, smoking a pipe and wearing a soft hat and a raincoat."

Tom shook his head despondently.

"You've got me again. *Might* 'ave bin the chap 'oo tried to get out through the wrong turnstile—and then might not."

Charlton's pulse quickened.

"What was he like?"

"Like either of the ones you've said."

With an impatient ejaculation, Charlton turned and went out to the car. Bradfield transferred himself to the driving seat and drove off with the Sergeant. They collected Peter Grey from his office, took him to Old Forge House, then brought him to the Tower, dressed in a raincoat, horn-rimmed spectacles and a brown felt hat. Charlton extracted the blinking Tom from his cubicle like a reluctant winkle from its cosy shell.

"Have you seen him before?" he demanded, pointing at Peter.

"Wait till I get me eyes used to the sunshine,"Tom answered. "Yes, I 'ave."

"Where and when?"

"It was 'im thought 'IN' was 'OUT.'"

The Inspector mastered a wild desire to swear. If Tom's evidence went no further than that, it was useless. He turned to Peter.

"Do you confirm that, Mr. Grey?"

"Yes," nodded Peter, "I tried to go through the wrong turnstile. But," he went on quickly to Tom, "don't you remember when I came here in the first place? I was dressed just as I am now. I gave you three pennies and you let me through. In front of me, there were a man and two children, and some people in a big car came along immediately afterwards. Don't you remember? For *God's* sake, man, say you remember!"

"I don't," said Tom woodenly. "I'd like to oblige a young gennleman, but I ain't going to tell no lies. That's not to say you didn't, but I don't call it to mind."

Peter snatched off his glasses and pushed them violently into the pocket of his raincoat.

"Then if you'll excuse me, Mr. Charlton," he said shortly, "I'll get back to my work."

"I'll walk down the hill with you. I have something to say to you. Bradfield, take the car down and wait for us in the village."

Peter fell in by his side. He sprang his question swiftly, with his glance seeming to be on the road in front of them.

"Where does your mother keep her clothes-line, Mr. Grey?"

The enquiry was received with a surprised laugh.

"In the summer-house, as far as I know."

"You haven't seen it recently?"

"No, but if you want to know anything, Mother is the one

to go to, or Mrs. Hope, who comes on Thursdays for a couple of hours."

"I'll see your mother."

He took Peter back to Lulverton, dropped Bradfield and the sergeant, and drove to Sheep.

The length of clothes-line hanging on a nail in the summer-house of Old Forge House was tagged with metal at one end, but the other end had been cleanly cut, not straight across, but at an angle. It corresponded exactly with an end of one of the pieces he had found in Waltham Hangar. On the wooden table in the summer-house were a few tiny, clustered strands and the table was scored where a sawing knife had cut into it.

"Very pretty, my friend," he muttered.

XV.

LARGELY STATISTICAL

IT is not to be wondered at that the Dictators of Europe supply the poorer citizens of their countries with free radio receivers, for, as a propagandistic or advertising medium, wireless broadcasting is unexcelled. The British Broadcasting Corporation does not concern itself with propaganda or advertising, but its programmes, whether they fall under the three general headings of news, education or entertainment, or whether they can be separately and more specifically described as Bach Recitals, have many millions of listeners.

So it was not, perhaps, so great a miracle that, by eleven o'clock that Wednesday morning, there had found their way to Charlton's desk in Lulverton police station seven more reports, which, when added to the rest, put him in possession of the names and addresses of one hundred and five of the Sunday's visitors to the Tower.

He took a fresh sheet of paper and wrote:—

BROUGHT FORWARD	39
Mr. and Mrs. Theodore Halfpenny and Mr. Jack Halfpenny, all of Lewes, Sussex	3
Mr. Geoffrey Scurfield and Mr. Harold Radforth, both of Welwyn Garden City, Herts	2
Señora Matilda de Guevara and Señorita Catalina de Guevara, late of Cartagena, Spain, but now of Foots Cray, Kent	2
Peter Grey of Sheep	1
	47
Visitors who left before 4 p.m..	58
	105

He was still one short of the turnstile figure, which, although it was something, was far too uncertain to weigh very heavily in Peter's favour. The missing No. 106 might have been Courtenay Harbord or some other person who plotted against him, but it might also very well have been a Mr. Ferdinand Fidgett, hater of radio, usually of Cockfosters, but now on a walking tour through Hampshire and unaware that the police were after him.

He filed away in the metal cabinet behind his desk the reports covering all the visitors who had left the Tower before four o'clock, and made another list of those of the forty-seven who had not yet been interviewed by himself or Martin. There were thirty-one of them, including Mr. Townsend of Whitchester, and their addresses covered a large area. When he had divided them into four sections and allocated these to Martin and his three detective-constables, Bradfield, Emerson and Hartley, he called the Sergeant in and gave him precise instructions.

"Take copies of those two photographs with you," he said, "and if you can find a witness who remembers having seen Harbord, or any other man who might have been Whiskers, on the balcony, you won't have wasted your time. And don't forget, I want those statements by noon tomorrow."

Martin decided against, "What a hope!" and substituted a smart, "Certainly, sir."

While he waited for this information to be collected, there was little that Charlton could do. He assembled the fingerprint evidence and sent the things up, by special messenger, to Scotland Yard, asking them for an early decision. He visited the moneylenders in the district, to find if one of them had advanced Harbord seventeen pounds. When they heard of the appointment with the buttonholed man on the Tower balcony, some were insulted, some amused, while others looked at him pityingly: but they all confirmed that they had never had any business dealings with the deceased young man. He took the numbers of the notes handed to him by Peter Grey and instituted inquiries at the Bank of England. He went to see Robson, Mrs. d'Eyncourt's chauffeur, to ask if he had noticed a man enter the Tower, as he drove up the hill from Etchworth village. Robson had not.

"You told me on Monday," said the detective, "that you arrived at the Tower at 4.10. Was that exact or only approximate?"

"Pretty exact, sir. Might 'ave been a minute one way or the other, but not more."

In the late afternoon, the man returned from Scotland Yard with the report of the Central Fingerprint Bureau. These were their findings:—

(1) The watch: Harbord. No others.

(2) The spirit gum bottle: Harbord and others.

(3) The spirit gum brush: Harbord, but fragmentary. No others.

(4) The pipe: Harbord. No others.

(5) The envelope: Peter Grey (very clear) and others (not so clear). Not Harbord.

(6) The cigarette-packet found in Harbord's pocket: Harbord (clear) and one other person (also clear).

(7) The cellophane found by Charlton outside the Tower: Harbord and others, but not the one other person mentioned in 6.

(8) The cigarette-packet found by Charlton in Waltham Hangar: Harbord. No others.

The Bureau had no previous record of any of the "others."

It is not necessary to record in detail the inquiries made by Sergeant Martin and his three assistants. The same questions were asked in Middlesex, Kent, Hertfordshire, Sussex; but the same vague replies received. It would be fun to tell of Martin's narrowly averted disaster with Mr. Townsend's parrot; of the remark with which Mrs. Herbert Haggett greeted Bradfield; of Emerson's lively conversation with Señor and Señorita de Guevara, in which, after numberless repetitions of "*No comprendo*" and "*No hablamos inglés,*" he finally shouted, "Damn this for a caper! You allee same speakee Flenchee?" But there is no space for those adventures.

By the Thursday midday, Martin delivered the reports and, for several hours, Charlton was busy with them. From all the mass of names and times of arrival and departure, he managed, by checking one statement against, perhaps, six others, to formulate a timetable that showed where every visitor had been during any particular minute of the Sunday afternoon. It might not have been completely accurate—that was too much to hope—but he felt that it contained no serious discrepancies.

"Well, Martin, my boy," he said when he had finished it, "there it is. If posterity remembers me for nothing else, it will surely remember me for this. Generations yet unborn will come to gape at it in the British Museum and it will be known as the Charlton Formula or Charlton Cypher or...."

"Charlton Athletic," suggested Martin, falling in with the spirit of the thing.

"I have given each 'key' visitor a number and, when there was no way of checking the times they gave us, I have assumed that they were telling the truth."

"No. 22, for example," said Martin.

TIME-TABLE

INDEX

p.m.	ASCENDING	ON THE BALCONY	DESCENDING
4.0		1-5 6-7 8-9 10-12 13-16	
4.1		1-5 6-7 10-12 13-16	8-9
4.2		1-5 6-7 10-12 13-16	8-9
4.3		1-5 6-7 10-12 13-16	
4.4		1-5 6-7 10-12 13-16	
4.5		1-5 6-7 10-12 13-16	
4.6	17–18	1-5 6-7 10-12 13-16	
4.7	17–18	1-5 6-7	10-12 13-16
4.8	17–18	1-5 6-7	10-12 13-16
4.9		1-5 6-7 17-18	
4.10	19–21	1-5 6-7 17-18	
4.11	19–21 22	1-5 6-7 17-18	
4.12	19–21 22 23–24	1-5 6-7 17-18	
4.13	22 23–24	1-5 6-7 17-18 19-21	
4.14	23–24	1-5 6-7 17-18 19-21 22	
4.15	23–24	1-5 6-7 17-18 19-21 22	
4.16		1-5 6-7 17-18 19-21 22 23-24	
4.17		1-5 6-7 17-18 19-21 22 23-24	
4.18		1-5 6-7 17-18 19-21 22 23-24	
4.19		1-5 6-7 17-18 19-21 22 23-24	
4.20	25–26	1-5 17-18 19-21 22 23-24	6–7
4.21	25–26 27–28	1-5 17-18 19-21 22 23-24	6–7
4.22	27–28	1-5 17-18 19-21 22 23-24 25-26	
4.23	27–28	1-5 17-18 19-21 22 23-24 25-26	
4.24	27–28	1-5 17-18 19-21 22 25-26	23–24
4.25	27–28	1-5 17-18 19-21 22 25-26	23–24
4.26		1-5 17-18 19-21 22 25-26 27-28	
4.27		1-5 17-18 19-21 22 25-26	27–28
4.28		17-18 19-21 22 25-26	1-5 27–28
4.29		17-18 19-21 22 25-26	1-5 27–28
4.30	29–31	17-18 19-21 25-26	22
4.31	29–31	17-18 19-21 25-26	22
4.32	29–31	17-18 25-26	19–21
4.33		17-18 25-26 29-31	19–21
4.34		17-18 25-26 29-31	
4.35		17-18 25-26 29-31	
4.36		25-26 29-31	17–18

p.m.	Ascending	On the Balcony	Descending
4.37		25-26 29-31	17-18
4.38	32-33	25-26 29-31	
4.39	32-33	25-26 29-31	
4.40	32-33	25-26 29-31	
4.41		25-26 32-33	29-31
4.42	34-35	25-26 32-33	29-31
4.43	34-35	25-26 32-33	
4.44	34-35	25-26 32-33	
4.45		25-26 32-33 34-35	
4.46		32-33 34-35	25-26
4.47		32-33 34-35	25-26
4.48		32-33 34-35	
4.49		32-33 34-35	
4.50		32-33 34-35	
4.51		32-33 34-35	
4.52		32-33 34-35	
4.53		32-33 34-35	
4.54		32-33 34-35	
4.55		32-33 34-35	
4.56		32-33 34-35	
4.57		32-33 34-35	
4.58		32-33 34-35	
4.59		32-33 34-35	
5.0	30-37	32-33 34-35	
5.1	36-37	32-33 34-35	
5.2	36-37	32-33 34-35	
5.3	36-37	32-33 34-35	
5.4	36-37	32-33 34-35	
5.5	36-37	32-33 34-35	
5.6	36-37	32-33 34-35	
5.7	36-37	32-33 34-35	
5.8		32-33 34-35 36-37	
5.9		32-33 34-35 36-37	
5.10	38-40	32-33 34-35 36-37	
5.11	38-40	36-37	32-33 34-35
5.12	38-40	36-37	32-33 34-35
5.13		36-37 38-40	

p.m.	ASCENDING	ON THE BALCONY	DESCENDING
5.14		36–37 38–40	
5.15	41–42	36–37 38–40	
5.16	41–42	36–37 38–40	
5.17	41–42	36–37 38–40	
5.18	41–42	36–37 38–40	
5.19		36–37 38–40 41–42	
5.20	43–44	36–37 38–40 41–42	
5.21	43–44 45	36–37 38–40 41–42	
5.22	43–44 45	38–40 41–42	36–37
5.23	45 46–47	38–40 41–42 43–44	36–37
5.24	46–47	38–40 41–42 43–44 45	
5.25	46–47	38–40 43–44 45	41–42
5.26		38–40 43–44 45 46–47	41–42
5.27		43–44 45 46–47	38–40 41–42
5.28		43–44 45 46–47	38–40
5.29		43–44 45 46–47	
5.30		43–44 45 46–47	
5.31		43–44 45 46–47	
5.32		46–47	
5.33			43–44 45
			43–44 45
5.34			46–47
			46–47

"You notice," Charlton said to the Sergeant, "that the last known visitors left the balcony just after 5.30. All their statements are pretty indefinite and there's no proof that they didn't leave No. 106 behind them. But I'll bet you fourpence that he'd slipped away long before that."

"It's not the *only* thing I notice," replied Martin. "I never thought statistics could be so revealin'." He tapped his finger on the timetable. "Look at that. 32–33 and 34–35 went up in sep'rate pairs, but, after the four of them 'ad had the balcony to themselves for twenty minutes or so, they all went down together—32–35 33–34 formation, I'll be bound!"

His round face screwed itself into a great wink.

"Furthermore," he smacked his lips, "the 36-37 couple took three minutes more going up than old mother 'Aggett. What might *they* 'ave been doing all that time? Carving their names on the wall? If you ask me, I'd say your No. 106 was a little chap wearing no clothes but a bow-and-arrow!"

The afternoon Charlton spent preparing a full report of his investigations to date, which he then submitted to Supt. Kingsley. Later, the Superintendent sent for him and they talked in private for an hour.

"The main question is at the moment," said Kingsley after following Charlton closely, "do we get an adjournment of the inquest? It's fixed for tomorrow, you know."

This Divisional-Superintendent was a bluff, hearty man, even bigger than Charlton, and the salt of the earth. When rank had not to be considered, Charlton called him "Tiny."

"I don't know what to suggest," Charlton admitted. "We've no strong case against anyone yet. Peter Grey's story was a strange one, but it sounded to me like the truth. Harbord was a malicious little devil and it would have been just like him to cook up a case against his cousin."

"But would he have committed suicide for the pleasure of knowing that this Grey fellow would hang for it? Sounds like the proverb about cutting off noses."

"Hatred of Grey might not have been his reason for taking his own life. It might have been forced on him by circumstances. He couldn't have been having a very happy time. Phyllis Greenhill had turned him down and he was being dunned by a man who was anything but a pleasant creditor. Quentin tried to persuade me that last Friday evening was the first time he'd ever mentioned repayment to Harbord, but I'll wager it wasn't. Then there was that other debt he told Grey about—not that I've been able to find any proof of it. There may have been other worries for Harbord and, finding himself with his back to the wall, with suicide as the only escape, wouldn't a man like him have said to himself, 'If I've got to die, I'll see to it that Master Peter suffers as well'?"

Kingsley looked quizzically at him.

"Do you really believe that?" he asked.

"Frankly, no," smiled the Inspector, "but we've no *proof* that Harbord didn't throw himself off the Tower balcony. We can't even be sure that he wasn't Whisk—the bearded man and that he didn't stay behind after Lee had locked up. Whatever one's private convictions, there's nothing to prove whether it was suicide, accidental death, manslaughter or murder. Until we're certain that Harbord did not go to the Tower at all or, or if he did, left before closing-time, there's no certainty that all the evidence I've collected against Grey wasn't cleverly prepared by Harbord before he took his life."

"I don't think much of the motives for suicide that you put forward, Charlton. What did they amount to? A broken love affair that was afterwards used in an attempt to obtain money by false pretences. Debts amounting to less than a hundred and twenty pounds, that his aunt would probably have settled, if it had come to it. What else? Nothing, as far as we know."

"Then what about the inquest?"

"How do you feel about it?"

"We don't want to have our hands forced, but I think we should be safe enough. If the jury understand the evidence, the verdict will be 'Murder against some person or persons unknown'."

As Charlton said this, he thought of Miss Mortimer and her new book.

"Our trump-card," he continued, "is the missing visitor to the Tower. As long as we remain one short of the turnstile figure, we're all right—I mean, of course, as far as the inquest is concerned."

"Then," decided Kingsley, "subject to the Chief's confirmation, we won't apply for an adjournment."

XVI.

MR. GREENHILL SPRINGS A SURPRISE

"OYEA! Oyea! Oyea!"

It was ten o'clock on the Friday morning. The voice of the coroner's officer rattled on like a mechanical toy:

"All manner of persons who have anything to do at this court before the King's Coroner for this County, draw near and give your attendance; and ye good men of the Jury who have been summoned here this day to inquire for our Sovereign Lord the King, when, where, and by what means a man said to be named Courtenay Harbord came to his death, answer to your names, as ye shall be called, every man at first call, on the pains and penalties that may fall thereon."

He handed out nine Testaments and the Jury took the oath. The inquiry was held, where all inquests in Lulverton were conducted, in a large room in the War Memorial Hospital. Besides the assembled witnesses, a number of members of the general public had come to watch the proceedings. They were glad, afterwards, that they had.

Mr. Samuel Trench, the coroner, took up the papers from his desk, tapped them into precise alignment and replaced them in front of him. Then he turned to the jury, who were in three rows of three in the corner to his right, and peered at them through the thick lenses of his spectacles. When he spoke to them, his tone was conversational:

"We are here," he said, as if they did not know already, "to inquire into the death of Courtenay Harbord, whose body was found at the foot of Etchworth Tower early last Monday morning. I understand that you are all acquainted with the Tower and with its surroundings?"

The foreman got to his feet. He was a schoolmaster.

"That is so, sir."

"Then we can proceed." He turned to his officer, a uniformed police constable, who had a roving commission and acted as general liaison officer. "The identification?"

The officer left his seat and shepherded Mrs. Grey to the witness-chair in front of Mr. Trench's desk. She took the oath and sat down.

Coroners can be divided into two main classes: those who read to the witnesses the statements they have already made to the police and ask for confirmation or, if necessary, amplication, of the details; and those who ignore the statements that have taken their officers so many wearisome hours to prepare, and ask the witnesses a series of questions covering the same ground. The answers are then written down by the old gentlemen in laborious longhand, while the whole court fidgets, yawns and blows its noses. Mr. Samuel Trench belonged to the first class and seldom required witnesses to say more than "Yes" or "No."

"You are Ruth Grey?"

"Yes, sir." She had been told how to address him.

"You reside at Old Forge House, Sheep?"

"Yes, sir."

"You are the aunt of the deceased, who lived at Old Forge House up to the time of his death?"

"Yes, sir."

"Do you identify the body of the deceased in the mortuary as that of Courtenay Harbord?"

"Yes, sir."

"Thank you, Mrs. Grey. That is all for the moment, but I shall recall you."

She went back, past Charlton, who was sitting near the Press table, to Judy and Peter. Old Tom Lee was next called, but was required, at that early stage, merely to confirm the discovery of the body and subsequent reporting to the police. P. C. Collins then told the jury about the false beard. Dr. Lorimer was the next witness.

"....and there you carried out an examination of the deceased and ascertained that he had been dead between eight and twelve hours?"

"Yes, sir."

"You later carried out a *post mortem* examination of the deceased and found that he had suffered the following injuries..." He took up a paper... "A broken spine, broken left leg, broken collar bone and broken left forearm. You also found a ruptured liver and injuries to the other organs, did you not?"

"Yes, sir."

"After considering these injuries, you can tell the jury that they are consistent with a fall from the balcony of the Tower?"

"Yes, sir."

"The position in which the deceased was lying was also consistent with the injuries he had sustained, was it not?"

"Yes, sir."

"But you are not able to say that these injuries could have been caused *only* by a fall from the balcony of Etchworth Tower?"

"No, sir."

"There is no doubt in your mind, however, that the injuries were the result of a fall from a height?"

"None, sir."

"There were no injuries that could not have been caused by such a fall?"

"No, sir."

"No abrasions on the wrists and ankles?"

"No, sir."

"Were there any signs of disease?"

"No, sir."

"Your opinion is, then, that the deceased came to his death by a fall, from which he sustained injuries grave enough to kill him?"

"That is my opinion, sir."

Mr. Trench swung round to the jury. "Any questions, gentlemen? No? Then that will do, thank you, Doctor. The Tower, as you probably know," he went on to the jury, "is a place of historic interest and, for the sum of threepence handed to the attendant at the turnstiles, one can climb the staircase and walk round the balcony, which is eighty-three feet from the ground. I shall now recall the witness, Mr. Lee, who, as he has told you, is one of the attendants."

As Tom shuffled past Charlton, with his well-filled pockets dragging down his jacket into two points, like the wings of an injured starling, he gave him a wink. Charlton looked the other way. It was no time for conspiracies.

"You were on duty at the Tower last Sunday afternoon?"

Tom nodded vigorously.

"Please answer my question," was the sharp order,

"Yes."

The coroner's officer stepped up to Tom and whispered in his ear. "What's that?" demanded Tom loudly. The officer whispered again and Tom looked at the coroner and said:

"Sir."

"At four o'clock, or two or three minutes either way, you admitted a visitor. He was brown-bearded and was dressed in a raincoat and a rough green felt hat. Was that so?"

He looked enquiringly at Tom, but the witness's face was wooden and unresponsive.

"Was that so?"

"Yes, sir." The words seemed to be torn from him.

"His appearance was, in every way, similar to that of the body you discovered the next morning?"

"Yes, sir."

"He bought from you a picture-postcard of the Tower?"

"Yes, sir."

"You have told the police that you recognized the deceased

as the bearded visitor to the Tower. Is there still no doubt in your mind?"

"Yes, sir."

"What do you mean by that?"

"No, sir."

"You mean that you are still convinced that it was the deceased who visited the Tower on Sunday afternoon?"

The old fellow wagged his head up and down.

"Answer Yes or No!" snapped Mr. Trench.

"Yes."

"It is your regular custom, when closing the Tower at night, to climb the staircase and make the circuit of the balcony, to ensure that no visitors have lagged behind?"

"Yes, sir."

"And you went through this routine last Sunday? ...I say, you went through this routine last Sunday? ...Are you dumb?"

"No, sir."

"You did *not* go through this routine?"

"Yes, sir, but I ain't dumb." This long sentence, delivered with reluctance, sent a subdued titter through the court. Mr. Trench hid his mouth behind his hand.

"And to the best of your belief there was nobody left inside the Tower when you finally locked up?"

"Not a soul."

"You are quite certain that the doors were securely fastened before you went home?"

"Yes, sir."

"And, when you arrived the next morning, you found them in the same condition. We know that it was not you, but a detective-inspector, who opened the doors and the outer gates, but I think you can tell the jury that everything about them seemed as usual."

Tom looked across at the jury, swallowed and said:

"Yes, gents."

"You have said that you were satisfied that the Tower was empty when you closed it; but—and I want you to think very carefully before you answer this question—do you remember the departure of the bearded man?"

The answer was sharp and prompt. "No, sir!"

Tom deliberately turned his head and the glance from his humid eyes wavered across the court and fixed on Charlton. "How's that?" it seemed to say. Charlton looked elsewhere.

"Or the departure of a man, either clean-shaven or moustached, who might have been he?"

"No, sir."

"You were not acquainted with the deceased?"

"No, sir."

"You saw the body, however, after the false beard had been removed and you have since been shown a photograph. But you cannot recall having seen him pass your office on his way out?"

"No, sir."

"You do not tell the jury that this bearded man whom you have identified as the deceased did *not* leave the Tower. You merely say that you did not notice him. Your attention was distracted, from time to time, by your Sunday paper."

"Saturday," amended Tom.

The assembly sniggered. One man threw back his head and laughed delightedly. Mr. Trench frowned at him.

"Kindly do not make that noise again," he said. "It is not only out of place in this court, but it will also disturb the patients upstairs." He addressed the jury. "The witness is right to correct me, but the point is immaterial."

The jury had no questions to ask this reticent witness and his place was taken by the Clafts, who confirmed having met the bearded man on the staircase, and afterwards by Mr. Matthews, the Clerk, and Philip Lambert, who told the jury about the keys.

Then it was Charlton's turn. He gave a brief outline of his

early investigations; how he had found the damaged watch on the dead man's wrist, the marks on his hands and the spirit gum, cigarettes and picture-postcard in the pockets. When he told them how he had unlocked the gates and doors of the Tower, the coroner asked:

"Are you quite satisfied that the locks had not been tampered with?"

"Yes, sir."

"Is there any other way of getting into the Tower?"

"No, sir."

"You afterwards climbed the stairs and carried out a close examination of the balcony and the upper cylinder. Please describe to the jury everything you observed."

"The upper cylinder is cut off from the main staircase by a grilled gate. The thick coating of dust on the stairs beyond the gate was undisturbed, so that no person, even had he had the key of the grille, could have hidden in the upper cylinder. I made a detailed search of the balcony, finding one Craven 'A' cigarette-butt and a clear imprint of a rubber sole that coincided with the sole of the right shoe worn by the deceased when he was found."

"You mean that it coincided, in so far as it was of the same make? There was no peculiarity that identified the footprint with that particular shoe, to the exclusion of all other pieces of footwear?"

"That is so, sir. They were of the same size and the pattern was identical, but the shoes were new and had no individual features."

"The floor of the balcony was dusty, yet you can tell the jury that, when you came to examine the shoes of the deceased, there was no film of dust on the soles."

"Yes, sir."

"In the circumstances, would you expect there to be?"

"Yes, sir. If the deceased had thrown himself off the balcony, there would have been no opportunity for the dust to be brushed away by some other surface."

"You found no footprints on the balustrade around the balcony, suggesting that someone had climbed over the upper grille?"

"No, sir."

"Would you expect the palms of the hands to become marked by rust after gripping the bars of the upper grille?"

"Yes, sir. I carried out a test at the time."

"Thank you, Inspector. That, I think, will do for the moment. We turn now, gentlemen, to the consideration of events leading up to the death of the deceased. You are to hear of his actions during the early part of last Sunday afternoon and of certain other matters that may enable you to arrive at a decision... Mrs. Grey?"

Again the coroner's officer escorted her to the witness-chair.

"Mrs. Grey," said Trench very gently, "we do not want to give you any more pain in this court than is absolutely necessary, but"—he cleared his throat—"I cannot avoid now asking you certain questions, so that the jury may have some idea of the state of mind of the—of your nephew, before this shocking tragedy occurred.... He came to live with you, I think, about five years ago, because his parents had died suddenly and left him unprovided for—penniless, I might almost say?"

"Yes, that is so."

"And you, with a generosity that earns the respect of all of us, took him into your home and have looked after him ever since?"

"Yes."

"He was unable to find—or did not seek—employment and was, therefore, entirely dependent on you for his food, his clothing, his pocket-money—in short, for everything. That was so, was it not?"

"Yes, but I was glad to be able to——"

Mr. Trench held up his hand. "We feel sure that you were. You were unaware, however, that your nephew had got himself heavily in debt?"

Her eyes opened wide, almost in terror.

"He couldn't have!" she cried. "He would have told me."

"Did you ever discuss with him the question of finding a salaried post?"

"Yes. He made several attempts to get a position, but somebody else always got there first."

"You never told him bluntly that the existing state of affairs could not continue?"

"Not as strongly as that. It wouldn't have been fair on the poor boy. I did say more than once that if only he *could* earn some money, it would be so much better for all of us."

"You gave him a fixed amount of pocket-money every week?"

"No. There was nothing regular about it. I gave him money when he asked for it."

"And sometimes his demands caused you—some inconvenience."

"It wasn't always easy without drawing on capital."

"He did not, at any time, ask you for a sum as large as ninety pounds."

"Good gracious, no! The most he ever wanted was three or four pounds."

"You did not give him five pounds one day last week?"

"No. I gave him two."

"Thank you, Mrs. Grey. I need not further prolong your ordeal."

She went back to her children, but Peter was next to be called.

"It is my usual practice," Mr. Trench told him, "to caution witnesses that they need not answer any questions that they think would involve them. Do you wish to make a statement on oath?"

An electric thrill ran through the court. It was a significant warning.

"Yes, sir," answered Peter without hesitation.

"Mr. Grey," was the first question after the oath had been

taken, "last Friday the deceased, who was aware that you were going up to London, asked you to oblige him by making a purchase on his behalf, did he not?"

"Yes, sir."

"This purchase was a false beard, which you handed to him on your return home."

"Yes, sir."

"The deceased gave as his reason for this unusual request that he wanted the beard to carry out a practical joke. That was so, I believe?"

"Yes, sir."

"He did not mention the name of his intended victim or when he proposed to play this joke?"

"No, sir."

"Gentlemen, it has been established, not entirely beyond doubt, but with reasonable certainty, that the beard bought by Mr. Grey was the one found on the face of the deceased... Mr. Grey, last Saturday evening, you had another meeting with the deceased, during the course of which he told you that he was in some financial difficulty. Will you kindly tell the jury the amount he mentioned to you."

"Seventeen pounds."

"To whom did the deceased say he owed this money?"

"A moneylender, who was pressing him hard."

"He did not tell you the name of this man, but he showed you two letters signed by some person whose name you could not identify?"

"That is so, sir."

"The deceased informed you, did he not, that he was in great distress about this liability and that he dared not confide in his aunt, for fear she should eject him from her house?"

"Yes, sir."

"But he told you that he had managed to find five pounds and hoped to stave off his creditor with that. He did not, however, reveal the source of this money?"

"No, sir."

"Now, Mr. Grey, be good enough to tell these gentlemen of the suggestion made to you by the deceased."

Peter repeated the conversation with Harbord and described how he had reluctantly agreed to give his assistance.

"And for fear this man you were to meet should be a notoriously, or obviously, bad character, you slightly altered your appearance before you reached the Tower by changing into another hat and putting on a pair of horn-rimmed spectacles. Was that not the case?"

"Yes, sir."

"But these precautions were wasted, for you failed to meet the moneylender's representative?"

"I waited on the balcony for about a quarter of an hour, sir; but he didn't arrive, so I went home."

"Thank you, Mr. Grey. That is all, for the moment—unless you have any questions, gentlemen? ...No? ...Mr. Quentin?"

Oliver Quentin was oily and entirely unconvincing in his air of deep grief. He told the jury with overacted reluctance of his scene with Harbord and of his demand for "something on account" by the Monday morning. He protested that he had done it because he had felt that the lesson would do Harbord good and had got as far as "*Facilis descensus*—" when Mr. Trench cruelly pulled him up.

"So you see, gentlemen," said the coroner, after Quentin had returned to his place, "that however well-intentioned the last witness may have been, he placed the deceased in an immensely difficult position. We have heard from Mr. Grey that there was another debt of seventeen pounds that must have increased his anxiety. But on top of that, gentlemen, the deceased had troubles of another sort. You are now to be told about them."

Mr. Greenhill, who had been patiently sitting through the proceedings with Phyllis at his side, was called to the witness-chair.

"A few months ago, Mr. Greenhill," said Mr. Trench when

the oath had been taken, "in fact, until Saturday, the 29th June, your daughter was on friendly terms with the deceased?"

"Yes, sir."

"Will you please tell the jury how their friendship was brought to an end?"

"Because I asked her not to see him again," chewed Mr. Greenhill. "I had decided that their association was undesirabubble."

"It is a father's privilege to advise his daughter in matters of that kind and we will not go into your reasons for so directing her."

Mr. Greenhill looked grateful for this concession and Charlton, glancing across at Phyllis, saw her heave a thankful sigh.

"But," went on Mr. Trench, "there is one other thing about which we must ask you to speak. Last Thursday evening, the deceased visited your house, during your daughter's absence, and you had with him a rather painful scene. Describe it, if you please, to the jury."

"He threw himself on my mercy. He said that he could not live without my daughter and implored me to consent to their marriage. I replied that I could never do that. My mind was completely made up and if they did marry, it would be entirely against my wishes. The young man assured me that he would never dream of taking such a step without my sanction, and then went on, almost sobbing, that if he could only get a real opportunity, he would make good and earn the right to my daughter's hand. He had been offered, he told me—in fact, gave me his solemn oath, a partnership in a prosperous bookshop in Paulsfield Square, the only stipulation being that he was to bring a hundred pounds into the business."

Mr. Greenhill paused and shook his head sadly.

"I know now why he wanted that money."

"You must not express your personal opinions in this court,

Mr. Greenhill," warned the coroner.

"I am sorry, sir. I spoke without thinking."

"Please do not let it happen again. The deceased suggested that you should put up the money for this enterprise and you refused, did you not?"

"I am afraid I did not give him a chance to suggest it, sir. I told him before he had the opportunity, that he must not expect any assistance, from me."

"How did he receive that decision?"

"I thought he had taken leave of his senses. He shouted that if I would not lend him the money and insisted on withholding my consent to his marriage with my daughter, I must put up with the consequences."

"Did he give you any idea of the nature of these consequences?"

"Yes, sir; but I shall be grateful if you do not insist upon my divulging them."

Charlton became suddenly interested. This was news to him.

"The jury have the right to know. You may write it on a piece of paper if you wish."

The coroner's officer supplied Mr. Greenhill with a pad and a pencil, and the old gentleman scribbled down a few words. The sheet was torn off and handed first to Mr. Trench, whose only comment, as his officer passed it on to the foreman of the jury, was:

"I see."

XVII.

NINIAN MCCULLOCH

THE coroner resumed his questioning of Mr. Greenhill.

"The deceased," he said, "did not tell you that he would take his own life if you continued to stand out against the marriage?"

"No, sir. As soon as he had threatened me with the results of my continued refusal, he flung out of the house, leaving me, as you will probubbably understand, in a state of great perturbation of mind."

"Thank you, Mr. Greenhill. I have nothing more to ask you. Any questions, gentlemen?"

A juryman in the second row leant forward to murmur into the foreman's ear.

"I quite agree," nodded the foreman and rose to his feet. "Will the witness tell us, sir, whether he verified the truth of the deceased's allegations."

"It was a monstrous lie!" exploded Mr. Greenhill. "I have been assured——"

"Mr. Greenhill!" snapped Trench. "I must warn you that hearsay is not evidence."

"We consider, sir," persisted the foreman, "that our question should be answered, if necessary, *in camera.*"

"Gentlemen," was the decisive reply, "I don't think it advisable to pursue this matter any further. We have been told by Mr. Quentin that the deceased owed him ninety-seven pounds and received an ultimatum from his creditor on the evening of the Friday before he died. We have heard of his unsuccessful attempt to borrow a hundred pounds from Mr. Greenhill. Whether, on the Thursday evening, he had any forewarning of the attitude later adopted by Mr. Quentin it is hard to say. Probably not. But there seems little doubt that he badly needed money and sought out Mr. Greenhill as a last resort. The charge that he so wildly made was very likely prompted by his failure to raise a loan. The next witness will prove to you that, whatever may have been his usual custom the deceased forsook the truth in one other particular during his interview with Mr. Greenhill." The foreman bowed and sat down. Mr. Greenhill was dismissed.

"Mr. George Stubbings!" called the coroner's officer. As George marched up to the witness-chair, he was, as he afterwards proudly boasted to his staff, one Milke, the cynosure of all eyes. As he took the oath, his clear, precise young voice reached every corner of the big room.

"... that the evidence I give to the court on this inquiry shall be the ..."

"You are the manager of a bookshop trading under the name of 'Voslivres,' which is situated in Paulsfield High Street on the corner of the Square?"

"Yes, sir."

"It is the only bookshop of any description in the Square?"

"Yes, sir."

"And you are in sole charge of it?"

"Yes, sir. The business belongs to Mr. John Rutherford, who built it up, but the entire responsibility now devolves upon me."

Charlton made a mental note to congratulate George on that speech.

"Mr. Rutherford is now in France, I think, but if he proposed to make any changes, there is no doubt that he would consult you first. Am I not right?"

"Yes, sir. Most decidedly, sir."

"The previous witness has given in evidence that the deceased told him that he had been offered a partnership in a well-established bookshop in Paulsfield Square. Will you now please tell these gentlemen that the bookshop in question was not, to the best of your belief, the one of which you are manager."

"It was not, sir."

183

"Thank you, Mr. Stubbings. That will do."

George paused, as if this short tenure of an important position was not to his taste; then dutifully returned to the body of the room. A glance passed between him and Charlton, and a very keen observer would have noticed the right eyelid of each of them quivered.

"That is proof, I think, gentlemen, that the deceased attempted to deceive Mr. Greenhill into giving him a large sum of money. This matter into which we are inquiring is full of complexities, but there has emerged one indisputable fact, which is that, when the deceased met his death, the difficulties that beset him were acute. You have been told, gentlemen, how he lived on the charity of his relations and how, in spite of generous allowances by his aunt, Mrs. Grey, he managed to get himself into serious financial trouble. You have heard how he was terrified that his aunt might lose patience with him and leave him to fight for himself in the world—a contest for which he seems to have had no other weapon than an aptitude for borrowing money without security."

The jury did not smile at this dry little jest. Perhaps they felt that it was not their place.

"Mr. Grey has told us that the deceased had other worries. He owed a moneylender seventeen pounds, of which he was able to repay only five—and even that small sum must have been lent to him, by whom we have not been able to discover. We can see that this hard-pressed young man was robbing Peter to pay Paul and then searching for someone who would enable him to reimburse Peter—a game that cannot be played indefinitely.

"But why, we ask ourselves, if he had the intention of flinging himself from the balcony, did the deceased arrange for Mr. Grey to visit the Tower at approximately the same time as he himself proposed to go? Why did he make such elaborate arrangements in order to repay part of a debt which, once he was dead, would not matter a very great deal to him? Was it, gentlemen, to throw suspicion on his cousin? Did he really owe seventeen pounds to a moneylender? The police cannot trace that he did. Mr. Grey, as he has told you, went disguised to the Tower. He has also told you that it was he who bought the false beard at the request of the deceased. The beard, together with the bottle of spirit gum for attaching it to the face, cost the sum of one pound, one shilling and sixpence. Is it probable, do you think that it was the intention of the deceased to put it to the frivolous purpose that Mr. Grey has told us he proposed? Surely a man, however blind to his responsibilities, would not lay out what was, in the circumstances, a considerable sum, just in order to play a practical joke on a friend, when it might have been used to help satisfy the demands of such of his creditors as Mr. Oliver Quentin?"

A more sensitive owner of the name would have been pained at the slight stress then given it.

"It is my duty, gentlemen," said Mr. Trench, "to bring these points to your notice. It remains for you to consider them carefully in arriving at your verdict. ..." He cleared his throat. "We come now to the events of the afternoon of last Sunday."

"Miss Judith Grey!" called the officer.

Judy described how Harbord had left Old Forge house at three o'clock. When asked by the coroner, she said that her cousin's manner had seemed quite normal and that he had told her of his intention to take a walk across the Downs. Mr. Trench made no reference to her talk with Harbord in the summer-house, and she was allowed to return to her seat. Robert Steeple, the conductor of the red bus, next told how he had put Harbord down at approximately 3.20 and had seen him climbing High Down in the direction of Waltham Hanger.

"Thank you, Mr. Steeple. Any questions, gentlemen? ... Inspector Charlton, will you please step up here again? ... We turn our attention now, gentlemen, to a subject whose importance may not, at first, be apparent. Members of the public who wish to ascend Etchworth Tower have to pass through the turnstile at the entrance; and, as some of you may know, the apparatus is so constructed that a mechanical record is kept of the number of persons who have gone through it. ... Please tell the jury, Inspector, the results of your investigations in that direction last Monday morning."

"Before the attendant or I entered the Tower, sir, I made a note of the total recorded by the turnstile. The full total at that time was 3,952. I also counted the money in the cash-box and found that it amounted to three pounds, six shillings and sixpence."

"Kindly stand down for a moment, Inspector." Charlton obeyed and Philip Lambert was recalled. "After the Tower had been closed to the public on Saturday evening last, Mr. Lambert, you called there to check the turnstile figure and the cash in hand, did you not?"

"Yes, sir."

"You recorded the totals in a book that you took with you, and left in the cash-box a certain sum in silver and copper, to enable the attendant to give change. Please now tell the jury the turnstile total at the end of the day's business last Saturday."

"3,846, sir."

"And the amount that you left in the cash-box?"

"Exactly two pounds."

"You have the book? ... Please let the jury examine it."

The officer took it from Lambert and handed it to the foreman. When all of them had seen it and it had been given back to Lambert, Mr. Trench continued:

"So you see, gentlemen, that if we take the total as at the end of Saturday last, which is recorded in the witness's book, and subtract it from the total already supplied by the Inspector, we can arrive at the number of visitors to the Tower last Sunday. I notice that one or two of you have been jotting down figures, and I think you will agree with me that the number of visitors is 106. This we can check with the receipts, which, after deducting the sum of two pounds for the cash in hand on Sunday morning, amounted to one pound, six shillings and sixpence: that is to say, one hundred and six times threepence. That, I think, is clear to you?"

The jury nodded as if they understood perfectly. Some of them did.

"That will do, thank you, Mr. Lambert.... Inspector? ... Please tell the jury, Inspector, how many of those 106 visitors the police have traced and questioned since last Monday morning."

"105, sir."

"A very fine achievement, don't you agree gentlemen? ... Accept our congratulations, Inspector."

He looked meaningly across at the Press table. It was not the first good turn the little man had done Charlton.

"It has not been considered necessary to summon all those visitors to this court, but I have here before me a full report covering all their statements. Some are here today to give evidence, but the majority, particularly those who left the Tower before the bearded man arrived—58 in all—are in no way concerned with the matter into which we are met together to inquire.

It would be unwise of you, gentlemen, to arrive at the hasty conclusion that this bearded man was the 106th visitor, for we have no proof of that. The swift action of the police and the far-reaching effects of messages broadcast by the B.B.C. have already supplied us with a wealth of evidence, but there may be somewhere in the world—even, by this time, dead—one man or woman who climbed the Tower last Sunday and does not know—or perhaps, will never know—that his or her testimony is being sought. Should such a person eventually come forward, it will become immediately certain—I use the word in all its implications, gentlemen—that the deceased did not pass through the turnstile and could not, therefore, have flung himself from the balcony; and it will be equally certain that one of those 105 witnesses was himself the bearded man and is, therefore to be looked upon with suspicion." Charlton waited patiently for this homily to end. Finally, Mr. Trench, satisfied that he had made his point clear, swung back to him.

"Now turn your mind, Inspector, to the watch that you found on the wrist of the deceased last Monday morning. I think you noticed certain things about it?"

"I did, sir. The unbreakable glass had been displaced and was lying on the grass underneath the body of the deceased. The minute-hand had been broken about halfway and the snapped-off fragment was also on the grass. The watch had stopped at 8.32. As in most modern watches, the winding-shaft could be used also as a hands-adjuster, by pulling it out a short distance. When I examined the watch, the winding-shaft was in that position."

"Thank you, Inspector."

"Mr. Andrew Selby!" the officer called.

The round-shouldered old man, whose face did not seem complete without his watchmaker's eyeglass, stumbled up to take his place in the witness-chair.

"You are Andrew Selby, a watchmaker, of 4, Low Pavement?"

"Yes, sir."

"I think we can say, Mr. Selby, that you have had considerable experience in your line of business."

"Over fifty years, sir. I began as a boy of twelve in the 80's."

"A long and useful career! ... Last Monday morning, Detective-Inspector Charlton brought you a watch such as he has just described, did he not?"

"Yes, sir. He did."

"It was an *Election* Swiss-made, silver wristlet-watch and the number of it was"—he raised the paper and peered at it—"183538. Is that correct?"

"Quite correct, sir."

"The Inspector has informed us that the minute-hand was broken, the unbreakable glass forced from the bezel, and the winding-shaft then in its hands-adjusting position."

"I quite agree with that, sir."

"Did your examination of the watch reveal any other damage?"

"No, sir. Apart from the broken hand, the watch was in perfect condition."

"Yet it had stopped at 8.32. How do you account for that? Had it run down?"

"No, sir. I should say that the watch stopped because the winding-shaft had been pulled out."

"Would it stop almost at once?"

"Not immediately, sir. It would continue to run from two to three minutes, maybe a bit longer, but it would eventually stop. When I pressed back the winding-shaft of the watch in question, it at once began to work perfectly again."

"Dr. Lorimer, in his evidence, said that the deceased came to his death as the result of a heavy fall. Would you reconcile the condition of the watch with such a fall?"

The old man's chin stuck out.

"No, sir! I most definitely would not!"

His listeners stirred and excited whispering broke out all over the room.

"Kindly give the jury your reasons, Mr. Selby."

"The most sensitive part of the mechanism of a watch is the balance-staff, which easily becomes damaged. If I knew that a watch had fallen from the great height that the deceased fell, I would willingly stake my oath, before I opened the back of it, that the balance-staff would be broken. But the balance-staff of the watch handed to me by the Inspector was undamaged."

"Would you expect to find the winding-shaft jerked out after such a fall?"

"Not unless it was particularly loose in its movement."

"Was that so with this one?"

"No, sir; and even if it was loose enough to be jerked out by the shock, I should be very surprised if it had not been snapped off."

"And the broken minute-hand—would you consider that a natural thing to have happened?"

"It's not impossible, sir, but I should hardly expect it. It would be far more likely to break off at the pinion than where it did."

"Where is the pinion, Mr. Selby?"

"It's where the hand is fixed on in the centre of the watch-face, sir ... No, I should say that the balance-staff and the winding-shaft would be much more likely to break first."

"The Inspector found the glass lying undamaged on the ground underneath the body of the deceased. You do not see anything unusual in it having fallen out?"

"Oh, no, sir. It's what I should expect. It doesn't need much of a jar to dislodge a watch-glass, especially one of the unbreakable type, which are more flexible and springy than real glass."

"So apart from that, you found that the watch under discussion had not only failed to suffer the damage that you yourself would have expected, but had also suffered damage that you yourself would *not* have expected?"

"Precisely so, sir."

"Which, gentlemen," said Mr. Trench, spinning round to the jury, "is a very extraordinary thing."

He turned back to the witness.

"If the jury have no more questions, Mr. Selby, you may stand down ... Inspector? ... Last Wednesday morning you went to what is known as the Tall Man chalk-pit?"

There was a sudden tension in the room. Even the habitual coughers fell silent.

"I did, sir."

"Will you please describe the features of this chalk-pit."

"It is just under a quarter of a mile to the west of the Tower and is on the northern side of High Down. The face is nearly, but not quite, perpendicular and, at its highest point, there is a drop of eighty-five feet."

"And during your visit, what was it that you discovered in a crack in the face of the pit?"

"An imitation briar-pipe, sir."

"You found nothing else? No evidence of a body having fallen there?"

"No, sir."

"But the ground was dry and hard, thus making it possible for a body to have fallen without leaving a trace."

"Yes, sir."

"From the Tall Man chalk-pit, you went, did you not, to Waltham Hanger, which is a clump of beech trees on the southern side of High Down, about half-way between Lulverton and Etchworth?"

"Yes, sir."

"There you discovered among the trees a small quill-handled brush, with the hairs of it stiff with some kind of hard varnish."

"That is so, sir."

"You also found, by a fallen tree, an empty Craven 'A' cigarette-packet, an accumulation of cigarette-butts and one match, as if some person had sat there smoking for a considerable time."

"Yes, sir."

"You later came upon a part of the Hanger, where the beech mast had been violently disturbed over an area of several square yards."

"Yes, sir."

"And you also found two lengths of rope, each of which had been tightly knotted, as if round the ankles and wrists of a person, and then cut with a knife. You satisfied yourself, did you not, that they had once formed a single length of rope and surmised that this length had been cut off a clothes-line?"

"That is so, sir."

"You went next to the house in Sheep village where the deceased had made his home and, on examining the clothes-line which you found hanging in the summer-house, you made quite sure that the single length I have just mentioned had at one time been part of it?"

"Yes, sir."

"When considering these facts," Mr. Trench addressed the jury, "we must bear in mind that Dr. Lorimer told us that the wrists and ankles of the deceased bore no abrasions."

There was a sharp double tap on the door at the far end of the room, and the coroner's officer hurried to answer it. While the court waited, a paper was handed in to the officer. He came back with it and laid it before Mr. Trench, who picked it up and held it close to his face to read it.

A feeling of disquiet took hold of Charlton and he shifted his position uneasily. Mr. Trench put down the paper and looked gravely at the jury.

"Gentlemen," said the little man, "after what has been said in this court today, it is necessary that I should pass on to you without delay the message I have just received. It is to the effect that, during the morning of Sunday last, a man hitherto unknown to us visited Etchworth Tower. His name—not that it really matters—is Ninian McCullough."

XVIII.

A DRAPER'S RELUCTANT CONCURRENCE

CHARLTON drew in a sharp breath. This was the one thing that he had feared. Before, there had been every chance that the jury would commit themselves no further than to return a verdict of murder against some person or persons unknown; but now, he felt sure, they would record a more definite decision. For what did Ninian McCullough's evidence prove? That the bearded man had not been Courtenay Harbord or some person unknown, but one of the hundred and six—and which of them was more open to suspicion than Peter Grey? Even Charlton himself, who had been firm in the belief that Peter was innocent, began now to have grave doubts. The case previously against Peter had been too circumstantial, too dependent on subordinate detail, to support a charge of murder; but this new fact was not only in itself of major importance, but it also gave all the other evidence against him a new and damning significance.

"For the third time, Inspector," Mr. Trench's voice broke in on his thoughts, "will you kindly stand down."

The next witness was a fingerprint expert from Scotland Yard, who confirmed the details already supplied to Charlton.

"And that, gentlemen," said the coroner, "is all the evidence I propose to call. Have you any further questions to put to the witnesses before I ask you to consider your verdict?"

They murmured amongst themselves. At length the foreman rose.

"We do not feel, sir, that we can arrive at a decision without being in possession of the details of the visitors to the Tower last Sunday afternoon. We quite understand that it was not possible to bring them all here today, but may we please know whether any of them could give any evidence having a bearing on this inquiry?"

"A very reasonable request. I am able to tell you that all relative evidence has been given this morning and that nothing else that the witnesses could tell the police has anything to do with this court. However, I see nothing against your having the copies of their statements, if they will assist you. There is also a timetable that has been constructed by the police. This, too, you may take with you when you retire."

"Thank you, sir. They will be a great help ... We should also like to know, please, whether the witness, Mr. Tom Lee, remembers passing the witness, Mr. Peter Grey, through the turnstile."

Mrs. Grey gave a little cry and Judy took her hand. Peter sat stiffly upright, looking straight ahead of him.

"Mr. Lee," said Trench abruptly, "will you please step up here?"

He had strict notions about the limited functions of a coroner's inquest and was displeased at the course proceedings were now taking.

"Mr. Lee," he said, "the jury wish to know whether you remember Mr. Peter Grey, whom you have seen here today, coming to the Tower last Sunday afternoon. You must bear in mind that he has told us that he was wearing a pair of horn-rimmed spectacles. Did you notice him or not?"

"No, sir."

The next question came from the foreman. "Do you remember him leaving?"

"Yes, sir. I do."

The foreman bowed to the coroner and sat down. "That is all, thank you, Mr. Lee ... Well, gentlemen, the witness has answered your questions. There seems nothing further to add. Have you already reached a decision, or do you wish to retire?"

"We should like to retire, sir, if you please."

"Very well."

An hour had elapsed and the nine members of the jury were still arguing in the room that had been set aside for them.

"But," said the Draper, "he doesn't look like a murderer."

"And what," demanded the Commercial Artist, who was young and had a beard, "*does* a murderer look like? Do you think you can pick one out by the colour of his hair or his size in collars?"

"They do say," observed the Licensed Victualler in a voice that was as slow and thick as cod-liver oil, "as you can tell 'em by their ears."

"Ears, bunk!" retorted the Commercial Artist. "Any man is a potential murderer, whatever the shape of his ears. Take Crippen. Did he agree with your idea of a murderer? Or Alfred Rouse, or that good-looking, curly haired, smiling fellow who did the girl in at Crumbles. What was his name? ... Patrick Mahon. Did *they* look like murderers? Given enough reason for taking the risk, and every one of us in this room would commit murder." He looked at the Draper. "Even you, sir."

By the Draper's expression, it appeared that he did not welcome this distinction: that he preferred to be a standard cut-throat like the others.

"Aren't we drifting away from the main question?" he suggested. "We are keeping the court waiting."

"The point I have been trying to make for forty-five minutes," fretted the Commercial Artist, "in spite of numerous interruptions, is that this man, Grey, although he *looks* a respectable, decent-living young fellow—and, I'll grant you, probably is, in other ways—had a *cast*-iron motive for putting his cousin out of the way."

"There I entirely agree with you," said the Veterinary Surgeon, who was large and leather-gaitered. "Harbord was nothing more than a parasite. Reading between the lines, I'd say that the rest of the family loved him about as much as a bott, yet, because the old lady hadn't the heart to throw him out, put up with him—until young Grey decided he couldn't stand it any longer."

"And took the law into his own hands," added the Journalist, as if he had just contrived the phrase.

"It sounds very likely," agreed the Bank Accountant, and the Nurseryman nodded.

"Couldn't he have used less drastic means?" suggested the little Draper.

"Nothing less would have done," answered the Commercial Artist. "It's no use urging a parasite to do the decent thing. He just doesn't listen. If they'd told him to pack his trunk and get out before he was thrown out, he would have said, 'Auntie dear, I know you wouldn't treat your helpless, penniless little nephew like that. Remember I'm your own flesh and blood.'"

"I'm not saying," conceded the Draper, who was a mild man, but, in his timid way, dogged, "that the deceased wasn't a young waster and no good to anybody but I do submit that they could have got rid of him without resorting to violence."

"If they had been united," said the Veterinary Surgeon, "they most likely could have done, but, whatever her private feelings were, Mrs. Grey would never have agreed. I'm certain of that."

"So young Grey," pronounced the Licensed Victualler, "saw this cuckoo in the nest was slowly but surely eating 'em out of 'ouse and 'ome, made 'is plans and then, when the moment was ripe, tipped 'im out of the nest, so that 'e broke 'is blinking neck and made more room for the others. And a good riddance, is what I say. Relations are all right in small quantities. Let 'em come to tea, by all manner of means. But dinner, no. It's too much for mother. And as for coming for years on end, it's no wonder murder was done last Sunday."

A silence fell on the seven of them, as they considered this point, and the voice of the Schoolmaster, who was their foreman, became audible.

"... and only the other day," he was saying to the Pastrycook, another boy told me that an unfrocked priest is a priest who has been dismantled. It's really amazing the ideas some boys get into their heads. There was another case in my class last term of a—"

He stopped and looked guiltily round.

"What are your views, Mr. Foreman?" asked the Commercial Artist blandly.

"I believe Grey did it," was the hasty reply, "and I think this gentleman is of the same opinion."

"I am that," said the Pastrycook.

"Gentlemen," remarked the Bank Accountant, who was a prominent local supporter of the Bank Officers' Guild and fancied himself as a second Winston Churchill, "will you allow me five minutes in which to give you a brief outline of the case, as it appears to me?"

On the spur of the moment, they could think of no valid reason for deterring him, so gave him their attention. He stood as bank-men do, with his right hand in his trouser-pocket and his jacket folded back under his arm to reveal his key-chain.

"Up to the moment," he began, "when the coroner told us of the last visitor to the Tower, I was convinced, in spite of all the evidence to the contrary, that Harbord had committed suicide, after having so arranged it that suspicion pointed straight to Grey. The finger-marked pipe in the Tall Man chalk-pit, the disturbances in the Hanger, the clothes-line—all these might have been clues planted by Harbord. Even the evidence of the watchmaker did not shake me much. I have heard about the evidence of specialists in such cases as this! But when I heard, gentlemen, of Mr. Ninian McCullough, I immediately altered my mind. Harbord could not *possibly* have killed himself, because he was not one of the hundred and six who entered the Tower. So, whereas before, Grey's visit there could have been explained by Harbord's desire to implicate his cousin, now the only interpretation to be put upon it was that

Grey invented the whole story to explain his presence on the balcony, and was himself the bearded man.

"There can be no doubt now that this bearded man was one of the hundred and six visitors. He was noticed by Lee when he went through the turnstile, and he was passed on the staircase a few moments later by that American couple ... I have just been running through the police reports, and I have noticed one very significant fact: the only man who visited the Tower *alone* between four o'clock and six was Grey. Everyone else had at least one companion, except a Miss Muriel Smith—and I don't think *she* could have been the bearded man!"

He paused for the laugh, but did not get it.

"Therefore," he continued, "Grey *must* have been the man in the beard—the beard that Harbord was wearing when they discovered his body."

"Not necessarily," the Draper reminded him.

"Everything suggests that it was, anyway."

"We've been given no proof of that. It's only presumptive," persevered the Draper.

"It doesn't really matter. Even if it was not the same beard, it was clearly Grey's intention to give the impression that it was—and that it was Harbord who climbed the Tower. The bus conductor saw Harbord making for Waltham Hanger. The police later discovered evidence suggesting that someone had been tied up and left to struggle on the ground—"

"There were no marks on Harbord's limbs," heckled the Draper, but the orator took no notice.

"What is, then, more likely than that Grey lured Harbord into the Hanger, overpowered and bound him, put on the false beard, went himself to the Tower, came back when it was dark, deprived Harbord of consciousness—"

"How?"

"Cut the ropes, carried him to the Tall Man chalk-pit, threw him off the top, then moved the shattered body to the foot of the Tower, for it to be found the next morning by the attendant.

"That, gentlemen," he ended modestly, "is how I see it."

"Hear, hear," the Commercial Artist applauded.

All the others, except the Draper, were of the same mind; and it took them seventeen minutes to get him to agree with them.

"But I still don't think he looks like a murderer," he said as he capitulated. The jury had filed back to their places and the coroner's officer had called for silence.

"Well, gentlemen," said Mr. Trench. "Have you arrived at a verdict?"

The Schoolmaster stood. "Yes, sir."

"What is your verdict?"

The whole assembly became completely still.

"Murder by Peter Grey."

Heads were immediately turned towards Peter, who started to jump to his feet, then dropped back into his chair. Mrs. Grey buried her face in her handkerchief and Judy put an arm around her.

"The cause of death, on the medical evidence," said Mr. Trench placidly, "was a fracture of the spine, and your verdict is murder against Peter Grey."

The coroner's officer handed the deposition to the foreman, who signed it. After the rest of them had written their names below his, the deposition was handed back to Mr. Trench, who carefully checked off their names with the list in his possession.

"Right," he said at last, and immediately his officer began to gabble:

"Oyea! Oyea! Oyea!

"All ye good men of this County, who have been sworn of this Jury, to inquire for our Sovereign Lord the King, when, where, and by what means Courtenay Harbord came to his death, having discharged your duty, may depart hence and take your ease.

"God Save the King."

Charlton's step was mechanical as he walked up to the

coroner's table.

"Get the women away," he muttered to the officer as he passed close to him.

Mr. Trench carefully blotted the warrant and handed it across the desk to him. Mrs. Grey was clinging to Peter, and sobbing on his shoulder. Judy, who was dry-eyed, helped the officer to take her from the court; and when Charlton went towards him, Peter was standing by himself, waiting.

"Peter Grey," Charlton heard himself say, "you have heard the verdict. I must now take you into custody and I must caution you ..."

Later that day, in an upper room of a house five doors away from Mr. Greenhill's "Pro Bono Publico," Mr. Edward Preston, late of Pentonville and Dartmoor, and known to his friends as the "Viscount", or more usually "Vike", was lounging back on the bed with his hands behind his head, while Albert ("Smoothy") Smithers, recorded at Scotland Yard as alias many of the names in the London Telephone Directory, which had always been his source of inspiration, sat upright in a cane-seated chair with a very beautiful smile on his face. On the floor lay an evening paper that Vike had just allowed to fall.

"Nice work," he said.

BOOK TWO

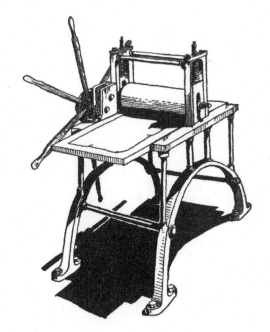

The
KILLING

XIX.

OVERSIGHT OF A SUB-BRANCH CLERK

COURTENAY HARBORD met Vike Preston and Smoothy Smithers ten months before they murdered him; and the casual acquaintance ripened into something approaching friendship after Vike and Smoothy had made the gratifying discovery that, although he had not had their opportunities, he was as big a scoundrel as they were.

During the religious service on the Sunday morning before they left the Moor, the two of them had arranged, by fitting to the tune of "Rock of Ages" words that would have greatly surprised Augustus M. Toplady, not to be seen in each other's company until three months after their release, and then to go into partnership. That was how they had come to live in the drowsiest corner of sleepy Downshire, in the unregenerate hope that they might be able to turn a dishonest penny without attracting the critical attention of New Scotland Yard. It was as well for the peace of mind of the villagers of Etchworth that they knew nothing of these ambitions, for they would not have slept quietly in their beds if they had known that one of the newcomers, Smoothy Smithers, had once been the most persuasive "con" man who ever sold a chimerical oil-well; and the other, Vike Preston, had made such a study of robbery with violence that the last night-watchman he had met professionally had lain for three days at the point of death with a skull fractured by Vike's jemmy; and only the united endeavours of the hospital staff had saved the watchman from death and Vike from an early morning appointment with Jack Ketch.

Vike was forty-one. He came from a middle-class family and had been given a good education. He had a fiery, impatient temperament, but a certain dash that had earned him his nickname. Smoothy's superficial polish was a part of his stock-in-trade, gained through a certain imitative facility added to a love for reading all kinds of elevating literature in the libraries of the prisons in which so many of his fifty-four years had been spent. It was only when Smoothy was really excited, which he very seldom was, that the veneer cracked and exposed the real Albert Smithers, the son of a drunken street-hawker, who had battered the boy's mother to death and had been hanged for it at Wandsworth in 1896.

They were, each in his different way, as dangerous as a couple of rattlesnakes.

For eighteen months, they worked well together and, by choosing the right moment and not being too proud to take on small stuff which, though it brought in only a modest profit, entailed very little risk to themselves, managed to live fairly comfortably. Then they met Courtenay Harbord.

At first, his manner deceived them and they took him for a simpleton with more money than sense; but after Smoothy had put forward a few tentative proposals that were guaranteed to produce a 300 per cent, return for the courageous investor, they found that this was not a plump pigeon to be plucked at leisure, but a carrion crow of particularly voracious habits.

One evening in the following March, after the three of them had grown tired of trying to cheat each other at pontoon, they fell to chatting and Harbord mentioned that his father had sent him to a school of photoengraving, so that he might lay the groundwork for a career in that trade.

"I bet they pushed you out after the first week!" laughed Vike. "I can't see *you* doing honest work."

"As a matter of fact," replied Harbord in his quick voice, "I got interested in the process and went right through the course. The fellow who took us said I'd go a long way if I kept at it."

"And have you kept at it?" asked Smoothy, who was not really very interested.

"No, but I've still got the experience."

"Might come in useful some time," Vike dismissed the subject.

It was only after Harbord had gone home to Old Forge House that Vike referred to it again.

"Smoothy," he said, laying down his glass, "we've still something left in the kitty, but that won't last for ever and these little tip-and-run jobs we've been doing lately aren't bringing in very much. I'm inclined to suggest something more ambitious. It's safe and quiet in Etchworth, but the life is deadly—for me, at any rate."

"I don't entirely agree with you," said Smoothy, "but I'll admit that I often think about Piccadilly Circus and the suckers who are walking round waiting for me to take it off them."

"Most of them have heard of your oil-well," gibed Vike.

"It doesn't matter. That's the amazing thing about the 'con' game. If you can spin the yarn convincingly, you'll always find somebody to listen to you. I remember once in the Long Bar at—"

"I don't want to hear that again," interrupted Vike. "It goes up five pounds every time you tell it. Let's come back to the main question. I wasn't very interested at the time, but it's occurred to me since that Harbord's technical knowledge might be turned to some account."

"What knowledge?"

"Photo-engraving."

"And what good is that? You're not thinking of printing Christmas cards and asking me to do a door-to-door canvass with 'em, are you?"

"Something much more profitable than that." He paused, then added, "Snide."

"What, Bank notes? That's damn risky, isn't it?"

"Of course it is, but it's worth it, if you can do it in a big way."

"But look at the tackle you want: cameras, printing-presses, paper—don't forget the paper."

"That could all be arranged," assured Vike.

"Listen."

They drew their chairs together.

Harbord was sounded out at their next meeting.

"This photo-engraving, Fly," began Smoothy, using the nickname they had given him. "Have you ever thought of putting what you know to any useful purpose?"

"Not while I can live in comfort without working," answered Harbord with a nasty laugh.

"Don't you sometimes think that comfort by itself is not enough: that a little *luxury* wouldn't come amiss?"

"Luxury? There's no luxury in the printing trade. *Experts* can't find a job, so what hope is there for me? Besides, I don't like work. Never did."

"Not if it brings you in a wonderful income?"

"Don't forget I've heard your yarns before, Smoothy. 'There's gold in them thar hills,' doesn't mean a thing to me."

"This isn't one of his fairy tales, Fly," promised Vike. "It's a business proposition."

"How much do you want?" asked the unbeliever. "A thousand or so?"

"Not a damn penny. All we're asking for is your help, and you won't complain at the amount we're willing to pay for it."

"It's something phoney, I suppose?"

"Naturally," said Smoothy without hesitation. Harbord had helped them in some of their enterprises and was under no delusions about them.

"What is it? Keep nothing back. I'm not easily shocked."

"Forging Bank notes."

Harbord whistled. "Flying high, aren't you? What's the penalty for that?"

"Eighteen months or so," lied Smoothy airily.

"If you see to the technical side of it, Fly," said Vike persuasively, "we'll attend to the distribution. We're already in touch with several useful men who'll take over the carrying."

"What about the plant? You can't forge notes with a bent hairpin."

"Tell us what you want and we'll get it for you."

"A 25 inch copper-plate press, for a start. Do you propose to smuggle *that* into Etchworth under your coats?"

"You shall have everything you need," said Smoothy calmly. "A camera and so forth."

"Shan't want that. Straightforward engraving on the copper-plate is the best way to do it. Photoengraving is all right for line blocks, but that's about all"

"But hand engraving on plates is confoundedly difficult, isn't it?"

"Of course it is. That's why you're going to pay me fifty percent of the profits."

"Fifty?" demanded Vike. "Have a heart, man. We've got to buy the plant and take the risk of having it found in this house. Say twenty-five?"

"Twenty-five, nothing. I'll take thirty-three and a third—and that's final."

"Fair enough," said Smoothy and Vike had to agree.

To men of resource, very few things are impossible; and, when they can avail themselves of all the benefits bestowed upon members of that strange freemasonry who live precariously beyond the Law, even the greatest difficulties can be overcome.

During the first week in April, the printing-press went into the cellar piece by piece. Respectably dressed little men, who looked like insurance clerks, brought it in a car while Etchworth peacefully slept, and they brought, too, all the paraphernalia of the trade. Where it came from, nobody enquired, but, when everything had been assembled, Smoothy paid the quiet little men hard cash for it, and they went away content.

"Well," said Vike, as he surveyed the apparatus, "we're the

death or glory boys from now on. The dees won't listen to our pitiful little excuses when they cast an eye over that lot."

Harbord did his part well. He took tracings of the watermarks and made line blocks in the acid-bath. Then the Machine Loam paper was damped, a block placed in position over it and heavy pressure exerted by the printing-press. The engraving of the copper plates was pure skill. He placed a gelatine sheet over a note and scratched a tracing. Plasticene was then smeared over the sheet, which was placed face downwards on the copper plate. Steady rubbing transferred the tracing to the plate and then Harbord got to work with the engraving tools.

When extensive experiments with inks had produced the right colours and Vike and Smoothy had got the trick of working the press, they turned out a series of convincing pound and ten-shilling Bank notes: unlikely, certainly, to get past cashiers and other keen-eyed experts, but quite good enough to deceive harassed bookmakers at crowded race-meetings and shortsighted old ladies in murky suburban sweet-shops. In fact, so successful were they that there came a considerable demand for the notes, and the carriers were willing to pay three shillings apiece, which showed Harbord, Vike and Smoothy a profit that repaid them for their trouble. The process of printing was slow, the output never being more than thirty notes a day, and they would have made more money at honest clerking; but that was *their* affair.

The great danger was being caught passing the notes to the carriers; and it was when Smoothy was beginning to fear that their regular trips from Etchworth might invite attention from the police, that Harbord met Philip Lambert at one of the Quentins' gambling parties. Lambert was then getting into serious financial difficulties, for there was nothing kindergarten about the select little gatherings at "Capri," where the regular winners were Mr. Oliver Quentin and the stool-pigeons who were allowed to make twenty pounds in an evening, on the distinct understanding that they afterwards refunded nineteen of them to their host. Mr. Quentin would have been a great success at Christmas parties, for he had a fine repertoire of clever card tricks.

Harbord reported on Lambert to Vike and Smoothy. "He's got himself in a jam," he told them, "and he probably doesn't mind how he gets out of it. He works at the Council offices, which may come in useful and, what's more to the point, he runs a car."

"Let Fly lend him some money," suggested Smoothy, the strategist, "and then, when he can't pay it back, we'll talk to him."

The plan was tried and worked out very well. Lambert's troubles had become even more acute by that time and he jumped at the chance to make some money. He was not, like Harbord, a congenital wrongdoer, but his character was weak. Smoothy, who had a genius for organization, arranged Lambert's part of the business. The important thing was to keep the carriers steadily supplied with notes, so he questioned Lambert about his duties in the Council offices.

"Is there any job that takes you out regularly?" he asked.

"It's funny you should ask that. There's been a strafe on about our not collecting the cash takings from the Tower a bit more frequently; and my boss, Matthews, has told me to make a special point of going there once a week."

"Just the thing. Has he fixed it for any particular time?"

"He told me today to go every Saturday morning."

"Then ask him tomorrow if he minds your going on Saturday evenings."

"But that would be in my own time," protested the wage slave.

"All the better for you," said Vike. "It would give the impression that you're a willing worker. That would please Sir Percy, wouldn't it?" he added wickedly.

Lambert jumped. "We'll leave him out of it, if you don't

mind," he said haughtily. "But Saturday evening seems damn silly to me. Why can't you make it some other time?"

"Because," answered Smoothy, "our complicated system wouldn't allow it. In any case, it's no concern of yours."

"All right, then; but don't forget the Tower closes at six. What do you want me to do?"

Smoothy told him the plan.

Until the end of June, things went like clockwork. Then there happened something that nearly ended in disaster. Courtenay came to Vike and Smoothy early in the afternoon of Friday the 28th with his face even whiter than usual.

"I've done a damnfool thing, Smoothy," he said. "I got a couple of our ten-shilling notes mixed up with my aunt's Guest House money and she's paid them into the Bank."

Smoothy and Vike kept their heads, but the mistake was serious. They had exercised the greatest care that none of their forgeries was circulated in the immediate neighbourhood. London, Birmingham, Manchester, Newcastle and other big, distant cities had always been their centres of distribution, so that the Downshire police should not become too watchful.

"Did the cashier pass them?" asked Smoothy with composure.

"He must have done, or Aunt Ruth would have said something about it afterwards."

"Which Bank was it?"

"The Sheep sub-branch of the Southern Counties. It's open twice a week for two hours. Lulverton is the parent branch."

"If they trace them back to her," growled Vike, "we can expect trouble before very long. I suppose you realize that, you blasted little fool?"

"I'm very sorry, Vike."

The young man was genuinely rattled.

"It would be interesting to know," drawled Smoothy, who was always unmoved in the face of danger, "why you were jiggering about with your aunt's money."

"You mind your own damn business!" flared Harbord.

"Easy," warned Smoothy. "It was only a friendly enquiry, you know. Little accidents like this are bound to happen, Fly. The thing is now: what are we going to do about it? If it had been just one note, it wouldn't have made much odds. Your aunt might very easily have been given it by a customer. But two are another matter."

"They might have been swung on her at different times," suggested Harbord hopefully.

"A carrier never goes to a place twice," Smoothy reminded him. "It isn't healthy. Mrs. Grey takes lodgers, doesn't she? The police couldn't prove that one of those hadn't given the notes to her."

"She has paying guests sometimes, Smoothy, but usually only in summer. The last one she had was a commercial, but that was over a month ago, so *that* wouldn't wash."

"Would a bill for food," queried Vike, "run a customer into more than half a bar?"

"The most expensive lunch is two-and-six. With extras, there would have to be a party of at least four."

"Carriers don't go round like a choir outing," said Vike shortly, "and they don't try passing two notes at once."

"They work, Fly," explained Smoothy, as one anxious to edify the young, "in pairs. One man holds the main supply and feeds it to the other a note at a time, so that if the dees get him, they find only one note on him—and they can't touch him for that."

"Then what are we going to do?" Harbord asked.

"There's only one thing we *can* do," was Vike's reply. "Let it ride. You've no suggestions, have you, Smoothy?"

"Watch and pray," said Smoothy devoutly.

XX.

THE RIFT IN THE LOOT

IN the long run, it would have been better for the little coterie of offenders against the Forgery Act of 1913 if Charlton had scored a knockout in the first round. But he did not.

At the close of business at midday on the Friday when Harbord was to bring grave news to Smoothy and Vike, the Sheep sub-branch clerk, whose name was Gough, locked up the office, said good-bye to the guard, who went off to cultivate his garden, and caught the blue bus back to Lulverton. In some branches it is the custom for a junior cashier to take over the additional responsibility of looking after a sub-branch. Before he leaves the parent branch, he takes from his till sufficient cash for his needs and, on his return, replaces any balance. But Gough was not a cashier at Lulverton, but a ledger-clerk, and was therefore dependent on cashier No. 1, to whom he had to give a just account of his stewardship when he came back from Sheep on Tuesdays and Fridays.

It was cashier No. 1, a clerk of long experience, who threw out the two notes that were causing their utterers such concern.

"Gough!" he shouted across the office. "You've passed a couple of dud halves."

"Blast it!" replied Gough. "That's the first time it's ever happened."

"I don't blame you," said cashier No. 1 magnanimously. "They're very nicely done."

The discovery was reported to Mr. Scott-Brown, who instructed Gough to advise the police immediately. Charlton called later at the Bank and talked to Gough over the counter.

"They obviously came from the same place," he said. "Have

you any idea who paid them in this morning?"

"Yes," answered Gough. "It was a Mrs. Grey,"

A lad of fourteen came and stood by Charlton's side.

"Yes?" said cashier No. 1.

"I want to join the Navy."

"Why?" smiled the cashier.

"'Cause I've walked three miles and I'm not going back and I want to join the Navy and you're the Recruiting Officer, aren't you?"

"No, we're not. You'd better get along to the Post Office. They've got all the particulars there."

"O.K.," answered the boy, and left the Bank whistling.

Charlton laughed. "You have some odd conversations sometimes, don't you?" he asked.

"'Odd' is just the word," cashier No. 1 agreed. "When I was on the counter in one of our Isle of Wight branches, I asked an old lady for twopence for a cheque I'd just handed to her. She flared up and said it was a disgraceful imposition, as cheques were only half that price in London. If you've ever lived on the Island, you may see her point of view. I *have* and I *did*!"

Cashiers' busiest time with customers is after the Bank has been officially closed to the public, and, as that moment had not quite arrived and Charlton had the public space to himself, cashier No. 2 edged along and joined in the conversation.

"Do you remember that woman," he said, "who rushed in and shouted that she'd only just got time to catch a train and would we please ring up her husband and tell him to turn the gas down in the oven?"

That started it. Every member of the staff had some tale to tell. Ledger-clerks and Security-clerks hung over the cashier's screen and the junior hovered in the background. Gough described how, when he went to Sheep, it was a regular thing for him to look after the landlady's baby while she slipped across Plestrium Dexter, and to take a large white and a small brown, if the baker called while she was out.

The doors were pushed open and seven breathless people piled in, each carrying a paying-in book. St. Augustine's clock down the road struck three. The Bank messenger went round the counter to close the doors and narrowly missed being trampled to death by another inrush of customers.

Charlton turned back to Gough. "You were going to tell me Mrs. Grey's address?"

"Old Forge House. It's a teashop in Sheep village."

"Thank you. If you'll have it made out, I'll sign a receipt for these notes."

And that was how Charlton came to meet Judy.

The front door of Old Forge House was open. He walked into the big room, which was occupied by a party having early tea. After he had stood waiting for a few moments, Judy came in with fresh supplies of hot water. She placed the jug on the table and turned to him with an enquiring smile.

"Are you Mrs. Grey?"

"No, that is my mother. Do you want to speak to her?"

"If I may?"

Judy showed him in to the small front room and closed the door. It was not long before Mrs. Grey joined him.

"I am a police inspector," he told her. "I understand that you paid some money into your Bank today?"

"Yes, I did. Why? Is anything wrong? Mr. Gough counted it very carefully and initialled my counterfoil. I do hope there's nothing wrong. If there is, why didn't they tell me themselves? There was no need——"

He arrested this torrent of words.

"I'm afraid," he said, "that two of the notes you paid in were clever forgeries. Mr. Gough was deceived by them, but they were discovered later."

"I must repay them," fluttered Mrs. Grey. "I hadn't the slightest idea that they weren't all right. Will you tell them that, please? I've read in the papers that there have been a lot of forgeries about. I must go and explain to Mr Scott-Brown."

"I don't think there will be any trouble about that, Mrs Grey," he smiled to relieve her distress. "The main reason for my visit is to find out how these notes came into your possession. Perhaps you can tell me?"

"I'm afraid I can't. I'm always changing notes for customers."

"You think you *were* given them by a customer?"

"I must have been. I keep my private money quite separate and always pay accounts by cheque."

"But if a customer gave you notes, his bill must have been considerable. Have you entertained any paying guests recently?"

Mrs. Grey shook her head. "Not for some weeks. A commercial traveller stayed here for a night, but I paid *his* money into the Bank a long time ago."

"Have you had any recent parties of visitors who spent more than ten shillings?"

"Oh, no! I only wish I had!"

"Do you keep any account books?"

"No. My statement from the bank is a good enough guide,"

"I think I should like a few words with your daughter. She has a certain amount to do with the running of the Guest House, I believe?"

"Certainly," said Mrs. Grey and went to fetch Judy.

But Judy was no more informative than her mother. She said she could not see how the notes had found their way into the cash-box, which was kept in the kitchen.

"Has anyone besides your mother and yourself access to the box?"

"Mother locks it up and keeps it in her bedroom every night; but during the day, we can all go to it—I, my brother and my cousin, Mr. Harbord."

"Is it likely that either of them served a customer when you and Mrs. Grey were not available?"

"It's not likely, but it's possible."

"Are they in now?"

"I believe my cousin is somewhere, but my brother's not back from the office yet."

"Perhaps you will find Mr. Harbord for me?"

That young gentleman was studying nature behind the bushes at the bottom of the garden, where he had prudently sequestered himself when he saw Charlton, whom he knew by sight, jump out of his car. He was a good actor and, when questioned by the detective, played his part to perfection. If he had not, he might not have died so abruptly three months afterwards.

"Your aunt," Charlton explained to him, "paid two forged ten-shilling notes into her bank today. She has told me—and Miss Grey has said the same—that there is nothing to show how they came into her possession. Can you throw any light on it? I'm wondering if you served a customer who handed them to you."

Harbord had his story all ready. He had not told his confederates the true facts, but several days before, when he had needed money badly, he had taken two notes from the cash-box and substituted forgeries, fully intending to change them back before his aunt went to the Bank on the Friday. Until Mrs. Grey had repeated at lunch some small piece of news that Gough had told her, he had completely forgotten about it. While he had been keeping himself out of sight in the garden, he had hoped that Charlton would not ask more than a few routine questions of Mrs. Grey; but now he saw that, if the detective went away without a convincing explanation of the presence of the notes in Old Forge House, he would keep coming back to nose around—and the Lord only knew what he might then discover. So Harbord fell back on the tale he had prepared.

"I think I can help you there!" he said brightly. "Early last Monday morning, when Miss Grey was at Lulverton and my aunt had slipped out—between customers, as it were!—to do some shopping"—he was more than glad that this had actually been the case—"a man came in and asked for a large Player's. He gave me a ten-shilling note and I had just fetched him the change, when another fellow appeared and said that he might as well have twenty Gold Flake himself. He asked his friend to lend him a bob, but the friend said that he'd lent him bobs before. The second one called him a miserable devil—it was all joking, you know—and pulled out a ten-shilling note of his own, which I changed for him. It looks as if I was the onion! The notes took me in, all right! Have you them with you?"

Charlton produced them and Harbord examined them closely.

"I still can't see anything wrong with them," he admitted with convincing candour. "No wonder so many people get caught. What gives the show away? The watermark?"

"Amongst other things. Can you describe the two men?"

"They were cyclists. Both about twenty-five or six, I should say. Londoners, by their voices. Not gawblimey, you know, but they dropped everything but their aitches. Those colourless, nosey voices. You know what I mean? Sort of secondary school with a dash of evening classes."

Charlton smiled. He knew the type and the description rather pleased him.

"They were wearing reddy-brown plus-fours, black alpaca jackets, open-necked shirts and proper cycling-shoes. Neither wore a hat and one of them—the second to come in—had curly hair."

"Would you recognize them again?"

"I should think so."

"You didn't get any idea of where they were going or where they had come from? Whether they were on a cycling tour or just out for the day?"

"I heard one say, while I was getting the second lot of

change, that he didn't think much of the Southmouth beds: he was bruised all over."

"Did you notice which way they went when they left here?"

"That way. Towards Eastbourne."

The inspector thanked him and he went back into the garden, so immensely pleased with himself that he forgot to kick the cat as he passed it.

Charlton saw Judy before he left the house.

"Are you going to clap us all in gaol?" she asked.

"Not just yet," he smiled.

"Doesn't a first offender get a Royal Pardon or something?"

"I'm afraid not. He's discharged under a recognizance and is usually placed under the supervision of the Probation Officer."

"That sounds a bit of a nuisance."

"It is, I assure you."

Peter came in just then and Judy introduced him.

"The inspector wants to ask you some questions, Peter," she explained.

"No, I don't, thank you. Mr. Harbord told me all I wanted to know."

After he had driven away, Judy went out to Mrs. Grey.

"Mother," she said, "do you know what a recognizance is?"

"Isn't it a promise to be on your best behaviour, dear? The grocer's boy had to give one when we lived at New Malden. He stole a bicycle and the first thing he did when they let him go was to steal *another* bicycle."

"Which just shows," laughed her daughter, "the importance of a recognizance. And who is the Probation Officer?"

"Some police court official, I suppose."

"You don't think it's likely to be a part-time job of a C.I.D. Inspector, do you?"

"I should hardly think so. Why, dear?"

"I was wondering if it would be worth while to commit some trifling crime."

She wandered aimlessly about the garden, taking care to avoid Courtenay, then came back to her mother.

"Don't you think he's *too* marvellous?" she said.

"Who, dear? The cat next door?"

"No, silly. Inspector Charlton."

"I don't know, dear. I was too worried to notice."

"Well, he *is*."

When the object of this enthusiasm arrived home that night and sat down to the meal prepared by the servant before she left, he thought to himself how confoundedly cheerless the place was. Molly, who had looked after him for so long, had married John Rutherford the previous Saturday and he felt very lonely. The strange thing was, when he came to think about it, that the previous evening he had been quite contented with his bachelor solitude.

On the Saturday evening, Harbord told Vike and Smoothy about the Inspector's visit.

"I don't like lying," grunted Vike from the depths of his chair.

"Getting a bit pie in your old age, aren't you?" jeered Harbord.

"My dear young sir," said Smoothy mildly, "neither Vike nor I have any moral scruples about lying. In fact, we have no moral scruples at all. Vike, I believe, had one once, but it died of loneliness. Lies, however, are like blameless reputations: they're difficult to live up to."

Harbord looked suddenly anxious.

"Do you think he'll find out that it was all moonshine?"

"I shouldn't be a bit surprised," answered Smoothy serenely. "If you hadn't opened your mouth so wide, he'd have nothing to hang on you, but once let him discover that nobody else in Sheep saw those cyclists, or that they did not sleep the night before in Southmouth, and we shall *all* spend our summer holidays in Glorious Devon. That man Charlton's the nosiest dee in the force. He'll be Divisional-Superintendent before he's finished."

"Unless I get him first," growled Vike.

The three of them sat busy with their thoughts. Then Harbord got up.

"I'm just going to pop downstairs," he told them. "Shan't be long. I want to put a new blanket on the cylinder."

When he had gone to the cellar, Smoothy picked up the evening paper and turned to the book reviews. Presently, there came the sound of heavy banging, and he looked over the top of the paper at Vike.

"What's he up to?" he asked. "You don't put a blanket on with a hammer."

"Knocking his brains out, for all I care."

"I don't like the look of him," admitted Smoothy. "He's rattled and he might get all three of us in the—D'you think we'd better go down?"

Vike jumped to his feet and Smoothy followed. They went out to the top of the cellar stairs.

"What are you doing, Fly?" Vike called.

"Just finished," was the answer.

Harbord came up the stairs, swiched off the light and followed them back into the room.

"Vike," he said, as they sat down, "I don't want to go on with this business. It's getting too risky."

"Don't be a damn fool!" protested Vike. "You mustn't let yesterday's trouble panic you. When you've been in this game as long as Smoothy and I have, you'll have got used to things like that. Smoothy was trying to frighten you just now, weren't you, Smoothy?"

"Merely my fun," nodded Mr. Smithers.

"You're probably used to it, Vike, but I'm scared of being sent to gaol. It would kill me. I've always had a soft time."

"*You* won't go to gaol!" laughed Vike. "Nobody's going to find out about us for a long while yet and by then, we'll have packed up and——"

Smoothy gave him a secret signal and he stopped short.

"We don't want to stand in your way, Fly," said Smoothy, "if you want to clear out. Vike and I can rub along very well without you. You're as free as air, as far as we're concerned. It only means we'll go halves instead of thirds."

"I don't want the money, Smoothy. I can't put up with the worry of it any longer. I was far happier when I hadn't a bean. I suggest we pack the whole thing up."

"Not on your life!" scoffed Vike. "Smoothy and I have just got the trick of spreading that ink, and we're on a good thing."

"You've *got* to stop before it's too late. If the police find you out, I'm sure to be dragged into it."

"Don't you worry, Fly," smiled Smoothy. "You're safe enough and we can look after ourselves. We can work the press like master printers now."

"But you won't be able to do it any longer."

"And why not?"

"I've just smashed up the plates."

XXI.

ON THE WAY TO SHEEP

VIKE sprang to his feet and glared down at Harbord.
"You *bloody* little fool!"

"I told you he was up to something," reminded Smoothy,
calmly lighting his pipe.

"Why the hell did you do that?" shouted Vike.

"Keep your voice down," warned Smoothy and his furious
partner swung round to him.

"You know what he's done?"

"Oh, yes. I understand quite well. He's just told us. Smashed
up the plates." He drew at his pipe. "No need to fly off the
handle, Vike. Sit down, there's a good fellow. You look like Ajax
defying the lightning. Fly will make us some new plates."

Harbord sat warily, ready to defend himself.

"Oh, no, he won't. I told you I was through—and I meant
it."

"You'll make 'em," menaced Vike, "or—"

"Vike," protested Smoothy, "do *please* sit down. This is not an
occasion for amateur dramatics. Let's talk this thing quietly over
with Fly. At the moment, he's not quite himself and strongly
against replacing the plates; but I think we can persuade him."

Vike dropped into his seat.

"It's no good threatening me," said Harbord.

"*Persuade* was the word I used. I'm not the one to threaten,
Fly. We've had a disagreement, but it's not too late for us to
come to terms.... How much do you want?"

"All I want is to clear out while I'm still safe."

"A fiver? There! That's a handsome offer for a few hours'
work—and we shan't ask you to do more than that.... Ten, then?
Five before you go home tonight and the balance when you've
done the job.... Come on, Fly!... Well, we'll make it fifteen, shall

we, Vike?... Fifteen pounds. What about it, Fly?"

"*No!*" said Harbord defiantly.

Mr. Smithers pulled out his wallet. "I've ten pounds here..."

"And you know what you can do with it!"

The persuader looked pained and tried another tack.

"You know, Fly, I don't think you're playing quite fair with Vike and me. You're leaving us to hold the baby. We shall have all that plant left on our hands—and not a chance to make a penny with it. You're not doing the sporting thing, Fly."

"Oh, cut out the Dear Old Coll, stuff, for God's sake!"

"Frozen assets. That's what our plant amounts to now, Fly."

"That's why I broke up the plates. *And I'm not going to make any more!*"

He got up and went out into the hall for his hat. Vike muttered something and was going to follow him, but Smoothy urgently waved him back. Harbord did not return, but slammed the front door behind him. They heard him walk down the path and along the road.

"Why the devil didn't you stop him?" demanded Vike, as the footsteps died away.

"Because, my dear Mr. Preston, the young gentleman has got us by the short hairs,"

"I could have scared him into it, if you'd given me a chance."

"Scared? He's far more scared of going over the wall than he is of anything we can do. I only agree with force when everything else has failed. Let's give him a few days. He'll come back with his tail between his legs when he gets hard up; and then it'll be our turn. You wait."

But despite this confident prophecy, Harbord stayed away. Three weeks passed and Vike got steadily more restless. Smooth's serenity began to infuriate him and at last he boiled over.

"I'm not standing any more of this! I'm going to drag the little rat here by the scruff of his dirty neck, and stand over him with a gun till he finishes those plates!"

Smoothy enjoined patience.

"*Patience*?" snarled Vike. "What's the good of sitting here like a pair of broody hens, with the carriers howling for more stuff at any price we like to name? If you had your way, we'd be working the trams at Southmouth!"

"There's a good deal to be said for *that*," answered Smoothy, as he opened his *Times Literary Supplement*. "How else do you think I got this watch?"

After reading for fifteen minutes, he looked across at Vike, who was savagely biting his nails.

"Why couldn't *we* make the plates?" he asked slowly.

"Because we don't know how. Mr. Fidgety Harbord insisted on being by himself when he did the others. Or perhaps you don't remember that?" he added viciously.

"You never know what you can do till you try."

"And a rolling stone gathers no moss. *I* know."

Mr. Smithers looked at him steadily.

"I have practically reached the end of my patience with you," he said with a restraint that made Vike shiver in spite of himself. "I have done such a foolish thing only once before. You may, perhaps, recall the consequences to a gentleman whose name, I think, was Armitage or Armstrong or something equally ridiculous." He smiled brightly like a fussy schoolmistress. "And now you and I are going to do some copper plate engraving."

Mr. Preston thought it wise to forget his annoyance. He had seen Armstrong after Smoothy had finished with him.

Nothing came of Charlton's further work on the forgeries. The roads of England are full of such pairs of cyclists as Harbord had described to him and, although he carried his inquiries to considerable lengths, he eventually abandoned them. All banks and shopkeepers in the neighbourhood were warned to be on the look-out for other spurious notes, and as no more local cases were reported, the matter was pigeonholed. There were more important things than that to occupy the time of a busy dee.

In London, though, and Manchester, Birmingham, Liverpool, Cardiff, Blackpool, Sheffield, Bradford and Wolverhampton, the C.I.D. were teased by the flow of forgeries that dribbled slowly, but continuously, into their ken. One of the carriers, an unassuming little man called Taffy Owen, was caught at Bromley in Kent, but he was the only one. Vike and Smoothy went through a few uneasy days, but Taffy Owen was no squeaker and took what he was given without a word. Then, of course, supplies became exhausted and there was a general lull, while Messrs. Preston and Smithers strove to engrave new plates.

On Tuesday, August the 13th, Charlton had occasion to visit the police station in Paulsfield. He afterwards drove along to the Square and went into "Voslivres" for a few minutes' chat with George, in whose conversation he always found unfailing entertainment. George put aside his book and jumped to his feet with a delighted grin.

"Nietzsche?" asked Charlton, nodding towards the book.

"No, sir," answered George, "it's called *Potassium Cyanide* and it's by a man called Patrick Dumayne."

"Never 'eard of 'im!"

"I think it must be a pseudonym, sir, *and* a woman. Only a woman would choose a mushy name like Patrick Dumayne. It's been in the shop for months, but that's always put me off. It's the fourteenth house-party murder I've read this year. They're always the same. The corpse has a large country mansion and, the day before he becomes a corpse, makes a particular point of sending out cordial weekend invitations to all his deadly enemies, so that, when the police arrive, everybody in the house has an apparent motive except the dear, white-haired old housekeeper, who has been with him for forty-eight years and has nursed a secret hatred for twenty-four of them, because he broke his poor mother's heart with Wine, Women and Song.

In this one, sir, it's the little country doctor, and I will give the author credit: she *did* keep me guessing until page eleven.... I sometimes wish, sir, that some daring author would make it one of the deadly enemies, just for a change."

"There's no hope of that, George. The great British Public would think it had been cheated."

George sighed heavily. "I am beginning to despair, sir," he said, "for the future of the novel of detection" he stole a furtive glance at Charlton—"*qua* detection."

With difficulty, Charlton turned a howl of laughter into a cough.

"You ought to write one yourself, George," he suggested.

"I would, sir, if I could only think of a plot."

"What about building one round a house-party in a large country mansion?"

George's broad grin admitted the tilt.

For ten minutes, they chatted idly about one thing and another. Then Charlton went out to his car. As he drove down the High Street, he saw Judy Grey walking along the pavement towards him. When she caught sight of him and smiled, he nearly caused a major traffic crisis by swerving into the curb and stopping dead. The driver of a lorry behind wildly swung the wheel to avoid him.

"Balmy?" he enquired at the top of his voice as he jerked by.

But Charlton had no time to spare for badinage. Judy stepped up to the open near-side window.

"This *is* a surprise," she said. "I didn't expect to see *you* in Paulsfield this afternoon, unless"—her voice became apprehensive—"you were following me, to see if I would lead you to the chief of the gang—the Big Shot."

"I can prove I wasn't doing that, Miss Grey," he grinned, "because we were going in opposite directions."

She waved the argument aside. "That's just a trick of your profession. Well, you won't find the Big Shot by trailing me, for I'm going straight home."

"Can I give you a lift? I'm going that way."

"That would be nice," said Judy, and he reached across to open the door for her.

As the Vauxhall gathered speed, she explained:

"I've just been paying a duty call on an aged friend of mother's and I was *not* looking forward to a horrible ride back in the bus. This is much nicer."

He took the new arterial road and it was not many minutes before they reached Burgeston village.

"Burgeston already?" said Judy.

"Yes. We shall soon be at Sheep."

"We're going the quickest way, aren't we?"

"Yes," he answered without enthusiasm.

"It's a glorious afternoon."

"Wonderful."

They left Burgeston behind, climbed Cowhanger Hill between High Down and its western neighbour, Dog Down, and saw compact, unlovely Lulverton lying below them. Conversation drooped badly until they reached the drab outskirts of the town. Then said Judy: "I shall be back early. The bus takes hours."

"A car is certainly more convenient. This one saves me a lot of time."

A traffic-light changed from green to amber.

"I expect you're always very busy?" asked Judy, as he slowed down.

The lights went to red. He stopped the car and turned his head to smile down at her.

"This is not the only way to Sheep," he said.

"I suppose it isn't," she agreed. "There must be other ways."

"Shall we try one of them?"

"Perhaps it would be... a better road."

"It's high time they made this one up."

The lights went back to green.

"Does it matter if it takes us a minute or two longer?"

"Not a bit. Mother's not expecting me just yet....
Anyway, it was *her* friend I went to see."

Amber.

"I know a very pleasant little run back to Sheep. ...It's much nicer than these main roads, although it's a slightly longer way round."

Red.

"Then let's go that way."

They turned their attention to the road in front of them.

"The lights are still against us," he complained. "They must have slowed them down. I've never been held up so long here before."

When the most unfairly criticized lights changed back to green, he turned the car to the right. Soon the tarred surface gave place to a macadam that was far rougher than the London road, but neither of them noticed a little thing like that.

At four o'clock they were still on their way to Sheep, which was, by that time, twenty-five miles to the south-east. Charlton scorned the main roads and kept to the lanes. The car zig-zagged across the country like a demented snipe. They glided through tiny villages and avoided anything that looked like a town.

"Where," said Judy at last, "are we?"

"On the way to Sheep," he answered guiltily.

"But where *are* we?"

"I warned you that it wasn't so quick as the other road."

"You haven't answered my question."

"Somewhere in Hampshire."

"Can't you be more precise than that? You might just as well say, 'Somewhere in the Arabian Desert.'"

"For all I know," he said, "we may be."

"Well, drive on to Stamboul."

"That's not in Arabia."

"Neither are we," she answered with incontestable logic.

They turned into an even smaller lane.

"We are approaching," he told her, "Westham St. Martin."

"That explains everything. I've never heard of the place."

"I haven't either, but I'm sure we shall like it."

They liked it so much that they stopped there for tea. There were only a dozen cottages, a tiny church and a shop in whose sunny window a tabby cat slept carelessly among the stationery, packets of Wheat Flakes and limp lengths of strip licorice. Hanging in a cottage window was a faded card advertising "TEAS." They went up the path and Charlton tapped on the door.

"No," said the woman who opened it, holding back four agape children, "we don't do teas any more, since the Castle was closed up and folks didn't come to see the flowers. A thousand pities it was, but there. Mrs. Arkwright does teas. Why don't you try 'er, now?"

"Which house is it?" he asked.

"Across the road there," she pointed, "three doors from the shop."

"Thanks very much. We're sorry to have bothered you, but we saw the notice in your window."

"'*Tis* a bit misleading," she agreed, as she thrust back her brood and closed the door.

Mrs. Arkwright was apple-cheeked, white-haired and bent-shoulders. There was no refreshments notice in her window.

"Mrs. Miles," she explained, "always sends those wanting teas over to me. Very good, she is, like that. Did you want tea in here or prefer it in the garden?"

The tear-off calendar on the wall, with no sense of shame, brazenly announced that it was Sunday, the 15th December, 1935, but made amends with the quotation, "True Glory lies in Noble Deeds." The room was small and stuffy, smelling as if a rodent or two had died inaccessibly under the floorboards. The small windows were tightly closed. The glass in them was plastered with fragments of defunct wasps, while the sill was a shambles of yellow corpses, some of them still wearing expressions of faint surprise. The oil-lamp hanging from the ceiling was a rallying point for a hundred flies.

Charlton looked at Judy and raised questioning eyebrows.

"Let's have it outside," she decided.

Mrs. Arkwright led them through into a little garden so stocked with flowers, vegetables and bullace trees, that there seemed no room for the rose-covered arbour of roughly put together trellis, in which there stood a crippled, warped-topped table. When the much mended, but snow-white cloth had hidden the table's infirmities, and their hostess had brought out a gigantic tea-pot and all the other trappings, they both discovered that they were hungry.

Two fat Rhode Island Reds, which seemed to have the run of the house and garden, came over to cock a speculative eye at the visitors and proved themselves deft snappers-up of unconsidered trifles. When the four of them had finished the scones and Mrs. Arkwright's sultana cake, and Judy had prevailed upon the pot to yield a fourth cup of tea for him, Charlton leant back in his chair, watching the smoke from his cigarette drift upwards. Except for the tentative clucking of the hens, as they experimented with their gutturals, and the humming of the bees that were going about their business, there were no sounds to break the stillness of the hot, sleepy afternoon. He heaved a contented sigh and Judy smiled complete agreement with his mood.

Everything, in short, was peaches.

Judy did not get back to Old Forge House until after seven.

"Why, dear!" was Mrs. Grey's greeting. "I was beginning to wonder what had happened to you."

The girl stopped at the foot of the stairs.

"I've been out to tea with a policeman," she said. It was Mrs. Grey's boast that she was not too old to appreciate her children's jokes.

"How absurd!" she laughed gaily.

"To the contrary," said her daughter, and went up to her room.

XXII.

BASE NOTES IN A MINOR KEY

"**D**AMN," said Vike, "and blast it!"

It was not an isolated ejaculation, but was frequently repeated in various forms, some of them to be found only in the most comprehensive of slang dictionaries. They had not made much headway with their engraving: in fact, they had made none at all, for Smoothy had decided that, before they tackled the copper plates, they must make the zincos for the watermarks. In spite of his partner's fretfulness, he plodded patiently on with his line blocks, depending, for his results, on the ability of nitric acid to chew its way into zinc, yet trying to limit its action to the parts that he wanted removed and to curb its savage eagerness to disintegrate the entire plate. It was his unhappy experience that, however carefully he applied the shellac to the portions of the plate intended to be kept intact, the slightest slip in banking up the shoulders with acid-proof resin—known to the trade as "dragon's blood" and to Vike by even more picturesque names—allowed the acid to get beneath them and eat them away like waves at the foot of a cliff.

Finally, after spoiling many square feet of zinc sheet, Smoothy gave it up.

"We've done our best, Vike," he said, pouring himself out a drink. "No man can do more. Now we've got to admit defeat and take it with a smile."

Vike did not entirely agree. He was quite prepared to acknowledge that he was beaten, but he was in no mood for smiling.

"We ought never to have tried. Even if we *had* been able to make the blocks for the watermarks, we should have fallen down on the engraving. That's a job for an artist, not for a couple of clumsy blunderers like us.... As I said from the start"—he thumped the table, so that both their glasses bounced—"the only thing to do is to get that little squirt along here and hold him at the point of a gun till he's done what we want."

Smoothy shook his head. "It wouldn't work. We'd never keep him quiet afterwards. He'd walk straight from here to the nearest police station.... If only we had some hold over him, we could put the screw on."

"Could we *fix* it?"

They sipped their drinks for a while. Then Smoothy put down his glass.

"Those two notes," he reflected, "and his yarn to Charlton about the cyclists."

"How can we use that?"

"Shall we ask him over, and see?"

Harbord, who had his own plans, accepted without demur their invitation to chat things over. He went to Etchworth on the evening of Monday, the 19th August.

"Fly," said Smoothy in a voice charged with an emotion not entirely false, "we're in a devil of a hole and you're the only one to get us out of it. For weeks, Vike and I have been trying to replace the plates you destroyed, but we have completely failed. Now we throw ourselves on your mercy."

"You can throw yourselves wherever you like, for all I care," replied Harbord. "Don't let us go over all that again. I came here this evening because Vike said on the 'phone that you had something important to tell me. What is it?"

"Last time we saw you, just after you had wantonly"—his voice shook again—"broken up property that was not yours to break, I offered you fifteen pounds to reinstate it. You refused. My partner and I are now prepared to increase that offer. Does twenty-five pounds interest you?"

It most certainly did. At that time, the acquisition of some ready money was Harbord's one ambition. Now that his income from the forgeries had dried up, he was finding life a trifle difficult, which was why he had agreed to see his old confederates. He did not answer Smoothy's question.

"Twenty-five pounds," repeated that placid man, "and a third of the subsequent takings."

"A pony isn't very generous for all that work."

Smoothy sensed a weakening of Harbord's resolve.

"We'll spring another fiver," was his instant offer.

"*Fifty* is not too much for such skilled labour."

"Fifty, then—and that's our last word."

"And a third of the profits?"

"Give it to him," growled Vike.

"That's a bargain, then," bustled Mr. Smithers. "Fifty down, standing in for thirty-three and a third. Splendid! This is quite like old times, I do declare! We'll seal it with a drink."

He was on his way to the sideboard when Harbord stopped him.

"Not so fast, Smoothy," he said coolly. "I don't accept."

Vike wriggled forward to the edge of his chair, while Smoothy turned from the sideboard. They both stared at Harbord in amazement. Smoothy was the first to recover.

"I recommend you to accept, Fly," he said quietly, "as we shall not increase it by another penny. In any case, fifty pounds is far more than we can really afford."

"My dear Smoothy," sneered Harbord, "don't forget it was you who brought up the subject. As a matter of fact, I wanted to find out just how far you two would go."

Mr. Smithers went back to his chair and carefully filled his pipe.

"You will remember," he said, throwing the match in the fireplace, "that towards the end of last June, you told Inspector Charlton a story that was not strictly true—a story that was, if you'll forgive my bluntness, a pack of lies. I think you will agree with me?... Has it since occurred to you that, if Charlton discovers your regrettable lapse, you'll find yourself in a position of some embarrassment? I'm not threatening you,

Fly—don't think that—but if you do this little thing for us, you won't be making it any worse for yourself. The penalty's no less for one offence than two."

"Specious, is the word for that, Smoothy. It was far too long ago for Charlton to prove anything against me now, but if I start mucking about down in that cellar and he catches me at it, it'll be another story. I've thought it all out and come to the conclusion that, whatever happens, I'm a white-headed boy of almost nauseating purity."

"You made the first lot of plates, didn't you?" demanded Vike furiously.

Harbord turned to him with an innocently enquiring expression on his face.

"Which plates?"

"The ones you broke up, of course."

"Broke up? I don't understand you, Vike. The only plates I know anything about are those you are now trying to persuade me to engrave for you. You must be confusing me with someb——"

"You lying little b——" burst out Vike, but Smoothy stopped him.

"Swearing won't get us anywhere," he said with a reproachful shake of his head.

"In no circumstances whatsoever," Harbord went on as if there had been no interruption, "will I break the law in the way you suggest, but I've another proposition to put before you."

He smiled at each of them in turn, enjoying himself mightily. They waited for him to go on.

"In the cellar below where we are sitting in friendly conclave, there is an accumulation of apparatus and materials that cost a great deal of time, work and money to get down there. It would take as much time and work, and nearly as much money, to get them out again."

"That's what I've been telling you," protested Smoothy.

"Even to the most ignorant person going down into that

cellar, it would be immediately clear what was, or had been, going on.... You were ready to pay me fifty pounds for a new set of plates.... I wonder if you'd pay as much to keep the police away from that cellar?"

"*The black!*"

Vike's hand went swiftly to his pocket and came out with a .45 Colt in it.

"Put that thing away." Smoothy's tone was mildly petulant.

"That's all right," Harbord reassured him. "I don't mind a bit, if it amuses him. I know he wouldn't dare to use it, even if he knew how. The presence of my poor remains in this house would be more difficult to justify than the shadow factory in the basement, even for *your* slick tongue, Smoothy."

The owner of that tongue never despaired of settling difficulties by unhurried discussion. He always sought a formula.

"Getting hard up?" he asked solicitously. "Why not let me lend you a pound or two? We don't bear malice, Fly. Live and let live, is the way I look at it. How much do you want till the ship comes home?"

Five notes were taken from one wallet and, after a careful and studiously offensive scrutiny, put away in the other. Smoothy courteously saw their guest to the gate.

"What did you want to do that for?" demanded Vike when he came back; and, from the answering smile, one would have thought that Mr. Smithers had not a care in the world.

"As I believe I have suggested before," he said, "our young friend has got us where he wants us."

"Why? There's nothing to stop us having a hand-press in the house, is there? We've got rid of all those plates you messed up and we could get the rest of the stuff away in an hour. Harbord must sleep sometimes."

"You're missing the point, Vike. I'm not apprehensive about the press. The police might have plenty of suspicions, but they'd have no proof. Have you forgotten that disastrous expedition to Guildford last May and our rather harsh treatment of the owner of a house called 'The Den'?"

"He got over it."

"But only just. It might have been better for us if he hadn't, because he was able to give the police a painfully accurate description of you and me. If Harbord invites the dees to our little retreat, they won't find what they expect, but they'll be more than glad to get in touch again with two such old friends as ourselves."

"I see what you mean," admitted Vike, "but I don't fancy having that little growth living on us. Why don't we clear out?"

A sentimental smile spread slowly over Smoothy's face.

"Ever since I was a ragged little guttersnipe in Hoxton," he explained, "I've yearned for a comfortable home. Most of my life has been spent in doss-houses and gaols; and now that I am enjoying something that I have never had before, I am loth to relinquish it, particularly when the alternative is the nomad life of a hunted criminal."

"You talk more like a book every day," was his partner's cynical comment.

"I love words for their own sake, Vike. I delight to hear them—I might almost say *taste* them—flowing out of my mouth like a ceaseless string of jewels: sometimes with the gentle beauty of pearls and at other times with the hard, glorious brilliance of diamonds. Actions speak louder than words—and noise is always to be avoided."

"Words won't get us out of this mess."

"Alas, no."

"Then why let Harbord get away with it?"

"You, Vike, who know the secret places of my heart, will appreciate the pang with which I parted just now with five hard-won pounds: but it was the only way to gain us time to arrange his journey to another and, I sincerely hope, a better world."

Mr. Smithers had found his formula.

It has been said that Smoothy Smithers had a genius

for organization, so it was natural that his plot to dispose of Harbord was worked out in elaborate detail. The long arguments he had with the forthright Vike, who wanted to butcher Harbord out of hand and then make a bolt for it, need not be recorded here. It is enough to say that Smoothy finally persuaded his partner that finesse was preferable to brute force.

This is how they went about it:

Harbord was first made to believe that they were quite prepared to accept his domination over them. On the 26th August, a week after his first successful attempt at blackmail, he came again, and Smoothy sent him away with a further generous "loan" and a fatherly warning not to come too often, as they were not millionaires. For all that, seven days later Harbord once more exacted tribute. On Thursday the 26th September, when he caught the bus to Etchworth on the same gay errand, the conspirators greeted him with anxious faces— or, at least, Smoothy did. Vike had been carefully rehearsed in a devil-may-care *rôle,* ready to side with Harbord and to jeer at Smoothy's timorousness.

"Why the gloom, Smoothy?" asked Harbord.

"Indigestion or just an uneasy conscience?"

"Come in here and close the door. . . . We've bad news for you, Fly. Charlton's on to you."

The sneering smile went from Harbord's face, but he kept his voice level.

"If he gets me," he drawled, "he gets you two as well."

"We know that, Fly. That's why we must sit down and talk it over quietly. . . . Cigarette? . . . We warned you, you know, that your story to Charlton might prove disastrous—and it has."

Harbord lifted his foot and studied the toe of his shoe. "I don't believe it."

"On my Bible oath," vowed Smoothy, "what I'm going to tell you is the truth. This is how it happened. You told Charlton that the cyclists had put up the night before in Southmouth.

That little addition to the story is going to get us all into trouble. Never let a lie depend for its plausibility on minor falsehoods, Fly; but let it stand magnificently by itself."

"Speech!" acclaimed Harbord, clapping his hands.

He was putting a brave face on it, but he was badly frightened.

Smoothy was unperturbed. "Charlton," he went on, "has been to every hotel and boarding-house in Southmouth. Don't ask me how I know, but thank a bounteous providence that I found out in time. He's been through all the visitors books and checked all those who slept there that night. None of them tallied with the descriptions you gave him."

"Entirely negative," said Harbord airily.

"I am told that our notes have attracted so much notice all over the country that Scotland Yard are arranging a special drive against us. Nothing would please them more than to find a scapegoat."

"I defy them to prove anything."

"Counsel for the prosecution won't find it very difficult, especially with Vike and me standing alongside you in the dock."

Vike stirred. "I think you're talking a lot of wet, Smoothy. Harbord's done nothing to make *me* like him. He's a tricky little twicer, but I've got to look after myself and I agree with him this time."

"Thank you for your heartening support, Vike," taunted Harbord. "The police haven't got a leg to stand on. Suppose those cyclists had really existed. Do you think they'd have let me know where they'd just come from?"

"There you are, Smoothy," Vike played his part.

"You hadn't thought of that, had you?"

There was no play-acting in Smoothy's perplexity. After a moment, he rallied.

"That won't help you. It would be a big thing for Charlton if he could catch us, and *he* would see to it that the evidence was cooked up against us. The dishonesty of the C.I.D. is a public scandal. He only needed half a chance. Now he's got it."

He played his trump-card.

"If only you had some idea of prison existence. Fly! The harsh discipline, the terrible conditions, the vile food . . . the *rats.*"

At this highly imaginative word-picture, Harbord surrendered unconditionally.

"I'll do anything you suggest," he said.

"We've only one course," answered Smoothy briskly. "We must turn Charlton's attention away from you. At the moment, he's not quite sure of his ground. We've got to switch him on to someone else. . . . But who?"

"I don't have to think," said Harbord maliciously. "My precious cousin, Mr. Peter Grey. I'd give a lot to see him sweating on the top line."

"Is that playing the game?"

"Playing the *what?* Who do you think we are—the Fifth Form at St. Dominic's? I've been waiting for a chance like this for years. . . . But I don't see how we can do it."

"Let us," suggested Smoothy, "examine the possibilities."

He talked for ten minutes and Vike was as ready with questions as Harbord.

"But how do I know," said Harbord eventually, "that this isn't a plot against me?"

"My dear Fly, how can it be? One word from you to the dees and Vike and I would be immediately apprehended."

"And if I know Fly," grunted Vike, "he won't think twice about saying it."

"You *bet* I won't!"

"If you play your part well, Fly," said Smoothy, "the scheme should work perfectly. I'll quietly give the police the tip and, when he comes away from the Tower with the dud notes in his pocket, he'll be arrested. You do exactly as I've said and leave the rest to us." Vike said, "It's damned dangerous."

Harbord still looked dubious. "I still think it won't help me at all. He'll tell the police the whole story and then they'll come back on me."

"And you will flatly deny every word of it. When you've shown him the letters, burn them. Believe me, Fly, when Charlton's caught Grey, the only man he'll be thinking about will be the bearded stranger. Impress yourself on the mind of the attendant and he's sure to tell the police about you afterwards. And don't forget, you must be out of the Tower again by ten-past four, or you'll have Grey seeing you."

"The bearded man," said Vike slowly, "will never be seen again. "I've got the idea now, Smoothy! It's damn clever. I'll say that for you."

"Who'll pass the notes to Peter on the balcony?" asked Harbord suspiciously.

"That will be Vike's job."

"Oh, no, it won't! You don't catch me walking round with a packet of snide in my pocket! It's your party, Smoothy, so *you* can do it!"

Mr. Smithers looked at his colleague with so much pained surprise that one would never have guessed that he himself had taught Vike the speech.

"Vike," he gently chided, "we can't expect Fly to take all the risk. Isn't it worth making an effort to keep out of gaol?"

"All right. I'll do it—and be damned to you!"

"I ... don't ... like ... it," said Harbord deliberately.

"Then perhaps you have an alternative suggestion that will not involve your cousin?"

Harbord was silent for a full minute.

"I'm on," he said at length. "I don't like the idea, but I like Peter Pie-face less."

"He'll wish," cackled Smoothy, "that he'd stayed at home and hanged himself with his mother's clothes-line. But perhaps she hasn't got one?"

It was a clumsy trick but it worked.

"It's in the summer-house," Harbord grinned with malice. "Nice and convenient for him *or* my charming *cousine*. . . . You'll have to give me some genuine money to pass on to Peter."

Smoothy got out his wallet and handed him five pound notes.

So was Courtenay Harbord's death arranged.

XXIII.

THE FORMULA

COURTENAY HARBORD never walked if he could ride, so he caught the 3.5 bus from Sheep and was put down below Waltham Hanger. In the pockets of the raincoat on his arm were the beard, the spirit gum and the rolled-up brown felt hat that he had bought in Southmouth on the Friday. He also had with him the cheap pipe and the packet of tobacco that he had got from an obscure little shop near Lulverton gasworks.

He skirted the Hanger until his entry into it would not be noticed from the road below, and made for the fallen tree described to him by Smoothy. It was difficult, without a mirror, to brush his face with gum and apply the beard, but he managed it. The moustache, he attached separately to his lip. Then he left the Hanger and went across the Downs towards the Tower.

For a clear understanding of the complicated events of that Sunday afternoon, it must be realized that the bearded man seen first by Tom Lee and afterwards by the Clafts, was Harbord himself. He was the man that Martin was afterwards to nickname "Whiskers" and he was the only bearded visitor to the Tower on that glorious autumn day. After the Clafts had gone on down the staircase, he ripped off the beard, leaving the moustache on his lip, and changed his green hat for the new brown one. He swiftly filled his pipe and lighted it, then continued up to the balcony, where it was his intention to make himself as inconspicuous as possible, until the descent of some fairly large party would enable him to leave the Tower with them, so that Lee might think—if he considered the matter at all—that he was one of their company and not the pleasant whiskered stranger, who had paused earlier to chat in a voice that was unwontedly slow and deep.

But time went by on the balcony and none of his fourteen companions seemed anxious to leave. He began to get restless for in a few minutes Peter was due to arrive and it would never do to be seen by him. The disguise was good enough for strangers, but Peter knew him too well to be deceived by a false moustache. But at 4.7 two separate parties made a united move. They were Mr. Theodore Halfpenny, of the Panama hat and the sad moustache, with his wife and grown-up son; and Frank Davison, Roy Davison and Mr. and Mrs. Brian Stevens.

Harbord insinuated himself between the two parties and went down the staircase behind Roy Davison and in front of Jack Halfpenny. A short way down they met Kathleen Harding and Jean Turner. One after the other, the eight of them went through the exit turnstile and drifted down the lane towards the village. It was a near thing for Harbord, for he had not left the Tower very far behind before Peter Grey reached it from the other side of High Down. A big car came up from the village and the Davisons and Stevenses, who were in front of him dropped into single file to let it pass. It was driven by Robson and in the back of it were Mrs. d'Eyncourt and Miss Mortimer.

In Etchworth High Street, Harbord cleverly broke away from the rest of them, dodged between the Memorial Hall and "Pro Bono Publico," and slipped across deserted High Down to Waltham Hanger. He found the tree-trunk again, pulled off the false moustache and, following the directions he had received, sat down to wait for Vike and Smoothy.

At 6.30 Vike came alone.

"Well," asked Harbord as Vike sat down beside him, "how did it go?"

"I passed the notes to Grey on the balcony, Charlton caught him and took him away." Vike's voice was dull and lifeless.

"That's great!" gloated the traitor.

"Not so fast. Charlton's got a warrant for *your* arrest, and he's looking for you."

"*What!*"

"For aiding and abetting. Smoothy and I'll be next, by the look of it."

"I don't care a damn about you! What am *I* going to do? Come on, man! Don't sit there like a dummy; What am I going to *do?*"

His voice rose almost to a shout and Vike looked apprehensively round. It was vital that they should not be seen or heard.

"Pipe down!" he snapped. "There's no need to go into hysterics. . . . Smoothy and I are clearing out tonight."

"You can't do that! You've got to stop and get me out of this!"

Vike pursed his lips. "I don't see what we can do. Charlton's got a man waiting for you at Sheep. As soon as you show your nose there, you'll be pinched."

"Where are you and Smoothy going?"

"That's no damn business of yours! I risked a lot coming here to warn you. Isn't that enough?"

"I'm coming with you. . . . I'd rather do anything than go to gaol. . . . If you try to stop me, I'll—"

"Cut it out, for Pete's sake! I've heard all that before."

"What time are you going?"

The answer was given as if unwillingly. "Ten o'clock. 'Screw' Capp, an old friend of ours, is picking us up in the car. Smoothy fixed it up on the 'phone.

I don't know how he'll take it about you coming with us. It's going to make it risky for us, now there's a warrant out for you."

"It'll be worse for you, if you go without me."

Vike rose from the log. "You wait, then, till I come back. I shall be some time, but I recommend you not to leave here."

"Don't you try double-crossing me! And before you go, give me some gaspers. I've run through nearly all mine."

"Haven't one on me. I'll bring some back with me. Craven 'A', aren't they?"

After Vike had left him, Harbord wandered about in deep and troubled thought. He waited for an hour, then, fretted by his anxieties, reached the conclusion that his old associates had tricked him and were, by that time, many miles away. . . . He had decided to go back to Old Forge House and give himself up to the detective he imagined to be waiting there, when he remembered what Smoothy had said about prison life. That recollection kept him lurking in Waltham Hanger until he heard a low whistle in the darkness and Smoothy and Vike approached him through the trees.

"My cigarettes?" was his first abrupt question.

They were handed to him by Vike, who was wearing gloves, and he opened the packet with eager fingers.

"Vike has told me," said Smoothy, flicking his petrol-lighter with his thumb and holding it to Harbord's cigarette, "that you want to come with us. Is that so?"

Harbord drew in a luxurious mouthful of smoke and nodded.

"We are setting up our hand press elsewhere," Smoothy went on. "You come with us on the distinct understanding that you engrave some new plates for us?"

"If you get me out of this, I'll do anything."

"Then you'll have to come as you are. There's no chance of taking anything with you. We've put our stuff in the car and it's waiting for us now by the Tall Man in Leaves Lane. It will be as well if we avoid conversation until we reach it. . . . Has either of you a watch?"

"No," said Vike.

"Yes," said Harbord.

"Please lend it to me until we get to the car." He held out his hand.

"Why?"

"So that I may keep my eye on the time without asking you.

I forgot to bring my own, which is a great pity. It was presented to me by a Choral Society to which I once belonged."

Vike controlled an ironic chuckle.

Harbord unclipped the watch from his wrist and passed it to Smoothy, who slipped it into his pocket with a gloved hand.

They left Waltham Hanger and climbed silently over the summit of High Down. The moon was in its last quarter, but they had no difficulty in picking their way. With Smoothy and Harbord abreast and Vike a step behind, they went down the hillside towards the Tall Man.

"We'll skirt the chalk-pit," murmured Smoothy, "and get down to the car that way. . . . Mind how you go, Fly. It's a bit dangerous just here. . . . Somebody's used most of the fence for firewood. . . . Come back a bit. You're too near the edge."

He took hold of Harbord's sleeve, as if to draw him away—and it all happened in a flash. Vike darted forward, got his arms round Harbord's neck and pulled him backwards. Smoothly bent down and caught his ankles. Vike released his throat to take an iron grip on his wrists: and with one great, united swing, they sent him flying over the brink.

He screamed rather shrilly as he went.

When they got down to him, he was dead. They were wiry men, but it took all their strength to carry him up the four hundred yards to the Tower. They marked his hands with rust from the front railings, then took him round to the other side and laid him down. Smoothy felt in the raincoat pockets and produced the beard, moustache and the bottle of spirit gum.

"How d'you put this stuff on?" he asked in a low tone.

"Isn't there a brush? It ought to be somewhere in his pockets."

Smoothy made a further search and found it. They got the beard and moustache fixed. It was not a pleasant task, but it caused neither of them the slightest tremor. The time was then just after ten o'clock. Smoothy, who still wore gloves, took the wrist-watch from his pocket, pulled out the winding shaft and turned the hands until they indicated 8.30, at which time that evening, he had taken care to chat with a neighbour over the fence, while Vike drank beer in the Tower Arms.

"We ought to smash it up a bit," muttered Vike. "His left arm was under him when we picked him up. Bang it on the ground just there."

It must have been a sub-conscious disinclination to damage property worth several pounds that prompted Smoothy to use so little violence that the glass was jarred from its bezel without stopping the watch.

"We needn't have worried about the glass splintering in the chalk-pit," he said. "This one's unbreakable." Again he was too gentle, perhaps, because he was hampered by the gloves. He took a pair of tweezers from his waistcoat pocket, gripped the end of the hand and twisted the instrument, so that the hand did not snap off at the pinion, but half-way along its length. He placed the fragment on the grass and put the glass near it.

"Did you stop it?" Vike whispered.

Smoothy examined it and then held it to his ear.

"It's not going now."

When he had reclipped the watch on the dead man's wrist, he ran through the pockets.

"Here's the tobacco," he muttered, "but there's no pipe."

"It must have slipped out of his pocket while we were carrying him here; but it won't make much odds if they do find it, only more evidence against Grey. Keep the tobacco, though."

"We'll leave the gum on him and drop the brush near the tree-trunk. . . . What about these Craven 'A'?"

"He can have those with me," replied Vike with an evil chuckle, and Smoothy replaced the packet.

They laid the body as they had found it on the bed of the chalk-pit, with his broken arm under him; and then, after a last look round, went across the empty Downs to Sheep.

Vike climbed over the wall at the bottom of the garden of Old Forge House and cut off the length of clothes-line in the summer-house. They took it back with them into the dark Hanger, where, when the torch they had brought had picked out a suitable spot, Smoothy bound Vike's wrists and ankles, then cut the ropes. They disturbed the leaves and left the knotted ropes and the spirit gum brush where Charlton later discovered them. The brown felt hat was taken away to be destroyed.

Before they parted for the night, Smoothy placidly recited: "Each morning sees some task begin, each evening sees its close; something attempted, something done, has earned, my dear Mr. Preston, a night's repose."

And his lips curved in a gentle smile.

BOOK THREE

106

The
GOLDEN EGGS

XXIV.

AFTER THE VERDICT

WHEN he had charged Peter Grey at Lulverton police station, Charlton went to his room and summoned Martin. His manner was confident and he showed no signs of his recent ordeal.

"Sergeant," he said briskly, "we have a great deal to do in a very short time. We'll start now."

Martin had been about to go to lunch, but he did not mention it. He was a wise man and knew exactly how far he could go.

"Grey has been found guilty by a fat-headed jury and I've just arrested him on Trench's warrant. I'm certain, Martin, that he didn't do it, and, as it's equally certain that Harbord *was* murdered, we must find the real offender as quickly as possible."

"Too right," said the Sergeant.

"We have not one scrap of evidence in Grey's favour. The worst thing against him is that the number of *known* visitors to the Tower last Sunday exactly equals the turnstile total for the day. Our first step is to find a weakness in that piece of elementary arithmetic. Our second step is to discover how Whiskers left the Tower. Messrs. Collinson and Dean of the B.B.C. justly argue that what goes up must come down. . . . I'll have another go at Lee and see if I can get something out of him. If *you* wanted to slip out of the Tower without being noticed, how would you set about it?"

"Well," said Martin, scratching his head, "they say there's safety in numbers. . . ."

"Precisely. Whiskers probably didn't know that Lee's powers of observation are negligible, so he wouldn't have dared to pass the office by himself. Where's my timetable?"

They found the sheet and Charlton pored over it. "On three occasions between four o'clock and closing time," he said, "parties of four or more left the balcony together. Whiskers very likely joined one of those. His only reason for going to the Tower at all was, on the face of it, to ensure that Lee would afterwards identify him with Harbord; so the less time he spent on the balcony, the better. The first lot of visitors to leave, after Whiskers had passed the Clafts on the staircase, was composed of two separate parties: Mr. and Mrs. Theodore Halfpenny and their son, Jack; and Frank and Roy Davison, with Mr. and Mrs. Brian Stevens."

'I questioned them, sir, and they never saw nobody 'oo might 'ave been either Whiskers With or Whiskers Without."

"We must see them again. Has T. Halfpenny a straggling moustache?"

"That's 'im. A great philat . . . philat. . . . Collects stamps. Couldn't keep 'im off showing me what 'e called 'is 'Brazilian Bull's-Eyes.' I tried to share 'is enthoosiasm, but give me pigeon-fancying or filling glasses of water up with pins. Stamps are all right for sticking on letters, but that's as far as they go, to my way of thinking."

"'A primrose by a river's brim,'" said Charlton regretfully, "'a yellow primrose was to him, and it was nothing more.'"

"Mrs. H. is a motherly old soul and, according to 'is dad, the son's serving articles. In the grocery line, by the sound of it."

The Inspector did not disillusion him.

"Frank and Roy Davison are twins and both nice boys, if you can keep them sorted out. Mrs. Stevens is their sister and Brian Stevens is *her* husband. 'Im and 'is wife are staying for a week or two with Pa and Ma Davison and the twins."

"While all those were on their way down," said Charlton, "two girls named Kathleen Harding and Jean Turner were coming up. *Their* statements aren't very helpful, but we'll have another go at them. *Somebody* besides the Clafts must have seen Whiskers inside the Tower."

Martin grunted. He was convinced of Peter's guilt, but was not saying so then.

"There's another thing, Martin. Have we had any news yet about those notes I took from Grey?"

"Not a word."

"You might stir them up. And while I'm away interviewing T. Halfpenny and the rest, try to work out some way by which 106 does *not* equal 105 plus 1."

"I'll do me best," promised the Sergeant.

The Davisons and their guests from Woodford Green had just finished lunch when the Inspector called at their house in Southmouth. Frank and Roy Davison, who were twenty-five, were both home from their offices for the meal, so Charlton was able to question his four witnesses at the same time.

"I am sorry to bother you again," he smiled, "but I wonder if you can enlarge upon the information you have already given my sergeant. You left the Tower at the same time as another party, which was made up of an elderly gentleman and his wife and grown-up son. That, I think, was so?"

"I remember the old boy," said Brian Stevens, who was one of those tall young men who go bald in the early thirties and look ten years younger in their hats.

"He was wearing a Panama hat and jacket made of grey. . . . What's the name of that stuff, dear?"

"Alpaca," his pretty little wife replied.

"That's it: but I can't remember who else was with him."

The others shook their heads. Mrs. Stevens was fairly certain about Mrs. Halfpenny, whose hat, she said, had been covered with imitation flowers; and although it was generally agreed that the old couple had not been alone, none was prepared to say whether the Halfpenny party had numbered three or four—or even more.

"Were you the first to leave, or did you go down behind

the Halfpennys? That," he added when they smiled, "is their name."

"*We* went down first," volunteered one of the twins, but, as only their family could tell which was which, Charlton could not be expected to know that it was Frank.

"In what order?"

"I was in front," said Stevens, "with my wife immediately behind me. That's right, isn't it, dear? You said something about having a soft thing to fall on."

"I was at the back," said the other twin, then added when he caught Charlton's slightly puzzled frown. "I'm Roy."

"What clothes were you wearing?"

"A brown felt hat and a grey tweed suit—flight grey."

"Were you carrying a raincoat?"

"No."

"Thank you. . . . So the order of your party was: Mr. Stevens, Mrs. Stevens, Mr. Frank Davison and Mr. Roy Davison. Do you all agree with that?"

They did, and he turned to Frank: "Who was immediately behind you?"

"My brother," was the prompt response.

Charlton's smile was rueful. "I'm glad," he said "that I don't have to deal with many twins! Mr. Roy Davison, who was behind *you?*"

"My answer's no more helpful than my brother's," said Roy. "I didn't turn round, so haven't the least idea who was following me."

"Mr. Stevens, did you notice?"

None of them had noticed. They and the Halfpennys had converged on the balcony door from different directions and Mr. Halfpenny had invited them, with a courteous wave of his hand, to precede his party down the staircase; but whether the old gentleman himself had directly followed Roy Davison, no one was prepared to say.

"When you left the Tower," was the detective's next

question, "which way did you go?"

"Down towards the village," replied Stevens, "where we caught a bus to Lulverton, had some tea and then came back here by train."

"How did you walk down the lane? I mean, what was your formation? You all understand, I hope, what I'm trying to find out? I've reason to suspect that a man left the Tower in the company of yourselves and the Halfpenny trio."

"I took my husband's arm," said Mrs. Stevens, "and we went first. My brothers straggled in the rear."

"We didn't straggle!" contradicted Frank. "We marched two-deep like a platoon of infantry, till we had to go into single file to get past a car that was coming up the hill. The lane's not very wide, you know."

"Was it a big saloon?"

"Yes," said Roy, "a dark blue one with a chauffeur driving and a couple of women in the back."

Mrs. d'Eyncourt and Miss Mortimer, thought Charlton.

"And you have no recollection at all of a young man of five feet ten, in a grey flannel suit, wearing or carrying a raincoat and probably brown-moustached?"

They were sorry, but they had not. Charlton shrugged his shoulders wearily. He was doing no better than Martin had done.

"I noticed," he said, "that you have a telephone in the hall. If I ring you this evening, are the four of you prepared to give up any other plans and devote your Saturday afternoon to assisting the police?"

"I was going to play Rug—" began Frank.

"We shall all be delighted to help," his brother-in-law firmly silenced him.

"Thank you very much. Please make a special point of wearing the same clothes as you did last Sunday. I'll ring you this evening: Southmouth 4296."

"How did you know that?" demanded Roy.

"It's on the instrument."

"What an eagle eye!" laughed Mrs. Stevens. "You ought to have been with us on Sunday, Inspector!"

He thought of Peter Grey in a police cell and of Judy comforting her mother at Old Forge House.

"I only wish I had," he fervently agreed.

He stopped at the "Feathers" for a hurried snack and a Guinness, then turned the black Vauxhall eastward and drove at a steady fifty to Lewes, the County town of Sussex. He pressed the bell at "Mendips," the Halfpennys' pleasant little house, several times without getting a reply; but at last Mr. Halfpenny, who had been enjoying an after-luncheon nap in a deck-chair in the garden, opened the door and stood blinking at him like a drowsy walrus.

When he had introduced himself, he was taken into the drawing-room.

"Is it about the Etchworth murder?" the old gentleman asked. "I understood from my son that a young man was arrested for the crime this morning."

"I'm making some incidental inquiries," was the evasive answer. "May I trouble you with a few questions? Perhaps I may see Mrs. Halfpenny and your son at the same time?"

"I will certainly ask my wife to come down. She is resting upstairs. But my son is at his office. If you will call round there, I am sure he will be pleased to help you all he can. He is with Swakeley's, the solicitors in the High Street."

When Mrs. Halfpenny made her appearance, Charlton said his piece again.

"I think you descended the staircase behind another party?"

"That is quite correct," replied Mr. Halfpenny.

"Can you describe any of them?"

"They were all young people, if I remember rightly, and there were one or two girls amongst them, were there not, my dear?"

"I believe there was only *one* girl, Theo, though I was so busy stopping myself from looking over the handrail, which I'm sure would have been too much for me, twisting down and down and gradually getting smaller and smaller, that I really can't be sure. We met two other girls on their way up."

"How many were there in the party in front of you?"

Their replies were simultaneous:

"Seven or eight," said Mr. Halfpenny.

"About five," said his wife.

"Can you be more precise?"

Mr. Halfpenny chewed his moustache as if he hated to have it on his face. Finally, he delivered his judgment:

"Seven or eight."

"I'm sure it wasn't more than five, dear," persisted Mrs. Halfpenny. "Perhaps the Inspector would like to ask Jack. He's more observant that we are."

"Did your son lead the way down the staircase, Mrs. Halfpenny?"

"Yes. I was in the middle, with my husband last."

"And on quitting the Tower, you walked down to the village behind this other party. They have told me that two of their number—a young married pair—went down arm in arm, while the remaining two young men walked abreast behind them. Do you remember if that was so?"

The old couple were desperately anxious to assist, but there was nothing that they could tell him. He thanked them and hurried off to see their son, before Mr. Halfpenny thought to show him his stamps.

He interviewed Jack Halfpenny at Swakeley's.

"When you were coming down the staircase," he asked, after his preliminary questions had proved unproductive, "did you notice anything about the person directly in front of you: whether he was tall or short, how he was dressed—and so on?"

"I believe—I only believe—that he had a light grey suit on.

It's difficult to tell how tall a man is when he's a step or two below you all the time, but I don't think he was very tall, for all that."

"Was the suit flannel or tweed?"

"That I can't say."

"Was he wearing a hat?"

"I think so. Yes, I'm sure he was."

"Was it a bowler or a soft felt?"

"Certainly not a bowler."

"What colour was it?"

"I'm afraid I can't tell you."

Nor had Jack Halfpenny anything to tell about the walk down to the village, except that he and his parents had talked most of the way about the eccentricities of the fourth Duke of Redbourn, who had built the Tower.

"Tomorrow afternoon," said Charlton, "I am arranging a conference at Lulverton police station. Will you please tell your father and mother that I should consider it a great favour if they and yourself could get there by three o'clock, wearing, if possible, the same clothes as you all wore last Sunday."

"You can depend upon it," said Jack, "that the A.P.'s and I will be there."

Lewes is fifty miles from London. At a few minutes after four o'clock Charlton drove across London Bridge into Gracechurch Street, turned to the left by the Crédit Lyonnais into Lombard Street and pulled up outside the Metropolitan and Provincial Bank, which lay between the great white Head Office of Lloyds and the red-bricked City Office of Martins, whose magnificent golden grasshopper seems for ever preparing to leap down Abchurch Lane.

Miss Kathleen Harding worked in the Bank's Income Tax Department, and her friend, Jean Turner, operated an adding-machine in the Branches Clearing. Charlton asked a messenger to find them for him, and in five minutes they came into the waiting-room. Both of them wore blue overalls.

"I want to ask you one or two more questions about your excursion to Etchworth Tower last Sunday," he smiled. "My assistants have seen you separately at your homes, but now I should like to speak to you together. . . . While you were climbing the staircase, you met some other people coming down, didn't you?"

"Yes," they answered together.

"How many were there of them?"

"Quite a lot," said Jean Turner. "We had a job to get by them, the staircase was so narrow."

"I'm afraid 'quite a lot' doesn't help me very much, Miss Turner."

"I should say at least seven," said Kathleen Harding.

"Yes," agreed her friend, "and probably more."

"Can you cast your minds back and think carefully. It is very important for me to know the correct number."

They ultimately agreed that it was either seven or eight, which seemed hardly worth while travelling so far to learn.

"You see," said Miss Turner, "when you're toiling up hundreds of stairs like those, you keep your head down and don't think about anything except getting to the top before your breath gives out. Practically all I saw were a lot of feet."

"I'd hoped," said Charlton with a patient smile, "that you would have much more than that to tell me, but now I've got to ask you to do me a service. Will you both come down to Lulverton tomorrow afternoon? Three o'clock at the police station. Your expenses, of course, will be paid."

"We'd love to," said Miss Harding.

"Try, please, to wear the same clothes as you wore last Sunday, if, of course"—he smiled down at them—"they're not out of fashion by now."

As he went along Newington Causeway on his way back to Downshire, a handful of urchins left the pavement in a body and ran out in front of the car. He jammed down his brake and just managed to avoid hitting a straggler, who was cheered by his friends on the pavement. This suicidal little pastime is called "Last Across" and is the delight of London boys and the terror of all motorists. After the incident, Chariton drove on with a thoughtful frown, but it slowly softened into a smile of satisfaction.

He got back to Lulverton and sought out the Sergeant.

"Any news?" he asked.

"For a start, sir," replied Martin, "they've traced those notes handed to you by the accused." He felt in his pocket and produced a folded sheet of paper.

"There you are, sir. Full details—and they make interesting reading."

Charlton's eyebrows went up as he read.

"*Very* interesting, Martin," he agreed. "Anything else?"

"Yes, sir. Bradfield's put in some fine staff work on the matter of Quentin. We've checked up 'is discoveries with the Yard and found that Quentin's quite an old chum of theirs. 'E was first in touch with them in 1919, then again in '25, '28 and '34. Keeping a common gaming house, was the way they described it, which means not letting the others 'ave a turn with the bank."

Martin felt again in his pocket.

"Here's the report on 'im, sir. Geography, excellent; 'Istory, inclined to slack: Algebra, fair and warmer. ..."

"Talking about mathematics," smiled his superior, "have you solved the problem of 106 and 105 plus I?"

The Sergeant shook his head gloomily.

"Not an 'ope, sir."

"I think *I* have," said Charlton.

XXV.

A FULL MORNING

JUDY telephoned Charlton at a quarter-past eight the next morning. Apart from their meetings that week, he had not seen her since they had taken tea together at Westham St. Martin on the 13th August. He had spent a thoughtful evening after that excursion, and had decided in the end that so inveterate a bachelor as he had no right to be playing Strephon to a Chloe twenty years his junior. So he had kept away from Judy.

Could he, she asked him now, see her for a few minutes as soon as possible? It was rather important. He told her that he could call at Old Forge House at half-past nine.

"No," she said quickly, "don't come there. I'm speaking now from a call-box. . . . Mother mustn't know. . . . Meet me in Leaves Lane just by the Tall Man at 9.30."

"I'll be there," he promised.

By nine o'clock he was standing in the Library at Paulsfield College waiting for Punchard 2 and Wood 1. When they came in and greeted him with self-conscious smirks, he put back the book he had taken down from a shelf.

"Which of you," he smiled. "is which?"

One of them was tall and pale, like a cabbage run to seed, and the other was a little boy with a circular saucy face, a snub nose and steel-framed spectacles.

"I'm Punchard," said the small one. "And he's Wood."

"Punchard 2 and Wood 1?"

"That's right."

"I am Detective-Inspector Charlton."

The two of them had spent the preceding days entertaining admiring groups of friends with increasingly exciting and circumstantial accounts of their interview with Martin. But here was no ordinary sergeant, but a full-blown inspector. They smiled in anticipation of further anecdotal triumphs.

"You were the two boys, I think, who visited Etchworth Tower last Sunday afternoon."

"We were, sir," said Wood.

"Yes, Inspector," said Punchard.

"You went together and later came away together?"

"Yes, sir."

"And which of you slipped past the attendant without paying?"

Their mouths fell open and they looked at him aghast.

"Was it you, Punchard?"

The boy swallowed with difficulty.

"Answer my question, Punchard! Was it you?"

"Yes, sir."

"It was my fault really, sir," Wood 1 came nobly to the aid of his stricken friend. "As we were walking up the hill towards the Tower, I dared him to get in without paying. He wouldn't have thought of it by himself."

"You know how it is when somebody dares you, don't you, sir?" asked Punchard 2 eagerly.

With a mighty effort, Charlton maintained his expression of stern disapproval.

"You might have got the attendant into serious trouble."

"I didn't think of that, sir. It was only done for a joke."

"Next time you're 'dared', young man, you consider the effects of your actions on other people."

"Yes, sir. I will, sir."

"Wood, have you threepence?"

The boy searched his clothes and produced a gallimaufry of small articles, which included no other coin than a Japanese sen with a square central hole. Then as if forced to fall back on his hidden reserves, he reluctantly extracted from his waistcoat pocket the cream of his collection, a bright bronze threepenny-piece.

"Give it to Punchard," instructed the Inspector.

"You, Punchard, will go to the Tower this afternoon, hand that coin to the attendant, climb to the balcony and stay there for not less than an hour. It is possible that, after that time, you will realise how disgracefully you behaved last Sunday. Don't you agree that that would be a satisfactory end to the affair?"

"Oh, absolutely, sir! That's topping of you! Thanks awfully, sir!"

"Now, tell me exactly what happened—and I warn you that it may be necessary for you to repeat everything in a court of law. A man's life will perhaps depend on your evidence."

"When Wood 1 dared me, sir, I said I'd have a shot at it, but he would have to keep the attendant's attention off me."

"How did you do that, Wood?"

"Punchard 2 stayed outside, sir, while I went in alone. I—"

"Wasn't there a motorcar just outside the entrance at the time?"

"Not right outside, sir. It was a little way down the hill. There was a chauffeur waiting in it, but he couldn't see what we were doing . . . I put my three pennies down on the turnstile, sir, but managed to jog one of them over the barrier thing. While the attendant was bending down, grovelling about finding it, Punchard 2—"

"Let him tell me himself."

"I crawled through the other turnstile, sir, and leapt across to the stairs. I was through the door and had closed it quietly behind me before the old man had picked up the penny."

An untimely note of elation crept into his voice, but he forestalled comment by adding:

"It was very wrong of me, sir."

The door of the library was opened and Dr. Roberts swept in, as only a gowned headmaster can.

"Well, Inspector," he said, and what is it now?"

Punchard 2 and Wood 1 froze. The "Bird" had looked a bit picky at prayers.

"Nothing very serious, Dr. Roberts," Charlton smiled. "I have just been asking these two boys a few more questions about last Sunday afternoon. I'm hoping that it won't be necessary for them to give evidence in court."

Dr. Roberts had that morning received an abrupt memorandum from the Chairman of the Board of Governors and was still simmering.

"They can surely have nothing of importance to tell you," he snapped. "I do not want to suggest, Inspector, that you are wasting your time, but you are keeping them from their studies, a delay that neither of these particular boys"—he petrified them through his pince-nez—"can afford."

Four retorts occurred to Charlton, but he discarded them in favour of: "I need not detain them any longer."

The Doctor waved his hand and the unhappy boys crept away to face the lesser perils of their form-rooms.

Judy was waiting for him in Leaves Lane below the Tall Man and he thought it a pity that she should look so sad upon so beautiful a morning. Hers was a face never meant for grief. . . . He pulled up the car and jumped out. Here and there in the fields, labourers were working and there was a distant hammering high above them to the east, where the builders were putting the finishing touches to the new grille-work on the balcony. The Indian summer persisted. The sun had chased the mists out of the valleys and it was going to be hot again.

"Don't say what you were going to say," Judy tried to smile. "I saw your face in the court yesterday and went home and cried my eyes out because of it. . . . I could *kick* that stupid jury!"

"I know he didn't do it. Give me a little while to prove it."

"You've *got* to, for if you don't . . ."

Her voice died away and she gazed past him across the fields.

"Don't worry." His deep voice was comforting. "Yesterday, your brother had no chance to defend himself. The jury returned that verdict on the flimsiest evidence and they should never have done it. . . . Things will be different when he has counsel to look after him. . . . There are roughly twelve kinds of evidence and the strongest of them is direct evidence, which is the story told by an eye-witness. Did anyone *see* your brother kill Harbord? When I hear that, I shall start to get anxious!"

"All the same, I'm terrified. Suppose he's convicted and . . . and hanged? It would be awful—awful for him, for mother and for . . . us."

The last word was said so quietly that he only just caught it. He stepped suddenly forward and raised his arms, but then he allowed them to fall.

"It'll never be as serious as that," he said lamely. "It's quite likely that the magistrates won't send him for trial."

"Have you seen him today?"

He shook his head.

"Where is he?"

"At the police station."

"Mother keeps on asking me if I'm sure he's all right and that they're looking after him properly. She's wondering, all the time, if he was warm enough last night. . . . It's about Mother that I want to talk to you. That's why I rang. Last night she sent a cheque for ninety-seven pounds to that poisonous Quentin person."

His hand jerked impatiently.

"You should have stopped her. I warned you against that."

"I didn't get a chance. She ran out to the post-box and then came back and told me what she'd done." She smiled wanly. "There's not much left now in the old oak chest, but Mother said she couldn't bear the thought of Courtenay leaving that debt behind him."

"She shouldn't have done it. That man's no more than a cheap sharper. . . . But leave it to me. I'll see what I can do. . . . I . . . I have an apology to make to you—"

"I said I didn't want to hear it," she interrupted.

"It isn't that. It's something else. . . . You remember I told you in the train on Tuesday that I knew where your brother was hiding? Do you know how I knew that?"

Judy shook her head.

"I guessed that your brother would ring you up and detailed one of my men to follow you and find out where you went. . . . After you'd left 51, Warne Road, he went in and had a word with the landlady. He rang my sergeant, who told me when I myself got through before leaving London. . . . I'm sorry I had to do that."

"Do you remember about the Big Shot?" she said and left it at that. "Now," she went on, "I must get back to Mother. She's in a terrible state."

"Can I take you?"

"No, I'll walk. The sister of the accused mustn't be seen driving with the officer in charge of the case." Again the tiny smile. "What *would* people say?"

"Frankly," he grinned, "they'd say quite a lot."

"Then we won't risk it. Anyway, it would take too long, even if we went the short way *via* Westham St. Martin."

"Rude child," he chuckled.

"Good-bye, then, and thank you for coming. I feel better now. ... You stayed away a long time, you know."

He was purposely dense. "I was here by 9.30."

"I don't mean that. You've been very neglectful since our car-ride together."

"I've been very busy. Crime is popular at the moment."

"That doesn't excuse you."

"There were other reasons. . . . I will tell you about them when I have found the man who killed your cousin."

"Is that a promise?"

"Cub's honour! Good-bye . . . my dear."

He looked at her for a moment, turned swiftly and climbed into the car. Judy stood without movement long after the sound of the engine had died away.

Mrs. Quentin, the Sergeant's vamp, received Charlton when he called at "Capri." Martin's description had been apt.

Even at that early hour, she was the living spit of one of Mr. Oppenheim's queens of espionage. A fat Balkan Sobranie was between her fingers. She must have lighted it a moment before the maid showed him into the glaringly palatial apartment.

"My husband," she drawled, "is not yet up. Perhaps I can tell you what you want to know?"

"I'm afraid not, Mrs. Quentin."

"Is it about Courtenay Harbord?"

He tried an experiment. "No."

The result was gratifying. She jabbed her cigarette in the ash-tray so savagely that it bent in the middle and the glowing end fell off.

"Then why have you come?" Her contralto voice was not quite steady.

"If you will ask your husband to spare me five minutes, I shall be able to enlighten him."

"He's still in bed. We were very late last night and I don't want to disturb him." She lighted another cigarette. "I'll give him a message, unless you would like to call back later?"

"That is impossible. My business with Mr. Quentin is urgent and with him alone."

"In that case," she said tartly, "I shall have to rouse him, but I think you are very inconsiderate."

She got up and went across the room with all the artificial undulations of a highly paid mannequin. He controlled the discourteous impulse to take a running kick at one swaying part of her.

Mr. Oliver Quentin joined him in a silk wrap patterned with the rich extravagance of Oriental art. His hair was immaculately sleek and his chin was as smooth as his manner. One would not have thought that he had been making up arrears of sleep while the detective chatted with his wife. One would have been right: he had been listening outside the door.

"Once again I have kept you waiting, Inspector," he effused, "but I fear I am not an early riser. My wife is constantly complaining about my lazy ways. . . . Now, how can I be of service?"

"Last Wednesday week, the 25th September, you drew some cash from your account with the local branch of the Metropolitan & Provincial Bank. The amount was twenty-five pounds, I think?"

"I believe it was. Why?"

"Can you remember what you did with the money?"

"Really, Inspector, that is a very great deal to ask. I spend money on a thousand and one things, and I can't be expected to recall every item. If you can be more precise in your enquiry, I will try to help you."

"At the inquest yesterday, Mr. Peter Grey gave in evidence that the late Mr. Courtenay Harbord handed him five one-pound notes. Two of those notes were among those drawn from your account on the 25th of last month. I am interested to know how they came into Mr. Harbord's possession."

Quentin's face broke into a wide, affable smile.

"That is quite easily explained," he said. "I have told you that I was always too good-natured and liberal with my poor young friend. The two notes must have formed part of one of my countless loans to him. You know that I was constantly getting him out of his difficulties."

"When did you give him the money?"

"My dear Inspector. How can I tell? He tapped me like a barometer."

His joke seemed to please him and he laughed energetically.

"I have certain written notes of my last conversation with you, Mr. Quentin. Allow me to quote from them. During last Thursday week, your wife reminded you that you had not seen Mr. Harbord for some time, and thereupon, you telephoned him and asked him to join you at bridge on the following evening. Am I right?"

"Perfectly."

"You did not see him on the Wednesday or Thursday neither did you see him on the following Saturday or Sunday. I am still relying on my notes, Mr. Quentin."

"Quite correct. I last saw the unfortunate young man on the Friday evening. That, I think, you will also find in your notes, Inspector."

"Precisely so. That was the evening when you had your serious talk with Mr. Harbord, demanding to know when he was going to repay some of the money he owed you."

"I did it for his own good. As I said in court yesterday, *Facilis descensus*—"

Again he was not allowed to finish the tag.

"You have made your motives," said Charlton sweetly, "abundantly clear. But it is beginning to appear that you did not give those notes to Mr. Harbord. You drew out the money on the Wednesday and the only occasion on which you saw him between then and the time of his death was on the Friday evening—and I have your assurance that no money changed hands at that meeting. Can it be that you are mistaken, Mr. Quentin?"

"I thought I had given it him then," the little man said uneasily, "but now it seems that I can't have done." He gave his head an irritable shake. "I don't follow all these questions, Inspector. How do you know that the notes Court gave that young scoundrel, Grey, were the ones handed to me by the Bank cashier? It can only be guesswork. Only notes of higher denomination can be traced through a Bank." He smiled as one friend at another. "I call your bluff, Mr. Charlton!"

"The notes were issued by the Bank of England to the Chief Cashier at the Head Office of the Metropolitan & Provincial Bank in Lombard Street. *He* is responsible for the distribution of notes to branches of his Bank, and was able to confirm that a bundle of new notes, including the two with which we are concerned, was recently supplied to their Lulverton branch. To enable the cashiers to find their 'shorts and overs' with minimum delay, it is the custom at that particular branch to pencil the numbers of notes given out on the backs of the relative cheques. That is why I am so sure of my ground, Mr. Quentin. Perhaps you can now recall some other way in which those notes could have found their way into Mr. Harbord's pocket?"

Quentin spread out his hands.

"You leave me entirely at a loss, Inspector. If I did not give those notes to Court, I cannot think how he got hold of them."

"Is it likely that Mrs. Quentin gave them to him?"

"Unquestionably, no. My wife has her own banking account and, apart from that, she has always set her face against my well-meant benefactions to Court. She is made of sterner stuff than I!"

"How did you spend the twenty-five pounds?"

"I have told you already that I do not know. Surely you can take the word of a gentleman?"

"I am not satisfied with your answer," said Charlton quietly, "and I shall stay here until I am. You have played with me quite long enough, Mr. Quentin. You remember perfectly clearly the person to whom you gave those notes and you are now going to tell me his name."

It was a battle of wills, and Charlton won.

"Very well, then," said Quentin after a stubborn silence. "It was a young man employed by the District Council and his name is Philip Lambert."

"Why did you give them to him?"

"You are really going too far!" protested Quentin. "I do not like this cross-examination."

"Why did you give them to him?"

"He asked me to lend him a fiver and I am always only too anxious to assist my young friends."

"When was this?"

"On the evening of the day when I drew the money."

"Thank you. I am glad that point is satisfactorily settled."

Instantly the friend of youth was on his feet and walking towards the door like a chubby mandarin.

"Just a moment, Mr. Quentin," Charlton restrained him. "There is one other thing before I go."

Quentin returned to his chair without eagerness.

"Have you yet opened your letters?"

"Yes. Bills, bills and still more bills! Life is all bills. I expect it's the same with you, Inspector?"

"Did you receive a cheque for ninety-seven pounds from Mrs. Grey?"

"As a matter of fact, I did. It represents a refund of the money I lent her nephew during his lifetime. All perfectly straightforward and a very prompt and proper action on the part of Mrs. Grey. One does not usually find ladies so businesslike in the settlement of their obligations."

"Mrs. Grey was not in possession of all the facts when she sent you that cheque. I must now ask you to hand it to me, so that it can be returned to her."

"That is ridiculous and I have not the slightest intention of complying!"

"You would be unwise to refuse, Mr. Quentin."

"Nonsense. You have no right to talk to me like that! You are a hired public servant and grossly exceeding your duty: I shall report you to your Superintendent."

He walked excitedly about the room.

"The matter was between Mrs. Grey and myself," he ranted on, "and I will not permit any intervention by a jumped-up jack-in-office of a country policeman. I have put up with your insulting manners and answered your unnecessarily officious questions because I am a law-abiding man; but I will not brook this last piece of damnable impertinence!"

Charlton leant comfortably back in his chair and smiled up at the furious man.

"For the first time, Mr. Quentin," he said pleasantly. "I realize that you are human. I previously imagined you to be some unidentified species of jellyfish."

"You impudent blackguard! I'll have you thrown out of the force for that! I'd like to know why you set yourself up as a champion of Mrs. Grey, when it was you who arrested that precious son of hers yesterday. I have no doubt that you were put up to it by that smug-faced little bitch of a daughter!"

The big man could move very quickly when he liked. His left arm shot out and his fist caught the dimpled chin with the clean click of a perfect brassie shot. Quentin yelped like a kicked dog and sprawled backwards on the settee, from where he slid to the floor with a wound where Charlton's signet-ring had broken the soft white flesh.

"You mustn't say things like that," said the detective reprovingly.

Quentin scrambled up and dropped on to the settee. He felt his chin tenderly and gasped when his hand came away smeared with blood.

"You've hurt me!" he wailed.

"I'm delighted to hear it. I have been wanting to do that for some time. Now will you please give me Mrs. Grey's cheque?"

The casualty pulled out a monogrammed handkerchief of fine linen and dabbed at his wound.

"I'm bleeding hard," he moaned, then flared up, "You've *wounded* me. I'll summon you for assault. Look!"

He waved the spattered handkerchief.

"Don't be a fool, Quentin," said Charlton easily. "You deserved what you got and that's an end of it. Now give me that cheque."

Quentin dug into the pocket of his wrap, pulled out an envelope and threw it on the floor at Charlton's feet. The detective picked it up, pulled out Mrs. Grey's cheque, read it, tore it into many pieces and sprinkled them thoroughly over the thick-piled carpet.

"There," he said, as if he had done a favour, "that will give the next vacuum-cleaner salesman who calls an opportunity to demonstrate his machine."

"You'll hear more about this!" shouted Quentin. "I shall write to the Chief Constable."

"Do, by all means, but don't forget to sign the letter with your right name, Mr. Lewis Weisenbaum."

Which seemed an appropriate moment to depart.

XXVI.

LEFT TO BRADFIELD

SO interesting and full of incident had been his interview with Mr. Oliver Quentin, formerly Mr. Lewis Weisenbaum, that Charlton arrived only just in time at the Petty Sessional Court, when Peter Grey was brought before two magistrates. The proceedings were brief. Charlton gave evidence of arrest and told the magistrates that, when he had made the arrest, the accused had answered:

"I have nothing to say."

The Clerk asked Peter if he had now any questions to ask the detective, and Peter, after looking Charlton slowly up and down, replied that he had not. He was then remanded in custody until the following Friday, when he could be brought before the full bench of magistrates, who would then decide whether he was to be sent for trial or discharged.

Peter was not taken back to the police station, but was removed to gaol, while Charlton, with the memory of the prisoner's contemptuous glance lingering in his mind, went along to the Council Offices and asked for a private interview with Philip Lambert. The young man was as perfectly dressed as ever and his hair-line moustache was no more robust than on their last meeting.

"Mr. Lambert," began Charlton, "between last Wednesday week and the time of his death, did you hand two one-pound notes to the late Mr. Courtenay Harbord?"

Lambert's voice was lackadaisical.

"Good heavens, no!"

"Did you see him between those times?"

"No."

"On that Wednesday evening, Mr. Oliver Quentin lent you five pounds, did he not?"

"An entirely personal matter."

"Unfortunately, Mr. Lambert, it is not. I am compelled to ask you what you did with the money."

"I really don't see why I should tell you." The tone suggested infinite fatigue.

"I cannot force you, but I recommend you to answer my question."

"It was spent on the things one usually spends money on, if that's any help to you."

"Was it used to pay Tom Starling for your losses on the St. Leger and the Doncaster Cup?"

"How the devil did you know that?"

"Was it?"

"No," was the unwilling reply.

"Then how was it used? If *you* didn't give those two notes to Harbord, you must have passed them over to somebody who did. Who was it?"

"I paid two weeks' rent to my landlady."

"Which one? Mrs. Ramplin or Mrs. Fenner?"

"Mrs. Ramplin, of course. I left Mrs. Fenner some time ago."

"So she was telling me," lied Charlton blandly. "What did this rent amount to?"

"Thirty shillings a week."

"That leaves two pounds. How did you spend those?"

"Oh, for God's sake don't keep on firing questions at me," said Lambert wearily. "I spent it on the Lord knows what: petrol for the car, cigarettes, drinks—and all that."

"It will become necessary, Mr. Lambert," said Charlton sharply, "for you to give this evidence in court, as it may also be necessary for you to explain what you were doing last Sunday evening and why it was you who suggested to Mr. Matthews that you should collect the cash from the Tower on Saturday evenings."

The bow was drawn at a wild venture and he could not be sure of the results. Lambert kept his languid pose and put up his hand to stifle a yawn.

"I really don't know what you're talking about," said the young man.

"I'll give you time to think it out."

By three o'clock on that Saturday afternoon, there had arrived at Lulverton police station all the persons Charlton had invited: Kathleen Harding and Jean Turner, the Davisons, the Stevenses and the Halfpennys.

"Ladies and gentlemen," Charlton smiled, "I am very much obliged to you all for coming here this afternoon and I hope, for my own sake as well as yours, that your time will not be wasted. With your assistance, I propose to carry out an experiment: something in the nature of an identification parade. Cars are ready outside to take us all to Etchworth Tower, where we will reproduce the events of last Sunday."

"Goody, goody!" cried Miss Harding and was frowned at warningly by her friend.

"I want you all," continued Charlton, "to behave exactly as you did then, and to tell me afterwards whether everything seemed the same, or whether there had been someone in your company last Sunday who was missing this afternoon."

Mrs. Halfpenny shivered dramatically.

"It all sounds very ghostly," she said and there was a strained note in the general answering laugh.

They went to the Tower in three cars driven by Charlton, Bradfield and another of his men, Emerson. It was now open again to the public. Tom was on duty in his cubicle and looked up at Charlton with a toothless grin of welcome.

"Good af'noon, sir," he said. "'Ow are things going? I'm glad to see you again, 'cause I wanter ask you 'ow I did at yes'day's prerceedings. You give me the straight tip to keep me mouth shut and I showed 'em, didn't you think?"

"You nearly got arrested for contempt of court, if that's anything!" laughed Charlton. "And another time, don't keep

winking at me. The coroner thought I'd put you up to it . . .
Now, I've a party of people outside and I don't want you to let
anyone else in for half an hour. Here's my authority from Mr.
Matthews. Shall I read it to you?"

"Give it 'ere," said Tom, holding out his hand. "I know me
A.B.C."

After much mouthing and following of the text with a
grimy thumb, he delivered the judgment that the document
was in order. Charlton went back to his group of helpers.

"Miss Turner and Miss Harding," he said, "will you please
wait here until my assistant, Mr. Bradfield, tells you to come
up? The rest of you kindly follow me."

He led them through the turnstile and up the staircase
to the balcony, on which there were several persons already,
including one who stood staring across the sea-plain with the
rapt expression of the young Roman soldier who was faithful
unto death. It was Punchard 2 doing penance.

Charlton looked at his watch, then waved his handkerchief
to Bradfield standing below, who started the Misses Turner
and Harding on their upward journey. Mr. Halfpenny and his
family were separated from the rest and, at a signal from the
Inspector, the two parties came from different sides towards the
staircase door. Mr. Halfpenny stood back and allowed Brian
Stevens to pass through the doorway. Mrs. Stevens followed
her husband, while the Halfpennys waited; then, when the
twins had gone after their sister, Mr. Halfpenny said to his son
in the sing-song voice so often to be heard on the amateur
dramatic stage:

"You go first, Jack."

He pushed his son forward and they followed the other
party down. When they had gone, Charlton strolled round the
balcony to examine the building operations. The workmen
had knocked off for the day, leaving the grille-work finished,
but the ladders for cleaning the vase were still erected. He
nodded to Punchard 2, who gave him a watery smile. The

boy probably imagined that he had come up there to make sure that he himself was obeying instructions, but, until he had caught sight of him, Charlton had entirely forgotten the punishment that had been imposed.

The girls arrived on the balcony and were going to speak to him, but he jerked his head warningly towards the other visitors. They waited until Charlton had seen the Halfpennys walk down towards the village behind the other party before the three of them descended.

The whole company drove back to Lulverton. Charlton's room was not a vast apartment and they rather crowded it, but he managed to find chairs for Mrs. Halfpenny and the girls. Everyone seemed to be on the point of bursting with important news.

"Now," he said briskly, "please don't all speak at once! Let us take the ladies first. Mrs. Halfpenny, have you anything to say?"

They all had something to say and, except for Jack Halfpenny, it was the same thing: throughout the whole course of the experiment, each one of them had sensed the absence of someone who had made one of their number the Sunday before. Charlton discounted their evidence. They had known, before they went, why the test was to be carried out, and it was highly probable that their minds had sub-consciously reacted. Happily, Jack Halfpenny had something less imponderable to say.

" I'd stake my last penny," he asserted, "that the man in front of me today was not the same one as last time. His shoulders were narrower and he was not so tall. I can't tell the difference between these two gentlemen"—he pointed to the twins, who were standing together—"but whichever it was I walked behind this afternoon did not touch the banister rail; and I've the clearest picture in my mind, now that I've gone down the staircase again, of the man in front of me last Sunday hanging on all the way down like grim death."

The Inspector smiled with delight.

"That's splendid!" he said. "I hope you'll be prepared to give that on oath in court? "

"I most certainly would," said Jack stoutly.

"Mr. Roy Davison, can you confirm that you descended the stairs last Sunday in the same manner as you did today: that you didn't hold on to the handrail?"

"I'm positive I didn't."

"Fine!" said Charlton. "And now that we have brought the proceedings to such a happy conclusion, I hope that you will join me in what I think we all badly need: a cup of tea."

"Marvellous!" breathed Mrs. Halfpenny, who had been visibly drooping.

"Don't forget," Charlton cautioned them, "that we mustn't mention this matter again. If we can spare time for conversation during tea, let us talk about the weather or our favourite film stars."

By the giving of which wise advice, he played right into the hands of Mr. Halfpenny, who, while they toyed with toasted tea-cakes and chocolate cream buns in a local tea-shop, entertained him with an interminable disquisition on Provincial British Guiana, Red Mauritius and English Penny Blacks. In spite of this preoccupation, however, Charlton had time to notice how Roy Davison—or Frank, as he could not be sure—saw to it that Miss Jean Turner wanted for nothing in the way of more tea or another fancy gâteau, and replied abstractedly to any remark addressed to him.

When, three months later, he read in the *Downshire Herald* of the engagement of Mr. Roy Davison (it *was* Roy, unless the reporter was misled) with Miss Jean Turner, and still later, a report of their marriage, with two photographs, one of the radiant bride and the other of a young man whose smile was so carefree that it must surely have been Frank, Charlton remembered that it was really he who had brought them together, and felt that there must be a moral somewhere, if one could only find it.

"Bradfield, my boy," he exulted later at the police station, "we proceed apace. If the bottom has not yet fallen out of the case against Grey, it is beginning to sag. We must do all we can to hurry it up—or rather, down . . . I have been thinking about those Craven 'A' packets."

He brought out his own cigarettes and offered one to Bradfield.

"There was something very strange about them," he went on when they had lighted up. "I've been making a few enquiries about the manufacture of cigarettes and have found out certain interesting things. You probably don't want to hear them, but, for all that, you're going to."

The young detective laughed.

"The more popular brands, Bradfield, are packed by machinery. The two parts of the packet, known as the 'shell' and the 'slide', are assembled and the foil-wrapped cigarettes inserted. The filled packets are then removed from the machine and transferred by hand in batches to another machine that wraps them up in their cellophane jackets and say a poor buffer lies low."

"Lies low," said Bradfield.

"The process is not entirely mechanical, I'll admit, but I consider that the chances of getting well-defined fingerprints on both sides of the packet are remote. Don't you agree?"

Bradfield nodded.

"We are concerned, in this case, with *two* packets: the one I took from Harbord's pocket, which we'll call A, and the one I found in Waltham Hanger, which we'll call—what do you suggest?"

"B," grinned Bradfield.

The answering nod was approving. "You'll go a long way, Bradfield, if you keep at it. B, then. I'll take it first. The only fingerprints on the shell of it were Harbord's. We could find no trace in the Hanger of any cellophane wrapping, which I found understandable, as it might very likely have been thrown away when the packet was first opened. Now we come to packet A. On the shell of that were not only Harbord's prints, but also those of other fingers. Outside the Tower entrance last Monday morning, I picked up a crumpled ball of cellophane. That also bore prints other than Harbord's, but, according to the experts, there was no similarity between them and the unidentified prints on packet A. Of course, there is nothing to prevent a wrapping from collecting any number of different prints, but *why*, Bradfield, were there any prints besides Harbord's on packet A?"

"It's all a bit too complicated for me, sir."

"Candidly, it's not very clear to *me*; but I have had one idea that may lead us somewhere. I have noticed, when buying cigarettes, that tobacconists or the assistants sometimes tear off the wrapping before handing the packet across the counter. It's a quaint little trick and one doesn't meet it every day. I wonder, Bradfield, whether that's what happened to packet A? If it was, packet A was not the one that Tom Lee saw Whiskers open."

"Something else strikes me, sir," said Bradfield. "If Harbord's fingerprints were on the ball of wrapping that you picked up outside the Tower, mustn't he have been Whiskers?"

"It could have been faked. The murderer might have got Harbord to take hold of the unopened packet. But I do believe now that Harbord *was* Whiskers. How he was persuaded to disguise himself and visit the Tower is, at the moment, a mystery . . . I am beginning to wonder, Bradfield, whether more than one man was concerned in Harbord's death. Those ropes in Waltham Hanger were merely a blind, I'm certain. There were no marks on his body as there would have been if he had been trussed up and left to struggle to the ground. So he probably went to the chalk-pit, not, perhaps, of his own free will, but under his own steam. You remember the conformation of that pit? The face was considerably off the perpendicular. He couldn't have been casually pushed over the edge, because that wouldn't have given him the straight drop that Dr. Lorimer insists on. If he didn't get well back from the edge and take a running jump into space, he must have been thrown: not just dropped over, but flung well clear—and that's not easy work for one man."

He pressed out his cigarette-end in the ash-tray.

"But that's all theory, Bradfield . . . I think, though, that it would be worth while to go round to all the local tobacconists. We may find a polite one amongst them who remembers selling the cigarettes to Harbord or to some other person in whom we can afterwards take an inquisitive interest. See to that for me, will you—and don't forget to take Harbord's photograph with you."

Bradfield jumped to his feet.

"Leave it to me, sir," he said with a confidence that he did not feel.

XXVII.

THE HUNT IS UP

"WHETHER a constable is nominally on, or off, duty," says the *Police Code,* "his responsibility to the public is the same, and he is bound to prevent and detect crime by all possible means."

A shrill, imperative telephone-bell got Charlton out of bed before eight the next morning. He had been hoping that, as it was Sunday, he would be allowed at least another half-hour's peace; and he swore quite bitterly as he got into his dressing-gown and, failing to find his slippers, went downstairs barefooted.

It was a man's voice at the other end of the line.

"I'm very sorry to ring you so early," he said.

Charlton had stubbed his toe on a chair-leg, but training told.

"Not at all," he answered civilly. "Who are you?"

"I daren't tell you my name on the 'phone, but we were talking to each other yesterday. May I come to see you this morning? I know it's Sunday, but the matter's urgent."

"I'll be here at my house at eleven o'clock," said Charlton and rang off. "I wonder," he thought, as he massaged his damaged toe, "what *he* wants."

The fine weather had broken and it was raining hard and steadily; but at nine o'clock, soon after the maid had cleared away the breakfast things, P.C. Bradfield brought sunshine into Charlton's home.

"Good morning, sir!" was his hearty greeting, as he disposed of his dripping hat. "I've found out something and thought I should report it without delay. It's great news, sir!"

"Try to be a little less boisterous," Charlton urged him. "I've just hurt my big toe and I want sympathy, not heartless rejoicing."

"Not seriously, I hope, sir?"

"Nothing much, really. Just a compound, comminuted fracture of the right hallux. Since my niece was callous enough to leave me for Mr. Rutherford, I've never been able to find my slippers—and now I'm crippled for life. . . . But enough of this foolery, Bradfield. Let's have this great news."

"I've traced those Craven 'A', sir, and I've found out something else."

"Tell me the something else first."

"Among the dozens of tobacconists I went to yesterday was a scruffy little shop in one of those back streets by the gas-works. As soon as I showed the proprietor Harbord's photo, he said he knew the face. Harbord went in last Thursday or Friday week—he couldn't remember exactly which—and asked for a cheap pipe and an ounce of Empire tobacco. The man tried to sell him a better pipe, but Harbord insisted that a shilling was all he was going to pay. Don't you think, sir, that that must have been the pipe that I found in the Tall Man chalk-pit?"

Charlton nodded agreement.

"Now the other matter, sir. After I had covered a good many tobacconists in Lulverton, Emerson took over the rest, while I went over to Etchworth. Only two shops in the village sell cigarettes and neither of them was at all helpful. Then it suddenly occurred to me that you can buy cigarettes in pubs, so I popped into the 'Tower Arms.'"

"And ordered a glass of beer that you propose to charge to expenses?"

"Yes, sir," said Bradfield unabashed. "I hadn't bought cigarettes at the other places I'd been to, but I asked the barmaid for a large Player's—and the first thing she did was to rip the wrapping off the packet!"

"I am agog. Pray continue."

"I said it was a trick you didn't often see in this part of the world and enquired if she made a habit of it. She said she had learnt it in London and always did it for customers she

284

liked. That started us off on a heart to heart talk and, when I could tear myself away, I took the packet over to Inspector Green at Whitchester for a quick decision. I'd been careful to keep my gloves on, so the only prints on the packet were the barmaid's. Inspector Green decided that they were identical with those on Packet A. We can get the Yard's confirmation later, of course."

"Fine work, Bradfield! Have you taken any further steps?"

"No, sir. By that time, it was getting late and I thought you'd prefer to see the girl yourself. She's really quite worth seeing, sir! Her name's Sheila Doyle—"

"And she comes from Ballymena."

"That's right, sir. You obviously know her. She lives at 27, Blackhill Road, Lulverton. I had to promise to take her to the pictures next Thursday to find that out."

"I'll go and see her now. Do you want a lift back?"

He put on his mackintosh and they drove through the rain to Lulverton. His last word of praise when he dropped Bradfield at the police station sent the young man off, as Charlton afterwards put it to Martin, as pleased as a tail with two dogs.

Sheila Doyle was everything that Martin and Bradfield claimed.

"Miss Doyle," he said, "I am a police inspector and on no account must you repeat anything we say."

Her eyes opened wide.

"Try to remember last Sunday. I understand that sometime during that day you sold a twenty packet of Craven 'A'. Was that so?"

"I sold several, sir."

"Can you recall whom you sold them to?" He took Harbord's photograph from his pocket. "Was *he* one of them?"

"No, sir. That's Mr. Harbord of Sheep, who used to come in sometimes. Last Sunday was the day he was killed. I didn't see him at all."

"Did any of your regular customers, who usually smoke Craven 'A', buy any last Sunday?"

"People are always coming and going, sir, and it's hard to remember what happened as long ago as that. There's only one I really remember. He's a man who comes in every night and I've never seen him smoke anything else but Gold Flake. I was a bit surprised when he asked for Craven 'A', for gentlemen don't usually like chopping and changing about. They stick to one brand for years. I made a joke about it to him and he said he was just starting to collect the cards, which was funny, because they don't have cards in Craven 'A'."

"What is this man's name?"

"I've never known it, but I can tell you what he looks like."

Mr. Edward Preston would have recognized the description that she gave.

"What time does he come in as a rule?"

"Half-past eight, most evenings, but on Sundays he usually drops in soon after opening-time, which is at 12.30."

"I'll be there myself on the stroke of time. As soon as he comes in, please say to me, 'Have you seen Greta Garbo's latest?'"

"Funny you should pick that," smiled the girl. "It's the one I'm going to see next Thursday."

He had the feeling that Miss Doyle was going to be disappointed. In the execution of his duties, Detective-Constable Bradfield promised to take girls to cinemas at the rate of four a week. He wondered whether, in this particular case, Bradfield would keep his word. If he did, Charlton was going to see to it that the cost of the seats was not charged to expenses.

"I hope you enjoy it," he said.

As a matter of fact, she did; but Bradfield did not escort her.

When he got back home, although it was well before eleven o'clock, his early-morning telephone caller was waiting for him. Philip Lambert had not shaved and he looked as if he had had a very poor night's rest.

"Inspector," he said, when he had taken the offered chair in Charlton's study, "how much do you know about this affair?"

The detective drew slowly at his cigarette.

"Nearly everything."

"I've had a filthy time since I saw you yesterday and I want, first of all, to apologize for my rudeness."

The air of insolent disdain had deserted him and he looked no more than a badly frightened young man.

"I wouldn't tell you yesterday who I gave those notes to, but I'm going to tell you now. Then I'm going to tell you the whole story, if you'll listen, and after that, I must leave the rest to you.

"I gave the notes to a man who lives in Lulverton and whose real name, I believe, is Albert Smithers. He is an ex-convict and has with him another old lag called Edward Preston. The notes I gave Smithers were a repayment of money I had borrowed from him. I have been associated with them for some time now, and Courtenay Harbord was mixed up with them, too. We were forging Bank notes."

"Quite," said Charlton calmly, as if he had not just received one of the biggest surprises in his life.

"Harbord made the plates and the line blocks for the watermarks, Smithers helped with the printing, and I passed them out to the carriers. Then Harbord left a couple lying about in his home, his aunt paid them into her account—and you'll probably remember going round to see them about it."

"That's what first put me on the trail," lied Charlton.

"It frightened Harbord so much that he broke up the plates and cleared out. The other two and I got rid of the notes we had in hand—and that was the end of it, so far as I was concerned. I've seen them occasionally since."

He broke off and was silent for a while.

"If that had been all," he went on," nothing on earth would have persuaded me to squeak like this: but I'm not going to stand by and see that fellow, Grey, suffer for what he didn't do."

Charlton did not swallow that fine sentiment whole. Lambert had not seen fit to confess until his own safety was endangered.

"Harbord tried to blackmail the others," continued Lambert, "and last Sunday evening they killed him."

"How do you know that?"

"Because I saw them do it."

Direct evidence! Charlton nearly whooped with joy. It was more than he had dared to hope. He went over and sat down at his desk. His manner was perfectly casual.

"Are you prepared to make a statement?" he asked, unscrewing his fountain-pen.

"Will it get me off the forging business?" demanded Lambert eagerly.

"I can promise nothing."

"It would finish my father if he ever knew. . . . At any rate, if you write out a statement, I'll sign it. Just before half-past eight last Sunday evening I called in at the 'Tower Arms' in Etchworth High Street. I was having my drink in the saloon when I heard Preston's voice. He was in the public bar on the other side of the partition. He ordered a pint of beer—"

"And then," interrupted Charlton, who believed in surprise tactics, "asked the girl for twenty Craven 'A'."

Lambert jumped perceptibly.

"My God," he said in wonder, "you know as much as I do."

"Very probably. But go on."

"I thought it strange that Vike—that's Preston's nickname, by the way. Short for 'Viscount', I believe. Smithers the other man, is called Smoothy, because he can tell the tale. . . . Well, I thought it was strange that Vike should want Craven 'A'. Harbord always smoked them and he'd broken away from

Preston and Smithers. I'd seen Smithers a few days before to pay back the money I owed him, and he'd said nothing about Harbord joining forces again. I never trusted any of them, least of all Harbord, and I began to think that they were all out to double-cross me. I was desperately hard up—still am, for that matter—and if they were taking up forging again, I wanted to be in it. It had brought me in two pounds a week."

He gave a helpless little gesture.

"I know it was all wrong, Inspector, but when a man's up against it like I am, he doesn't worry much about his methods. I owe money all round and I'm very nearly desperate."

"I can help you with one piece of private advice, Mr. Lambert, which you'll probably not take, and that is: Keep away from Mr. Oliver Quentin. He's a thimble-rigger of the first order. He'll go on lending you money until he's got you just where he wants you—and then you'll have to look out for yourself."

It was hardly his job to give fatherly advice to a confessed law-breaker, but Lambert was a much more pleasant young man now that fright had swept away his arrogance; and Charlton, who had a wide humanity, was sorry for him.

"Go on with your story," he requested.

"I heard Preston say good night to the barmaid, gave him a couple of moments start, then followed him out. He didn't go back home, but slipped between 'Pro Bono Publico' and the Memorial Hall. It was dark by that time, of course, and he made off across the Downs, with me just far enough behind not to lose him. After he'd gone some distance, I heard low voices and thought he must have met Harbord. . . . The two went on together and finally disappeared into Waltham Hanger, leaving me wondering what to do. I felt certain they were up to something, but I didn't dare follow them into the Hanger. I hung about for a few minutes behind a gorse bush, then saw three of them coming out from the trees. There was a bit of a moon and I had to be jolly careful to avoid being noticed, but none of them looked round as they climbed the hill and went down the other side."

He stopped speaking and looked queerly at the Inspector.

"What happened after that has given me nightmares ever since. . . . I suddenly heard a frightful scream that made me stop dead. . . . There was silence after that and I crept forward to find out what had happened. . . . Before I realized it, I was on the very brink of that chalk-pit by the Tall Man. I could see them clearly down below and dropped flat, so that they wouldn't catch sight of me against the sky. Preston and Smithers picked up Harbord's body—he must have been dead by then—and started to carry him away. It took them a long time to get him to the Tower. . . . I followed them all the way. When they got there, they laid the body down. I couldn't catch everything they did after that. . . . Eventually, they left him—and nearly caught me. I hadn't expected them to come back on their tracks. I dropped flat on my chest again and they passed within a few yards of me. . . . I waited for five minutes, then slipped down to my car, which was still outside the 'Tower Arms.' . . . And that's all."

"You are certain that the two men were Smithers and Preston?"

"I'll swear it."

"Did it occur to you to go at once to the police?"

"Don't you see the position I was in, Mr. Charlton? I knew that, if they were arrested, the whole story would come out—and that would have been the end of me. . . . When you came round to the Council offices on Monday morning, I thought it was all up. I tried to put a brave face on it, but I was stiff with fright."

Charlton finished the statement, blotted it and handed it to Lambert for his signature.

"Whatever else you do now, Lambert," he said, as the statement was passed back to him, "keep all this under your hat. I'll see you later. There's one more thing before you go. How did Smithers and Preston pass the notes to you?"

Lambert gave him details of the clever arrangements that Smoothy had made, and was sent away with an easier mind. Charlton went to the telephone and asked for the Old Forge House number. Judy answered.

"You mustn't say a word to anybody," he murmured into the transmitter, "but everything is all right now. You may dance round the room, if you like. *I'm* going to."

He hung up the receiver and executed a graceful *pas seul*.

On the stroke of 12.30, he pulled up his car outside the "Tower Arms." The doors had only just been opened and the saloon bar was empty and fresh smelling when he went in. Sheila Doyle was already working the handles in the public bar, but she soon came to him.

"Good morning," he smiled. "'White Horse' and soda, please."

Both bars began to fill and it was a quarter to one before Sheila approached him in his corner.

"Have you seen Greta Garbo's latest?" she asked, as she wiped a glass.

"No. I saw one of hers some time ago. What was it called, now. . . . ?"

She leant across the counter towards him.

"He's standing at the left-hand end of the public bar," she muttered. "You'll have to peep through the door."

He drew back his head and laughed heartily.

"No, did he really?" he asked incredulously. "I bet she was wild, wasn't she?"

"So the story goes," laughed the girl, and turned to serve another customer.

He went immediately, for fear Preston might leave.

As he went along the passage, he paused and pushed open the door of the public bar. Several men turned their heads, but he glanced casually round, as if in search of a friend. He took a look at his man without appearing to, then allowed the door to close.

When he had got back into his car and was about to start the engine, a man ran out of the building and came up to the open window. It was Mr. Greenhill's handyman and he was no more prepossessing than when Charlton had seen him on the previous Monday.

"Mornin'," he said.

"Good morning, Philp. Do you want me?"

"Not bloomin' likely, but the Guv'nor does. 'E said 'e was going to look you up tomorrow, but seeing you poke yer nose into the public, I thought I might as well tell you the glad noos. 'Oo were you rubberin' about for just now? A bramah?"

"I don't want any of your rudeness," Charlton answered sharply.

"Question withdrawn. Never does to interfere with other people's amures. Will you pop along and look the Guv'nor up now? 'E's jumping anxious to see you, with 'is old face wobbling about like an 'alf-set vanilla blancmange."

"I'll go along there now."

He had no wish to see Mr. Greenhill then, but he was curious to know why his company was so much sought after.

"While you're turning the charry round, I'll tell 'im you're on the way. That'll give 'im time to lock up the spoons."

He went off along the road, marching on his heels with his toes turned out and whistling merrily as he went.

Mr. Greenhill received Charlton in the same over-furnished room as on his previous visit.

"It is very obliging of you, Inspector," he said, "to call upon me. Philp has told me that he met you in the High Street and I fear he has been too presumptuous. I merely happened to mention to him yesterday that I proposed to visit you—without, of course, revealing my reason—and he has now taken the law into his own hands."

"It doesn't matter at all, Mr. Greenhill," smiled Charlton. "I'm always pleased to be of assistance. What can I do for you?"

"You can give me your advice. At the present time, I am on the horns of a predicament, if I may use the phrase, and I look to you for guidance. You have a fuller knowledge of this world than I have. . . . To come to the point, Inspector, I am troububbled about my daughter."

Charlton had more important things to do than listen to Mr. Greenhill's anxious confidences. His face, however, suggested nothing but attentive concern.

"After my daughter's disturbing experience with that ill-fated young man, Courtenay Harbord, I am loth to see her enter into any friendship that may reach the same disastrous conclusion. Recently a young man has been paying her formal attention and before I give the association my unqualified blessing and approval, I wish to find out a little more about him."

His worried expression lifted and he smiled.

"There is a story," he said, "of a man who was asked for references by his new landlord. For one of them, he gave the local police. The landlord told him later that he had sent a letter to the police station, but they had written back to say that they had never heard of the gentleman in question. 'I have lived in this neighbourhood for thirty years,' said the tenant, 'and now the police tell you that they have never heard of me. Could you wish for a finer reference than that?'"

Charlton laughed as convincingly as a man ever can when he has heard a story for the fortieth time.

"That," said Mr. Greenhill, "is why I wish to consult you. If you, in your official capacity, know nothing about this young man, I think I can safely place Phyllis in his care; but, if on the other hand, you have something against him, I earnestly beg you to tell me what it is. His name is Philip Lambert."

The morning was full of surprises and this was not the least of them for Charlton. Phyllis had told him of her friendship with Lambert, but he had never thought that such a situation as this would ever arise.

"That is a difficult question, Mr. Greenhill," he managed to say at last. "I have only met Mr. Lambert a couple of times, but he struck me as being a very respectable young man. His manner is, perhaps, a little supercilious and off-hand, but that is a failing with a good many of the younger generation. Isn't his father Sir Percy Lambert, the Whitchester J.P.?"

"So Philip himself has told me, but if that is the case, why is Philip working as a junior clerk for the Lulverton Urban District Council?"

"Many wealthy men send their sons out to business. It gives them experience."

"I do hope that is so with Philip; but I have been in grave doubts whether his father did not tire of his excesses and send him packing. It is a relief, however, to learn that he is, in your Opinion, a respectabubble young man. May I now offer you a glass of sherry?"

"Thank you, no," Charlton smiled.

Many times on his way back to Southmouth for lunch, he laughed aloud. He had said the only possible things to Mr. Greenhill, but after Lambert's confession that morning, the whole situation became pure comedy.

It was very, very funny.

XXVIII.

A TOUCH OF MELODRAMA

THE affair, although its previous pace had been pedestrian, had quite a stirring finish and one that was talked about in Downshire—in fact, all over the country—for a good many more than the statutory nine days.

That Sunday afternoon, Charlton sought out Supt. Kingsley and laid all the new facts before him. The Superintendent decided that no time was to be lost and Charlton accordingly laid immediate plans. A 'phone call to Scotland Yard put him in possession of the strange, eventful histories of Albert Smithers and Edward Preston.

"But remember," was the warning, "when they're cornered, there's nothing kid-glove about their methods. Preston's got no subtlety—he's straightforward smash-and-grab—but don't be deceived by Smithers's high-flown blah. He'll talk you into a doze and then act like lightning. *We* know him and we want him badly."

"You shall have him," Charlton answered courteously.

Half an hour after this assurance had been given, Vike and Smoothy sat chatting together. Vike was restless, but Smoothy the picture of tranquillity.

"The point is," Vike was saying, "are we going to get away with it?"

He had made the same enquiry many times since Harbord's death and Smoothy's answer had always been:

"Only time will tell."

"I got a shock this morning," Vike now went on, "when Charlton poked his nose in the bar. I thought he was after me."

"The Harbord murder, my dear Vike, is probably not the

only matter with which Charlton is concerned. He may have been on some betting-slip inquiry or something of that kind. He may even have been looking for someone to buy him a drink. You should have offered him one."

"I'm getting sick of this waiting. Why don't we make a bolt for it?"

Smoothy looked horrified. "That is the last thing we must do, Vike! Apart from the fact that I love my life in Etchworth, if we left suddenly now, we should be playing right into their hands. Ask yourself, my dear fellow, what *can* they have against us? Every single scrap of plant and material has been removed from the cellar and taken away to a safer place. The unfortunate Grey boy has been charged with the murder and, although I doubt if he will be hanged, will certainly receive a long term of imprisonment. In a few weeks, the whole unhappy affair will be forgotten and we shall be safe to pass the rest of our lives in the quietude and peace of this little village, doing good when we can—"

"Put a sock in it!" suggested Vike.

"We must not run away, Vike. Don't forget that Guildford misadventure. Once let the police know where we are and, whatever the outcome of the Harbord matter, we shall certainly go over the wall for the Guildford job. . . ." He continued on a different theme. "What I cannot understand is how that turnstile worked so well to our advantage. Had it not been for that, the unfortunate young man—"

"Don't keep calling him unfortunate," snarled Vike.

"Surely no better word describes his position? But let me call him luckless. Had it not been for the (to me) unexplainable fact that the turnstile disproved any suggestion of our late colleague having entered the Tower last Sunday, this—ah—luckless young man would not now be awaiting trial. It is a solemn thought that this soulless piece of apparatus should have intervened on our behalf. It is an almost literal case of *deus ex machina.*"

"I thought I was pretty tough," Vike admitted, "but this business is getting me down. . . . It's the waiting. . . . Charlton's like some great cat. You don't know what he's up to, or which way he'll jump. . . . I've got a touch of Harbord's complaint, Smoothy. I don't want the law to get hold of me. . . . It's got hold of me before. . . . And it wouldn't be gaol this time."

"Play the man!" Smoothy encouraged him. "'One who never turned his back but marched breast forward, never doubted clouds would break—'"

"For God's sake, shut up!"

"That poem has always been a great inspiration to me, Vike. 'Never dreamed, though right were worsted, wrong would triumph. . . . ' I fear I have not lived up to that noble ideal, but it is something to have tried. In this life, Vike, poetry is a bulwark, a refuge and a sure defence."

"I prefer a gun. If the dees come after me, I shall use it."

"I do not favour your practice of keeping a loaded firearm on your person, but I will admit that I have transferred my automatic from the drawer of my dressing-table to my pocket. I agree with you when you say that you wish to evade the clutches of the law; and, in the unlikely event of our connection with Harbord's death being discovered, I shall take every possible step to avoid arrest. I am not given to melodramatic pronouncements, Vike, but I shall see to it that I am not taken alive. It will not be a pleasant experience, yet it will be less distressing than being hanged . . . If I cannot live at my ease in this comfortable home, I do not wish to live at all. . . . But I hope and believe that it will never come to that. Charlton has got his burnt offering and that is all he really cares about."

He looked wistful.

"It will be a pity to die," he said. "How do those lines go? 'The garlands wither on your brow; then boast no more your mighty deeds; upon Death's purple altar now See where the victor-victim bleeds—'"

Vike jumped up with an oath. "I can't stand you any longer!"

"Don't stay for me, Vike. I have my paper. Why don't you take a brisk walk? The rain won't hurt you."

"Oh, go to hell!" snapped Vike.

He went out into the hall snatched down his mackintosh and Smoothy winced as the front door slammed behind him.

For a man with such a conspicuous record, Edward Preston did not put up a very good show. He had not gone many yards along Etchworth High Street when the black police car slunk up behind him. Young Emerson, who could crumple a tobacco-tin like paper in his hand, slid out of the back seat and Sergeant Martin followed from his place beside the driver. Vike spun round as they closed in on him.

"What's your game?" he asked.

"Am I speaking to Edward Preston?" Martin politely enquired.

Vike laughed shortly. "No, you're not."

"I've reason to believe that I am. I'm a police officer and—"

Emerson caught Vike's arm as his hand went to his pocket and Vike winced with pain. Martin tapped him on the shoulder.

"I arrest you," he said, "for the murder of Courtenay 'Arbord and we don't want any 'alf-larks, young fellow."

Vike began to struggle, but Emerson put great motherly arms around him and persuaded him into the back of the car, where P. C. Hartley was ready to receive him with the handcuffs. They took his gun away, the car was turned, and they drove swiftly back to Lulverton.

Martin turned round to where Vike sat wedged between Emerson and Hartley, and gave him the usual warning.

But Vike held his tongue.

The other car had stopped outside the Memorial Hall, and the driver sat waiting with the engine ticking quietly over. Bradfield disappeared down the passage by the side of the hall, to cut off any retreat by the back door. Charlton opened the gate, walked up the path and rang the bell. In a moment or two, Smoothy, carrying his paper between his fingers, opened the door. Charlton's foot went forward.

"Albert Smithers," he said, "you know who I am. I arrest you for the murder of Courtenay Harbord."

Smoothy's face showed nothing but bewilderment.

"I really think you have taken leave of your senses!" he said. "Surely you know that my name is—"

"I am going to take you into custody and—".

Smoothy took a pace backwards and Charlton stepped after him.

"I must warn you that any—"

Suddenly Smoothy reached up to a coat-hook and brought the hall-stand pitching down between them, blocking the narrow passage. He turned and ran along the hall; but at the kitchen door he paused and groped in his pocket . . . The gun crashed and Charlton ducked an instant before the bullet shattered a leaded pane in the front door.

Bradfield was waiting where the Downs began, at the bottom of the short back garden. He heard the shot and shinned over the fence. When he neared the house, the door was wrenched open and Smoothy came out with the gun still gripped in his hand. As Bradfield leapt at him, he fired. The detective threw out his arms and fell forward. Smithers jumped to avoid him and raced down the garden.

Charlton got the hall-stand out of the way and ran along the hall and through the kitchen. He stopped short when he saw the wounded man and bent over him.

"Carry on, sir!" urged Bradfield faintly.

The hunted man had climbed the fence and was making for the Tower. Charlton stood for a moment in the rain, then ran back through the house and out to the car. He jumped in and they shot along the High Street. Smithers had cut across the grass and was half-way up the lane before the car skidded round into it. He turned his head when he heard them behind him and stopped dead. They were thirty yards away when he raised his gun. The big, black car was roaring straight at him, but his hand was steady as he pressed the trigger. A star splashed across the windscreen and the driver fell forward with a grunt over the wheel. His foot slipped from the accelerator, the car stopped and began to slide backwards against the compression. Charlton leant across to pull on the handbrake. Another shot hit the windscreen and went past his head into the bodywork. He opened the door and got out.

Smithers was running again and was a good way ahead. Charlton cupped his hands.

"Lee!" he roared, "Shut the doors!"

In his cubicle, Tom went on reading, but looked up from his paper when Smithers appeared.

"Let me through!" the man panted.

"Threepence, please," said Tom.

Charlton had torn off his mackintosh and was getting very close. Smithers put a foot on the turnstile and clambered over.

"Look 'ere—" began Tom, but Smithers lifted the gun and shot him.

The Inspector slowed down when he heard the report. It was suicide now to dash into the Tower. He went quietly forward and stood by the railings, listening. . . . He heard nothing but the rain. Taking a chance, he peered round the corner. Inside, it was dim and he could not be certain that his man was not still lurking at the foot of the staircase . . . He stepped suddenly across the entrance to draw the fire, but everything stayed silent . . . Smoothy might be running up the stairs. It was a risk, but Charlton took it. He walked boldly through the entrance. Nothing happened while he went through the turnstile in the way that Tom had taught him.

The old man was crumpled up in his cubicle and the keys had disappeared from the nail. Charlton took a swift stride across to the staircase and began to climb. . . . Half-way to the top, Smithers, with blue lips, sat gasping on a stair. He soon caught the sound of his followers' footsteps and got up to lean over the handrail. He waited with gun ready until Charlton came in sight, then fired. The crash of the shot in the hollow shaft was terrific, but the bullet ricocheted off the wall behind the detective, who bounded up after him.

Smithers snatched his arm back, but the rail caught the stock of the gun and jerked it out of his hand. He swore furiously as it fell down the well of the staircase. After that, it was just a race between them. Charlton was fresher, for he had not run all the way from the village, but Smithers had thirty stairs' lead. This was reduced to twenty before he reached the grille. Gasping for breath, he feverishly fitted the key in the lock and turned it. The gate swung open. He pulled the key out, but there was not time to lock the grille behind him.

Charlton's lungs were nearly bursting and coloured lights were dancing before his eyes, but he hung on. He reached the grille ... There was still a chance, for Smithers had to undo the padlock on the trap-doors. ... But as he struggled up the stairs in the cylinder, a clinging mass of flags and bunting dropped down over his head and shoulders. Blinded and choked by the dust, he tore at the fabric ... When he had freed himself, a fit of coughing doubled him up and, by that time, Smithers had climbed the funnel through the vase and was searching in the darkness for the padlock.

As Charlton reached the landing, Smithers pushed back the trap-doors. The detective jumped at the iron ladder and clambered up hand over hand. Smithers caught hold of the lip of the vase, pulled himself off the last rung and slammed down the trap-doors behind him. With his eyes filled with the flying rust particles, Charlton went up the remaining rungs and pushed at the doors, but the other man's weight was holding them fast.

"And now you can come down again, Smithers!" he shouted.

"You'll never get me!" the answer was yelled.

"I've cheated you of your prey, Mr. Detective-Inspector!"

He was standing upright on the flaps and bent forward to peer over the flames round the lip of the vase, which reached just above his knees. Down past the cylinder and the balcony, with its new horizontal grille, he could see the ground a terrifying distance below. For a moment, his resolution faltered. It would not be a pleasant death . . . Then suddenly, as if not giving himself time to draw back, he moved to the edge—and the flap from which his weight had just been shifted flew up with a crash.

He glanced round, then stepped up on to the lip of the vase. As he bent his legs for the spring that would take him over the flames, Charlton, who was on the top-most rung, sprawled across the closed flap, clutched a grip on a trouser leg and pulled him backwards. Smithers turned like a maniac, kicked him in the face, leapt back on to the lip and scrambled over the flames, which bent under his weight.

Roped outside the vase were three builders' ladders resting on the sloping ledge at the top of the cylinder. Charlton, his face streaming with blood, struggled up and saw Smithers disappearing down one of them. He sprang across to another . . . His hands slipped on the wet uprights and, clinging desperately, he shot down until his feet touched the ledge. Smithers had reached the bottom and was gripping the ladder with one hand. Charlton released his own hold and worked his way along the slippery stonework. With his free hand, Smithers wiped the rain from his face and grinned horribly.

"So you would like to come with me?" he said. "I will wait for you."

Inch by inch, Charlton edged to his left. His position was one of fearful peril, for Smithers could push him off without losing his grip on the ladder. He got to within two feet of the crouching, watchful man, then jumped sideways at him with an arm wildly grabbing at the ladder. He missed it and Smithers closed with him. They struggled for a moment on the ledge before they toppled together into space.

Philip Lambert had seen the two police cars leave Lulverton and had followed them to Etchworth in his Riley. He had witnessed the arrest of Preston, heard the shooting and seen Charlton hurry from the house to the waiting car. He had been behind when they had driven along the High Street, but had paused at the end of the lane where, with his windscreen wiper sweeping from side to side, he had watched the ensuing events.

When the sound of more shots came from the Tower, he left the car and ran across to the telephone-box as P.C. Collins had run on the previous Sunday morning. . . . Within a minute, Martin and his assistants were racing back from Lulverton. Lambert pushed his way through the crowd of villagers who had gathered at the end of the lane, started his engine and drove up the hill. He bumped off the road to avoid the stationary police car and pulled up outside the Tower. He peered over at old Tom lying in his cubicle and vaulted over the turnstile.

As he stepped warily up the stairs, he could hear nothing. . . . The opened grille gate attracted his notice and he crept into the upper cylinder. On the landing, he paused and looked up. He saw the grey sky through the open trap, but there seemed to be nobody there. . . . After standing for a moment in doubt, he shrugged his shoulders and placed his foot on the lowest half-circular rung.

He got to the trap and peered over.

Down below, Charlton was working his way slowly round the ledge, while Smithers waited. He saw them come to grips and drop backwards off the stonework; and heard clearly above the crash as they hit the new grille-work, the sharp crack of Charlton's breaking arm.

Smithers was unhurt by the fall that had landed them both on the grille. He was nearer to the corner than Charlton, who was hanging by his left, uninjured arm, with most of his body dangling over the edge.

Lambert swung his leg over the flames.

Smithers knelt on the bars and leered at the detective, who was urgently seeking a foothold on the lower rails.

"This is the end of your distinguished career, Mr. Charlton," he sneered.

He reached forward and was levering Charlton's fingers off the bar, when Lambert sprang on him from behind.

Sergeant Martin could not keep up with the others on the staircase. . . . Hartley followed Emerson on to the balcony. Above them, Lambert and Smithers were wrestling madly on the narrow grille-work, while Charlton stood on the handrail, with his fractured arm hanging loosely by his side, grimly determined not to lose consciousness.

Emerson pulled himself up on to the handrail below the fighting men, waited for an opportunity and grabbed at Smithers' arm. He dragged it down between the bars and twisted it savagely, so that Smithers screamed.

"Be quiet, can't you?" Emerson rebuked him.

Lambert crawled away from the prone man and lay panting on the grille. Hartley had his arms round Charlton, who was sagging dangerously, Martin reached the balcony. Smithers began to struggle, but yelled with pain when Emerson wrenched his arm.

"Martin," Charlton managed to gasp, "there's some rope in the cylinder."

"Can you hold on a bit, sir?" Martin shouted, as he came back with the rope.

"I'm all right. Look after Smithers."

The Sergeant lassoed Smithers' writhing legs and tied them firmly to the bars. Then he did the same with the arms, leaving the man spreadeagled on the grille-work. Emerson was freed from his task and they threw a supporting rope around Charlton.

Excited crowds were gathering below and Etchworth High Street was thick with cars that had brought the curious from all around. Martin shouted down:

"Get the ambulance, somebody!"

He passed a truncheon up to Lambert, who had been violently sick.

"If 'e tries any funny business," he said, "give 'im a fourpenny one with that."

The builders had fitted a manhole in the new grille-work. It was locked.

"See if the key's with the one in the trap-door padlock," said Charlton weakly.

Emerson climbed the funnel and brought back the ring. The new key was on it and he turned it in the lock. There followed ten nerve-racking minutes while they hauled Charlton to safety. The broken ends of the humerus were grinding together all the time, and he was unconscious when they laid him gently down on the balcony, with his head on Martin's jacket.

The Sergeant heaved a great sigh of relief and, regardless of the rain, swaggered round in his shirtsleeves to the other side of the balcony. He looked up.

"All right, Mr. Lambert," he said. "Give 'im the K.O. and we'll get 'im down."

Smithers glared at Martin as Lambert raised the truncheon. The Sergeant grinned up at him.

"Well, I never did!" he said in extravagant surprise, a moment before the blow fell, "if it isn't Mr. Greenhill!"

XXIX.

AND IN CONCLUSION …

THERE is very little more to be told.

Vike Preston had, of course, been Philp, the gardener. He had lodged five doors away from "Pro Bono Publico" and it had been in his bedroom that the first recorded conversation between him and Smoothy Smithers had taken place.

"Phyllis Greenhill," whose real name was Emily Webster, was arrested in Lulverton as an accessory, but there was not sufficient evidence against her to get a conviction. Harbord had never been in love with her. Their affair had been arranged by Smoothy to supply Harbord with an excuse for paying frequent visits to "Pro Bono Publico." The dance in Buckingham Park had coincided with the breaking up of the forging partnership. She had described to Charlton how she had sent Harbord away that evening, but it was only an attempt to explain the discontinuance of his regular calls at the house.

It was through the agency of Emily Webster, who was on the books at Scotland Yard as an accomplished shoplifter, that the spurious notes had been transferred to Philip Lambert every Saturday evening. She had met him in the lane when he had made his visits and had passed over the packets during their weekly joy-rides together. He could not have got much pleasure from these trips, for he had hated the sight of her.

Nobody died on that Sunday afternoon. Bradfield, the driver of the police car and old Tom Lee all recovered, although it was many weeks before Tom was able to get about again. By then, young Bert Parsons had settled down as permanent attendant at the Tower, and Tom was forced to accept his pension.

On the following Friday, Peter was brought before the full bench of magistrates and discharged.

Philip Lambert, as an eye-witness, played an important part

in the trial of Smithers and Preston, but his connection with the forgeries was never made public. Charlton gave him a gold watch, which was a powerful enough token to win him Sir Percy's complete forgiveness.

But to revert to Sunday, October the 6th. Two hours after the transpontine matters described in the previous chapter, Judy visited Charlton's cubicle in the Lulverton War Memorial Hospital. He smiled happily as she came in and she ran to kneel down by the bed.

"Darling," she breathed, "you frightened me."

"Not nearly as much as I frightened myself," he answered. "When I'm well enough for you to eat my grapes, will you come and see me again? I have a question to ask you."

"You may forget it then. Won't you ask me now?"

With his free hand, he motioned her closer and murmured in her ear. She drew back and looked at him searchingly.

"You're quite sure you're not light-headed?" she said.

"Perfectly sure. I need somebody to help me find my slippers."

"In that case," smiled Judy," I'd better say. Yes."